A FRAGILE LOVE

"M-may we meet here sometimes?" Lisbet asked awkwardly after a while, desperate to pull the threads of their disintegrating relationship back together. "Arrange a schedule? Just sit close, talk . . . remember . . . ?"

Forrest smiled a smile both fond and full of rue. "Are you returning to the role of innocent already, my dear Lisbet?"

He moved close again and, extending a forefinger, ran it from her brow to her chin, then slowly down to the place where the locket nestled. She could not see the shape of his hand in the night, but she knew it well, its lean perfect shape, its clean square nails. With a little sigh she clasped it within her own.

Drawing her face up to his, Forrest bent his head to kiss her. It was an aggressive kiss, deep, selfish, and swift, and when she reached out to embrace his neck and prolong it, he drew immediately away to elude her touch.

At her cry of protest, he laughed wickedly.

"And now, Lady Thorpe," he said simply, strolling away in the darkness, "you find out that two can play the game."

DEBORAH SATINWOOD

LOVE'S SECRET FIRE

ZEBRA BOOKS
KENSINGTON PUBLISHING CORP.

ZEBRA BOOKS

are published by

Kensington Publishing Corp.
475 Park Avenue South
New York, NY 10016

First Printing: April, 1993

Printed in the United States of America

To my father, for giving me his love of history.
To my mother, for giving me her love of reading.
To my husband, for giving me encouragement.

Chapter One

England, 1883

With their ice-tipped fur rippling beneath a glacial breeze, their undulating forms scarcely visible in twilight's fall, a pair of white foxes darted across the snow. Catching a scent, they paused, their movement so quickly arrested that each held a nimble paw suspended. Their noses twitched, their ears quivered, and their long slanted eyes gleamed silver with some primeval knowledge, or with a secret long kept dark.

Oddities they were . . . or were they merely specters? Whatever name they claimed, they caused an eerie chill to freeze the blood and tingle the spines of witnesses.

No less affected than any other was the tall, grim-faced intruder who had happened into their wintry world. Intrigued, he maintained his narrowed scrutiny of the creatures until the sting of snow made him blink, but when he reopened his eyes they both had disappeared without leaving so much as a trace. He knew the legend about them, the one claiming they were the restless spirits of two young lovers drowned in a stagnant pool, but he shrugged carelessly even as he recalled it. Legends he did not believe in.

Yet, curiously, he had sighted this elusive pair once before, on the eve of his banishment from this hamlet nearly two decades ago. The shameful exile was still so raw a wound that his wide shoulders stiffened all at once, and his eyes glinted with the same cold cynicism as they had on the day of that unjust eviction.

"Twenty years," he hissed, his tone marked with both wonder and asperity. "Twenty damnable years."

He moved on through the haunted copse, following a path obscured by white but forever etched in memory. The tracks his boots left were an uneven set, for war had lamed one of his long lean legs. With an unlikely sort of grace, he dragged the crippled member along behind the sound one, his gait a rhythmic step and sway that barely rocked his frame. The pain he suffered with it was a curse, a curse that would have driven an undisciplined man to distraction; he bore it in stony silence with barely a flinching muscle. If nothing else, life had taught him fortitude. Indeed, his regiment had once sworn that their steel-nerved captain could endure hell itself, if asked.

His destination loomed near. With a sweep of discerning black eyes he took in the shrouded landscape, unwittingly searching for the curl of smoke from blackened chimneys, listening for taunting voices, anticipating the sting of humiliation. Were *they* there even now, characters frozen in time, waiting with stones clutched in their hands and menace in their looks? Were their teeth still bared in laughter and their eyes agleam with cruelty?

Of course they were, they and their shadows. They had called him Anvil, a name he had resentfully endured all the days of his boyhood. The odd-shaped birthmark he bore upon his shoulder had prompted the tag—it was the devil's own mark, the villagers claimed.

"Anvil! Anvil! Anvil!" He could still hear their taunt-

ing jeers. *"Won't you come out and forge old Dobbin's shoes?"*

With remembered shame he put a hand to his coat-clad shoulder, rubbing his fingers over the dark brown stain in the same way he had as a child, furtively and out of habit. His eyes hardened and he lowered his hand. The mark he could not erase, but years ago he had ridded himself of the hated name. Now he answered only to Capt. Forrest York.

He sucked in a slow breath, expelling it as vapor. There . . . Just over the rise nestled the familiar cottages, their rectangular shapes huddled together defensively, their plots of dead gardens uniform, their snow-coated eaves and ivied walls unvarying. A stranger may have termed the village quaint, even charming, but he remembered it differently. He swung his gaze, finding the black crenellated tower that rose above the humbler abodes. Centuries old, it stood sentinel over the chimney tops and wind-scarred trees, its silhouette the same as always . . . hard, indomitable, unforgiving.

"Why? Why in the name of God have I come back here?" he mouthed silently. Was it to stride defiantly through the streets once more, dare anyone to sneer? Was it to find even a shred of spiritual peace he had been unable to find anywhere else? Or, he asked himself with a tinge of familiar self-scorn, was it to lay a ghost to rest at last?

Unable to answer his own musings, he went on, a dark solitary figure limping across a field of ice-coated grass. Suddenly movement caught his eye, and he adjusted his gaze in the evening's dimness.

A tiny figure traversed the hill only a hundred paces in front of him, a figure running clumsily in the deepening snow. The runner seemed to be a girl in a heavy cloak and trailing skirts, or a woman whose form still retained the lissomeness of youth. Her garb was pale gray like the snow shadows, its billowy folds aglimmer with ghostly light.

Was she substance, Forrest wondered, or only a part of that white, spellbound world of the foxes? Recently he had suffered plenty of delusions, raving out of his head upon a blood-stained cot, and now he dashed a hand across his eyes to reassure himself that this fleeting vision was real and no wraith.

As he continued to follow the woman's course with his eyes, he wondered at her hurried progress, the purposeful, almost desperate nature of her flight. Curiosity piqued him, and merely on the whim of impulse, he changed his direction to pursue the fleeing lady.

His own pace was not as speedy, indeed, it could not have been with the encumbrance of his injured leg. But steadfastly he followed the deep tracks she left, hobbling through ice-bound copses and over wind-rippled drifts until at last, and with much chagrin, he sighted the fugitive again.

A still, slim figure, she stood poised upon a precipice, her feet daringly planted upon a piece of jagged stone jutting outward from the hill. Before her stretched a panoramic snowscape so magnificent and vast it seemed to swallow up her slender form.

A stiff breeze swirled up from the valley and flapped her hood suddenly, blowing it back against her shoulders to reveal a tangle of hair whose volume appeared too heavy for the slender bowed neck and whose color was akin to gold. Her arms she held at her sides, the small gloved fists clenched tightly as if with suppressed emotion. Her shoulders rose and fell with quick shallow breaths.

When she turned her head a bit, just enough to provide her unseen companion with a dusky silhouette, Forrest was disturbed by its distressful lines and stepped nearer to view her better. She seemed to be contemplating with a fixed stare the descent of stone dropping only inches from her shoes. Forrest knew well the treacherous plummet there, the river that snaked silver beneath it. Many desolate dawns had found him in this very place . . . eons ago.

But what the devil was the woman doing, he pondered, his unease rapidly mounting. The very posture of her body, the slumped shoulders and drooping neck suggested forlornness. Did she think to throw herself over? *Was she considering suicide, for God's sake?*

Suddenly she swayed. Instinct spurred him. He lunged, snatched at the hem of her swirling skirts in an attempt to pull her back from the edge. But his step was not as quick as it had once been, and the effort was a vain one. With horror he saw her slight, gray-cloaked figure disappear over the cliff edge and hurtle downward.

He lost not a moment of time. Even as he witnessed her plunge through the river's icy glaze, he unclasped his greatcoat and, together with jacket and gloves, threw it aside. Then, taking two steps, he leaned forward and propelled himself outward, arcing his body into a dive to follow the other's fall. She had shattered the thin crust of ice and its shards floated in brittle shapes upon the river's surface. His own entry into the frigid current stunned him momentarily, its numbing chill shocking his nerves and its depth robbing him of breath. As he resurfaced, he spat a mouthful of water from his paling lips and grunted against the pain of cold. Treading water, he glanced about for sight of the woman, finding at last the gleam of her hair as it bobbed amidst the pewter waves. He guessed her to be fifty yards or so away from him and, seeing her struggle weakly, knew the pull of sodden clothes and the deadly cold would drown her in only minutes.

Stroking strongly, his arms pulling with the current,

he reached her in what seemed hours but was certainly only seconds, and with a mighty stretch clenched at her waving hair. But he retrieved not a strand, for she was sinking beneath the surface with alarming speed. Almost as if with deliberation the long fair locks he had meant to catch eluded him.

He cursed and stroked again, diving downward into the gloomy depths, keeping his eyes open wide in an attempt to locate a flash of pearl skirts. With furious kicks, he went deeper, his muscles stiff and uncooperative, his extremities already numb.

Where was she? he despaired. Had she sunk to the river bottom or had the current carried her forward beyond his reach?

When his lungs were near to bursting, he returned for air and, sucking in another breath, searched the eerie ribbon of river again. No movement broke the wintry crust ahead, no ripple marred the surface around him. She must be floating below somewhere, with the cold paralyzing her limbs and water filling her lungs. Had breath already left her? Was she dying?

Quickly he dived once more, stretching his hands downward in a sweep to explore the depths. Something soft and tenuous brushed his fingertips, and he snatched at it, catching nothing more than a handful of liquid ice. In a second attempt his fingers closed over and captured some unseen object. Was it the waving stem of a water plant . . . or a lock of golden hair?

He yanked hard, dragging his prize upward with him as he kicked his way to the surface with renewed hope. By the weight of the thing he towed, it would seem that he had found his drowning lady. He prayed he was not too late.

Putting his arm beneath her chin, he drew her up, holding her face above the lapping waves, hoping to see her eyes flutter or her mouth gasp for air. But the sculpted features were as frozen and pale as marble, the lips tinged with blue.

Losing no time, he swam ashore with his fragile burden, laying her down upon a snowbank, crawling up to kneel at her side. As he did so, a blast of northern air gusted, freezing into rime the moisture upon the woman's lashes. His own body was beset by uncontrollable shivering, and he clenched his jaw against it, feeling for a pulse in the white drooping neck. Swearing, he abandoned the effort, for his fingers were so numb he could not have discerned a vital throb had there been one there. Hastily he turned her facedown and, pressing his hands to her back, desperately fought death for her possession.

"Breathe!" he shouted at her unresponsive form. *"Breathe, dammit, breathe!"*

At last, at his continuous pushing against her ribs, a stream of water trickled from her open mouth, followed by a gurgle of sound that rose upward from her chest. He leaned to put an ear to the full, discolored lips. A soft, warm vapor seemed to wend upward and touch his cheek . . . just the barest breath.

Quickly he gathered her in his arms and struggled through a snowdrift, searching for a negotiable path upward. A few paces downstream the way to the cliff edge seemed less steep. With luck he could just manage it.

When the wind pierced his drenched shirt, a convulsive chill shook him, and he faltered, dragging his lame leg in its water-logged boot and hugging the unconscious lady closer to his chest. Once, not many months ago, he could have agilely climbed the ascent in spite of the present difficulties; but war had left him less sound. Only three steps up, and disaster threatened when he slipped on a slickened stone and almost fell backwards. Regaining his balance with difficulty, he paused to catch his breath before finding a surer foothold. At last, after a few more precarious steps, he reached the overlook.

Carefully laying down the woman, he shrugged into his jacket, then drew on the gloves, grimacing as he covered his frozen fingers. The woolen greatcoat he folded snugly around his patient, and lifting her up, he cradled her in his arms once more.

Nightfall tinted the snowscape now, and the scattered trees quivered like tall black skeletons. Trudging beneath them, Forrest directed his staggering steps toward his rented cottage, for time could not be wasted while he knocked on doors to learn the victim's address. Recalling his agent's directions, he judged the cottage to be no more than a half-mile away. He only hoped its cupboards would provide plenty of clean linens, abundant blankets, and ample firewood.

"And what I could do with a dram of whiskey . . ." he muttered between rattling teeth.

When he came to a signpost, he turned westward instead of following its pointed tip, focusing his eyes in the gloom to locate a green-painted gate set between two cedars. There! Framed between their spires stood a cottage, its welcome form steep-gabled, cross-timbered, and dark above a rising moon.

Never slowing his labored pace, Forrest bent his head low, assuring himself that the woman's chest continued to rise and fall. He rejoiced, for it seemed as if she were clinging to life—if only with feeble effort. Arriving at the gate he put his hip to its latch and nudged it open, crossing the short space to the cottage stoop. After balancing the senseless woman upon his knee, he thrust his hand into his breeches pocket, fumbled for the key, and unlocked the door. Darkness greeted him. That, and a musty odor someone had attempted to tame with potpourri. A stair rose before him and, pausing not at all in his hobbling step, he ascended it in search of a bed.

One right turn put him in a narrow corridor marked by two open doors, and he shouldered his way into the first, halting briefly to get his bearings. Moonlight shimmered through a lace-hung curtain, spilling diagonally upon a barren wood floor and the coverlet of a four-poster bed. The room's furnishings were of another age, he noted, well-used and mismatched, but more than adequate.

Taking his gloves between his teeth Forrest pulled them off, letting them drop willy-nilly. That done, he divested his patient of the greatcoat, her cape and skirt, and lastly the ruined silken blouse, shoes, and stockings. His hands never hesitated, nor were they anything but impersonal as they completed their unfastening of hooks and buttons.

However, the damp, lace-edged undergarments did give him pause—not because of any modesty on his part—but in consideration of the lady's own should she wake. Leaving them, he laid her gently between the sheets and covered her thin, fair length.

Behind him there was a hearth, and atop its rough-carved mantel he discovered matches. Fortunately, some thoughtful soul had laid the wood, and in a matter of seconds he had coaxed it into flame. When amber light illumined the room, he took stock of the simple furnishings in a glance, searching for extra blankets. The chest at the foot of the bed proved a haven for knitted shawls, woolen caps, and assorted mittens, and finally gave way to a stack of folded quilts, which he draped one by one over the frozen form whose shape barely raised the covers. Then, as he repacked the contents of the chest, he discovered a silver flask of whiskey lying on the bottom. He grinned, thinking some secret tippler had stashed it there for midnight indulgences. He blessed the sly imbiber and, after pausing to swig a good measure of the spirits down, retrieved a towel from beside the wash basin. Returning to the bedside, he gently lifted the masses of fair hair strewn like seaweed about the woman's faded face and squeezed out the ends so they would not drip and wet her pillow.

The fire popped and roared, gradually sending out its warmth to dispel the dreadful cold. Flexing his fingers, discovering them revitalized, Forrest leaned to find his patient's pulse, unwittingly brushing her ear and the delicate curve of her jaw. Her flesh was soft, very soft, and he realized how long it had been since he had touched a woman. Sighing, he felt for the throb of a vein and found it faint.

"You're still as cold as ice," he muttered to the unlistening ear. Shaking his head, he added softly, "I'd give my horse to know what you were brooding about on the cliff tonight. What made you jump?" With a frown, he drew forth her wrist and chafed it. "Were you lonely . . . afraid? Have you lost someone . . . ?"

Shrugging at her unresponsiveness, he sank down upon the coverlet, still with her hand in his. He saw she wore a wedding ring and with idle curiosity turned her finger to better catch the firelight, examining the huge gold band. It was a grotesque piece, its design clearly medieval, with two twisted serpents holding a ruby within their open fangs. The gem was so red and pure and cold it could have been a drop of frozen blood.

"Hmm," Forrest murmured. "Worth a fortune, I'll wager. A smart fellow could get a few thousand pounds for it if he asked in the right places." He turned her hand, obscuring the ring. "Damned ugly piece of work, though, if you ask me."

The silver flask was conveniently close, and he reached for it, removing the stopper with his teeth and savoring a drink with a lusty "Ah!" Before long its fire relaxed him and, tilting his head back against the headboard, he closed his eyes. What tragedy, what grim circumstances would drive a woman to suicide, he ruminated, absently rubbing some of the soreness from his knee. His return to Winterspell had put him in a thoughtful mood, and pictures of his past came flooding back to him in a gentle rush.

Recalling his own trials over the years with a sort of bland amusement, imagining them much different from the troubles of his wealthy guest, he laughed shortly. "Good Lord, when I think of all the times I've reached rock-bottom . . ."

Sighing, he propped his legs upon the bed, easing the lame one with care, raising the knee of the other. Exhaustion assailed him fully now, and with a lazy slur and a need to talk, he continued his one-sided dialogue. "I remember going two months without tuppence in my pocket once—damned strange how I'd forgotten about it 'til now." He sighed and took another drink before rambling on. "But that was years ago of course—just after I jumped ship in Madrid. Great learning experience, as they say." Derisively he smiled and put the bottle to his lips, then raised an arm in an exaggerated salute. "One I shall strive never to forget! After all, 'tis quite an accomplishment for any lad not to get caught pickpocketing a Spanish don."

Shrugging, he continued, his tone a self-mocking one. "That same year, after I'd worked barefoot in a vineyard all season, I decided to borrow a pair of boots from a Spanish sailor . . . the devil if he and six of his pals didn't beat the hell out of me for it. Uncharitable fellows, Spanish sailors. Oh—and something else you should know about me," he added matter-of-factly, "I've been thrown in gaol a few times—though in several different countries."

He knitted his brow and glanced down at the haunted face of his silent companion. "You spend too much time brooding about things you can't change, I'll wager. Now when I brood I just spend a few nights gettin' drunk as a lord—bad advice, I know. Learned not to make a habit of it after I drank myself into oblivion once and afterward had a three-week memory loss. Never have tried to do away with myself, though." He smiled a little grimly. "Afraid hell would be worse, I guess."

He straightened and, as if hoping to find secrets there, absently opened the lady's palm. Though unable to see its finer details, he noted the fingers were of the slender variety so often found in artist's hands. Her arm was thin as well, and with his rough knowledge of the body beneath the covers, he knew her feminine curves just as meagerly fleshed. He wondered if she had been declining food lately . . . deliberately starving herself.

"What secrets do you hide, milady?" he asked quietly of her sleeping form, tucking her hand back beneath the covers and touching her cheek with the back of his hand. "What is *your* private torment?"

Upon the snowy pillow, touched with fire colors, her face remained impassive.

Her rescuer sighed. Retreating down the stairs with her bundle of wet clothes, he paused once to grip his knee when pain locked it, holding his breath before releasing it with a slow, racked groan. Any thoughts he had of going out again, tramping through the snow to notify the village of the lady's whereabouts, quickly evaporated. His leg would never hold up, and he was loath to leave his patient alone. After all, she had tried to kill herself tonight.

Through the darkened rooms touched with glossy moonbeams he walked, his uneven stride purposeful as he went in search of the kitchen. Along the way he found an oil lamp, which he promptly lit and carried with him. Through a cursory glance he saw that his rented cottage contained a small drawing room, dining room, and study, all furnished in an unpretentious but comfortable way. It would suit well his Spartan needs once he had lit the fires and chased the chill away.

The kitchen was spacious, and from what he could see during his search for cups, saucers, spoons, and tea, its larder and cupboards were well and thoughtfully stocked. After laying a fire, he rummaged about the drawers for string and tied a line across the hearth for the lady's dripping, notably expensive clothes. Then, spending a few moments stoking the oven, he put the kettle on and waited until it sang. Thinking optimistically, he poured two cups of hot tea, added coarse brown sugar to one, and placed them on a tray. As an afterthought, he grabbed a tin of biscuits from the cupboard—God knew his guest needed the nourishment.

Once upstairs, he noticed immediately she had moved. Her waxen, oval face was turned slightly toward the window now, and one hand lay upon her breast atop the covers. Yet her eyes remained closed, the lashes spreading fans upon white cheeks.

He set the tray down, then quietly moved to stand beside her, raising the lamp so that its gleam shone full upon her features, for in the wintry gloom he had yet to see them clearly. The light put sorrel tones in her water-darkened hair, turning it to shades of honey. A few of its wisps framed an intelligent brow that was gently rounded and unlined. Her cheeks were hollowed but finely boned, her chin noticeably pointed. Where the nose was straight and unremarkable, the mouth was generous and bowed, provocative in its fullness. Though her ordeal in the elements had put a pall upon her flesh, robbing it of its natural color, it had also lent an ethereal quality. Some master carver could have fashioned it, wielding delicate tools until it resembled a little stone goddess resting prone upon a marble pedestal.

Forrest stared. He raised a finger to touch the soft parted lips, then cupped the brow and smoothed it with a searching, unsteady hand. The jaw and neck he stroked with his knuckles, the eyelids he brushed with a thumb. Lifting a strand of her hair, he let it slide through his palm, scrutinizing its color, its texture—all with a look of sudden terrible wonder upon his face.

"My God . . ." he breathed, stepping back.

Slowly he lowered the lamp and set it aside. His eyes had grown bright, feverish, sheened with moisture as they turned from the lily-pale face to stare at the moonlight on the floor. The muscles in his face strained, his complexion paled, his mouth drew down, a sound escaped from his tightened throat.

He had the look of a man in pain.

Chapter Two

Someone was wailing. . . . It was a mournful sound, plaintive and desolate, its notes raw and loud one moment, soft and keening the next.

Had she been weeping? Yes, yes, she had been . . . earlier in the silent, winter-dead garden. Her head had throbbed, more so than usual, and she had sought ease in the cold sharp air. But there had been no peace along the powdery paths; the bare branches had clacked overhead, the wind had whined, and a flock of crows had cawed angrily in the snowdrift that covered last summer's herbs.

Lisbet turned her head a bit. It still ached, and her limbs seemed very weak, too sore and feeble to stir themselves. Indeed her entire body seemed strangely light, as if it were floating atop a cresting wave. Images of ice and swirling water flashed behind her eyes at the thought, and she instinctively gasped for air before shutting out the visions. She did not want to recall whatever it was threatening to resurface in her memory. She wanted only to sleep again, fall into a state of oblivion, dream dreams forever.

But reality intruded, prodding her reluctance until she opened her eyelids.

What was this . . . ? A low ceiling with rough beams slanted above her head, yellow light playing softly across its length. It was not the garlanded, blue-painted ceiling in her room at home; none of the ceilings in Wexford Hall were so crude as this one. Her eyes roved slowly downward. An unfamiliar quilt covered her, one plum-colored and worn, and between the peak her toes made at the end of the bed, she could see a fire burning in an unknown hearth. Beside it, a never-before-seen chair sported lace arm covers, and next to it squatted a needle-pointed footstool. Tea things rested upon a small oval table with dropped leaves and beneath it a pair of gloves lay abandoned upon the floor. She noticed they were large leather gloves—not her own—fawn-colored and stained darkly with water.

With a strange sense of unreality, she moved her gaze past an old-fashioned oak wardrobe, past a washstand to a dark rectangle of window. She studied it hopefully, but through the lace drape only a night sky showed, adorned by a moon whose guileless face gave no clue of her whereabouts.

Dizzy, she began to slide her eyes shut again, but as her lashes dropped, she noticed a leg stretched out beside her bed. Dove breeches encased its long length, and they were very damp and clinging. Knitting her brow in perplexity, too befuddled to be alarmed, she examined the bare foot. It was long and strongly formed, its ankle crisscrossed with newly healed scars. She noted further that the outstretched leg was held stiffly straight, while its counterpart was raised in a more relaxed posture. Nearby, standing upright, were a pair of black riding boots dripping puddles on the floor.

A wave of nausea suddenly seized her. She was disoriented. And so tired. How easy it would be just to drift into sleep again, let darkness sweep her into oblivion. *But who sat beside her?*

Slowly she tilted her head back and let her eyes follow the line of masculine leg upward. Its owner slept sprawled in a rocking chair. Looking uncomfortable, his head leaned back over its wooden backrest, exposing a dark column of neck interrupted by a prominent Adam's apple. In an almost absurd way the gentleman's lengthy frame overran the piece of furniture; indeed, his balance looked precarious. Both arms were folded across his chest, their wrists exposed by the rolled-up sleeves of a creased white shirt. The hands were well-shaped, squarish, and wore no rings.

Lisbet's gaze moved upward. His hair was dark, and the ends were wet, dripping tiny beads of water down his temples to the hollows below his ears. With the slant of his head and the contrasting light and shadow playing over it, his face seemed particularly angular, his chin harshly straight-cut. Deep lines scored either side of his mouth, strain furrowed his brow, and the gauntness of his cheeks suggested recent illness or some personal misfortune. Nature had gifted him with a remarkably handsome face, Lisbet thought, but life had made its expression hard.

She stared curiously at his exposed throat and crossed arms, thinking them unusually browned. Who would have sun-darkened skin during an English winter?

Gently she rocked her head from side to side, laying a languid hand across her brow. Confusion racked her. Who was this man? Like the room and all its furnishings, she did not know him . . . or did she?

Perhaps he felt her observation, for suddenly his eyes flew open, instantly alert, deeply black. Slowly he raised his head from its distressing angle and stared at her intently as if questioning what he saw.

"Wh—" Lisbet found she could not get the words around her tongue and tried again. "Where . . . ?" It was little more than a creaky whisper, but apparently adequate enough to get an answer.

"You are in my cottage," he replied in a low, quiet tone, as if that were sufficient explanation.

"Your cottage . . . ?"

His eyes scrutinized her. "I believe they call it Laurelpath."

She nodded, relieved to hear a familiar name in unfamiliar surroundings. "I know it. Named after . . ." she swallowed, for her throat was raw, "after the daughter of its original owner."

Leaning forward, her host tilted the runners of the rocker so he could examine her more closely. "Your memory seems intact. Thank God. I was beginning—" his voice was odd, "I was beginning to fear I'd lost you."

"Lost me . . . ?" she queried, pushing aside another frightening vision. "Where had I gone?"

Her companion smiled, but the smile was sad and held no brightness. Yet . . . just for a moment, Lisbet thought with strange excitement, the grooves on either side of his mouth had become something other than lines of stress. They were dimples . . . unexpectedly boyish dimples.

She blinked, concentrating upon the face before her. Its image blurred and grew as wavery as an object viewed through still, shallow water. It whirled, dizzying her, blending with flashes of the past like dye cast into a whirlpool. She kept her eyes affixed to the vision as if her very life depended upon it, for this dear face had been lost to her a very long time, and now, by some miraculous act of God, she was able to behold it again.

"Forgive me," he was saying, the words drifting to her ear as if from a great distance. "I've neglected to introduce myself." He paused and continued wryly. "But it's been an extraordinary day, to say the least. My name is York, Captain Forrest York."

Despite his comment Lisbet said nothing. She was unable to speak. Her head swam, her pulse hammered so madly in her temples she feared she would lose consciousness. Did she exist in reality, or had she slipped into some nebulous otherworld? Was *he* real . . . was *she?* Had she swung back in time or far forward into a dream she had dreamed before?

"Here, drink this," her host commanded, taking hold of her head and raising it up off the pillow.

She felt the smooth rim of a cup pressed to her lips and opened her mouth, trying not to gag as warm liquid trickled down her throat. It was tea, very sweet and strong—just as she liked it. Sputtering a little, she put the back of her hand to her mouth, never taking her eyes from the man seated beside her on the feather tick.

He had come back. . . . No, she told herself, *it is only that you have wished for his return for so long. And yet . . .*

He started to move away, and she spoke quickly, wanting to draw him close to her again, so close she could touch him if she needed to. "May I have more tea . . . ?"

Saying nothing at first, Forrest pulled the topmost blanket off the bed and, lifting her shoulders, draped it about them solicitously. Until then she had not realized she was clothed only in her undergarments.

Too disturbed to address the topic, she silently drew up the cover. At the same time feminine instinct caused her to put a hand to her hair. Feeling the long mussed strands straggling down her back, she slowly lowered her arm again. They were wet. Why were they wet?

As if no thought of impropriety had occurred to him, her companion proceeded to prop her up with gentle but impersonal efficiency, retrieving an extra pillow from a cedar chest and sliding it behind her shoulders. Silently he handed her a comb—his comb—fished from his hip pocket.

With self-consciousness she ran it through her knotted locks, realizing her arm was nearly too feeble to accomplish even such a simple chore.

"Can you manage the cup yourself?" Forrest asked after she had finished her little task of vanity.

She nodded, wrapping her fingers about the warm china and greedily swallowing every drop of tea.

"How about a biscuit? They're a little dry, but sweet."

"Er—please."

He passed her a plate from which she took two biscuits. Devouring them both, thinking vaguely that nothing had tasted so good to her in ages, she dusted the crumbs from her fingers and asked for another. "You said—" she spoke through a mouthful, "you said your name was . . . ?"

"Forrest York," he supplied, speaking with succinctness but regarding her oddly.

For awhile she remained silent. "The latest tenant of Laurelpath," she murmured at last. "You arranged to lease it in London last month." Nothing in the village of Winterspell was a secret for long . . . very little, anyway.

"Correct on both points," he affirmed, indicating neither surprise or offense at her knowledge. "And . . . your name?" he queried softly.

She lowered her eyes. Even after all these years she still had difficulty saying it. "My name is Lady Thorpe."

He seemed to ponder the title, as if turning it over in his mind. Then his eyes dropped to his thigh, where they studiously regarded a tear in his breeches. "Lady Thorpe," he repeated. "You're married then."

"Nearly nineteen years."

Solemnly his eyes touched hers again. "Nineteen years . . . a long time."

"Yes," she said in a trailing whisper. "A very long time."

"Your husband must be frantic."

Beneath the sheets her fists clenched. How could she have forgotten? For a time it was as if she had been transported into a warmer, safer world, one she did not want to leave.

"Yes," she affirmed, staring at the quilt until its plum-colored patches grew fuzzy and danced with ugly images. "He will be . . . most distressed. Wh-what time is it?"

Forrest glanced at the mantel clock. "Three A.M. You will have been missed quite a long time. I apologize for that, but," he indicated his outstretched leg with a nod, "I have a lame knee which prevented me from journeying to the village and leaving word. Besides . . . I thought it unwise to leave you alone."

He regarded her expectantly as if she were to glean some significance from his remark and respond to it. But her condition was a topic she was not yet ready to discuss.

"At any rate," he went on after she made no reply, "at first light I'll walk over and notify your husband."

"Have you no horse or carriage?" she inquired, unwilling to let him hobble the mile distance to Wexford Hall.

"I do, but he'll not be delivered until later. I was making my way here on foot this evening when you and I . . . met. Do you not remember?"

He pinned her with a piercing scrutiny. Beneath it, Lisbet began to recall, letting brief flashes of the past few hours seep through to her consciousness. Even as she stared, the blackness of her interrogator's eyes turned silver until it resembled an ice glaze upon the surface of cold deep water. A roar rose in her ears and her throat closed. She was suffocating. Quickly she shut her eyes, banishing the visions that panicked her. She knew there were questions she needed to ask of this man, details as to her being here in his cottage, but she could not bring herself to ask them. If she did, she would have to open wide her memory and face its unpleasant contents.

Forrest reached to measure the pulse in her wrist, and as if dissatisfied with the rhythm there, he began to vigorously chafe her hand.

"Rest awhile," he said, replacing her arm beneath the quilts. "You're dangerously weak from your ordeal. Foolishly I've tired you by allowing you to talk so long. Lie back. Sleep. In an hour or so you may sit up again." With that, he deftly pulled the extra pillow from her back and forced her to recline.

"No!" she said too sharply, struggling to rise up on her elbows. If she were to sleep again, fall into one of her heavy slumbers, he may be gone when she awoke. She might find herself lying upon the shadowy bed at Wexford Hall with its cold satin drapes closing out the light. "I don't want to sleep!" she cried. "Please don't make me sleep!"

Quickly Forrest put a reassuring hand to her shoulder, pressing her back. "Steady on. Don't upset yourself. I only thought you'd feel better if you slept. But here—" He turned to pour another cup of tea, adding a good measure of whiskey to it. "Maybe this will clear the cobwebs."

Grimacing as the fiery stuff went down, Lisbet at last experienced a gradual calming of nerves. She was embarrassed over her behavior, ashamed of the hysteria that seemed to loom so near of late. A moment ago she had come dangerously close to blurting out her private torment, that shameful secret best kept hidden. What if Forrest York were to pry?

Hastily composing her features, Lisbet willed herself to relax and change the subject. Not only did she want to steer his interest away from her troubles, she was curious about her host—madly curious. "Tell me about yourself, Captain York," she began, mustering enough strength to speak. "I . . . feel as if I'm somewhat at a disadvantage. After all, I know virtually nothing about you, while . . ." Her sentence trailed as she became aware of her barely clothed body beneath the sheets.

"I understand," he said, coming to her rescue, seeming to repress a smile. "But you know my name, and you know I am newly arrived here as the tenant of Laurelpath Cottage. What else about me could possibly be of interest to you?"

She hesitated. "Have you a wife . . . children?"

"No."

"Where have you . . . where do you come from?"

His look was direct, his voice earnest, but his eyes sparkled briefly as he spoke. "No place. I come from no place."

Lisbet smiled a tiny smile, and her eyes warmed as if with a confidence shared. "I think you're being evasive. But let me guess a little about you." She glanced at his brown arms with their fuzz of sun-lightened hairs. "You have lately been in a warm climate."

"Yes. I have been in one warm climate or another for—" he stopped himself in midstream, "many years."

"The South of France, perhaps?" she queried, remembering suddenly how the guessing games of childhood used to delight her. "No, you would have traces of the accent had you been there long. How about Spain, or Greece? Have you traveled to the Mediterranean? I have always wanted to see the Acropolis—oh, and Crete of course."

"I've seen all those places."

"All of them? I envy you. But where have you lately been?"

"I'll give you a clue. Pyramids."

"You have been to *Egypt?*" Lady Thorpe said wonderingly.

"Yes, but don't be jealous. It was hardly a pleasure trip."

"Business?"

"Yes. A most unpleasant sort of business."

"A death perhaps?" she asked cautiously, not wishing to be indelicate.

Rising, Forrest went to stand beside the fire, replying seriously. "There were many deaths, I'm afraid."

Lady Thorpe turned her head upon the pillow to observe his firelit profile. His eyes appeared clouded as they contemplated the dance of flames. His posture had stiffened, become straight-spined and square-shouldered all at once, like a soldier's stance. He has retreated from this room, Lisbet thought. He has journeyed to a land of shimmering sands and fiery sunsets and found the scenes there painful.

"The British military saw action in Egypt recently," she said quietly, wanting to draw him back to her. "You were amid the fray, weren't you?"

He took a poker from its stand beside the hearth and stabbed at the glowing embers. "Congratulations, Lady Thorpe. You have won the game."

And your leg?" she persisted, wanting to know all that had happened.

"Wounded in the line of duty," he acknowledged without taking his eyes from the fire. "And please don't waste your pity on me. I don't resent the sacrifice of my knee, so why should anyone else?"

Hurt by his brusqueness, Lady Thorpe said nothing, and for a time there remained a strain between them.

Her now-somber companion added logs to the fire, shifted them to their best advantage, and replaced the poker. Then he drew aside the curtain so the waning moonlight and approaching dawn could fall full upon the room. The night sky had given way a little, allowing the encroachment of morning's sapphire and lavender palette. Hovering above the treetops, the moon was quickly losing her silver brilliance.

"Hmm," Forrest murmured, staring out the window. "There's a light flickering through the trees below. I believe it's a lantern light. Someone seems to be coming through the woods in our direction."

A moment or two passed and he continued to watch. "It's a search party, surely. Two men are winding in and out of the brush down there, shouting and hunting about the trees and in the undergrowth. No doubt they're looking for you." He turned from the window to face her, and when his next words came, they seemed ponderously spoken. "I must go down to meet them now."

Lady Thorpe opened her mouth to utter a plea. Then she firmly closed it. For one wild moment had she actually meant to detain him, ask him not to reveal her whereabouts, ask him not to leave her? Fool! Did she really believe, even for the briefest spell, that she could keep from returning to Wexford Hall? Did she really think anyone, even *he* could keep her from her duty?

Huddling beneath the faded quilt, twisting the ruby ring upon her finger, Lisbet watched sorrowfully as Forrest York leaned to slide on his boots. She noticed he had no trouble with the first, but the second he eased on gingerly and with excruciating care. When he turned to exit, she saw he could scarcely set weight to his lame leg, could scarcely drag it forward, yet only the paleness of his face revealed his suffering. Not even his eyes flinched with the torment of it, nor did a gasp escape from between his lips, nor did his shoulders hunch.

But he had always borne pain with a stoicism not found in many, she thought with an ache in her heart. He had always stood flinty-eyed and square-shouldered to face every adversity. Even when narrow minds had inflicted scorn and prejudice upon his youthful heart, he had faced them bravely.

Slowly a stream of tears slid down Lady Thorpe's cheek. She let them fall unheeded, putting a fist to her teeth to smother a sob. How well she remembered standing at a distance, wide-eyed and terrified, watching the punishment meted out to a rebellious little orphan lad. How well she recalled witnessing his repeated humiliations. He had been so maligned, so ill-used, and yet, no beating, no harsh words, no embarrassments had ever quenched his spirit. Nothing, *nothing* had ever broken him, not isolation, not deprivation, and now, not even war.

She heard the *tap, scrape, tap, scrape* of his steps downstairs. Now that there were no witnesses, she wondered if he would allow a grimace of pain to twist his face. No, she decided; it would go against his nature.

Turning her face to the window, seeing the dawn rise inexorably before her eyes, she wished she had even a tenth of her rescuer's courage. How well she could use it now.

Chapter Three

Earlier Forrest had discovered a back exit to his cottage. The small, arched door there resisted his push, and he put a shoulder to it, freeing it from the frame. Not surprisingly, ice had formed all around its edges, and snow had drifted against its lower half. Stepping out, dodging a fall of powder from above, Forrest rested a hand on his hip and surveyed the view. The beauty of earth draped with a coat of nature's white always awed him. He breathed deeply of the dawn's raw and violet air, realizing all at once that he had missed the cold during his long sojourn from England. Only a few miles from here he had pitched snowballs across a kitchen garden and watched forlornly as a little girl had built snowmen with her nanny.

The sudden sentiment irritated him, and he swatted an icicle hanging from the eaves, letting it fall like a long glass spear into a mounded drift. For good measure he swatted another, and another. Pent-up emotion roiled just beneath the surface of his self-control, and the violence of his actions, the tenseness in the muscles across his shoulders eloquently betrayed it.

Getting hold of himself, sighing in frustration, he

stepped off the stoop and laboriously crossed the snow-covered yard, his boots crunching upon its icy surface. The low picket gate he swung open with a shove of his hand, sending it clattering on its hinges. Looking toward the woods, he searched for the elusive flicker of light he had seen earlier from the window. There . . . like a firefly, it wavered in and out of sight.

Raising his arms, cupping both hands about his mouth, Forrest shouted out an alert.

Almost instantly, two men emerged from the trees, their lantern casting an arc upon the snow, their capped heads lifted in his direction. After peering with distrustful faces through the tangle of shrubs edging his yard, they exchanged a few murmured words and trudged forward.

"Are you looking for Lady Thorpe?" Forrest called out as the well-bundled pair neared.

"Aye!" the taller of the two yelled. "Do you know where she is? Have you seen her?" The speaker was a tow-headed lad in need of a haircut with a rifle slung over his shoulder.

"She's inside," Forrest replied after a slight hesitation. Had he a choice, he would not have told them.

"Thank the saints!" exclaimed the lad's bandy-legged companion. Out of breath, he plowed through the last stretch of snow and, together with the boy, came to stand at Forrest's side. "The master's been afeared she were dead these past hours. 'Taint like 'er to wander off. Been out all night in the cold, we 'ave, lookin' behind every tree an' shrub for 'er. When she didn't return home last evenin', the master flew into a blitherin' rage. Fired the coachman, 'e did, for not insistin' that she ride. Every man on the estate's been routed out of 'is bed and sent to—"

"How did she come to be here?" the lad asked Forrest, cutting into the older man's dialogue. His voice and his widely spread stance displayed belligerence. "Was she here with you all night? Why hasn't the master been told?"

Forrest regarded the young man calmly, taking in the wide adolescent shoulders, cocksure posture, and distrustful blue eyes. A handsome, well-formed boy, he thought discerningly, a boy ready to test his budding manhood and, in the process, just asking for trouble.

Forrest gave him a cordial, but slightly cautioning smile. "I'll give answer only to Lord Thorpe, lad."

The boy's gloved fingers tightened upon the rifle stock. Beside him, the calmer man put a staying hand upon his arm. " 'E's right, ye know, Scottie. 'Tis only the master's business."

"Can you bring a carriage around for her?" Forrest asked, addressing the elder man.

"Aye. Right away we'll go back to Wexford 'All. But I must ask ye so that I might inform the master—is Lady Thorpe well? She 'asn't met with an accident, 'as she?"

Forrest hesitated, choosing his words with care. It would not do to reveal the details of Lady Thorpe's ordeal. Within hours the precise words exchanged between the new tenant of Laurelpath Cottage and the servants of Wexford Hall would be repeated by every busybody in the village. Amidst her other problems—whatever they may be—the lady hardly needed such a scandal.

"She's well," he said reticently, knowing his next words would set tongues wagging regardless of how he phrased them. "But bring her a change of clothes, if you will. And she could do with the services of a lady's maid."

"Why would she be needin' a change of clothes?" the lad asked suspiciously, immediately balling his fist. "If you've harmed her—"

"Scottie," the older man interposed, firmly taking the

boy's arm and pulling him towards home, "ye're wastin' time."

With a rude jerk, the youth took his elbow from the other's grasp and, throwing Forrest a hostile glare, turned sharply on his heel.

Shrugging in the classic gesture of an experienced man exasperated with youth, the boy's partner apologized. " 'E ain't really so bad. Just feelin' 'is oats. You remember 'ow it was."

Forrest nodded. He did indeed. Yet it wouldn't hurt the young pup to be taken down a peg or two, he thought, eyeing the arrogant youth's swagger with a frown.

He stood a moment more, watching the two coat-clad backs grow smaller against the landscape. As they tramped the lane the pair seemed to be having a lively discussion; their heads bobbed, their arms waved. Even at his distance, Forrest could hear the lad hurl a cheeky remark at the older man, and though its exact contents were indistinguishable, Forrest got the gist of it. He grinned. The brat reminded him of himself, twenty years ago.

In the distance, across three gentle hills of snow, he could just distinguish the slate roof and smoking chimneys of Wexford Hall. The remains of the grin faded from his mouth and his eyes grew bleak. The weight of what he had just done assaulted him like a blow. He had relinquished Lisbet. Letting his head drop to his chest in a moment of helplessness, he fought the surge of old frustrations. Suddenly it was as if no time at all had passed since his youth, it was as if he stood facing again an invisible foe that could not be vanquished.

Resisting an urge to touch the devil's mark upon his shoulder, Forrest raised his head and stared fiercely at the brightening sky. He made a vow to heaven. It was a private vow and savage in its sincerity.

Time's passage may not have altered circumstances, but it had surely altered Anvil.

A moment later, with his stiffened knee dragging, Forrest returned to the cottage, knocking the snow from his boots onto a kitchen mat before making his way to the stairs. Giving their steep ascent a baleful stare, he negotiated them with reluctance, knowing he must go to bid Lady Thorpe farewell. It was a task he did not relish, for not only did he hold grave concern for her well-being, he felt toward her a violent possessiveness as instinctive to him as breathing. She was despondent, in trouble, and he yearned to crush whatever threatened, using raised fists, flashing eyes, and savage words if necessary. However, he feared her mysterious burden was a thing she would not share.

Besides, she had a husband. It was his place to give her succor, comfort, protect her. Forrest would not be a welcome interference into the problems of their private lives. Yet, what if Lord Thorpe himself were her threat?

"I'll press her for answers, by God!" Forrest declared under his breath, hating to be thwarted. "One way or another she'll be made to tell me what plagues her."

Up to now he had refrained from probing too deeply, giving the fragile Lisbet time to recover and regain strength. Frankly he had hoped she would volunteer explanations; he had hoped she would speak of her attempted suicide and the terrible distress leading up to it. But she had not, and time, as always, was speedily running out for them. Shortly, her husband would come for her, carry her away, return her to the situation she found unendurable. Then she would be out of Forrest's reach, perhaps forever.

Arriving at the top of the stairs now, he slammed his fist into the oaken bannister. Aggressive, defiant, sometimes recklessly disregardful of consequences, he found it nearly impossible to stand by and watch the course of life flow by. He was a fighter: self-preservation had always demanded he be. These last years his only saving grace had been the wisdom of experience, which mercifully had gifted him with a measure of prudence and patience—if not much.

Lady Thorpe was reclining tranquilly when he reentered the bedroom, her long-lashed eyes fixed on the shadowy ceiling with a soft, pensive stare he could not interpret. Though his limping entry had been far from silent, she seemed not to have noticed it, and for the briefest moment Forrest stood poised upon the threshold. The scene spread before him was one he had envisioned countless times in the last years, especially during bouts of hardship and loneliness. Firelight gilded every corner of a clean, pleasantly furnished room, a hearth kept the cold at bay, a bed with starched linens and embroidered pillowcases invited comfort. And there, with skin like cream and hair unbound, a woman waited . . .

He faltered forward, crossed the room, and quietly dragged the rocking chair forward until it met the bed's edge. Lady Thorpe turned her head to look at him, observing him through liquid eyes composed of flecks of green, gold, and brown. Her stare was direct, fervent, and communicated a silent appeal. He wished he knew for what it appealed, and looked deeply into the hazel depths, searching, seeing the dreadful sadness there, experiencing it himself. He thought his own eyes must be a mirrored reflection of all she felt.

"They'll be sending a carriage for you directly," he said.

She looked heavenward, fixing her gaze just as if she could see through the ceiling. He noticed the hollows above and below her eyes, the arch of her fine-lined brows. Her nostrils flared like those of a startled mare, her chest rose and fell rapidly beneath the covers, and her hands gripped the quilt so that the knuckles turned white.

Chilled by the unnatural detachment of her stare, the stillness of her body, Forrest eased down upon her bed and took her rigid chin between his thumb and forefinger. His hand was unsteady, his usually fine set of nerves slowly shattering. He knew his time with Lisbet was quickly winging away. "Lisbet . . . ?"

Her lashes fluttered and beneath their shadow her gaze slowly swung to his.

"Do you trust me?" he asked gently, stirring her hair with his breath.

Unblinking, she nodded.

Squeezed by time, he spoke urgently. "Then tell me what you fear."

Her full, dry lips moved, but no words came.

Forrest's brows drew together in anxious concern. "You know I'll do whatever I must to keep you from harm. You've only to tell me who or what threatens you." Stroking her brow, he added in notes of anguish. "You believe that, don't you?"

A shimmer of tears brightened the gold-green of her irises, then slowly, brilliantly, spilled over.

"Tell me, Lisbet."

Her chin quivered at the sound of her name upon his lips, but she only swallowed and turned her cheek away into the pillow. "Th-there is . . ." Her breath trailed. "There is nothing."

Outside a sound marred the perfect morning stillness—the distant churn of iron-rimmed wheels furrowing a snowy lane.

"They're coming," Forrest warned, glancing toward the window. "We've only a little time left together. You must talk to me, let me help."

Lisbet grew still. Her lashes lowered to her cheeks

and her head rolled to one side. Strangely, Forrest thought, she seemed to be slipping into sleep again. Before his eyes her complexion drained and turned waxen until all traces of the fairest rose vanished from it. Finally her breathing slowed so that the covers barely stirred.

He watched the phenomenon of her mental retreat closely, realizing with astonishment that it was not sleep at all into which she fell, but some eerie trancelike state. Appalled, he stared, understanding that she was willing herself into unconsciousness, retreating from reality into some other world, a world that to her perhaps seemed a safer one than this.

Urgently he raised her limp shoulders off the bed, uncaring that the quilt slid down to barely cover her modesty. In an effort to rouse her from the stupor he shook her shoulders roughly, shouted her name, his fingers biting into the tender skin of her arms. She stirred enough to whimper, but her head lolled back in the manner of a rag doll, its honey stream of hair waving upon the pillow like pale golden streamers.

"Look at me, Lisbet! Look at me, for God's sake! Please!" He gave her another shake. "What are you doing? Don't drift away like that. Come back. Come back to me!"

Her eyes flickered, closed, then opened again. She viewed him through their slits.

Outside, harness bits jingled. A rough-accented voice shouted out a command for a carriage team to halt. Boots crunched in the snow.

"They're out there, Lisbet," Forrest warned again in a menacing voice, hoping to provoke her courage. "Do you hear them? I can't stop them coming unless you give me good reason." In a desperate attempt to pierce the dark oblivion she had so willingly passed into, he slapped her cheek. Then he grabbed her arms roughly and dug his fingers into her bare flesh with such force that they marred its whiteness. "Why did you try to take your life last night? Why have you given up, Lisbet?"

She stared up at him but gave no answer.

"Why?" Forrest repeated. Shaking her, ignoring the knock at the door downstairs, he accused, "You remember what happened last night. You remember jumping into the river—I know you do. You just refuse to think about it! *Why?"*

Her face crumpled; a small sob escaped like a breathy sigh from her throat. As if in denial she turned her head from side to side against the pillow. "I-I . . ." Her whisper faltered. She put a weak, trembling hand to her breast and spoke, her voice slow, tremulant, slurred. "I-I was wearing a locket . . . a g-gold locket. It fell from its chain as I stood to enjoy the river view at twilight. I leaned to catch it . . ." her sentence ended in a sigh. "I fell."

He did not believe her. "No," he said.

At the door below, the heavy-handed rapping had increased, grown persistent. Impatient voices rose above the banging, demanding to be admitted.

"I must go and let them in, Lisbet," Forrest hissed, angry with her passivity, enraged by her apathy. His time for her had flown but her stubbornness had not budged a bit. Desperate, unable to relinquish her quite yet, he slid his hand beneath the quilts, feeling the smooth sheet her body had warmed. He searched for her hand. Meeting skin as soft as velvet, feeling the fragility of small knuckles and oval nails, he enfolded her flesh in his. Breath escaped him at the contact. He lifted her fingers to his mouth, held them pressed there with his face twisted in anguish. The grotesque ring with its blood red stone—another man's token—cut into his palm as if warning him, and he squeezed it harder, smothering its ruddy glint.

Lisbet seemed to be struggling to rise up out of her darkness. Her eyes bored into his now. Not since he had brought her here had they been so bright, so clear and lucid and filled with life. Suddenly as his lips moved against her hand, she reached up and, in a violent gesture, tore at the collar of his shirt. A button snapped from its thread, the linen cloth gave way, and there, bared for her to see, was the dark symbol that marked him.

Her eyes widened. They glowed. They devoured the brown-colored shape with their ardent stare. Her lips moved, drawing in gasps of air. And then, in a frantic, clawing fierceness, she put her hands about his head and plunged her fingers deep into his hair, pulling his face to hers.

"Anvil! Anvil!" she cried.

Her embrace was like that of a wild creature, the press of her hands upon his head relentless. For an instant Forrest was stunned. And then he possessed no restraint. With a ferociousness that more than matched hers, he pressed his cheek to hers, clenched her hair, and groaned soft broken words. He slid his arms beneath her, lifted her a little, locked her fragile frame against his chest, and rocked her. Their embrace was desperate, filled with pain. The separation of years had put an obsessiveness in their touching, a hopelessness in their longing. There were no kisses. Their coming together again was beyond lust, far beyond physical boundaries.

"I must go, Lisbet," Forrest breathed raggedly, pulling back, struggling to recapture his sanity. "I must go and let them in." Threats to summon the constable were being made by those on the doorstep. No longer could Forrest keep the world at bay. He sat up, hastily reordering his shirt to cover his mark of shame, and made to go.

As if he had betrayed her with his words, Lisbet turned her head away.

No more eager for a separation than she, unable to bear her censure, Forrest groaned and moved close once more. The hand he brushed against her cheek was a despairing one, but his voice was stern. "I can't keep you from your husband, Lisbet, you know that. You have given me no grounds to do it. Save that of—" He broke off, his eyes bleak.

Downstairs his front door rattled against its frame.

Lisbet said nothing in reply. Slowly she rolled to her side, drew her knees up to her chin in an age-old posture of childhood, and stared at the pair of gloves upon the floor.

With his shoulders slumping in defeat, Forrest sighed. Then he left her to whatever private misery she so tenaciously guarded.

Sometime later, Forrest stood at his window. With wintry eyes he watched a coachman carry Lady Thorpe to her brougham, watched her lady's maid bustle about making certain her charge was duly wrapped against the cold. An attentive footman opened the polished black door and pulled down the step.

Every ounce of muscle in Forrest's body strained to dash outside and tear Lisbet away from their impersonal arms. Every instinct screamed for possession of her. He yearned to knock the coachman from his perch, send the other servants flying, drive Lisbet away himself. But not to Wexford Hall, not to any place within sight or sound or memory of Winterspell village.

With a curse of self-condemnation, he slapped the

butt of his hand down hard upon the window frame, rattling the glass. The dreams he dreamed were for fools. He had dreamed them before and learned well the lesson of their futility, felt sharply the sting of their disappointment.

Even as the brougham grew small in the distance, his eyes smoldered, then turned cool again, then evolved to a thoughtful black. "Strange that her husband didn't come," he murmured low in his throat. "What sort of bloody fool is he, I wonder, not to come?"

Then the churn of wheels faded from his ears and as leaden clouds gathered to blot the sunlight, he turned his back on the view. Crossing into the kitchen, limping to the line of damp clothes strung before the hearth, he touched first a lacy petticoat, then a silk stocking, and lastly the gray woolen gown. Sliding his hand within its folds, finding a pocket, he withdrew a small, polished object wrapped in a tattered handkerchief.

A stray sunbeam escaped from the clouds and darted through the window, glinting upon the cheap, heart-shaped piece of gold in his open palm. Thinly fashioned, its surface was dented, and tiny scratches marred its burnish. Long since the clumsily etched engraving had worn away and disappeared, leaving nothing but an aged patina. The flimsy clasp was broken and there had never been a chain.

Forrest closed his hand over the trinket. He clenched it so fiercely his flesh warmed its metal. With a terrible anguish his eyes shut and his belly knotted.

God help him. He knew she had lied.

Chapter Four

Two hours after Lady Thorpe's departure, with the morning still young and pale-colored, Forrest smeared a dollop of shaving lather on his jaw. Earlier a postboy had delivered his trunks and saddle horse, and after unpacking Forrest had set out clean clothes for the call he would be paying later . . . a very important call.

That no message from Wexford Hall had been delivered this morning baffled him. He had fully expected a tersely penned summons from Lord Thorpe demanding his immediate appearance at the Hall. What husband would not want an explanation of all that had transpired during his wife's overnight stay at a bachelor's cottage? For that matter, what husband would not march to the door with a brace of pistols in his belt and a demand for satisfaction?

Was Lisbet's spouse a simpleton without the sense to be suspicious? Or was he the cold, detached sort of aristocrat who divided his time between a mistress and the gaming clubs of London, and had little care for his wife?

It hardly mattered what sort he was, Forrest decided, becoming careless with his razor. Invited or not, Lord Thorpe would receive a visit today. He need never know that the reason for the call involved more than a polite, follow-up inquiry regarding the countess's health.

He need never know that Captain Forrest York coveted his lady wife with a fierceness approaching obsession.

All at once the harsh sound of a key grating in the lock of his front door shattered Forrest's turbulent thoughts.

"What the devil—" he murmured, putting down his razor and shrugging hastily into a freshly laundered shirt. Not bothering to wipe the cream from his chin, he descended the stairs with shirttails flying, hurling curses at both his stiffly uncooperative knee and his brazen intruder.

"Who in the dickens is it!" he roared. That someone had the audacity to wield a key in his own front door and interrupt him before he had even got the coffee brewed was enough to unleash his temper to the fullest.

Hearing the hinges of the door squeak open and footfalls cross the threshold, he bellowed with even more outrage. "Haven't you the decency to knock!"

Halting abruptly with two steps to go, he found himself face-to-face with a woman, a thin, dour-faced sort wearing a prim black bonnet. Her face was long and angular, her figure straight and spare, and the spectacles resting upon the tip of her nose threatened an imminent fall. Unstained white gloves glared upon her hands, and in the crook of her skinny arm she held a basket.

"Well!" she said abruptly in a judgmental tone, perusing him with a critical eye. "I'm glad ta find yer not a lazy bones inclined to lie abed all day—not ta say ya couldn't use a little sleep by the looks of them eyes." She glanced at the knee he held suspended. "What's wrong with yer leg?"

Forrest eyed her dubiously, and limping down the

last two steps, stood with his arms folded. The reply he gave her was a terse one. "I've never had the luxury of lying abed all day, madam, and the knee's a bit worse for wear. Now who the hell are you?"

As if in no hurry, his visitor set down the basket, removed her cape, and hung it neatly on a coat peg beside the door. With her back to him she answered. "Agatha Peacock."

Forrest thought it a most unlikely name; not a bit of color brightened any part of her severely clad person. "Who gave you a key to my cottage?" he demanded crossly, feeling the lather begin to dry and tighten on his face. "And more to the point, who do you think you are to *use* the blasted thing?"

She removed a long, wickedly sharp bodkin from her hat, set it and the headpiece upon a scarred huntboard, and draped her gloves across the crown. Retrieving the basket, Mistress Peacock then pertly raised her long boney nose and proceeded at a brisk pace toward the kitchen, throwing words over her shoulder. "Yer agent sent me a key, o' course. Ya said ya wanted the place cleaned, didn't ya?"

"I asked to have it cleaned before I arrived, aye," he found himself explaining, hopping along in her wake on his one sound leg.

"And was it?"

"Of course it was."

"Well, who do ya think *did* it?" Arriving in the kitchen, she put her basket on the table before pushing aside its gingham cover and drawing out a plate of buttered currant buns.

Forrest eyed them, his mouth watering. He had eaten nothing since yesterday afternoon, and even that meal had been only a cold one of bread and cheese.

"Are ya implying now that ya *don't* want the cottage cleaned?" Agatha queried with her hands on a pair of meager hips. "Do ya mean ta clean it yerself? If ya do, I dread ta see the state of the floors and the furnishings in a fortnight or two. Never seen a man yet as could clean properly."

Frankly Forrest had intended to keep it himself. He valued his privacy to a high degree, and the last thing he desired was a Winterspell villager snooping about his cottage and reporting everything she saw to her long-nosed neighbors.

Agatha's spectacled blue eyes seemed to accurately read his hardening expression. "If yer thinking I got a waggin' tongue, I don't. I'm a spinster livin' alone—except for a one-eyed cat—and very few of the overfed old crows of this village'll give me the time o' day." She sniffed. "For some queer reason, they rate themselves above me, as if havin' husbands and brats is something ta be braggin' about. They're a mean lot, I tell ya, all of them. Just because I ain't got a family of my own, don't make me a freak, now does it?"

Had her complaint not been so poignantly understood, Forrest would have smiled. As it was, he could sympathize only too well with her ostracism. "No more a freak than I," he drawled with more irony than she could appreciate. Then he reached to steal a bun from the plate.

" 'Course," the housekeeper continued dourly, "even if I had a mind ta, I couldn't add much ta the gossip already flying round the village streets. Why, look at ya—ya ain't been here a day, and already there's talk of a scandal. Word of the queer goings-on in this cottage spread this mornin' like a house afire."

Though her tone was a dutifully disdainful one, Forrest thought he detected a creeping note of admiration in it. Swallowing a bite of food, frowning as shaving cream blended unappetizingly with bread, he shrugged. "No immorality was committed."

Agatha pursed her lips and nodded toward the assortment of feminine garments still strung above the now-cold hearth. "Oh . . . ? If that old gossip-monger Martha Tewkesbury were ta peek her glinty eyes through yer window right now, she'd have more scandal than she could flap her lips about in a year."

"And what tales have her lips already been flapping?" Forrest asked matter-of-factly, limping from one cupboard to another in an attempt to locate a canister of coffee.

In her efficient way Agatha produced one from her fertile basket and, after tossing him a cup towel to wipe the lather from his face, set about to brew a pot for him. "Why, they say Lady Thorpe spent the night with you after she'd told her husband she was goin' for a stroll over by the river."

"And why do they say she stayed the night with me?" Forrest asked, lowering himself into a chair to ease his throbbing knee.

Agatha paused in her task, pressed her thin colorless lips together, and without a blush, let her eye travel the length of his masculine frame. Not a word fell from her tongue; apparently the pointed gesture of assessing his maleness was to stand as her answer.

"They must credit me with staggering seductive powers," Forrest replied with more sarcasm than contempt, helping himself to another bun. "After all, I only arrived in the vicinity an hour before I brought the lady here."

"After young Scottie's description of ya they're all fair dyin' to get a glimpse for themselves," Agatha pronounced, removing from her basket roast beef and raw vegetables for a cold supper. "Wouldn't be surprised to find a few of them females hangin' from the trees outside right now, a-spyin' on ya." Opening a narrow closet and producing a well-used broom, she attacked the spotless slate floor.

Forrest suspected Agatha herself was 'fair dying' to know why Lady Thorpe had sheltered at Laurelpath Cottage, but those details he would share only with Lisbet's husband. Then *he* could then decide what tasty morsels to feed the villagers, if any at all.

"What do you know about the occupants of Wexford Hall?" he questioned his housekeeper, tapping the ready source of information bustling just beneath his nose.

Agatha employed her broom more vigorously, swiping at the crumbs of currant bun lurking under Forrest's sprawled legs. "Humph!" she snorted, rolling her eyes heavenward. "Strange lot, *they* are."

"Oh?"

She cocked her head as if considering. "They ain't like other folks, that's all. They're peculiar."

He wondered with a sort of dry humor if she used the people of Winterspell as her standard for normal behavior. "What sort of man is Lord Thorpe?" he prodded smoothly, indicating no more than casual interest. "Is he considered a good man—you know, a generous husband, kind father, all that . . . ?"

"He's never been a father," Agatha declared, shaking her head with its mouse-colored topknot. "All these years and his lady has never once conceived."

Forrest closed his eyes briefly against a rush of emotion. He was glad the lady had not conceived, he was glad the lord's seed had never swelled in her belly and been nurtured at her breast. He could not have borne seeing a child with another man's eyes in its face clutching at her trailing skirts and calling her Mama. Not after—

A tiny clatter suddenly interrupted the savage turn of his thoughts, and he took himself in hand, knowing he had been caught within the threads of a spell, an ancient, dangerous spell threatening to reawaken.

"Do ya take sugar in yer coffee?" Agatha repeated. "Or cream?"

"No," he said with vagueness, belatedly realizing a cup of the fragrant brew steamed near his hand. "No. I prefer it black."

"You've been ailing, haven't ya?" Agatha asked suspiciously. "Not takin' proper care o' yerself. Have ya seen a surgeon?"

He laughed with no humor. "This last year I've seen more surgeons than you can shake a stick at."

"Ya don't say?" Agatha exclaimed. "Well, it don't look ta me like they done ya much good." Then suddenly, as if unable to contain curiosity a moment longer, she blurted, "What're ya doin' in Winterspell anyway?"

Forrest raised the cup of coffee to his lips, and discovering the liquid too hot, set it down again. With a raised brow, he inquired, "Gathering fuel for gossip, Mistress Peacock?"

She huffed and crossed her arms.

"Very well," he conceded. "I'm here to do some writing for the military, complete a journal. And you have my permission to relate that to the village gossipmongers." He tried the coffee again. "Perhaps I'll even write something about one of *them*—something . . . scandalous."

Agatha put a hand to her powdered, slightly fuzzed cheek and patted it as if it were growing hot. "My, my, but you are ripplin' the waters in the pond."

He lifted a lean, well-muscled shoulder, then neatly turned the dialogue back to the Hall. "You were speaking earlier about Lord Thorpe, I believe . . . ?"

With her tongue touching her upper lip, she spread her hands upon the table top and contemplated their boney, work-worn shape. "Most would say he's a decent man. 'Course, he rarely shows his face outside the gates of Wexford Hall. But he's quite openhanded with his wealth. Just last month he donated money so's we could order two stained-glass windows for the church. But that sort of spendin' is nothin' to the kind of spendin' he does on his wife." Agatha snorted. "He fair smothers her with fine things—I've never seen the likes of it. New carriages, blooded horses, costly jewels, Russian furs—more stuff than any woman could use. Why, he brought two seamstresses all the way from London for her special use," she imparted with obvious disdain, "just in case she should suddenly take a fancy to some new style in them dress catalogues."

Folding her barren hands, she settled them primly in her lap. "The strange thing is, she has nowhere to wear her finery—we ain't got no Assembly Hall or fancy ballroom here, ya know—and we ain't even got but one paved street for her three carriages."

Forrest digested every word of gossip Agatha divulged. Her description of Lord Thorpe hardly suggested an abusive husband. On the contrary, her picture seemed a rather flattering commendation of the fellow, even if he was extravagant.

"As husbands go," he concluded, eyeing her carefully through his lashes, "it sounds to me as if the lady could hardly ask for better."

Rising, Agatha stuffed her gingham cover back into the now-emptied basket and retrieved the coffeepot from the stove, freshening Forrest's cup. "I'll say no more, for as I told ya at the onset, I'm not the gossipy sort. Wait till ya've seen the man, then judge him for yerself." Clicking her tongue, she added, "Don't know which lot is queerer, the one at Wexford Hall or that mad menagerie in the Tower."

With that, she departed from the kitchen like a stiff

breeze, declaring it her intent to retidy the upstairs bed that Forrest had already, with perfectly mitered corners, made himself.

He had wanted no other to smooth out the worn embroidered sheets upon which Lisbet had lain.

An hour later, well-dressed against the cold, Forrest tramped the snow-packed surface of his yard, his step more halting than yesterday, the sting of crisp air reddening the cheeks that sickness had paled. Across one shoulder he toted a well-oiled saddle, and in his hand he carried a new black bridle.

The sun had deigned to show her face today, spreading yellow beams across winter's landscape, gilding ice, and scattering glitter upon the snow. With his breath making silver clouds in the brightened air, Forrest paused to take stock of his surroundings, noting the newly thatched roof of the rough-timbered cottage, the green hollies skirting its rectangular foundation, and the remains of an old stone well behind the wash house.

A few yards away his horse nickered softly, its wild-maned head crooked expectantly over the gate of a livestock pen. Forrest's purchase of the thoroughbred had been an impulsive extravagance, one of the few he had ever allowed himself. Chestnut, with four white stockings and a starred face, the animal was of the best steeplechasing stock in the country, and Forrest whistled to it in greeting, knowing he would soon have to make arrangements for its board elsewhere. The cottage had no proper place to house a blooded horse used to the attention of pampering grooms.

Bobbing its head, the high-strung creature sidestepped as Forrest settled the saddle upon its back. "Save your energy, old boy," he said. "Soon enough you'll work up a lather on that red-gold hide." Then, setting the boot of his healthy left leg to the saddle, he eased the right over the cantle and kept it dangling, unable to bend it to the stirrup iron.

The cottage drive took them out onto a twisting lane whose narrow, snow-veiled ruts snaked through a line of barren maples. Far beneath them, wending its way through an icy valley, glinted the river, and in the distance where land met sky, a crumbling bridge spanned its width. The sight seemed as familiar to Forrest as a memory from yesterday, and he marveled that his recollection of the past was so keen, marveled that a mere glimpse of a bridge could cause the agony of old emotion to return with a forceful knotting in his belly.

He had been born to this hamlet—at least, he thought he had. Thirty-six years ago a vicar had climbed a hill to the Norman church and, opening its door, been disturbed by a mewling cry. Thinking some small animal had wriggled its way through a broken window, the old man had investigated, inspecting the pews, the font, and lastly the apse. There, placed precariously upon the finely carved altar, swathed in nothing more than the altar cloth itself, lay an infant. It had been a male child, newly born, with no traceable identity other than a birthmark, queerly shaped.

That stamp of the devil, as some had so quickly sought to term it, had become the infant's only name, and had remained a brand of disgrace and abasement all the years of his boyhood. Only one heart in Winterspell had been merciful enough to offer the outcast a permanent home. Lady Tattershall of Wexford Hall had taken pity on the unclaimed, unwanted baby and brought him to her estate. There he was raised by no one in particular, his early care entrusted only to the mercy of off-duty scullery maids and rough-handed laundresses. When he was old enough to toddle, he was put to good use, doing simple chores like picking strawberries in springtime or scattering grain for poultry. Later, after Lady Tattershall's death, he had been required to work at much more taxing employment, and though he had never avoided hard labor, experience eventually taught him that no one had ever been more a slave than he.

There had been one bright spot in his early years, however, a warm, doll-toting little personage much his own age, who, like a star, infatuated him with her shine. But like any light in the heavens, she was untouchable, for she was the lord and lady's dearest treasure, their only child.

Worshipfully gazing at her from afar at every chance, Anvil had noted each feature of her curl-framed face and long-lashed eyes, every detail of her clean pink-sashed gowns and white-eyelet pinafores. And then one day, when they were both much older, he had come upon her in the woods by accident.

It had been his habit in the brief twilit hour between toil and sleep to wander beside an old stone bridge straddling the river. While lending him sufficient cover, the arched bridge provided a view of Winterspell Tower, that ancient structure that had always enthralled him in some dark, unhealthy way. The secluded place in the shadow of its battlements became his sanctuary, the one spot on earth where an anguished, lonely foundling could sit and dream the dreams of every child.

Appropriately it was here where the little girl of Wexford Hall had first entered his empty world. She was perhaps seven or eight then, and, surprisingly, much more intriguing at close range than she had ever been distantly. Like a shy woodland doe, she had only stared at him for awhile from behind a tree, and like a spell-struck idiot he had stared back. Finally he had extended his hand and offered from a purple-stained palm the handful of blackberries he had gathered. Timidly she accepted them like a great prize and, giving him half back, insisted he share them with her. With that simple gesture of equality, that act of kindness, Anvil's lonely heart had convulsed and beat more strongly than it ever had before . . . and given itself over to her forever.

Sadly, in the midst of their innocent feast, her father had discovered them. While his daughter looked on in horror, the enraged Lord Tattershall had whipped Anvil with his riding crop, beat him so savagely the boy had been unable to work for a fortnight. But the brutal punishment did little to deter Anvil from pursuing his beloved playmate. The urge to fight hardest for that which was denied him was in his nature, and in the days following the beating, the ill-used boy grew more determined than ever to see the lord's daughter.

To his astonishment it seemed the little girl was as eager for his company as he was for hers. Not two months after his flogging, while Anvil pondered Winterspell Tower with his back against the bridge, he felt her presence near. Turning, he found her sitting quietly a few yards away, watching him with liquid, uncertain eyes. He had smiled and gone to take her little hand in his, and contentedly they again shared berries. Afterwards, ignoring danger, they contrived to meet at regular intervals.

It was in his thirteenth year that Anvil first noticed a difference in the way he felt about his forbidden companion. His love was greater than ever, to be sure, but upon accidentally brushing his hand across her slightly swelling hip, he had experienced a splendorous new sensation. It thrilled him so that he trembled, but frightened him as well, because he realized his longing for her had taken on a new and powerful meaning, one that she did not yet understand. Carefully he controlled the force that stirred him, fearful of its consequences, while waiting patiently for the current that kindled his being to awaken in her own.

Their meetings grew less frequent over time. She was guarded more alertly, while he was doled more work. From necessity they grew more clever in their strategies to meet, more sly in eluding discovery. All the while nature was changing them, squaring his shoulders and rounding her curves. As a token of his maturing love he gifted her with a cheap gold locket won in a game of cards. No longer did he hide his longing for her; no longer was she ignorant of the intensity of that longing. Nature fueled them. Obsession drove them. It was inevitable that youth and forbidden love would have their way.

One evening she had arrived with a sacrament book in her hand and solemnly shown him the pages of the rites of marriage. He had needed no prompting to repeat the vows with her, for long ago he had confessed his love and, with the idealistic fervor of youth, sworn to wed her one day. Their ceremony beneath the bridge had been as grave as any performed before the altar in a church, their exchanged kisses at its conclusion no less ardent for lack of a license sanctioned by law.

In the aftermath of their first coming together, even while they lay entwined and damp-browed upon their mossy bed, the unwary lovers were discovered. While looking for poachers, the strange, wild-eyed master of Winterspell Tower had stumbled upon them in the half-light. He had at first been astounded, then gleeful at the find and, with his musket steadily aimed, torn Anvil from his beloved. The boy's degradation was extreme and increased when he was paraded naked through the village streets and into Wexford Hall. There he was viciously whipped once more by the furious Lord Tattershall before his bundled clothes and prostrate form were thrown like so much rubbish from the gates.

A flock of crows flew from their cover beside the road now, startling Forrest out of his reverie. He and the stallion had reached their destination.

Before them, unaltered and indomitable, Winterspell Tower rose up like some monolithic pillar dropped down from heaven. Forrest felt his neck tingle at sight of it, experienced the same rush of fascination that had disturbed him as a child. He knew its features intimately—the number of its arrow slits, the color of its limestone blocks, the texture of its ivy-cracked mortar. In his wild, solitary youth, he had trespassed upon its grounds often enough to know many things about it. Yet, with a strange persistence, it retained its air of mystery.

Forrest swung his gaze a little, following the line of the long gray shadow cast by the Tower spire. It lay upon the snow like a stain, pointing a crooked finger at the river and at a bridge crumbling beneath its weight of years.

Slowly he dismounted and, faltering upon his crippled leg, limped down to the river's edge. Even as he walked he felt as if he were crossing over the boundaries of time, returning to a place in the past from which he had never quite departed. Though he had encountered distant shores and countless faces, a part of him had always remained here.

With bleak eyes Forrest stood staring, giving himself up to a flood of grief, that peculiarly tenacious type of grief that time can never heal. Just for a moment he wished he could return to his youth, wished he could feel again the hope of childhood, the simple faith in life. Just for a moment he yearned to turn back the clock, live again in the time when Lisbet had been his own.

For a long while he stood beneath the bridge, listening again to the whispering voices echoing off its arches, tasting again the ripening blackberries twined upon its stone, seeing again the ghost of a smiling face.

Here in this place the thing he had loved best in the world had been torn from him, and even now, decades later, it remained the only thing he had ever loved.

With a sigh he turned about, drawing the collar of his coat more closely about his neck. Then, with a uneven step, he retrieved his horse, turned it southward, and headed for Wexford Hall.

Chapter Five

For a moment Forrest paused outside the scrolled gates of Wexford Hall and, with a gaze so hard it would have frightened many, stared at its distant door. The door was an oaken one, set within a fine Georgian façade of mellow stone, fronted by a dozen steps and a pair of marble lions. To most it would seem no more than a stately entrance to a grand estate. But to Forrest York it represented hatred and evil, and symbolized all the grief and isolation still buried beneath his heart.

With the nudge of an ungentle heel he sent his horse forward, traveling down that straight graveled road where nary a weed dared sprout. He had last traveled it twenty years ago—except then, of course, he had been naked, his hands shackled and his nose bloodied, his ears filled with the catcalls of a crowd wielding stones.

"Knock the devil down!" one onlooker had screamed. "Knock 'em senseless! 'E's Satan's own, 'e is, marked with the Dark One's sign!"

"Either kill 'im or send 'im away from our village!" cried another. "Else 'e'll be sullyin' *our* daughters next! Just look at 'im! You can see the evil in 'is eye."

But the villagers had cheered loudest when the Marquess of Winterspell, at the end of an aged musket, had delivered Anvil to the imperious Lord Tattershall for further punishment. With one collectively held breath, the throng had waited, watched as the door swung open and the master appeared.

"What's the meaning of this disturbance?" he had demanded of the marquess in an impatient tone.

Upon being told of the crime and presented with its perpetrator, the enraged lord had uttered a curse so loud it reverberated like cannon through the wood. Then he had snarled and, with the wild eyes of some fiendish judge from hell, thrown wide the door of his court so that all could watch the meting out of justice. Beneath the gaze of every villager, beneath the tender eyes of his hysterical daughter, the nobleman had laid a whip to Forrest's hide, lashed it fourteen brutal times—the number of Lisbet's natal years.

Remembering caused perspiration to bead upon Forrest's brow even in the cold, and he went pale with anger, feeling a rage so strong and violent he shook with the struggle to keep it bridled. When a movement from the estate caught his eye, he jerked his head up as if threatened, seeing a figure framed within a second-story window. But just as quickly as it had come, the figure disappeared, glided back into shadow, leaving no clue of identity.

When a groom came around from the stable, Forrest relinquished his mount and inhaled a few hard breaths before limping up the familiar stone steps. His forceful knock summoned a stiff-faced butler who ushered him inside, then took his coat and gloves and bade him wait.

And so he stood once more in the vast hall that had seen him so debased, saw again the cold marble tiles and lofty ceilings that had witnessed that chilling scene so many years past. Yet great changes had been wrought. Where once the Hall had been simply furnished, it now dripped with ornamentation. Gold-leaf molding festooned every wainscoted wall; silver vases, porcelain figures, and ancient urns glinted in painted niches; and a massive crystal chandelier trembled at every draft. Romanesque sculpture stood in dark corners, and the walls were hung with crimson silk. The whole effect suggested not only great extravagance but vulgar gaudiness.

"The earl will see you now," the butler announced from a doorway, standing expressionless as Forrest moved to follow.

Down a corridor they went, passing more marble busts, more toga-draped sculpture, and more cascading chandeliers. Upon their arrival at a closed mahogany door, the butler nodded his head.

"The earl awaits you inside." He retreated, his footfalls quietly tapping polished tiles.

Forrest put a hand to the latch and stepped across the threshold.

A long, overfurnished library spread itself before him. Within it, flames blazed in the hearth, figurines danced upon spindle-legged tables, fringed pillows adorned every chair, and beside a monstrous potted palm, a cockatoo fussed atop its golden perch. Laden bookshelves marched from floor to ceiling, their volumes richly bound in the finest leather and stamped with gilded titles. At the windows the tasseled drapes were drawn, shutting out every ray of winter light and casting gloom in all the corners.

In the midst of the library stood a massive desk of French design. A multibranched candelabrum reflected off its satiny top, fluttering wildly with the draft Forrest brought. Behind the desk a huge leather chair faced backwards.

Forrest scanned the room for movement, searching sofas and chairs for sign of his host, all to no avail. Yet he sensed a presence here.

Disliking such theatrics, he scowled and, turning his attention once more to the reversed desk chair, stepped forward to take a closer look.

And there, motionless upon its leather arm, rested a miniature hand with lace framing its tightly curled fingertips.

". . . 'Though from upper day thou art a wanderer, and thy presence here might seem unholy, be of happy cheer!' "

A strangely lisping voice uttered the words, and though it seemed masculine, its tone was curiously high-pitched for that of an adult.

Hardening his jaw with impatience, Forrest wondered what strange game his host played, wondered why the fellow did not turn about and show himself.

And then the chair swiveled slowly around, so that the light of a dozen candles revealed its mysterious occupant. And a *singular* occupant he was! With his diminutive height, hunched shoulders, and extraordinarily ill-proportioned visage, he seemed a character straight from the pages of a frightening children's book. His face was unlike any Forrest had ever seen, being disfigured with a high-domed brow, sagging cheeks, and full cherry red mouth. His eyes were huge and brown and drooping like a hound's, the pink rims of the lower lids being much in evidence. His garb was of another age and quite flamboyant with its ruffled shirt, puce brocade waistcoat, and bold striped cravat. Upon his stubby fingers rings set with gemstones of every shape and color shimmered, accentuating hands that were dark and dreadfully misshapen.

Forrest narrowed his eyes and firmed his mouth, attempting to mask utter astonishment. He had envisioned some imperious aristocrat here, fine in face and figure, who would be his match in height. He had expected to face a man whose powerful presence, stern-jawed face, and cruel mouth would hint at the cause for Lisbet's unhappiness. Frankly he had even looked forward to confronting such a man.

Instead, he had found . . . whom? He scrutinized the person before him with incredulity, seeing a man who was half his size, a man who, at best, might be termed curious in appearance—at worst, grotesque. By no stretch of imagination, however, could this odd personage be considered a threatening figure.

Feeling as if the wind had been taken from his sails, Forrest let a breath slide through his teeth.

His host seemed to take no notice of his chagrin. Within his crooked hands he held an open book, and he perused its dog-eared pages so absorbedly Forrest wondered if he had forgotten the presence of his guest.

When at last he snapped the volume shut, he looked up from its cover and declared, "Keats, of course. Extraordinary fellow, don't you think? One of my favorites."

Obviously not expecting an answer, the dwarf smiled, revealing pointed teeth. He stroked the cover of his poetry volume, and his bejeweled fingers sent arcs of rainbow color sparking off the ceiling. "You're pondering several questions, I'll be bound, fine sir," he said. "One of which is, 'Can this creature be Lord Thorpe, Earl of Tilbury? Can this naughty trick of nature be wed to the fair and gentle Lisbet?' "

Tilting back his sparsely haired head, he roared with glee as if enjoying the merriest of jokes. "Hee! Hee! Hee! The answer is yes, of course! I *am* Lord Thorpe—the very same. And the fair Lisbet is indeed my very own, my dearest flower."

It was a rare occasion that caught Forrest York off guard. And though he had never been one to judge character by appearance, Lisbet's choice of mate astounded him. Regaining composure, he stepped forward and began an introduction of himself.

"I know who you are," Lord Thorpe cut in, waving a tiny hand. "Lisbet has told me about you . . . much about you."

Forrest wondered *how* much and for a moment felt betrayed. He said coldly, "I must apologize for not immediately notifying you of Lady Thorpe's accident and of her whereabouts—"

"You needn't apologize," the gnomelike gentleman cut in, rising up from his chair with a creak of leather and a rustle of satin knee breeches. He adjusted his waistcoat, pulled it snugly down over a rounded belly, then checked the time upon his silver pocket watch. "Have you taken tea, Captain York?"

When Forrest replied negatively, Lord Thorpe toddled to the door and, with great aplomb and a flourish of his arm, issued an invitation. "It will be served in the drawing room in precisely six minutes. I should be honored to have you join me." He raised a crinkled brow. "It is a rare treat to have visitors here. But having seen me, I daresay you arrived at that conclusion already."

"And Lady Thorpe?" Forrest inquired, not to be detoured from his purpose. "Will she join us?"

The little man gave him a twinkling glance and quoted, " 'Stand ye calm and resolute, like a forest close and mute, with folded arms and looks which are, weapons of unvanquished war—' "

"Shelley," Forrest supplied drolly, making his host chuckle in delight. "One of *my* favorites."

Of all the rooms glimpsed in the refurnished Hall, the drawing room intrigued Forrest most. It was packed with furniture in the Dolphin style, that fanciful design created earlier in the century to commemorate Nelson's naval victories. Forrest had seen examples of it once in India while delivering dispatches to an admiral's house and had never forgotten the unusual embellishments characterizing its graceful curves.

With a glance he took in the rest of the room, noting with appreciation the huge gilt-framed paintings depicting ocean scenes and sailing ships, and the collection of ship accouterments displayed all about. Most whimsical of all was the brass-trimmed porthole which was cut in the opposite wall. It allowed the room its only source of natural light, for the velvet curtains on the other windows were just as tightly closed as those heavy coverings in the library. Sunlight, it seemed, was an unwelcome visitor at Wexford Hall.

"Be seated, be seated, fine sir," Lord Thorpe invited, waiting for Forrest to take a chair before lowering his round little figure onto a settee. "We shall be joined by my fair flower very soon." He raised a finger suddenly and closed his eyes tight, exclaiming, "Ah! 'He knew whose gentle hand was at the latch, before the door had given her to his eyes.' "

A whisper of silk sounded then. Forrest glanced up expectantly. Hovering upon the threshold in dark blue silk, her cheeks flushed, her expression uncertain, stood Lisbet. In contrast to her ornate surroundings and the garish, outdated garb of her husband, she was severely attired, wearing no lace, no furbelows, no jewelry save her wedding ring.

The sight of her caused Forrest's chest to constrict, and just as he had done last night, he compared the girl he had carried in memory so long with the vision of this woman standing quietly before him. There was no question the woman was lovely, yet her loveliness was not of the vibrant, blithe sort of lost days. Now her skin was pale with lack of sun, her hair snooded to keep its dance of curls confined, and her eyes fraught with some unnameable care.

As she moved, he noticed how graceful and unobtrusive was her walk. Once it had been buoyant, the skipping gait of a free-spirited girl. The contrasts sobered and disturbed Forrest. He felt a queer sort of pain, a sorrow over her lost liveliness. Yet, in spite of all the changes, he found he loved her no less.

Slowly he came to his feet and set his jaw, hardly trusting himself not to betray his emotion with a look, an impulsive word. At the same time Lord Thorpe hastened to his wife's side, taking her hand and bowing over it in a comically formal manner.

"My dear," he said in his reedy voice, "look who has come to call—Captain York, your rescuer—or do you think of him as a guardian angel?"

Lisbet met the visitor's eye, her gaze faltering beneath his direct and telling regard. Her eyes were liquid, brimming with moisture, and the skin beneath them was smudged a pale pink, a sign perhaps of recent tears. Words seemed to hover upon her trembling lips, which were full and dewy and parted.

As Lord Thorpe released her hand, Forrest took it, bending to place a gentlemanly kiss just above the cool and drooping wrist. The smell of flowers clung to her skin as if she had just splashed scent from a bottle.

"Lady Thorpe," he greeted her in a husky voice.

Beneath the touch of his possessive fingers, her hand fluttered and her eyes dilated until they looked black. Faintly she shook her head in warning.

But she need not have feared. For her sake Forrest would do nothing, say nothing to arouse her husband's suspicions.

Lord Thorpe lingered near like a small anxious shadow, and Forrest stepped aside dutifully, watching as the aristocrat again took Lisbet's fingers and drew her close. One misshapen hand reached up to brush the length of her silk-clad arm, caress it in a long loving stroke, but she nudged it away in a movement so subtle, a less aware onlooker would not have noticed it.

Forrest's fists clenched in a reflexive action. In spite of Lisbet's cool response, the sight of another man exercising his husbandly rights over her caused the cold prickle of jealousy to stiffen his spine. An instinctive urge made him want to shove Thorpe away and take his place beside this woman who, since boyhood, he had considered his own.

"Are you feeling better, my love?" Lord Thorpe whispered to his wife, his dark balding dome barely topping her shoulder. "If you aren't inclined to entertain today I'll escort you back upsta—"

"No," Lisbet answered quickly, her voice thin and breathy. "I'm fine. J-just some tea . . ."

"Of course, love. Here it comes now."

A tea trolley was wheeled in by a crisply uniformed servant, who unloaded onto a serving table a set of damask napkins, an elegant silver service, and buttered scones.

Lisbet sank down upon a chair, declining, Forrest noticed, the sofa to which her husband had led her. Looking dolefully at her with his large sagging eyes, the little man went to sit alone.

"Can you pour, dear?" he asked solicitously. "Or do you feel yourself too weak?"

For answer she merely took up the silver pot and tipped its steaming liquid into three china cups. Taking hold of the first, she stretched her hand out and offered it to Forrest, but her fingers shook so violently tea spilled over, splashing out of the saucer onto her slender fingertips.

Taking hold of the cup, Forrest dabbed at her hand with his napkin, watching her with concern. He could not fathom what ailed her, for she did not appear ill in a physical sense. But nervousness obviously beset her, its telltale signs in the quiver of her hand, the flutter of her lashes, and the twin spots of color staining otherwise colorless cheeks.

"My dear," Lord Thorpe began again, leaning forward to touch her sleeve like a fretful child, "I really must insist that you go up and rest a bit more. You—"

"No."

Her refusal was definite, her mouth thin with stubbornness.

Forrest glanced at Lord Thorpe. He almost felt sorry for the man. Deep within the ugly brown eyes, there glowed a soulful, naked worship of Lisbet which Forrest likened to a penitent gazing upon the sculpted face of a Madonna.

So that is the state of affairs, he mused. Lord Thorpe adored his wife, there could be no question of that, and from all appearances he treated her tenderly and with respect. Why then did she have reason to consider suicide?

"So, tell me, Captain York," his lordship addressed him now. "How do you find our quaint little borough?"

Forrest set his cup down and answered smoothly. "I'm afraid I haven't been here long enough to pass judgment upon it."

"Diplomatic of you," Lord Thorpe drawled, picking up two lumps of sugar with silver tongs. "Especially when it has already passed judgment upon you." He dropped the sweetener into his tea with a plop and shrugged his humped, uneven shoulders. "Of course, I pay little attention to such gossip. Having lived life more as a spectator than a participant, I learned long ago to judge men by their characters rather than by their—er—outer trappings, you might say. Who better than I can understand that the flesh may not characterize the soul?" His smile held a sad and ancient wisdom.

Grudgingly Forrest found himself admiring the man's candor.

The dwarf regarded his guest. "My wife tells me you are widely traveled."

"I have seen much of the world, yes," Forrest answered. "I just returned from the Middle East, as a matter of fact."

"Compliments of the Royal British Navy, I understand."

"Yes." Forrest's eyes flickered in Lisbet's direction, but she avoided meeting them. Was no part of their past, no part of their newly found present left to them alone? Had it all been shared in whispers between the lady and her lord upon some shadowy bed? Had she withheld nothing from her husband?

"I have ventured out beyond the boundaries of merry old England only once," Lord Thorpe continued conversationally. "And, oh, what treasure did my travels reap!" He turned his eyes to Lisbet and they sparkled as if truly beholding the brightest of treasure troves.

"W-we met in Italy," Lisbet put in suddenly as if needing to explain. "My father took me there when I was . . . when I was but fourteen." Her voice quavered, and after glancing askance at Forrest, her eyes lowered down to her interlaced hands. "I confess I didn't enjoy it as I should have done. But I was homesick. Papa was displeased over my attitude and lectured me often. He couldn't understand my misery, my yearning for . . . for Winterspell."

With her simple words, related so casually, she had told Forrest much, revealed to him her despair and loneliness following their brutal separation.

"But you were very young, pet," Lord Thorpe commiserated. "And travel is wasted upon youth." He looked at Forrest. "She was a child bride—barely fifteen when she consented to be my wife. I brought her back to England immediately, where we took up residence at my Surrey estate until her father died. She insisted upon returning here, and," he leaned to pat her shoulder, "since I am unable to deny my precious pet anything, I agreed readily enough."

"Permit me to inquire as to your health, Lady Thorpe." Forrest changed the subject with pointed emphasis. "Have you recovered from your . . . ordeal?"

She set down the cup and put a hand to her high-collared throat. "Yes, I-I've recovered, thank you," she faltered. "So clumsy of me to fall."

"And all for a valueless locket," lamented Lord Thorpe, shaking his balding head. "Can't think why you were so fond of it. Girlish piece, it was. And when I've given you so many expensive jewels." He plucked distractedly at the buttons upon his velvet jacket. "Well, at any rate, the blasted thing's gone now, into the river."

When Forrest turned his eyes to Lisbet's face, she looked away.

"Of course, we owe you a most profound debt of gratitude, Captain York," his lordship continued. "You saved my lady's life, risked injury or death to do so. Words are inadequate to express the depth of my thanks, and though a gift is hardly a worthy offering for a thing so precious as a life, I would like to present you with one anyway—as a token, if you will."

"That's quite unnecessary," Forrest declined, not unaffected by the man's sincerity. "My only wish is that the lady will try to keep herself safer in the future." Again he fixed his gaze upon Lisbet. Without words he told her he knew she had suffered no accident.

"I have a fine pair of silver dueling pistols—French, turn of the century," Lord Thorpe persisted. "Can I not persuade you to take them, Captain York? A military man such as yourself could appreciate such things far more than I."

Forrest shook his head and delivered a polite reply

that was not without its subtle warning. "You are most generous, Lord Thorpe, but knowing the countess is again safely under your protection is reward enough for me." He made to rise. "Now I must be going."

With a clatter Lisbet put down her cup. In a frantic rush of words she addressed her husband. "Perhaps—perhaps there is one thing you could offer Captain York that he would accept, Sylvan."

"And what is that, my dear?"

Coming to her feet slowly in a soft rustle of silk, she said, "Laurelpath Cottage has no stable. If Captain York keeps a horse, perhaps he would make use of our own stable and groomsman, at least until the weather grows milder."

"Well, how about it, York?" Lord Thorpe asked. He shoved stubby hands into his pockets and rocked back upon his heels to better view the taller man.

Forrest considered. The mile walk, even upon an injured leg, he dismissed easily. Prudence he dismissed as well. The boarding of his horse at Wexford Hall would provide him with a convenient excuse to be near Lisbet, allowing chance meetings, glimpses of her strolling in the garden or gazing out a window. Meager rewards, he admitted, but better than nothing at all. In spite of the realization that he was placing himself in a situation strikingly similar to another one twenty years past, Forrest agreed.

"Then shall we tour the stables?" the lord suggested.

"Yes, let's do," Lisbet answered in a tone brighter than any she had used in years.

After seeing his wife properly bundled against the cold, Lord Thorpe led the way through a snow-veiled garden adorned with a menagerie of mythical stone statuary. Down its meandering pathways they went, then across a cobbled yard. Presently they entered the musty confines of a shuttered stable where horses snuffled and stamped in almost every stall. Even an inexperienced eye could see the value of the beasts, Forrest thought with an appreciative eye.

"I don't ride myself," Lord Thorpe explained, pausing to pat the soft nose of a dappled gray. "But, when she feels up to it, Lady Thorpe does. I see to it that she has any size, shape, or color mount she could ever fancy," he added with pride, touching her white unblemished hand with a dark imperfect one. "Isn't that so, my pet?"

"Yes, Sylvan," she answered with a dutiful nod. Then she glided on.

In the half-light at the opposite end of the corridor, a young man stooped to rub liniment upon the legs of a thoroughbred, his tuneless whistle piercing the straw-fragrant air. Lord Thorpe raised an arm to hail him.

"Scottie, lad, look sharp! I have a guest with me—Captain York, it is. He'll be stabling his horse here at the Hall for as long as he cares to. You're to look after it good and proper for him, do you hear?"

The boy slowly set down the bottle of witch hazel and raised up from his work. When his eyes fell upon Forrest, they flashed with instant dislike. Had the lad leaned forward and spat at his feet, Forrest would not have been surprised.

Regarding him levelly, in just the same manner he had stared down countless callow recruits, Forrest spoke, a tinge of raillery in his voice. "The horse's name is Flambeau. He likes to be groomed twice a day. He also likes extra straw in his loosebox and is partial to a bran mash in the morning and oats in the evening. Oh, and add a little molasses to those oats. He has a sweet tooth." Forrest's eyes glinted. "Feed him breakfast at an early hour, if you please—around dawn. I'm partial to early rides and exercising him on a full belly won't do."

Eyes blazing, Scottie drew himself up, shoulders squared and tense. His face grew red and his jaw clenched.

"Do you have something to say, lad?" Forrest prompted, folding his arms.

The boy widened his stance and thrust out his jaw. "Maybe I do," he began contentiously. "Maybe I—"

"Scottie!" Lord Thorpe cut in, his childlike voice rising in ineffectual warning.

Quickly Lisbet stepped in the midst of them.

"Scottie," she said quietly. "Fetch my gloves for me, please. I've left them in the house."

"Impertinent rascal!" Lord Thorpe exclaimed when Scottie had stalked away. " 'Pon my soul, I can't think why you insist upon keeping him on, dear," he complained to Lisbet. "He's been nothing but a nuisance since he was a wee mite. I'd have thrown him out on his ear before he was in breeches if it were left to me. What do you see in the lad?"

As if she were experiencing a rush of strong emotion, color rose up and pinkened Lisbet's face. "He has no family, Sylvan," she said in a low tense voice. "Nowhere to go. You know that."

"We are not a charity," Lord Thorpe countered testily. Then, as if remorseful over his intolerance, he quickly added, "But then, you're soft-hearted, love, and I must remember that. Indeed, I fear your tender heart has been to my own advantage from the start."

Making no reply to the sentiment, Lisbet turned her eyes toward the stable door and watched her young charge's retreating figure. "Perhaps he could drive Captain York home," she suggested suddenly.

"Indeed, yes," the earl agreed. "Put the lad to good

use. I only hope the captain is not too put out by his surly presence."

"I have no doubt Captain York can hold his own in a contest of will," Lisbet said, meeting Forrest's eye with a ghost of her girlish charm returned.

"No doubt," Lord Thorpe conceded. "But don't hesitate to put him in his place, York. Give him a good cuff to the ear if need be."

"The lad and I will get on fine together," Forrest replied in response to Lisbet's apprehensive eyes. At the same time he could not help but wonder at her strange devotion to the insolent young groomsman.

A short while later a stone-faced Scottie drove the curricle from the carriage house to the sheltered portico on the east side of the estate. With a smart tug on the lines, the lad halted the pony and waited for Forrest to climb up.

"It's been a pleasure, Lord Thorpe," Forrest said, turning to his host.

Sketching a formal bow of respect, the dwarf regarded Forrest with his unhandsome eyes, his expression serious and genuine. "It has been an honor to meet you, Captain." He took Forrest's strong, well-formed hand in his own twisted one. "Thank you for my Lisbet's life."

The words struck Forrest in a painful way, and he found himself almost shamed. Silently he pivoted to face his hostess. When she would not meet his eyes, he took her hand and squeezed it, making sure to shield the gesture from her husband with the positioning of his body. He yearned to speak to her openly, though what he would have said he did not know. To express more than the most formal words would be inappropriate, and for Lisbet's sake, he must not risk pricking the earl's suspicions.

"Keep yourself safe," he whispered at last. All his concern, all his love were in the words.

"I will," she breathed, and then with her lips only added, "for you I will."

He pressed her hand hard, and for a few seconds she clenched his in return, holding so tightly, so desperately, he thought she would not let him go.

It was with a heavy step that he climbed into the curricle. Lord Thorpe raised an arm in salute, quoting cryptically, " 'Away, he is not of our crew. I wept, and though it be a dream, I—' "

Before the eccentric could complete the verse, he sputtered, choked violently, and grabbed at his throat with a frantic hand. The veins in his face bulged, his eyes rolled back in his head, and his chest began to heave. Then he collapsed upon the pavement, a satin jumble.

Immediately Forrest rose up and would have leapt over the low door of the curricle, but Lisbet stopped him with a word.

"No!" she cried over her shoulder, even as she knelt in a cloud of skirts at her husband's side. "He suffers these spells often. They are not as serious as they would seem, and I know what to do." With practiced hands she began to loosen the cravat about Lord Thorpe's quivering neck. "He wants no one else but me."

"Sylvan . . ." she keened, crouching above his convulsing, prostrate form. "My poor, cursed dear." With that she put her hands upon his shoulders as if to restrain his spasms, reaching once to wipe the froth of spittle from his mouth with her hem.

Still poised at the door of the curricle, Forrest hesitated, then made to step down again.

"No, Captain York, please!" Lisbet repeated, turning around. "Can't you understand? Spare him some shame, at least. He would not have you see him this way." She looked at Forrest pointedly and added in a low voice, "Nor would I."

Her words stung, reminding him forcibly that he was an intruder with no claims upon a woman married to another man. Cursing his own foolishness, he climbed back into the curricle and with a curt nod prompted Scottie to go. One last time he glanced at the disturbing scene behind him, saw the incongruous sight of lovely woman and her quivering, garishly clad mate.

What had he expected?

Had he hoped to find Lisbet at the mercy of a cruel despot, a sadistic husband from whom he could snatch her away? Had he hoped to find her miserable, desperate to escape a loveless union? *Yes!* But more than anything, he had intended to rectify the past, reorder with the strength and wisdom of manhood what the boy Anvil had been helpless to change.

Instead he had found an adversary he couldn't hate. And he had found the woman who belonged to him beyond his reach again. Only this time she was not caged behind locked doors, guarded by a powerful father.

This time she was imprisoned behind a far more formidable boundary. An emotional one . . . one she had erected herself.

Chapter Six

A mile away Lisbet closed the door to her bedroom and sagged against it. Her limbs quivered with such violence they seemed unable to support her weight. Putting a hand to her throat, she closed her eyes and thanked God she had had the strength to get through the day.

Anvil's arrival at Wexford Hall had been no surprise this morning, indeed she had expected it. But no amount of preparedness had lessened the impact of his presence. the forcefulness of her feelings for him. Sliding her hand within her skirt pocket, she closed her fingers tight about the thing hidden there, then opened her palm to stare at it.

As he had said goodbye to her this morning, Anvil had returned the locket, pressed it to her hand just as he had done long ago on one of those halcyon days made sweet by youthful innocence. It had remained the only part of him she had been able to keep. It had been her talisman. For years she had kept it sewn in her petticoats, concealed from her father's eyes—and later, Lord Thorpe's curiosity. More recently, knowing how Sylvan indulged her in everything, she had dared to take it out, wear it about her neck, carry it in a pocket.

But no more. Now her husband thought the locket lost on the river bottom, for her story to him had been the same one told to Forrest York. If Sylvan discovered the charm, he would ask questions, want to know why she had lied about dropping it, want to know the real reason Captain York had found her drowning in the river. Her husband had no idea, no inkling of the state of her mind.

Lisbet passed to the looking glass and paused, automatically smoothing the tendrils of hair escaping about her cheeks, pulling down her cuffs, straightening her high collar. Staring at herself, at her wide hazel eyes and colorless face, she likened herself to a wraith, a strange, fading image of the girl she once had been. Most terrifying of all, her mental self seemed to be dissolving as well. Sometimes she even thought herself a sleepwalker, floating about in a state somewhere between reality and dream.

Quickly she breathed deep and pinched her cheeks, forcing the rosy hue of past years to resurface on her flesh. What did Anvil think of her? Did he believe her as beautiful, desirable, enchanting as before? The image of him spun before her eyes now, blending with his younger form. How magnificent her love had become! How tall and broad and commanding! Gone was the adolescent whose age and circumstance made him prey to viciousness; gone forever was the defenseless outcast. In his place stood a most formidable man.

And yet, Lisbet mused with both sorrow and relief, the eyes of that outcast had never changed. They were just as haunted as before, as if they contained a thousand hurts, a thousand furies.

She shuddered, yearning to go to him, hold him as she had done before, calm the restlessness that plagued his spirit. She wished she could flee Wexford Hall this instant, run down the snowy lane and into Anvil's arms. And then the two of them would go away, far away. In another land they would lie together in sunshine beneath azure skies, kiss and laugh and dance away endless days as they were meant to do.

The soft smile died on her lips. A faint snuffling sound penetrated the door connecting her room with Sylvan's. He would be sleeping fitfully, his malformed shape tossing about the satin sheets in its child-sized gown. Lisbet shut her eyes tightly, wanting to force out all thoughts of her husband; but they would not relinquish their hold of her. With a racking sigh she let the gold locket slither back within her pocket, the gesture a symbol of her acceptance of duty. She could not abandon Sylvan. The reasons were many and complex, but one prevailed over all . . .

Below, the echo of hooves clattering upon icy gravel arrested her attention. Scottie, with a flex of his strong young hands, maneuvered the horse and curricle toward the coachhouse. For a moment Lisbet watched, noting the squareness of the young man's frame, the maturing of facial features which, only yesterday, had seemed so childish. He was like his father, she thought proudly, so very like his father.

Her eyes were aglow surely, and she looked away. She would have to watch herself, guard her feelings for Scottie more vigilantly than ever before. No one must guess them—not Sylvan, not Forrest York, not even the boy himself.

It would bring destruction to them all, every one of them.

Snow descended upon Winterspell again, repowdering the patches sunshine had struggled to melt. Forrest stared at the whitening landscape from the leaded window in his study. Cold seeped through the diamond panes and raised the flesh on his arms. He rubbed them, shivering.

In spite of the cold, he planned to ride to the village, ostensibly to visit the stationer's, but also to look again upon the place of his birth. He wanted to see the crooked avenue where village boys had mocked his name and thrown horseshoes at his back with taunting laughs. Through the eyes of a man he wanted to observe again the faces of those who had scorned him, determine if they were as twisted with malice as his memory recalled.

Over shirt and riding breeches he donned his heavy greatcoat, then slid gloves over his hands as he began the trek toward Wexford Hall. The day before yesterday he had sent a message to Lisbet via the postboy, asking after her own and Lord Thorpe's health. Her reply had been polite, reassuring him all was well. Yet her words had been so stilted and impersonal he wondered if she ever intended to see him again.

His journey to the Hall did not take long. His knee was less stiff, owing mostly to two days of Agatha Peacock's tiresome insistence that he sit with it propped upon a pillow. To give her credit, she had fussed over him like a mother, and since he had never had such attentions, he allowed them with a strange softening of heart toward her. Not that he let Agatha know of this softening. Both of them were too emotionally reserved to relinquish their pretended irritation with one another.

Few were about outside Wexford Hall when he arrived there. Going straight to the stable, pushing wide the double doors, Forrest paused for a moment while his eyes adjusted from the brightness of snow to the dimness of the building's interior. His horse was close to the front and stood with his head crooked over the loosebox. Immediately Forrest noticed extra straw padding the floor and traces of bran mash stuck to the wooden trough. Hiding a private smile, he ran a hand over the chestnut neck made sleek by a recent grooming.

"You won't find anything awry," Scottie accused defensively, stepping out of the shadows. "I know how to take care of horses."

"I'm sure you do," Forrest said, glancing up. He took a bridle from its peg and slipped it over Flambeau's head, applying pressure at the corners of the steed's mouth to make him accept the bit. "Is Lady Thorpe about?"

"And what if she is?" the young man challenged.

"I just asked," Forrest answered tightly, with as much tolerance for the boy's insolence as he could muster. "And, since you seem to be unoccupied at the moment—except for your endeavor to rile my temper of course—would you mind fetching my saddle for me?"

Giving him an impudent look, Scottie turned. Then, hooking thumbs in his loose trousers, he sauntered away, leaving the older man to wonder if he went to get the saddle or not.

"Disrespectful whelp," Forrest muttered. "Godawful manners. Worse than mine ever were." In mild surprise he raised his brows when the boy ambled up carrying a saddle in his arms.

Wordlessly Scottie swung it atop the loosebox rail, disdaining to transfer it directly to the other's hand.

"Has Lord Thorpe recovered from his seizure?" Forrest asked, unperturbed by the insult. He settled the saddle on Flambeau's back.

The groomsman shrugged. "He always does."

"Does he suffer them often?"

"Every fortnight or two. It scares the wits out of the maids. They think he's possessed by devils. All that frothing at the mouth and rolling of his eyes." Scottie snorted with disgust.

"It hardly has to do with devils. It's simply a disease, and it doesn't discriminate between rich or poor, high-born or low. They say Bonaparte himself suffered such fits."

Scottie seemed unconvinced and heaved himself up to sit upon the rail. "Still, Lord Thorpe's a queer sort of fellow, any way you look at it. In the village they call him Toady, say his place is in a circus."

"And you agree?"

Scottie lifted a shoulder. "Sometimes."

"Because he's unusual in appearance?"

" 'Course. Why else? He is a freak, ain't he?"

Forrest tightened the girth of his saddle. He was tempted to repeat the same sentiment regarding freaks he had expressed to Agatha Peacock. "If the respectable citizens of Winterspell say he is," he quipped instead with heavy sarcasm, "then far be it from me to say he's not. But," he added with a raised brow, "Lady Thorpe certainly doesn't seem to consider her husband the least repugnant."

As if galvanized by the words, Scottie drew himself up, his fists tensing. "That's because Lady Thorpe is near a saint!" he declared forcefully. "There's nobody, *nobody,* as good as her. Those old harridans who turn their backs on her in the village ain't even good enough to touch her skirts."

"Turn their backs on her?"

"That's what I said," Scottie answered sullenly, reaching to pull his brown tweed cap low across his brow.

Uneasy, Forrest probed deeper. "One would think Lady Thorpe the most respected woman in the neighborhood. After all, she's titled and—"

"She ain't never been respected," Scottie cut in rudely. "Not since she was a girl and—" As if thinking better of enlightening his companion, Scottie suspended the sentence and finished, "People here have long memories, that's all. Besides, I 'spect those old women are just jealous of all she's got. Have to hand it to the master on that score, he takes good care of her. Not a week goes by that he don't order some new piece of furniture or a bonnet or a fancy doodad from London just as a surprise." Scottie cocked his head to one side and spoke disapprovingly. " 'Course, he don't go anywhere with her, probably because of the way folks stare and point at him. I drive her to church myself sometimes, but even there nobody speaks to her much. Except the vicar, of course."

"Of course." Forrest pondered this information with a frown. He found it disconcerting that Lisbet could still be so maligned after twenty years.

Beside him Scottie shifted on the slender rail. "So why are you here in Winterspell?" he asked abruptly. "And how long do you mean to stay on?"

Forrest stifled an exasperated sigh and drawled, "If you ever make one tactful remark to me, lad, I swear I'll feel compelled to offer you congratulations."

With his unshaven jaw as stubborn as that of a bulldog, Scottie persisted. "You didn't answer my question."

"I didn't intend to." Forrest adjusted a stirrup strap with a strong tug of his hand. "And let that be the end of it."

But the youth seemed to have no intention of letting the matter drop. "You're not thinking to make trouble for Lady Thorpe, are you?" he demanded, jumping down from his perch and blocking Forrest's exit.

The older man stepped close, his head topping the boy's by several inches. His words were as bland and patient as the ones he'd used with countless young midshipmen acting too big for their breeches. "Don't stick your young nose where it doesn't belong. It's liable to get bruised, if you know what I mean."

Bristling, throwing back his shaggy head, Scottie regarded Forrest with a contempt far more adult than childish in nature. "I've seen the way you look at her," he accused. "You do anything to harm her, *anything,* and I'll—"

"You'll what?" Forrest leaned so close the lapels of his greatcoat brushed the buttons of Scottie's shirt. The boy tilted his head back in order to meet the older man's eye. His firm young mouth opened, then closed again.

"On second thought," Forrest said in the driest of tones, "*Don't* tell me. Make it a surprise." In one agile move, he swung himself onto the horse's back and took up the reins, so that Scottie had to step hastily backward to avoid the animal's hooves.

"Thanks for the saddle," Forrest flung amiably over his shoulder, exiting the building in a clamber of hooves. "And for the conversation—delightful as always."

When a string of curses rang out behind him, Forrest grinned, then murmured drolly beneath his breath, "The poor lad can't even curse properly—pitifully inadequate vocabulary. Guess I'll have to teach him a few of my cruder sailor's blessings one of these days."

As he guided his horse through the gargoyle-infested gates of Wexford Hall, he could not resist staring upward at its second-story windows. It was early yet, only an hour past dawn, and he wondered if Lisbet slept still. With effort he prevented himself dwelling too long on a fragile body warm beneath the sheets, honey hair mussed, the peace of sleep on parted lips. He must put away such thoughts. Lisbet was not his, she would never be . . . except, of course, in his own cursed mind.

As he neared the village a time later, coming within sight of its shuttered windows and timbered walls, the silence of it struck him. He had an odd, and likely accurate impression, that behind every glinting window curious eyes stared. Slowing his pace, he looked from left to right at each humble cottage. Icicles hung from all the eaves, from the gateposts and from the aged, bent trees. Even as he watched, the houses seemed to crouch beneath their blanket of snow, slide closer together until their upper stories projected so far out over the lane, sunlight had only a narrow entrance.

Nothing's changed in this ungodly place, Forrest thought. *Nothing. It's been as frozen as some bloody glacier for twenty years.*

And then he began to see them—those who had called him Anvil, labeled him the devil's spawn. At the corner a man halted his snow shoveling to glower at the intruder. A woman with a basket on her arm stepped back beneath a lattice, following Forrest's progress with suspicious eyes. From under an age-yellowed cap, an ancient dame glared at him. Though none of them could know his identity, they viewed him in the same discolored light as they had always done. Their minds were distrustful of all who were strange or different. There was a meanness about them, an ignorance Forrest had always loathed and never understood. Though his travels had broadened his own perspectives, showed him the natural wariness of mankind toward strangers, never had he found hatred to be quite so twisted a thing as in Winterspell.

The village boasted a row of shops, including those of a baker, butcher, confectioner, and cobbler. At the end of the line was a small stationer's, its sign reading BATTER'S LTD. Pulling his horse up, easing his leg over the cantle, Forrest dismounted.

He could see someone within the shop, a man's

shape flitting about behind the glass with the stealth of a ghost. Tracking the untouched powder of the walk with his boots, Forrest opened the door and stepped inside. Above him a bell jangled.

From behind a high counter, wearing spectacles made opaque by reflected light, a shopkeeper regarded him mutely, crossing arms across his waistcoated chest and offering no welcome.

" 'Morning," Forrest said shortly, coming to stand close, putting his large gloved hands atop the counter. "I'd like a half-dozen tablets of paper."

"Don't have any paper," the stationer replied, making no attempt to hide ample merchandise stacked on shelves behind his head.

With eyes as wintry as the day, Forrest regarded him, and with no change of expression, removed two notes from his pocket. Slowly he slid the money forward until the edges of it nearly touched the other's hand.

The stationer's face subtly twitched. He swallowed. Had his eyes been visible, Forrest knew they would be darting toward the street view, looking to see if anyone could witness this exchange. Then in one furtive movement, the clerk reached his fingers forward and pulled the notes free of Forrest's hand.

"The paper'll be delivered to you," he stated in a low tone.

Forrest knew he would find a box on his doorstep tomorrow, quietly dropped there under cover of darkness. "Don't put yourself out," he drawled, bidding the clerk goodbye with a sardonic half-smile.

Then, making no attempt to save the stationer from his neighbor's questions, he lingered for a moment in front of the establishment, gazing openly around, meeting the eyes of everyone who dared to stare.

At a leisurely pace he guided his horse away from the

unpleasant muddle of buildings, wandering far, seeing again all that he had not seen with manly eyes. And though the remembrance of past cruelties put a bitter taste in his mouth, he was not so jaded that winter's beauty went unnoticed.

The air grew cold. After an hour it began to seep through Forrest's outerwear and nip his fingers and feet. With thoughts of a hot drink and dinner, he turned southward, following a rough strip of lane alongside a densely forested wood. Before he had gone far, two riders came into view, one trailing the other at a distance of fifty yards or so. Immediately Forrest recognized them, and urging Flambeau forward, made to overtake the pair.

He could see the startled stare Lisbet gave him, her eyes wide and bright even within the shadow of her hooded cloak. He could see indecision in their depths, too, and, before thoughts of escape could form in her mind, he spurred Flambeau across her mare's path.

"Lady Thorpe," he greeted, his eyes holding hers.

"Captain . . ." she breathed, as if air had gone from her lungs.

Her horse was the color of pearl, he noted, like the habit she wore. Her gloves were of a darker gray, and the small boot peeking from beneath her hem was black. He wondered why she always dressed as if she were in half-mourning. Damned waste of beauty, he thought, wanting to pull the hood from her hair and let the sun touch its gilt.

Scottie pulled up beside them, his horse snorting, sending puffs of steam out into the air. Glowering at Forrest, he addressed Lady Thorpe.

"The earl will be anxious, my lady," he warned, flicking another belligerent look in her companion's direction.

For a lon moment, Lisbet vacillated, her hands

clenching the reins more tightly. She could not take her eyes from the captain. His dark harsh-cut face, his black eyes and hair were so stark, so splendid against the white of snow they took her breath away. As a girl she remembered how his wild spirit and sullen eyes had fascinated her, how his lonely mystery had answered some call in her heart. She had been unable to resist him then; she could not resist him now. She told herself a few moments alone with him would not matter. Like a stolen treat she could savor them, then later enjoy their sweet memory. There was nothing wrong in that. In no way would a brief canter alongside Captain York betray Sylvan or give her cause for guilt tomorrow.

"Go home, Scottie," she ordered in a low tone. "I'll follow you shortly.

When the lad remained unmoving, his eyes darting distrustfully to Forrest, she spoke in a more reassuring way. " 'Tis alright. I'll come to no harm. Go now."

With obvious reluctance, Scottie departed, but not before throwing a largely ignored warning glare in the older man's direction.

Neither Forrest nor Lisbet moved until the groom was well out of sight. All the while Forrest watched his love of past days intently, waiting until her eyes slid up to meet his. A tension seemed to stretch between them, as if both withheld such explosive feelings the tiniest crack would unleash catastrophe.

"You really must take that boy in hand, you know," Forrest said at last, to ease the strain. "His attitude's rotten. Does you a discredit. And one of these days he's going to get the devil flayed out of him by someone with a temper shorter than mine. Has the manners of a swine, for God's sake. Tell you what," he continued, feigning seriousness, "I know a recruiting officer who'd be happy to sign him up for the Navy. After he's done a four-year stint swabbing decks and being lashed a few hundred strokes with a cat o' nine, he'll come back beautifully disciplined."

At first Lisbet seemed taken aback, offended, prepared to argue vehemently in Scottie's defense. But suddenly her face changed, and she began to laugh. She laughed until tears coursed down her cheeks. Forrest had not heard that lovely bell-chime sound in twenty years. Had the sweetness of it not been so poignant, he would have joined in her fit of unreasoned hilarity.

Her laughter gently faded. The uneasy silence returned. It had been no good trying to joke with her, Forrest thought. It had only delayed what needed to be said. Time was too precious for superficial things. He supposed neither of them knew quite what to say, now time had given them the chance. Each wanted to express feelings too deep for words, each wanted to share all the lost moments of two decades of life.

Impossible. Impossible.

Wordlessly, as if by some mutual consent communicated by thought, they turned their horses off the lane and entered the woods single file, Forrest in the lead.

The little woodlet was like an arctic wonderland, its frozen, silver-blue glaze overlaying black and gray. A great hush lay everywhere. Overhead, blackbirds arced upward in an arrow. A faint wind sobbed, and the tiny icicles hanging pendant from frozen leaves tinkled like a thousand bells.

Forrest halted his horse, allowing Lisbet to edge closer. Her knee nudged his and their eyes met again. The intimacy of the winter gloom enveloped them, stirring their blood. For a moment they continued to ride slowly, side by side, their legs rubbing now and then, the thread of tension between them coiling tighter.

"It's no different, is it?" Forrest said at last, his voice

as brittle as the air. "Winterspell, I mean. It's no different."

Lisbet released a soft breath that floated as vapor. "No. Nor will it ever be." She glanced at him. "But then, did you expect it to be changed?"

"I don't know. . . . Perhaps I only thought to see it through different eyes."

Lisbet touched a glove to her nose and edged closer to Forrest's warmth. All at once she longed to throw her arms about him, draw him close, be enveloped in his hard embrace.

"What have you done these many years?" she asked with sudden fervency. "Where have you been? Not a day passed that I didn't wonder where you were, how you fared . . . how you felt."

Forrest fixed his eyes ahead and shrugged. "I've just wandered, wandered everywhere. Europe, the Americas, Africa, Asia. I've been a sort of global gypsy, you might say."

When she stared at him, he grinned boyishly. "Damned waste of a life, isn't it? At first I signed aboard merchant vessels, swabbed desks, rigged sails, jumped ship when it suited me. Then, when I felt the wanderlust subside a bit I joined the military. They found me a handy fellow to have around." He looked at Lisbet askance, his dark eyes touched with the barest glint of humor. "I'll have to tell you why someday."

"You must have had many adventures, met many different kinds of people."

"Many."

Lisbet looked down at the oiled black reins threading through her fingers. "Has there ever . . . been anyone?"

His head turned and he regarded her curiously, pleased with the tremor in her tone. "A wife, you mean?" he asked with a remote smile. "No. I haven't made many attachments in my life—found them too . . . cumbersome. Besides, I never stayed in one place long enough to cultivate more than passing acquaintances."

Pausing, he looked ahead again and let a measure of his control slip. "I've only loved one woman, Lisbet. I even exchanged vows with her."

The words sent pain slicing through Lisbet's heart. He seemed to be blaming her for her marriage. Did he think she had forgotten the vows they exchanged long ago, dismissed them easily before falling into the arms of Sylvan? Did he think she had forgotten the fidelity they had sworn to each other?

If he accused her, he was being unfair, and she wanted to tell him so. But she did not, for she knew he had no way of knowing the tragic turns her own life had taken.

She reined in her horse, waiting until Forrest looked at her questioningly and halted his. Then, reaching out, she clasped his hand where it rested at the pommel.

His knuckles tensed, resisting her touch. When she met his eyes, she was astonished to find both anger and accusation sparking them and watched them grow ever blacker and brighter, as if the fires of hell flickered somewhere deep within their depths, burning up the softness.

For a moment she did not know what to say. She shook her head in denial, devastated by the bitterness she saw on his face.

"Anvil . . ." she whispered instinctively. "Anvil."

For a moment the word seemed to revolve them backwards in time, hurl them through space in a gentle whirl that ended beneath an old Roman bridge. The memories were vivid there, beautiful and ugly.

"Anvil is gone," he declared harshly. "He will never come back."

Lisbet leaned closer, the movement sending an eddy of snowflakes down from her hood. "No! He is not gone," she countered with a vehement cry. "He has always been here . . . right here." She put her fist upon her breast, then reached across to touch the broad curve of his own. "Didn't you feel it? Even during all the years you've been away from me, didn't you feel it?"

He stared at her, his eyes fierce beneath their straight brows. They seemed to be searching out her thoughts, judging them, confirming the truth of what she had said.

Seconds passed. Forrest's chest heaved beneath her hand. And then he slowly raised up in his stirrups, leaned toward her, and put his hands about her head. Drawing her face to his, he sought her lips with his own.

He kissed her deeply, hungrily, pulling her forward across the space between their horses. Together they slipped from his saddle to the ground. He put himself atop her, his black coat spreading out about her hips.

For a moment he merely held her face between his hands, his eyes tarrying upon her brow, her nose, her mouth. Impatiently he tore his gloves off, letting his fingers touch where his eyes had been. His flesh was warm, strong, calloused with years of toil. Lisbet would have liked to have closed her eyes beneath the pleasure of it, except to do so would be to lose sight of his face.

Following his lead, she slid her own hands free of gloves, then touched his jaw, tracing the roughness there. She explored the smoothness of his temples, the texture of his thick and dusky hair. It was as if the two of them touched for the first time, and yet their features, each to the other, were as familiar as their own.

A sound rose up from Forrest's throat. My God, he thought, how can I still love her with such desperation?

I'm no longer a calf-eyed boy. I've had no lack of women. But why must this one woman—the one I cannot have—obsess me even after twenty years?

Putting his arms beneath Lisbet's fragile shoulders, heedless of the deep snow, he embraced her so hard that breath sailed from her lungs. She clasped him just as despairingly, clawing the fabric of his coat and burying her cheek within the hollow of his neck.

When their lips joined again, they seemed to become a part of the wilderness setting, become a part of the untamed tangle of nature. Their kisses were wild, stolen things. And where their reuniting in his cottage had been beyond physical boundaries, now it was a carnal reawakening, made all the more desperate because her marriage forbade it.

Again and again Lisbet touched her lover's face, marveled at its handsomeness. And with each caress of her hand, the ruby ring flashed arcs of fire upon the whiteness of the snow. She wanted to yank it off, dash it to the ground, fling it deep into some pool of ice. But she could not. Her duty would be broken, her honor lost, her conscience forsaken . . . her husband ruined.

Struggling beneath Forrest's weight, breaking his possessive hold, she put her hands to his chest and shoved. "No . . ." Her eyes pleaded with him, conveyed unspeakable distress. "Do not ask this of me, Anvil! Please! I want us to see each other, be together, but . . . I can't belong to you anymore!"

With his face a mask of bewilderment and anger, Forrest released her, watching while she covered her eyes with her hands and turned her back upon him.

The two of them sat apart then, in the hard crust of snow.

"You ask much of me, Lisbet," Forrest said finally, his voice shaken and grave. "Perhaps too much. I'm not who I was. I'm not a boy. I don't bend to the will of others anymore, and I've never had the luxury of acquiring many gentlemanly restraints. Truthfully you'll probably find me a more unscrupulous scoundrel than you ever did before."

He shifted a bit in the cold snow, idly brushing the white powder off his coat. "I'll tell you something. After leaving this place without a penny in my pocket, I set out to conquer the world, do great and glorious things. Anvil would find a way to get to America and work in the gold mines, I told myself, or he would seek his fortune in the West Indies, or he would find diamonds in Africa. After a few years, with a fine suit of clothes on his back and a purse full of silver in his hands, he would return to Winterspell a very rich and envied man."

Forrest looked at her, smiling a rueful smile. "We're damned fools when we're young, aren't we? Instead of sailing off for the gold fields, I wandered through the villages of Yorkshire asking for work—on my knees at times. But no one obliged me. After all, why should they have taken notice of a ragged, smart-tongued brat with no shoes on his feet and all the anger of hell in his eyes? Why should they have done more than look at me with disgust when I begged in their clean, respectable streets?"

He stopped speaking, rested one hand on an upraised knee and absently traced lines in the snow with the other.

Though there had been no self-pity in his voice as he related his hardships, Lisbet's eyes filled. "What happened to you then?" she asked.

"I went to London."

"And did you find work there?"

Forrest lifted an amused brow at her question. "Have you ever seen the poorer streets of London, Lisbet? No? Well, let's just say as a boy in straitened circumstances, I was in very good company."

"What did you do?"

"I stole." His eyes twinkled a bit at her dismay, and he added. "I became quite good at it, too. Started out picking pockets and ended up swindling rich young bucks in a series of various—and rather imaginative—schemes."

Lisbet grew quiet at that, and Forrest thrust his hands in his pockets. It was cold sitting in the snow. It made his knee throb and his nose run. He sniffed, watching Lisbet beneath his brows.

Huddled in her cloak across from him, she stared at his face, appalled, and he sensed she wondered why he was telling her these unsavory things about his past. He did not fail to detect a flash of pity in her eyes as well, and hated it.

"I'll tell you something about hunger, Lisbet," he said shortly. "You'll do anything to get rid of it, ease its constant gnawing. And somewhere in the process, you stop bothering with the pangs of conscience. After awhile stealing doesn't even seem wrong anymore. It becomes justified to your way of thinking—even righteous."

As if wrung by compassion, she reached out for him then, circling his waist with her arms and resting her head upon his shoulder. Her gentleness made Forrest's eyes smart, and he wondered furiously why it was he had always needed Lisbet when he had never needed anyone else in the world.

He drew her back from him, shook her a bit, made her look into his eyes. "Do you understand what I'm saying to you, Lisbet?" he asked with harshness in his tone. "Do you understand that in a way I'm starving now? I don't have any scruples where you're concerned—not a blasted one. I never have, even knowing the consequences, even suffering the consequences. I'm a danger to you—I'm a danger to us both."

He tightened his hands upon her shoulders. "Ask me

to go away, to leave Winterspell now, and I will do it."

"No!" she cried, flinging herself into his arms. "I'll never ask you to leave! Never!"

Rocking her in his hard embrace, he murmured ardently, "Then let me hold you at my side like this . . . just for a little while. I'll not ask more than that now, I swear. It's just that I've wanted this so long—God, there have been times when I thought I would lie down and die from the pain of wanting it."

"I know," she nodded, her face awash with tears. "I know."

And then together they sat quietly upon the snow in the cold white woodlet.

As snowflakes covered their heads, drifting down about them, they could have been two creatures of the landscape . . . two white foxes perhaps. And yet, if an onlooker were to peer more closely with curious eyes, he would not mistake the despairing, huddled forms of two ill-starred lovers.

Chapter Seven

Even beneath the noon sun, the landscape of Winterspell lay ice-bound. Forrest sat at his desk staring out the window, the nib of a pen suspended over note paper half-covered with his bold undisciplined scrawl. After his medical leave, the military had commissioned him to organize a mapped journal of his travels in Arab lands, complete with sensitive information, and he had begun his writing shortly after breakfast. But concentrating was hard going. The names of African cities and Algerian villages seemed as elusive as straying sheep, perhaps because he did not try overly hard to catch them. His thoughts lay elsewhere today, not terribly far from where he sat.

Pondering the frigid skies and glittering snow, he fought off thoughts of Lisbet, mentally recounting a sojourn through a torrid desert where he had nearly been flayed alive by stinging sands. In some ways he missed the arid heat and the exotic peoples, he missed wandering through mysterious lands rarely penetrated by Western man. Perhaps he would return to them someday, an anchorless man in a sea of strangers. He didn't know. At the moment the future stretched before him like an empty plain.

Putting aside his pen, Forrest drained the last of his

coffee and stretched his stiffened knee, idly watching a trio of sparrows peck at the ice in a bird bath outside. The bowl rested askew on its pedestal, so that the birds half-hopped and half-slid across the surface. Forrest grinned at their antics, and after setting down his cup, grabbed an unfinished cinnamon bun from his plate and headed outside.

He had not bothered to don a coat, and the air chilled him with its brittle breezes. Squinting against the brightness of sun on snow, he gazed across the frozen land toward Wexford Hall, where chimney pots and roof lines made a sharp silhouette against flat oyster skies. All night he had lain awake thinking of Lisbet. All night he had cursed himself, wondering what sort of fool he was to repeat the folly of his boyhood. Why did Lord Thorpe's wife utterly obsess him, craze him with a need to possess? Why did he still, after twenty years, feel he must have Lisbet for his own, no matter what the repercussions? Already he had suffered untold miseries for love of her; to resume the relationship now would be doubly complicated and treacherous.

He had no answers, and yet he had few qualms. For a man who had faced death countless times in many creative forms, danger held little sway these days.

Stepping out into the powder, Forrest took hold of the bird bath pedestal and twisted it about, leveling the base. Crumbling the bun he had brought out, he tossed it across the snow for any feathered songsters hungry enough to return. Then, before he had dusted the crumbs from his fingers, the faint sound of crackling foliage reached his ears.

His spine prickled, alerting instincts he had learned to trust in earliest boyhood, instincts that had saved his life more than once in both raging battles and sleepy courtyards.

Pretending to busy himself again with the positioning of the bird bath, he used his peripheral vision to scan the edge of the woodlet. A line of trees bordered his rented property, and deep in the knotted underbrush there crouched a motionless girl.

He sighed, blowing out air from his lower lip in profound exasperation. He hoped to high heaven this wasn't a sign of events to come. The last thing he needed was the cabbage-headed citizens of Winterspell spying on him every time he so much as stepped out into the yard.

Crossing his arms in irritation, he fixed his eyes on the gawker. For a few seconds she returned his steady gaze. Then, in an extraordinarily agile move, she sprang up from her hiding place and darted through the brush. Out of sight she went, zigzagging through the nest of thorny shrubs and hawthorn with a remarkable display of gazellelike grace.

"Hell of a place, Winterspell," Forrest murmured with an incredulous shake of his head. "Hell of a place."

He turned to go inside, but noticing a forgotten shovel propped by the stoop, took hold of it to clean the steps. He had barely scraped the first one when he felt eyes on his back again, and pivoting, found the odd girl standing not more than ten feet away. He had no idea how she had managed to get so close without his knowing it, but considering her extraordinary appearance, perhaps he should not have been surprised.

Never had he seen anyone, man or woman, who had such a creature-wild look. He knew no other way to term it. Being of exceptional height and of slender build, the girl possessed an animalistic litheness, complemented by a strange foxlike face. To accentuate the untamed image, her hair rioted about her face in moon-pale snarls, nearly obscuring eyes that were peculiarly slanted. He could not fathom what sort of apparel she wore; layers of green cloth hung loosely upon her frame, defying any fashion book of the present century.

Forrest narrowed his gaze. The snow surrounding her feet seemed to be turning pink. Looking more closely, he saw drops of blood descending steadily, one by one, from beneath her clothes.

"What the—" As Forrest moved forward, his visitor stepped back. At the same time, however, she thrust something out at him from the folds of her skirts.

A large, long-eared hare lay lifelessly cradled within her arms, its head lolling, its two front paws mangled and bloody.

Guardedly the girl watched Forrest through the tangle of hair. He could see her muscles tensing for flight even while her expression beseeched assistance.

"Have you come to bring me the hare?" he ventured, making no further move to get near.

She nodded.

"Did you find it in the woods?"

Again she nodded.

"Is it for my supper?" he inquired smoothly, just to clarify things.

Vigorously she shook her head in denial, stepping back.

"Then do you wish me to bind up its paws?" Forrest proceeded with exasperation, feeling as if he were playing some new, unconventional parlor game.

She regarded him for a moment with a skeptical tilt of her head, then gave a slow nod.

Forrest held the door open. "Then come inside."

At his invitation she planted her feet in an obvious show of disobedience.

"If you won't come in, then what in Hades do you want me to do?" Forrest grumbled under his breath, adding a private comment that the most bizarre collection of characters on the face of the earth surely resided in Winterspell.

"Suit yourself," he snapped at last in defeat. "I'll be back in a minute."

In his bedroom he retrieved a small leather-bound trunk from beneath the bed. It had been his habit to collect medicines from the various cultures crossed in his travels, and he had recently organized them and recorded their uses. Some he had seen employed with remarkable results, others were no more than valueless potions given to him by shamans, holy men, and quacks. Hefting the trunk to his shoulder, he carried it downstairs, snatching up his greatcoat on the way.

When he stepped outside again, he found the girl sitting comfortably on his stoop.

"Well, we've made some progress, at least," he murmured, watching her as she stroked the soft fur of the hare's back. She seemed not to mind that its blood continued to spread a stain over the garments she wore.

When he opened the lid of the trunk, its contents immediately caught the girl's fancy; indeed she seemed so intrigued she might have been ogling a pirate's cache of jewels. Though her head was bent low, concealing her expression, Forrest could see by the reflexive opening and closing of her fingers that she longed to touch. He supposed the tiny withered roots and the glass vials in their rainbow colors tempted her, those, and the amulets of cloudy stone strung on loops of braided hair. She bent lower and lower, her silver locks falling across the trunk like a tattered curtain.

"What's your name?" Forrest asked, eyeing her with curiosity.

She remained busily occupied, ignoring him.

"All right, so don't give me your name." With a considering stare, he drawled, "I could tell you mine, but I'm sure you already know it. Being a Winterspell resident, you probably know a few other particulars about me, too, like the size of my boots and how many pairs of breeches I own."

She kept her face averted.

Forrest sighed, gently easing from her lap the dying hare, which she seemed to have forgotten since the opening of the trunk. "Let's see what we can do for your friend here," he said. "Hmmm . . . pulled it out of a trap, eh?" With a soft cloth he cleaned the animal's wounds, thankful that pain and blood-loss rendered the creature docile. A raging case of rabies he did not need.

"Let's see," he continued in a droll tone, sorting through the vials while the girl watched with avid eyes. "Shall we try a compress of cobwebs . . . or vervain . . . or adder's tongue? None of them, you say? Then perhaps something a bit more scientifically acceptable."

Laying out antiseptics and gauze, Forrest worked efficiently. Traveling alone in strange and dangerous places had often found him mustering resourcefulness in dressing his own wounds and purging fevers. And whoever the deuce had sent those poorly paid charlatans along with Her Majesty's Royal Navy and into battle zones had given him a whole new respect for the oblivion of a certain Oriental painkiller. He had learned early on that a little knowledge of medicine and pharmacology in war never hurt, to phrase it appropriately.

Dressing the hare's injuries, he doubted the thing would ever hop again, providing of course, it lived. In truth, he thought it best to put it out of its misery. However, he kept that piece of pessimism to himself and bandaged it up anyhow, much in the way one patches a doll broken beyond repair for the sake of a child. Also, he could not help looking at the beast's poor mutilated flesh with a degree of compassion, remembering his own knee that some cannon-wielding maniac had almost smashed to smithereens.

Once the hare was as near restored as it would ever be, he tenderly deposited it back to the girl's lap. By this time she had dared touch the items inside the trunk, and though Forrest eyed her rifling with consternation, he noticed she took pains to handle everything with care. The amulet of coral she seemed to find particularly fascinating, running her square unmanicured fingers over its ridges and examining it minutely.

The thing was a worthless piece, really; perhaps he should give it to her.

"Do you like that?" he asked.

Predictably, she nodded without looking up.

"All right, then I'll make a bargain with you," he said, not hesitating to employ bribery to its fullest extent. "If you tell me your name, you may have it."

All at once she tilted her chin up, and with a jerk of her head, tossed the wild, pale-colored forelock away from her face.

Her features were unique, unexpected, Forrest thought. While piquantly beautiful, they were disturbingly untouched by time. Her eyes were rarest of all; though seductively slanted, their depths contained an unnatural innocence. It struck Forrest that they resembled those of a fox kit, who, while possessing instincts and craftiness, had no understanding whatsoever of anything outside its own familiar habitat.

"Gretchen!" she proclaimed abruptly, giving him the impish smile of a woodland nymph. Without further ado, she reached up, yanked the amulet from his fingers and looped its braided chain around her neck.

Forrest grinned with rue. "You obviously had no trouble at all understanding the terms of the deal." He shook his head and sighed. "Females. Dangle a bauble before their eyes and they'll give you anything."

Gretchen ignored his comments. She sat fingering the worthless charm and humming to herself, occasionally sparing a stray caress for the poor hare lying limp as a pelt across her knees.

Standing up, Forrest dusted the snow from his seat and closed the lid of the trunk with a snap. "Well, Mistress Gretchen Whoever-You-Are, I'd like to stay and chat longer, but I really must get back to work. The Navy frowns on giving quid to old bashed-up officers who don't do anything to earn it."

By this time, he was beyond expecting a response from his unusual guest and opened the back door, saying without further ado, "An honor to meet you, and all that. See that you watch that animal, so he doesn't end up in somebody's cooking pot before winter's end."

Tucking the amulet in the neckline of her ragged garb, Gretchen sprang up from the stoop with a hop, embraced the hare to her chest, and galloped off. Within seconds her tall, darting figure had disappeared through the snow-shrouded foliage.

His thoughts still with the girl, Forrest limped inside, where he promptly collided with Agatha Peacock.

"Blast it all, woman!" he exclaimed, steadying her by the arm while attempting to maintain his own precarious balance. "I swear you and everyone else in this dismal excuse for civilization get some sort of depraved pleasure in sneaking up on me."

Agatha drew herself up in the manner of an enraged hen. "I did not sneak up on you." As if mortally offended she wrenched her arm away and added, "Just because *some* people around here have nerves as jittery as those of a cat with string tied round its tail."

Forrest scowled. "Try dodging pot-shots from every wild-eyed Berber and Christian-hating Arab this side of Hades and see how your nerves come out after a decade or so." Hobbling to the table, he pulled out a chair with a noisy scrape of wood on slate, and plopped down. "Got anything for dinner?"

"Maybe."

"Maybe yes or maybe no?"

From beneath her brows Agatha gave him a look of contrived sternness. Then she went to the old black stove and slammed a pot atop it. "How about a little *rabbit* stew?"

"Very amusing," Forrest said between his teeth.

"So you got acquainted with our Gretchen, did you, eh?" The housekeeper reached up to remove a cold shepherd's pie from the larder. "What'd ya think of her?"

"She fits right in with the other natives," he pronounced blandly. Then in a more serious tone, "For awhile I thought she must be mute."

"Oh, she can talk up a storm when she has a mind ta. 'Course, half of what she says don't make sense ta anybody but her." Taking cracked tulip-patterned dishes from a shelf, Agatha added, "She lives at the old Tower, ya know."

Forrest looked up. "The Tower?"

"Sure. She's the old marquess's granddaughter."

Forrest pondered the information with interest. "How old is she?"

"Oh, twenty or so, I guess. She was already livin' at the Tower when I arrived here ten years ago." Agatha cut a slice of pie and eased it on to a plate. "Gretchen's a strange one, all right. Runnin' about the forest like a wild animal. Totally improper behavior. And her clothes!" The housekeeper shook her head. "Some say she's half-witted, o' course. But I don't know . . . I'd call her more simple-minded, like."

"What's the difference?" Forrest drawled, as if he were loath to find out.

Agatha cocked her head and considered, clapping a

work-reddened hand to one meager hip. "Don't know exactly. But she don't seem at all stupid, ya know, just . . . childlike."

Forrest nodded. "Actually she gave me much the same impression. A beautiful young woman with the mind of a small lass."

Agatha went to a cupboard, and sorting through preserve jars, selected one packed with peaches. In an automatic gesture she handed the container to Forrest, who torqued the lid with an easy twist of his wrist and handed it back.

" 'Course," the housekeeper continued, "the village boys circle round her like stray dogs after a—" Putting a hand to her cheek, Agatha appeared astounded over the word that had almost slipped from her mouth.

"Bitch in heat . . . ?" Forrest offered helpfully with an innocent raise of brows.

The housekeeper spread butter on a roll with more enthusiasm than necessary and nodded her head. "Well, you can imagine how they all take wagers on which one of 'em—I mean, who'll—well. . . ."

"On who'll be the first . . . ?" Forrest again supplied, wondering if women were afraid of dropping dead if they repeated even the mildest euphemisms.

"P-precisely," Agatha affirmed with a prim, scornful sniff. "She's scared to death of 'em, poor girl. Why, I'm surprised she even got close ta you today." She eyed him over her shoulder. "Considering the way ya look, an' all."

Forrest let that pass and tossed a napkin across his lap just as Agatha set a plate of food before him. "You said Gretchen lived up at the Tower. Who's there with her?"

"Why, the old marquess, of course," she replied.

"The marquess? But he was ancient when—" Forrest abruptly cut off the remainder of the sentence. Agatha did not know his past connection with Winterspell, and he preferred to keep it that way.

"He's still ancient," she went on, apparently noticing nothing strange about his unfinished comment. " 'Course, he could be dead for all anyone'd know it. He's such a recluse, we almost forget he's alive at times." She clicked her tongue. "Now there's one who's balmy in the crumpet."

Forrest remained silent, staring out the window in a sudden fit of brooding. He did not quite trust himself to speak. Long ago, assuming the man dead and buried, he had believed his hatred for the Marquess of Winterspell dissolved. But now, to know that the one who had yanked him from Lisbet's embrace and paraded him naked through the streets still lived . . .

Hatred seemed to coil again within his chest like a poisonous thing, a thing that demanded justice and revenge just as violently as it had done twenty years ago. Forrest closed his eyes for a moment, wishing he could forget it all, the enmity, the bitterness. God, how tired of the past he was—how tired of *feeling.*

The rattle of pots and pans shook him rudely from his reverie. Agatha bustled about the kitchen, tidying where nothing required tidying as if needing to keep her hands busy.

"Agatha," Forrest said, watching her over his untouched plate.

She turned, arrested by the solemnity in his voice. "Yes, Cap'n York?"

"How about filling up another plate and dining with me?" he suggested kindly, smiling the broad smile that women on at least five continents had found irresistible. "I may even manage to make myself tolerably charming for the duration."

"Oh, pish," Agatha retorted, flushing. But she eagerly took up another plate and sank down beside him.

* * *

Later that day Forrest asked his housekeeper to procure supplies for him from a list he had made. If the villagers continued to charge him the exorbitant prices they seemed to reserve for unwelcomed strangers, he would be beggared in less than a fortnight. Sending Agatha would surely save him money.

An hour or so after she departed, he fetched his horse and headed for Winterspell himself. Last evening Flambeau had thrown a shoe, and by the looks of it, would soon loose another. There was no avoiding a visit to the village blacksmith. It was only to be hoped the new set of iron shoes would not cost the same price as two pairs of custom-made Wellingtons in Bond Street.

For awhile Forrest stood inside the blacksmith's stable watching the leather-aproned farrier heat, pound, and shape iron bars to fit each of Flambeau's hooves. The smell of hot metal and cinders and horseflesh filled the confined space, making the barn a warm contrast to the cold without, so that Forrest found himself quite enjoying the red glow of the workman's fire.

When the faint sound of shouting voices penetrated the clink of the hammer, Forrest only idly strolled to the outer door. Stepping through, he stood for a moment lounging against the jamb, surveying the crooked lanes and cross-timbered shop fronts. He spotted Agatha, her gloves as white as always, toting her wicker basket, pausing to look at a fringed shawl displayed in a bow-fronted window. Not catching sight of him, she went on, entering the bakery across the street while her plain black skirts swished in a no-nonsense stride.

Forrest's eyes swung back to the narrow street, noticed the circle of old women gossiping beneath a sign post, the clerk scraping ice from his step, and the knot of adolescent boys loafing at the corner. He also noted the fine carriage parked at the curb a block away, its glossy finish as black as ink. Its accouterments were shiny brass, the inner rims of its high, delicate wheels gold-edged. Matched bays with tails flowing to their fetlocks stood harnessed before the grand equipage, and atop the box, dressed in simple green livery, sat Scottie Stone.

Forrest scrutinized the street yet again, this time for sight of Lisbet. Was she in the bakery, the grocer's, the cobbler's shop? Wherever the devil she was, he wanted to find her, take her by the arm, and with no particular gentleness, kiss her mouth with all the pent-up frustration driving him mad.

Suddenly he saw the door to the apothecary shop swing in. Lisbet emerged, her slender form draped in a hooded, chocolate-colored cloak; in her hand she clutched a package. Her head was bent low, so that Forrest saw only the pretty curve of her chin and the tip of her nose. After glancing right and left, she turned in his direction, making for her carriage at a brisk pace. Forrest straightened slowly, uncrossing his long legs. As intended, the movement caught her attention and caused her to look up. Their eyes met, her step faltered.

At the same time the huddle of boys on the corner began to stir, stepping off the curb and milling about the carriage. Forrest shifted his stance, and turning his gaze from Lisbet, followed their suspicious movements with unease.

All at once, one of the scoundrels raised a fist, pointed to Lady Thorpe, and called out the vilest obscenity. Another and another repeated the filthy word. In a flash Scottie jumped from the carriage and dashed headlong into the fray, bringing down one of the boys in a jumble of kicking limbs.

With a grim face, Forrest moved to cross the street himself. But before he had gone three yards a pair of white-gloved hands gripped his arm. "*No,* Capt'n York," Agatha hissed, hanging on to him. Her basket spilled, tumbling potatoes and jelly rolls to the ground. "Ya'll make it worse, don't ya see!" she cried under her breath. "Ya'll make it worse for *her.* Think of what you're doing!"

Forrest hesitated, his eyes following Lisbet. She was running for the carriage now, her small booted feet moving quickly beneath heavy skirts. The group of miscreants rushed forward in a mob, closing in, creating an ugly circle about the expensive equipage. The carriage team tossed their heads and pawed, shying in the traces, straining against the brake with haunches bunched for flight. Then, just above their ears, a large rotten apple sailed through the air and, for a moment, seemed to hang suspended. Just missing Lady Thorpe, it finally landed with a thud against a carriage wheel.

In a swirl of brown wool Lisbet wrenched open the vehicle door, dashed inside, and slammed it shut, just as another, better-aimed missile soiled the shuttered window.

No stranger to such cruel shenanigans, Forrest boldly limped across the same snowy cobbles that had once been the scene of his own humiliations. He was not oblivious to Agatha's warning, nor was he rash to the point of brawling with unwhiskered boys, but neither would he leave Lisbet unprotected. The first foul-tongued yokel to put a hand on her carriage would find himself flattened in short order, age and reputations be damned.

He glanced again in Scottie's direction, marking the groomsman's participation in the melee. The lad had entered into fisticuffs with a youth close to his own size and strength, and with one blow to the other's jaw, sent him sprawling. Receiving a bloodied nose for his effort, he then took on a second troublemaker, laying the fellow out with one forceful jab to the belly.

"Anyone else!" he challenged now, with blood coursing down his chin. He stood with chest heaving, long legs apart, fists raised, eyes ablaze. The once neat uniform was torn and wet with melting ice.

All about him the crowd grew quiet and motionless. The remaining boys appeared younger than Scottie, some as young as ten. None were near as tall or well-formed, nor did any seem anxious to take up the gauntlet. With eyes darting aslant, the ruffians passed a silent message of retreat. Slinking away, pulling their woolen caps low, they dispersed, dissolving into side streets like cowardly little shadows.

Standing all alone, Scottie wiped the blood from his nose with a handkerchief. Then with a weary step, he tapped upon the carriage window. Receiving assurances from within, he climbed aboard his box, released the brake, and took up the lines. With as much dignity as possible, and ignoring the smug stares of the Winterspell elders who had watched the action in the darkness of their doorways, Scottie bore his defamed lady home.

"There's not one of 'em Scottie Stone can't bring down," Agatha said quietly, coming to join Forrest again.

"Aye, he's good with his fists," Forrest acknowledged absently, so suffused with anger he could scarcely concentrate on the words. "But what the hell was behind this outrage? For God's sake, can't she even come into the village without being treated like some Piccadilly whore? I'd like to string up every last one of those filthy little blockheads and leave 'em dangling by their toes for a fortnight."

Agatha lowered her head, her gaze fixed upon the

slush covering her neat black shoes. "Lady Thorpe's always been somewhat ostracized here. Something about her past. I've only heard bits and pieces o' it, but there was a boy once—"

"She's still being pummeled with rotten apples for something that happened almost twenty years ago?" Forrest interrupted, his mouth taut with wrath.

"No, not exactly."

"Well, *what,* then?" he demanded, turning on her, barely in control of his temper. He could not know that his handsome face was marked clearly with a certain, unmistakable emotion.

Agatha looked up at him, her direct, myopic eyes magnified behind their rounded spectacles. She took a breath. "I'll tell ya why they called her a name today, why they threw apples at her head. She was seen yesterday afternoon . . . lyin' in the woods with you."

Chapter Eight

The mythical beasts of the topiary garden stood be-whiskered with hoarfrost, and yet upon each branch, tiny droplets of moisture formed and shivered beneath the afternoon sun. The intricate shapes of the knot garden slowly emerged as well, their patchwork of snow dissolving to reveal green yew.

Lisbet hardly noticed the heralding of spring. She hastened on slippered feet down the garden pathways, going ever deeper into the labyrinth of shrubbery, wishing she could walk forever, flee forever the demons that pursued her. There were so many of them—some as real as the stone dragons fronting the terrace, some as nebulous as the snow shadows beneath her swishing hems.

She feared she would go mad with them all! And this pain in her head, this throb that seemed to dizzy her more each day . . .

She walked on, inhaling frigid breaths of air. She wondered what would it be like to be free, to breathe the hot winds of a desert land if she chose, to bask in the sun upon a palm-studded terrace. She would never know. Even her long-ago trip to Italy had been no more than a blurred, heart-rending sojourn, beginning with seclusion and ending with terror. Since then she had not once escaped Winterspell, not in nearly eighteen years. And now, it seemed as if even the miserable streets of the village of her birth were barred to her. The boundaries of her existence were drawing ever inward inexorably, threateningly.

Passing beneath a skeletal canopy of great oaks, whose monstrous branches twisted like serpents and groaned in the winter wind, she began to run. Her billowing cape brushed frost from the rigid needles of pines, sent ice crystals tinkling, while her feet left a faint blue trail upon white.

And then she was seized suddenly, pulled back from her forward flight by strong and steadying hands. She twisted about and gasped as if one of her pursuing demons had materialized, ensnaring her in its trap.

"Good lord, but you make it difficult for a lame man to catch up with you." Forrest York's amused, deep-pitched voice calmed the very air, broke the spell that drove her, brought sanity where confusion had ruled.

"Forrest!" She laughed with a sudden thrill and stared up into his face. How vital he seemed, how indomitable! He stood so tall before her, his shoulders beneath the heavy greatcoat broad and square. And his dark face with its hint of ruthlessness suggested utter maleness. Lisbet had a sudden notion that the captain would have been savage in battle, more than a match for the most merciless foe.

But there were some dragons even he could not slay, she thought with a sobering shiver. She must remember that, she *must* . . .

"Why were you running, my love?" he asked softly, his eyes fond and tender. "Have the Hounds of Hell been loosed here in the gardens of Wexford Hall? Are they nipping at your heels? Tell me, and I'll send them back to their fire and brimstone, by heaven! Did I ever tell you I could knock the eyes off a potato at fifty paces with a slingshot?"

Melting into his arms as if it were the most natural of instincts, Lisbet pressed herself against the roughness of his coat and clung there. How she wanted to unburden her heart, tell him about the excruciating headaches that plagued her, tell him about her life with Sylvan! But she could not. To pull out and share one secret from her knotted web would be to unravel them all.

"Keep your slingshot in your pocket," she answered, forcing lightness, keeping her face buried in his coat. "I just needed a bit of air. I've been detained indoors all day, you see, and when I finally got out, I felt so invigorated I began to dash along the path quite recklessly." She put a hand to her throat. "Undignified of me, wasn't it, acting like a schoolgirl?"

Forrest drew back, holding her by the arms, looking down at her face. The laughter left his eyes. "I always liked you as a schoolgirl."

He was resistless in this mood. She put a hand to his cheek and ran it along the curve of his jaw, telling him with a look that her memories were as poignant as his.

Lisbet," he said, frowning, taking her hand. "About the scene in the village . . ."

She bent her head at the words as if ashamed that he had witnessed her humiliation.

"The cause of it was entirely my fault," he went on softly. "More than anyone, I should have remembered how the snooping sods of this place—"

She put her fingers to his lips to silence him, for what had occurred had been no more his fault than hers, and she would not let him accept the blame. When he tightened his hold, however, she pulled away. They could ill afford another indiscretion.

Touching his hand, she began to stroll the path

again. Forrest limped along at her side, his stride so conditioned and strong that its halting seemed barely perceptible. If it pained him to walk, he gave no sign of it.

Beyond the orchard, they skirted vast rows of iris whose stalks lay ice-glazed and brown, then beds of roses, whose fragrance would not reawaken 'til June. A small pond, its surface silver-blue with ice, lay nestled between a circle of yews, and Lisbet halted there at last, feeling sheltered, screened as well as one could ever be from the treacherous eyes of Winterspell.

Forrest stood beside her. He bent his head, staring at the leaves frozen in the rigid pond, shoving his ungloved hands deep within his pockets. The quiet between them stretched long.

Did you come to ride today?" Lisbet said at last.

"Ostensibly. But more than anything I wanted to see you, talk with you."

At the seriousness in his tone, Lisbet glanced up at him with a frown.

"I want you to tell me about Sylvan, Lisbet," Forrest said steadily. "I want you to tell me about your life with him."

Shaken by the sudden unexpected question, uncomfortable discussing her marriage, she looked away.

Forrest made a move to take hold of her arm, but reading her uneasiness, let his hand drop back to his side. After holding her in his arms the other day, he had felt strained to the breaking point in the effort to keep himself from her. Damned fool that he was, he had wanted countless times to storm the walls of Wexford Hall like some warrior of old and bear her away, leaving the small eccentric Earl of Tilbury standing ineffectually behind. The very thought of her marriage, of a husband and his intimate rights over her, roused Forrest to the fiercest peak of jealousy.

His mood was not helped by the events of the past three days. Since that outrage in the village, Forrest had paced the floors of his house, thinking, brooding. Many things had crossed his mind, including the notion of a swift, silent departure from Winterspell. He really had no right to interrupt Lisbet's life, after all. His intellect told him that leaving would be the wisest course, and his intellect was rarely wrong. But last night he had let the battered, more tender organ in his chest do his thinking for him.

He wanted Lisbet heart, soul, and body—nothing less. He wanted to take her away from Winterspell, away from Wexford Hall, away from her husband. He did not want her to be ostracized any longer, despised by all in the village, made to suffer insult when she should have been offered respect. He would see her happy, take her to Greece with him or Venice or Spain. He would show her wondrous sights, all the treasures he had seen alone and wished to share. And he would never let her go again.

There was no one to stop him. Lord Thorpe could be evaded easily. So could any detective, no matter how well-paid. If Forrest chose not to be found, he would not be, nor would Lisbet. No, there was no one to halt him in his plan . . . except Lisbet herself—if she chose to do so. And would she?

He wasn't sure. There was much he did not understand about her, much she would not let him know.

"Tell me about Sylvan, Lisbet," he repeated, steeling himself. He realized he was afraid of what she would say, but he must know her feelings for Lord Thorpe before proposing his plan to her. He must know if she loved her husband.

Lisbet stilled. "What would you have me say about him exactly?" she asked awkwardly.

In a low, tight voice Forrest answered. "I want to

know what it is that makes you care so much for him."

Lisbet glanced up with chagrin. She saw his jaw pulsing erratically, and the lines on either side of his mouth were taut. It occurred to her that he had wanted to ask these questions since his return to Winterspell, but he had held them back until now. Her answer was important to him, vitally important. In an aching rush, she realized that he was jealous, tormentingly jealous.

She shifted on the uneven ground, the snow seeping through her shoes and freezing her toes. She felt an overwhelming sense of desolation all at once, as if she stood upon a swinging bridge and could move neither right nor left without a fatal fall. And yet, at all costs, Forrest must know where her duty lay. Her happiness, even his happiness could never come before it.

"There is much about Sylvan that is . . . difficult to explain," she faltered, hardly knowing where to begin. "He is far more vulnerable than most people can ever understand. While he has all the same feelings, the same hopes and dreams as other men possess, he . . . he is trapped within a form that is his very nemesis. He lavishes excessive gifts upon people and charities so they will forget the way he looks. Since birth he has been the object of ridicule, a pariah even within his own family. And he has been utterly alone and friendless." Her voice lowered and she inhaled a shaky breath. "I am his only friend, his only love. He says he lives for me. And I believe, were I to leave him, he would die."

There . . . she had said it.

Beside her, Forrest clenched his fists in his pockets. So that was the way of it. She would not go with him, he realized grimly. Nothing he could do or say would persuade her to leave her husband.

Feeling frustrated and bitterly disappointed, he

longed to seize her by the arms and ask, *And what of me, Lisbet . . . and what of me . . . ?*

Instead, he merely lifted his lip in a rueful half-smile and thought, *Well, Anvil, old chap, you are the odd man out again.*

"Do you love him?" he asked rigidly, staring hard at her.

Dismayed that he would ask, she looked away from his piercing regard. "Forrest, I—"

"Why did you marry him, Lisbet?" he pressed, his voice brittle. "What made you marry him?"

She tensed. What could she say? Not the truth, never the truth. "My f-father arranged it," she stumbled. That, at least, was not a lie.

"That would have been less than a year after you were with me, wouldn't it?"

"Y-yes."

"And yet you were agreeable to your father's arrangement, his choice?"

Lisbet shivered. His voice was as cold as the air. It made her feel faithless and wretched. "At first I refused," she said stiffly, attempting a defense of herself.

"And then . . . ?" he persisted in a near-taunting voice.

"And then I agreed," she snapped. She could deliver pain as well as he. "I agreed. I *agreed.*"

"You agreed," he repeated through his teeth. Turning, he leaned toward her, his dark eyes sullen and demanding. "And now are you happy with the choice you made?"

Happy? Did he need to ask? Couldn't he see? "No," she answered, the word flat and empty. "No."

He had wanted to hear her say that. She could see it in the sudden flicker of his eyes; she could hear it in the breath he released.

For several moments he said nothing more, only

shifted his weight as if his injured knee ached with standing. When he spoke again, his voice had altered. Anger still touched it—and yet, so did the barest edge of agony.

"You could have had anyone, Lisbet. *Anyone.* Any blasted duke in the kingdom would have asked for you—one with piles of money, a seat in Parliament, and bloodlines as pure as those of some damned thoroughbred horse. You could've had your pick."

His mood seemed to change yet again, grow darker. He snorted cruelly, then rubbed a restless hand across his jaw before shoving it back inside his pocket. "Hell, surely that little matter of my . . . deflowering proved no deterrent. With a bit of feminine guile you could have deceived some pretty-faced young duke just as easily as you did that poor disfigured earl you selected."

Lisbet struck him hard across the cheek for his disrespect. Her ring scratched his flesh, drawing a thin line of blood to the surface. But only the corner of his eye flinched with the sting.

"What is your point?" Lisbet demanded through her teeth. "Would you have liked it better if I had married someone with your rutting good looks? Would that have satisfied you in some perverse way? Is your pride bruised because you think Sylvan is less of a man than Captain Forrest York?"

Forrest did not move, but his expression held all the ferocity of a wild and wounded beast. For a few seconds both man and woman remained motionless, eyes glaring, oblivious to everything except the sight of each other. They did not hear the wind above their heads or the drip of melting ice or—at first—the distant cry of a voice.

"Lis-bet!"

At last Lady Thorpe stirred, putting a hand to her heart, and looked about in fear.

"Lisbet, my pet!" the reedy voice called from behind them. "Where have you hidden yourself?"

Through the trees she could see Lord Thorpe now, a miniature figure in a green velvet coat and knee breeches, his yellow hose as bright as daffodils where he stumbled over the snow. In anxiety she glanced at Forrest and breathed, "My husband . . ."

A bitter smile curved Forrest's mouth and his black eyes glittered. "Don't worry, my lady. As I do not relish the trouble of explaining my presence any more than you do, I shall make myself scarce."

But when he moved away, Lisbet put a frantic hand on his arm, clawing the stuff of his sleeve to hold him. Suddenly she did not want him to stalk away angry and cold. She wanted to make amends, tell him she loved him, wipe the wound on his cheek.

He was waiting, looking down at her with a wry, saturnine tilt to his mouth.

In a gesture of remorse, she raised a hand, making to gently wipe the blood away.

Seizing her fingers, he jerked them away from his face, the violence of his emotions clear. "Do you know why I came here today, *Lady Thorpe?* I came to ask you to leave the country with me, pack your trunks, and sail to some decadent paradise in the arms of your lover."

When her eyes narrowed, he smiled brutally. "That's right. I had hoped to persuade you to abandon your husband and live a life of scandalous immorality with me. But didn't I warn you, my lady? Didn't I tell you I was unscrupulous? I even quite gallantly offered to leave, but you declined in a most desperate and touching way as I recall. And so," he finished silkily, "it appears you must ever be on your guard against me."

He lifted a dark brow. "Now, I believe your husband is calling."

"Lis-bet!"

She swung about. At the end of the pond, her husband crashed through the foliage, grunting with exertion. Distraught, she glanced toward Forrest, still loath to let him go.

But already he had disappeared.

"Lisbet, Lisbet!" Lord Thorpe cried in a tone both petulant and distressed. "Why have you been so contrary today, my pet?" With his eyes accusing, he trotted up to her, reaching for her frozen hands. "And you've forgotten your gloves again. So forgetful, so forgetful. Shall I scold you?"

He tugged upon her arm like a fond but exasperated parent. "Come inside, come inside," he panted. "Sit beside the fire with me. Soon it will be dark."

Dinner that night was one of the most harrowing meals Lisbet had ever endured. The dining hall seemed colder and more cavernous than ever, its purple velvet drapes closed tight, its single chandelier spilling tarnished gold across the table. A feast sumptuous enough for a king and queen burdened the lace cloth, including salmon mayonnaise, roast mutton, jellied capon, spinach souffle, sauteed mushrooms, and creamed peas steaming gently on polished silver. Crystal glinted, snowy linen glared, while conservatory lilies nodded their waxen heads above a porcelain bowl. The sculptured centerpiece of silver, weighing at least sixty pounds and representing the fall of Icarus, seemed gaudy and bright. And in contrast, away from the table, gloom ruled every corner, edging the garlanded ceiling with violet-black.

In a mechanical move of her arm Lisbet put food to her mouth, nearly choking upon its richness. She had yearned to go to bed, escape to that curtained recess usually so detested. But she feared Sylvan would trail after her, insist upon holding her hand. And she couldn't bear his touch, his avid attentions tonight.

Not with the vision of Forrest so close behind her eyes.

" 'Pon my soul, pet," Sylvan said now, noisily consuming his leg of lamb. "Are you wearing *that* gown again? You should throw it out. Doesn't become you. So plain. I declare, you will wear the simplest wardrobe. I can't fathom it. Always thought women were fond of frills and furbelows."

"I like this gown," Lisbet murmured in stubborn argument. It was her habit to wear the plainest garments. When she had married Sylvan as a young girl, she had done whatever she could to make herself less noticeable.

"At least wear some jewels with it, then," Lord Thorpe grumbled. "Not that your beauty requires adornment, of course. But I like to see you wear the baubles I buy."

"Yes, Sylvan," she said with an automatic nod, wanting to shut out the sound of his voice. She was growing sleepy the way she often did at supper, experiencing that dreadful, heavy somnolence she hated. But at least the ache in her head would lessen. And, perhaps, if she slept soundly enough, she could escape haunting thoughts of Forrest York. Unless, of course, he came to disturb her dreams . . .

"Sleepy, my dear?" Sylvan inquired.

She made an attempt to raise her chin, force her lashes up. Her husband smiled at her. The candlelight from above touched the features of his hideous face, the bulbous nose, the domed forehead, the odd protruding eyelids.

Wiping his lips with a napkin, he commented. "Your naughty protégé got himself into another scrape today.

Dashed impossible lad, that Scottie!" He waved a butter knife with his misshapen hand. "I found him this morning brawling with the kitchen boy behind the coachhouse. Knocked the poor clod senseless, he did. Laid him out like a corpse. The gardener had to dash water in his face to bring him round. Then, without even an apology for his behavior, Scottie stomped off on his own, going wherever it is he goes to do his sulking. And that brings to mind something else . . ."

Lord Thorpe frowned, tapping a finger to his chin in a musing fashion. "I overheard the footman remarking to a maid that Scottie had been fighting in the village. Do you know about that, love?"

Lisbet reached for her wine, her hand setting the burgundy atremble in its goblet. Hastily she sipped. Pray God the rumors about Forrest had not reached her husband's ears. "H-he's just a spirited young man," she defended, struggling to keep her voice calm. "The village boys are always fighting. He's no different."

Sylvan rapped his elfin fingers on the table thoughtfully. "I suppose you're right. Although when I was a lad, I never raised my fists to anyone—'course, I would've liked to. But even an ugly curiosity like me has brains enough to recognize futility when he faces it."

Lisbet regarded him with vague surprise. Except for a few, best-forgotten occasions, Sylvan took care to avoid self-pity.

The dishes were removed then and dessert set out. At sight of the raspberry trifle, sugared violets, and chocolate comfits, she averted her eyes, feeling nauseous. An inexplicable fear nagged at her stomach as well, for if Sylvan suspected her feelings for Forrest, he would surely banish him from the property, making Wexford Hall more a prison for her than ever. She looked up at her husband to judge his thoughts, watching while he speared a berry on his fork and popped it into his mouth.

His soft, drooping brown eyes met hers as he ate. He smiled softly, waiting for her to smile back. When she did not, his face sagged, and he put down his fork.

Lisbet looked away, feeling despicable, wretched. Sylvan's idolization was a thing to which she never grew accustomed. She abhorred his ardent expressions, his beseeching eyes, his clinging presence. Sometimes she thought he loved her to the point of sin. He believed her good, pure, beautiful, proclaimed her his very life, his only reason for existence. And she loathed it.

Yet she wondered how she could despise him for his love. How could she even contemplate abandoning him simply because of his abnormalities—or because she loved him so much less than she should? Only a woman devoid of conscience would do these things. It was contemptible enough that she yearned constantly to escape him, that she had to steel herself against his every touch . . .

"Come and sit with me beside the fire, my sweet," he invited now. He slid down from the velvet tasseled cushion that gave him added height in the chair. Walking round the table and its sixteen ever-empty chairs, he disappeared in a shroud of shadow before reentering the island of candlelight. Mutely he drew back Lisbet's chair, offered his arm with a practiced raise of his little elbow, and bowed.

Extending her hand downward, she took hold of it. Beside her Sylvan cleared his throat and raised his head. Then, as if he were a king escorting the fairest princess in the land, he led her through double mahogany doors, across echoing marble tiles, and into a splendorous saloon where an orange fire blazed. As he and his lady stood beneath a ceiling painted with Pan-dora and her open jar, twin mirrors caught their ill-matched image.

Only one chair sat poised beside the hearth; Sylvan had had its mate removed. Climbing upon its tapestry seat, he patted his satin-clad knee. "Take your place, my dove. I have missed you sorely today, missed looking at you. You seem so restless of late, always strolling or riding or pacing the gallery. You must tell me why."

Lisbet eased down upon his lap, disliking this ritual established at the onset of their marriage. But it had been a compromise then, a way of avoiding something else, something a girl of fifteen could not agree to face on her wedding day.

"I suppose I'm just anxious for spring," she said, needing to give an answer.

He took her hand in his. She had long ago grown used to the feel of his flesh against her palm; its unusual shape, even the roughness of it, bothered her no more. For she truly did see beyond Sylvan's differences, beyond his eccentricities. She knew him simply as a man, upon whom the world turned scornful eyes.

And in some strange way, a way inexplicable to her, Lisbet loved the gentle, misbegotten Earl of Tilbury.

"What day is it?" he asked now, just as she knew he would.

"Saturday."

"And the month?"

"March, of course."

"Ah . . . March. Then only a few months more, a few months more."

He said nothing else, but this game of questions and answers held significance for them both. The anniversary of their wedding fast approached; they were to celebrate it specially. Sylvan counted the days like a child eager for Christmas; Lisbet counted them much differently.

On this midsummer's eve, Lord and Lady Thorpe would complete what had begun so many years ago in Italy. When dusk approached, they would climb the stairs side by side, they would extinguish the lights, draw the bed curtains tight.

And then, at last . . . they would lie down together as man and wife.

Chapter Nine

Thwump! Thwump! Thwump! Forrest wielded an ax with a rhythmic swing of his body, feeling perspiration wet the place between his shoulder blades even in the cold. Always a man of action, he relished the physical exertion of chopping wood, and in less than a quarter-hour had almost finished splitting the huge oaken branch that had broken from its mother tree beneath a weight of ice.

The past fortnight he had spent every morning working at his desk, an activity requiring a great measure of personal discipline, for passivity was not his natural inclination, especially after years of constant travel. Every afternoon he rewarded himself with a vigorous ride down lanes made soggy by an early spring, then repaired the pumps, door frames, or whatever else needed mending at the cottage. The activity did much to vent frustration.

Gradually his days had fallen into routine. On her housekeeping days, Agatha took supper with him in the kitchen, pestering him into relating tales of adventure and war as if it were quite the most entertaining activity she had enjoyed in years. And in the evenings, when darkness fell and he had banked the fires high, Forrest sat alone. Sometimes he perused a book or whittled sailing ships or polished his boots till they gleamed; sometimes he simply stared into the flames and felt loneliness more acutely than he had ever done before.

Never had he allowed himself quite so much time for reflection, and now that he did, it seemed he had little to show for a man of thirty-six. He would have liked to have a woman to sit beside the fire with him, he would have liked to have had children. He thought of all the women who would have been happy to oblige him, he thought of the one who would not.

Since the scene in the garden with Lisbet, he had studiously avoided Wexford Hall, even kept himself from gazing at its upper-story windows and wondering where the lady was. Yet he still thought of her with a nagging constancy. She was like a poison in his blood, one he did not know how to purge. In spite of her rejection of him and her decision to remain in her husband's keeping, Forrest could not bring himself to leave Winterspell, separating himself from her forever.

Now he put the ax aside and, wiping sweat from his brow, bent to stack the firewood. Suddenly a distant crack rent the air. He straightened, listening. Moments later, from the general direction of Wexford Hall, another report echoed through the trees.

Thinking it prudent to investigate, Forrest went inside, retrieved his revolver from a desk drawer, and shrugged into a brown tweed coat. Then he set off down the lane.

Following the intermittent sounds of shots, he came upon a clearing and, for a moment, stood watching the activity there. It seemed target practice was in session.

Scottie Stone wielded a pistol and, after carefully realigning a row of colored bottles on an outcropping of rock, stood back and took aim. Four shots later he had managed to shatter not one piece of glass.

Forrest grinned and shook his head, casually strolling up behind. "Try this," he said blandly, pulling the revolver from his coat and extending it in offer.

Starting, Scottie whirled, embarrassment over his poor performance apparent in his reddening face. With distrust he regarded Forrest as if expecting the older man to make some disparaging remark. When none came, his eyes fell to the revolver, flickering with interest.

"Go ahead, it's loaded," Forrest prompted. "Or don't you know how to use it?"

Spurred by the question, Scottie laid his own weapon down and grabbed hold of Forrest's. Then hardly taking time to aim, he squeezed the trigger and delivered a bullet into the trunk of a nearby tree, missing wide the row of bottles.

"Bull's-eye," Forrest proclaimed in a quite serious tone. "I believe you hit the knothole. Doubt I could have done it myself at this range."

As if highly suspicious of the remark, the youth glanced sharply at Forrest. He opened his mouth to say something, then shut it, obviously too flattered by the compliment to admit the truth of the matter.

Forrest indicated the ancient dueling pistol. "Where did you get that thing?"

"Lady Thorpe gave it to me," Scottie said challengingly.

Picking it up, Forrest turned it over in his palm. "Hmm. . . . not a bad piece. If you're shooting at pirates." He set it aside and invited Scottie to use the revolver again. "This time target the bottles. And if you were to change your grip just a bit—"

"I don't need any instructions on how to use firearms," Scottie declared with his usual brand of insolence. Again he pulled the trigger and missed his target.

"I can see you don't," Forrest drawled, crossing his arms and changing his stance as if expecting to be there for awhile.

All right, then show me," the young man grumbled, obviously torn between dignity and the desire to learn. "But don't do any long-winded preachin' on the subject. I can't abide it."

Forrest grunted. "Preaching has never been one of my strong points, believe me." He put his hand atop Scottie's, adroitly readjusted the boy's grip, then stepped back. "Now, again."

This time the bullet buried itself in a rock just inches below the line of bottles.

"Blimey!" Scottie exclaimed, pleased with his marked improvement.

Beside him Forrest raised his brows and suggested a stronger expletive.

After looking at him in surprise, Scottie turned his head away, unable to conceal a grudging smile. "Did you do a deal of shooting in the military?" he asked, just barely maintaining a sullen tone.

"Yes." Forrest's voice held a hint of dry humor. "But I did a great deal more out of it."

"Were you ever shot yourself?"

Forrest laughed. "My body could have done adequate service as a sieve once or twice."

If that information caused Scottie to experience a twinge of respect for the soldier, he masked it behind a churlishly uttered question. "Do you consider yourself a good shot?"

"Fair."

"I'll wager you can't hit six of six," Scottie dared, confident.

A smile pulled at Forrest's lip. "I'll make a bargain with you. If I hit them all, you'll come to my cottage on your days off and help me build a stable for my horse."

"And if you lose?"

"Name your price."

Scottie met Forrest's eyes squarely, his usual belligerence showing in the clench of his strong young fists. "If you lose, you stay away from Lady Thorpe."

Forrest regarded the youth in silence for a second or two, then conceded. "Very well."

From a distance Lisbet watched the two men. Huddled in her hooded cloak, she stood behind a hedgerow, the drab color of her garments blending with the stunted evergreens. Mud edged her hem and stained the fine leather of her shoes, and she had trod upon a clump of brave crocuses proclaiming spring. But she was too starved for the sight of Forrest York to notice. She had not seen him in a fortnight, not since that terrible scene in the garden where she had been forced to make her loyalty clear.

Though it could not be helped, she knew she had hurt him with her words concerning her fidelity to Sylvan. Forrest's anger and brusqueness were to be expected, but his avoidance had been a surprise. She had never dreamed he would stay away so long and with such obvious resolve.

After only a few days of his conspicuous absence, she had grown fretful, then distraught, taking long strolls about the stableyard hoping to intercept him on his rides. She yearned to arrange a rendezvous, apologize, and reconcile. But he always managed to elude her. Last evening desperation had nearly driven her to risk disaster and run to his cottage.

Now he was near. And he was with Scottie. In vain she tried to catch a word exchanged between them, interpret an expression, wondering if their conversation was amiable. It appeared to be. Forrest stood close to Scottie, his frame tall and square, his demeanor calm and patient. In a steady dialogue he pointed out the particulars of his revolver, then demonstrated its reloading before handing it back to the younger man.

Lisbet bit her lip and clenched her hands inside her sable muff. To see the two men together in such a way caused remorse to rend her heart. At the same time, the gleam of pride shone in her eyes, moistening them until tears rimmed the lashes.

They should have had each other all these years. They should have loved each other.

Bowing her head, she thought how unjust life had been, how costly its mistakes. She had deprived Scottie of his father; she had deprived Forrest of his son. And now they could never know of their intimate connection, never. If she were to unveil the truth, the boy would loathe her; if she told Sylvan, he would be devastated by the lie she had guarded so long. And Forrest . . . ?

She would not be surprised if he cursed her for keeping from him the knowledge of a child.

"Out taking the air again, my pet?"

Lisbet started like a skittish hare. Sylvan had come up behind her, his long, plum-colored cloak dragging over the greening sod like a royal train. Upon his head he wore a large black bowler, which, instead of lending him dignity, only made him look like a child dressing up.

"Ah, I see our dashing captain is instructing Scottie in the finer points of weaponry," he said when Lisbet offered no reply. "Can't believe you gave the lad a pistol, my dove. As hotheaded as he is, there's no predicting what he'll do with it. Perhaps Captain York will at least lecture him on safety."

For a moment he watched the two men below, then smiled excitedly. "Look! Seems as if the captain is preparing to demonstrate."

Furtively Lisbet dashed the moistness from her eyes and watched father and son. Like any fond mother, she yearned with a straining heart to see a bond form between the man she loved and the son she had borne him.

She saw Forrest reload his revolver. He performed the procedure with such practiced movements, she thought he could have done it blind. Casually, with no particular care, he raised the weapon, aimed, and fired.

The six colored bottles seemed to disintegrate almost simultaneously in a shower of exploding glass.

"By Jove!" Sylvan exclaimed. "Dead on target! Didn't miss a one of 'em." He began to toddle forward through the muddy grass, holding his hat to his head with one hand and waving with the other.

Lisbet trailed a bit behind. To stand amidst her son and her husband and Forrest York, to remain unperturbed while conflicting emotions battered her heart would not be an easy thing.

"Good show!" Sylvan called, catching Forrest's attention. "Deuced good show. Shall we have the pleasure of another?"

Forrest smiled cordially but shook his head. "I believe Scottie and I have had enough practice for one day. Don't you agree, lad?" He leaned to pick up the boy's discarded pistol and clapped it to his hand. "And remember, I shall expect you at the cottage ready to work on your day off."

Without acknowledging Forrest's remark with so much as a nod, Scottie shoved the pistol within his pants and stalked off.

"Beastly manners," Sylvan growled, watching his retreat. "I should like to take a strap to him."

"He's a bit out of sorts," Forrest said casually. In spite of himself, he let his eyes fasten upon Lisbet, consuming every inch of her appearance to make up for the fortnight lost. "Little matter of a lost wager," he added in a low voice.

"That he's a poor loser comes as no surprise to me," Sylvan said with disgust. "One would think the boy at least clever enough not to gamble with a seasoned man like yourself. May I see that revolver?"

Forrest passed it to his hand.

"American, isn't it? Colt?"

"Yes."

"What model?"

"Frontier."

"Ah." Sylvan handed it back. "You must come up to the Hall and dine with Lady Thorpe and me, tell us how you came to have such a specimen."

"I'm hardly dressed to dine," Forrest temporized. He looked at Lisbet, judging her response, his eyes cool. Truth to tell, he wanted more than anything to sit across a candlelit table from her; at the same time he was loath to put himself through the torture. She did not meet his eyes.

"No matter!" Lord Thorpe replied, taking his wife's arm. "I insist you come. It will please my dearest pet as well as myself. Won't it, dear?" he asked, squeezing Lisbet's arm in a show of affection. "You enjoy the captain's company immensely, do you not?"

"Of course," Lisbet said faintly. Then she lowered her head to avoid Forrest's mocking smile.

Lisbet had never dressed for dinner with so much anticipation. She allowed her lady's maid to bathe her with tea rose soap, then arrange her hair in an elaborate coiffure in which a profusion of curls cascaded over the delicate point of one shoulder.

"Use the tongs, Mary," she ordered the astounded servant.

Not since childhood had she worn her hair in anything but snoods or tightly coiled knots. She bade the maid cinch her corset extra tight as well, then applied the faintest trace of scented powder to her throat and bosom.

"Take out the jade green gown, Mary, the one with the underskirt of pale rose. I shall wear it tonight."

When the astonished maid's hand stilled momentarily upon the wardrobe latch, Lisbet rushed across the carpet and pulled open the mirror-fronted door herself. "This one," she instructed impatiently, stroking the costly Japanese silk. "Take it down. Quickly. I haven't time to spare. Oh, and get my emeralds from the jewel case, too."

When the dozen yards of rippling green fabric were slipped over Lady Thorpe's head and smoothed in place, when emeralds blazed at wrists and throat, she moved to the cheval mirror, adjusting it to get a better view of herself. She could not remember the last time she had primped, the last time she had worn a pretty-hued gown. And she had worn an extra petticoat as well, so that her skirts belled out from her waist like a full-blown flower from its stem.

Peering close at her face, she frowned. "Rouge . . . get me the rouge, Mary. Then you may go."

Hardly able to keep her mouth from gaping, the servant obeyed, rummaging through the cluttered drawers of the elaborate French vanity before finding the unused paint amidst equally untouched powder jars and crystal atomizers.

With a trembling hand Lisbet took it from her. After the flustered servant departed, the lady discreetly applied color. She noticed that her hazel eyes glittered at her from the looking glass.

A dangerous notion seized her. She straightened and with slow deliberation began to unfasten the pearl buttons at the back of her gown, struggling only with the last. Using a feminine tilt of her shoulders, she let the silk slide down over chemise and petticoats to the floor.

Returning to the wardrobe, she sorted through its contents again, finally touching velvet. Almost reverently she drew out a magnificent crimson gown, simple in design but flattering in a most daring way. For a moment she held it to her breast, her mind racing. Then, she put it on.

It warmed her with its plush weight. She could feel hot color rise high in her cheeks as if a sudden fever raged in her body, a recklessness to which she was unaccustomed. With its boldness the fever seemed to burn away her virtue, her constancy, her reserve, but she did nothing to smother it.

Slowly she stepped before the mirror again.

For the first time she felt as if she were seeing herself as the woman she might have been. Standing amidst the opulent splendor of her room, where fringed cushions, hand-painted screens, and Oriental vases framed her image, she resembled an exotic enchantress. She was vibrant, striking . . . seductive.

With all the age-old instinct of a woman desiring the attention of a man, she draped her hair more artfully over a bare shoulder, fastening diamonds to her ears. Then, feeling the prick of daring, the thrill of temptation, she raised her hands and unclasped the emeralds.

Tonight she would wear another charm.

Hastily she removed it from the pocket of her cloak, threaded a golden chain through its ring, and secured it about her neck. Its gold was tarnished and cheap, its design plain, but it winked brazenly between her breasts. A man's eye could not fail to be drawn to it . . . his mind wonder at its meaning.

Forrest York belonged to her. She would not allow him to go out of her life again.

Downstairs Forrest paced the length of the drawing room with all the restlessness of a confined tiger. He had been waiting nearly an hour for his host and hostess to change, and although refreshment had been brought in beside a fire that was warm and inviting, he could not seem to settle. Sloshing brandy into a glass, he downed it, wondering for the thousandth time why he had been born with such a galling predilection for trouble.

The wide paneled door swung open at last. Forrest glanced up to see Lord Thorpe and. . . . At first he thought the man must be escorting someone besides his wife.

She stood in the half-light, which slanted obliquely across her gown, her bosom, her face. The soft velvet of her costume was so rich and deep it seemed to pulsate crimson. It trailed behind her, falling in voluptuous folds, its bodice scooping down from the shoulders to form a heart-shaped point. Above it Lisbet's flesh gleamed like pearl. Where her hair had been severely knotted before, now it tumbled in a shiny riot of curls behind one ear, brushing the curve of her shoulder.

She gazed at him from beneath half-lowered lashes, the hazel of her eyes glittering green, the light in them full of the ancient appeal he had seen in the most practiced courtesans. And nestled in the cleft of her bosom, a locket glinted gold . . .

His blood rose. Every nerve in his body responded to the deliberately flaunted allure.

Lord Thorpe seemed disconcerted himself and yet equally beguiled as he fluttered about his wife like a nervous schoolboy.

Forrest ignored him, his eyes burning into Lisbet's. *What was she doing? Did she think to taunt him, punish him for his coolness, his avoidance? Well, he was not some callow youth with which to be played. He had learned early on how to handle teasing women, beginning with the bored, uninhibited wives of his senior officers.*

Recovering himself with a smooth readjustment of his features, he bowed over her hand. "Lady Thorpe."

"Captain . . ." she breathed, meeting his eyes.

" 'Our sweetest songs are those that tell of silent thought!' " her husband quoted in a thin, unsteady voice, taking Lisbet by the arm again. "The footman has announced dinner. Shall we proceed?"

The table settings, the service, the furnishings of the dining room were fit to grace a king's palace, and yet Forrest scarcely noticed them. Whenever he chanced to meet Lisbet's eye, a slight, enigmatic smile would touch her lips, madden him with both anger and yearning. He told himself that whatever game she played, he could play it, too, and doubly well. He was only sorry it had to be played across his host's table.

"Now, Captain York," Lord Thorpe began, adjusting himself upon his tasseled cushion. "You must tell us more about this revolver of yours. I have read about the model, but never had the occasion of seeing it. Have you been to America, by chance?"

Forrest slid a napkin across his lap, waiting while an elaborately liveried footman dipped creamed soup into his Sèvres bowl. "I've been to the States several times, as a matter of fact, but I didn't acquire the revolver there."

With a graceful move of her hand, Lisbet dipped a spoon into her soup, held it suspended near her lips, and breathed, "Then where did you get it, Captain?"

Every ounce of Forrest's masculinity was aware of her presence across the table. He did not have to look up to remember the arch of her brows, the curve of her upper lip, the texture of the skin across her throat. He did not even have to hear her voice to recall its low beguilement.

He cleared his throat. "Three years ago," he began, "I was traveling in Morocco. It is a place foreign to us in almost every way, with snake charmers, sheiks, and slippered pashas behind the walls of its cities. Its people are extremely religious and yet savage in their treatment of anyone caught in an offense. There are tribes who are intolerant of all things Western—and particularly Christian—in nature." He gave a wry smile. "And when I say intolerant, I mean it in the strictest sense of the word."

"Being dark," he continued, "I naturally dressed myself in native garb and, with a mastery of the language, blended well enough. There was a certain caravan heading for Fez, and having business there, I joined it. Unfortunately a group of Foulahs journeyed with us. They are a barbarous lot, not above waging petty wars, staging executions, and indulging in thievery." He raised his glass, touched it to his lips with a sardonic smile and added, "Much like our own esteemed Parliament, come to think of it. At any rate, I noticed that one of their members had a Colt revolver, which he quite boastfully explained had been the recent property of an American calvaryman. Apparently the misguided Yank had gone to Morocco seeking high adventure without first doing his homework."

"You mean he should have gone in disguise?" Lord Thorpe questioned with avid eyes.

"I mean he probably attempted a Methodist conversion on the steps of a mosque."

Sylvan clapped his hands and laughed with childlike enjoyment. "Capital! Quite so, quite so. Go on."

"Well, as you might have guessed, the American was promptly eliminated for his sacrilege to Islam. The rather stupid Foulah brute I mentioned earlier won possession of the gentleman's revolver, though exactly what democratic process decided this, I can't fathom. It certainly had nothing to do with his skill at shooting."

"Was he a worse shot than Scottie?" Sylvan sputtered, wiping soup from his grinning lips.

"Considerably," Forrest drawled. "As the caravan moved through the desert, I saw him take pot-shots at granite stones from time to time. He never managed to hit one of them, not even the boulders."

While Sylvan chuckled, Forrest selected stuffed pork from a platter and went on. "There came a point when I got the distinct impression that I was shortly to meet the same fate as the American. Seems I'd talked in my sleep—in English, of course. Fortunately, however, a group of Moorish robbers made a timely appearance and drew swords on us. As the esteemed marksman of my story seemed unable to get a shot off, I took it upon myself to borrow the revolver and send the thieves to Hades myself." Forrest raised a brow. "Amazing how my status rose amongst the crowd."

"So you were given the revolver?" Sylvan finished.

Forrest shook his head. "It's true that some Middle Eastern cultures are generous givers of gifts, and I wish I could say the Foulahs were so impressed with my talents that they handed over the gun, but—"

"You stole it from them." Lisbet phrased the sentence as fact, as if knowing the conclusion.

"Without a qualm. In the dead of night."

Silence reigned while two pairs of eyes locked across the table.

"I envy you your adventures, York," Lord Thorpe declared, his houndish eyes alight with excitement, empty of suspicions.

Lisbet leaned forward slightly in her chair. "And the ladies in that part of the world, Captain York?" she asked in deliberate, breathy tones. "Are they always veiled?"

Forrest looked at her, watching as she slid a hand upward and toyed with the locket at her breast. Her eyes seemed dilated, her movements unnaturally languorous in spite of her lively color. He wondered if she had been drinking more than she should.

"The ladies are always veiled in public."

"And when they are not in public . . . ?" She suspended the words, but the question was clear.

Forrest gave her a smile as inscrutable as her own

had earlier been. "Only a few men—a very select few—are invited behind those walls, Lady Thorpe."

Lisbet's eyes sparked with a gleam of jealousy, then lowered.

"Such an exceedingly different culture from our own," Sylvan said, clumsily cutting into his curried chicken. "I admire you for your courage, York. Damned dangerous place to put yourself, sounds to me."

"And will you be going back there?" Lisbet asked quietly, touching the locket again with her fingertips. Her eyelids were heavy and shadowed, her gaze alight with an utterly seductive gleam.

Forrest's hand stilled upon his spoon. He glanced pointedly at Lord Thorpe, then back to Lisbet.

"Perhaps," he said, his eyes dark with satisfaction. "If the whim should seize me."

Shortly thereafter, stretching social etiquette, Forrest took his leave. His temper was sore, his passions roused, and the mile walk through a sudden spring downpour did nothing to soothe them. Nor did his mood improve at his arrival home. A pile of old rusted horseshoes were dumped upon his doorstep.

Someone in Winterspell remembered him as Anvil.

Chapter Ten

Forrest touched the brand on his shoulder in the instinctive gesture of bygone years and, with his boot, sent the horseshoes flying off the step. That someone in Winterspell still harbored enough maliciousness to continue this childish prank caused anger to gather like a maelstrom in his chest. All the old helpless fury returned in one swift gale, all the old bloodlust begged for retribution. The force of it stunned him, for he had thought himself beyond it long ago.

Stepping inside the shadowy cottage where raindrops slashed the windows and made a thrumming sound against the timbered walls, Forrest's toe struck yet another iron shoe. It had been thrown through the window, sent glass flying everywhere, and allowed the deluge outside full access to the clean slate floor. Picking up the offensive object, he opened the back door and, raging, hurled it out toward the woods. As it landed with a splatter against the flooded earth, he cursed every inhabitant of Winterspell, its ancestors, and future issue with all the eloquence of an Arab camel driver.

His knee throbbed. Pulling out a chair, he let a hot breath of air hiss through his teeth, then leaned a forearm on the table. A shard of glass pricked through his sleeve, and with a yowl, he clapped a hand over the trickle of blood on his elbow. The blood was dark and crimson . . . as dark and crimson as a velvet gown.

"Teasing, conniving Jezebel!" he roared. Visions of Lisbet remained with him still, tormenting his senses, and he spoke to the brazen countess as if she stood in all her finery before him.

"You hoped to play me for a fool tonight, didn't you! You taunted me, mocked me, had me staring at you like a cockeyed boy, flaunted what I cannot have. And for what? What point did you make with your game, what satisfaction did you gain from it?"

Forrest pounded his fist into his thigh and, pushing himself up, limped to and fro, to and fro about the glass-strewn room. "Were you here with me now, my lady," he growled through his teeth, "I would take you by your naked white shoulders and shake you until your teeth rattled."

Flinging open the back door, he stalked outside, heedless of the rain that pelted his head and ran in rivulets from his hair. Wind swayed the trees, and lightning danced through the clouds, illuminating the fierceness of his face.

For a long while he simply stood in the middle of the yard, oblivious to the elements while he contemplated with a dark eye the flickering outline of Wexford Hall.

"Come, my love, and sit with me beside the fire. The way you always do."

Lisbet remained motionless, standing by the French doors as if she would escape. Rain drummed steadily upon the paving stones, coursed from the eaves in streams, made mud of the flower beds. A low rumble of thunder rattled the panes before rolling away like a retreating drum. At the same time the rain diminished, falling in drifting beads that clung to the glass and made the landscape like a scene viewed through finest gauze.

"Did you not hear, my love?" Sylvan persisted from his chair beside the hearth. "Come, sit with me."

"No, Sylvan," Lisbet said tensely, daring to defy him. "I don't feel like sitting up tonight. I want only to go to bed."

Ever her shadow, he came to stand near, his silver buckled shoes absurdly old-fashioned, his cinnamon waistcoat clashing with a burgundy jacket too long in the cuffs. At the top of his high domed head, a wisp of hair frizzed out, and upon his chin, a spot of mustard dried. Looking at him caused Lisbet to feel both revulsion and pity, both protectiveness and guilt.

"Did you have an enjoyable evening, sweet?" he asked her with slight uncertainty in his piping voice. Brushing the warm velvet sleeve of her gown with his knobby hand, he added, "Did you enjoy Captain York's company?"

She clenched her lacy handkerchief and made her answer vague and light. "He's an interesting dinner companion."

"Indeed. And quite a handsome fellow. Intrepid and brash. Rather moody, I suspect, and always on his guard. He seems to have been alone much of his life, too. Being the good judge of character that I am," Sylvan added officiously, "I have decided our Captain York is a mystery."

"A mystery?" Lisbet repeated with unease.

Sylvan shrugged his crooked shoulders. "Well, he seems to have no ties, no family. If he's spoken of his origins, I've never heard him." He slid his hand in hers. "Have you?"

Pretending idleness, Lisbet glided to a table and flicked through the pages of a ladies' journal. A tiny smile curved her mouth. "As a matter of fact, I have heard him say. He said that he came from . . . nowhere."

Ha!" Sylvan exclaimed. "Didn't I tell you he was a shadowy figure?"

"Some men are more private than others," Lisbet answered vaguely, wanting to close the subject. She turned, her hips pressed against the table edge. "And now I believe I shall go upstairs. It has been a long day, don't you think?"

Sylvan detained her, rushing across the room in his uneven totter. Taking her wrist, he lifted it, putting it to his cherry lips, and kissed its straight blue veins with ardor. Then as he often did, he trailed a stubby, horny-nailed hand over each of her fingers, from knuckle to knuckle and back again, as if marveling at their perfection.

"You're lovely tonight, my pet," he whispered against her palm. Leaning close, he spoke so that his breath warmed the hollow at the base of her throat. "But the locket you wear . . . I thought you had dropped it in the river."

She managed to laugh, but it was a short, nervous sound. "I-it had fallen into the pocket of my cloak, Sylvan. Can you imagine? All the time it had been right there, if I had only known to look."

He nodded, putting his hand to the ivory swell just above the charm. Possessively he let it rest there, palm open. "You tempt me sorely tonight. Ah . . . how you do tempt me, my dearest love."

She swallowed, staring down at the darkness of his flesh upon the fairness of hers. Her body began to shiver as if with a winter chill, and her face ached with the effort to keep it rigid, devoid of aversion. "Sylvan . . ."

As if unable to stop himself, Lord Thorpe began to

gently stroke her shoulders, follow the intriguing line of delicate collarbone to the downy spot beneath her earlobe. He then let his fingers slide down again to the place where the locket lay. "Please, Lisbet," he murmured in an anguished voice. " 'Tis not so long until midsummer's eve, you know."

With an unsuppressible shudder Lady Thorpe stepped back. Simultaneously her husband clutched at her hands and lowered himself on his knees, putting his misshapen head into the plush folds of her skirt.

"Please!" he wailed. "Do not shrink from me. You are my life, I adore you." He pulled at her hem, crying in the tormented tone she knew so well. "I love thee! I love thee! I love thee!"

"No, Sylvan!" She attempted to disentangle his fingers but he only squeezed them tighter, looking up at her with his pouched, red-brown eyes. As always pity overwhelmed her.

"Lie at my side through the night, if nothing more!" he beseeched with a frantic clawing at her hem. "Let this ugly, cursed form, this vile creation of the devil know what it is to feel you so warm and so perfect against it. Oh," he moaned, rocking on his knees, "I am no man, I know, I know. I am no man. . . ."

"Oh, Sylvan, you mustn't. You mustn't!" Lisbet cried, putting her hands on his bowed unhandsome head and kneeling down before him. His behavior had been the same on the day of their wedding—how vividly she remembered it!

Throughout her short courtship with Lord Thorpe, she had been outwardly controlled, sitting beneath her father's stern and watchful eye even while she quivered inside with dread at the notion of marrying such an odd, ill-featured man.

"Remember!" her grim-faced sire would say each day before the prospective suitor called. "You have no choice in this matter, Lisbet. At fifteen years of age, you are ruined in England. Do not think that news of your despicable liaison did not travel far and wide across the drawing rooms of my peers. Do not think the gossipmongers of Winterspell kept the scandal to themselves. You, a daughter of a viscount, a gently bred lady of quality, letting herself be pleasured by a vulgar stable hand—a filthy son of a whore!"

Mutely she had sat beneath her father's raving chastisement, her heart growing colder while outside on the terrace the Italian sun blazed as hot as fire.

"You have destroyed your chances," Lord Tattershall had continued, his wrath so great the veins across his nose reddened. "And yet you seem utterly taken aback by my harshness. Did you believe I would allow you to return home, be scorned by every decent matron, be snidely propositioned by every young blade in polite society? Did you think I'd leave you unwed and spoiled, to lie with the village boys when the urge came upon you? Perhaps you thought I would let you marry that common, black-eyed lout who put a belly on you!"

He had snorted, leaning to spit upon the glistening terrace tiles.

When Lisbet had raised up her eyes, daring to meet his merciless gaze, he had grabbed a lock of her hair, cruelly twisting it about his hand. "You will marry this man I have found for you. He is at least higher in the peerage than I and has money enough to rival Croesus. I hardly care that you must look at his hideousness the rest of your life—it is just as you deserve. Remember, I have the child, that bastard of a bastard you seem to love so much. Obey me, and I shall allow you knowledge of his whereabouts. Disobey, fail to wed Lord Thorpe, and the child will disappear to a place you will never find."

Lord Tattershall had strolled to the terrace then,

taken stock of the view, and sauntered back inside. "I care not what you do after the wedding," he continued, waving his hand. "Tell Lord Thorpe about the child if you choose. But remember, he will have reason to kill you for your deceit. No man, not even one as ugly as he, likes to find out his bride has come to him after bearing a beggar's son."

Lisbet had shuddered. She would do anything to keep from losing her child. Minutes after Scottie's birth, after her father had allowed her to hold the infant to her breast, he had taken him away to use him as a bargaining chip.

Of course, she had known her illegitimate child could never be acknowledged, but at least if she obeyed her father he would allow her access to the boy. She would be able to follow his progress over the years and send him gifts. Losing Anvil had already devastated her; she would not lose his son as well.

And yet during her first meeting with the ill-formed earl, it had been all young Lisbet could do not to gasp and beg her father to relent. She had cringed as the dwarf bowed over her hand and kissed it. Only his pitiful self-effacement, his gratefulness, and his unfailing kindness had allowed her to keep her wits. In spite of herself, she had felt touched by a grudging compassion even then.

But a highly strung girl of fifteen can only stretch compassion so far. On the night of her wedding to Lord Thorpe she had grown hysterical when he touched her, slapping his hands away and cowering in a corner. He had pursued and put his hands upon her nightdress, causing her to cry out in terror and huddle against the floorboards in a small quivering ball.

Undone by her revulsion and overcome by despair, Sylvan had begged for her love, demeaning himself. In abhorrence, Lisbet had watched him tear at his hair, curse himself vilely, then curse the fate that had given him a monster's form.

Finally she had screamed until the hotel employees beat upon the door.

Now as she stood in the drawing room of Wexford Hall, her eyes grew bright with recollection. She bent her head. Her husband sobbed like a child at her feet, prostrating himself on the floor, his face pushed to the rose-patterned carpet, his imperfect hands outstretched like a supplicant's before an idol.

"Sylvan, do not do this to me!" she cried, recoiling. "Get up, get up now. Don't do this to me! You know I cannot bear it!"

Wheeling about, she broke the grip he had upon her gown. In a swirl of crimson she ran for the stairs, taking them two at once, slipping on the glossy marble. Fleeing to her room, she shut the door and leaned breathlessly against it, her arms raised to the panels as if to keep a stronghold secure.

A noise startled her and she whirled about. But it was only a gusty breeze rattling the drapery cord against the open casement window.

She let out her breath and slumped against the wall.

Her bed stood ready, its embroidered pillows plumped, its coverlet turned back as if inviting her to slip inside. But with its heavy fringed curtains it looked a smothering place. She let her gaze travel the length of the room, where bric-a-brac danced upon every table and rugs vibrated with rich color. Huge oils framed in gold hung everywhere, leaving only an inch or two of wall between them. Venus at her bath beckoned slyly from one canvas. From another, Persephone smirked even as she descended into Hades, and the Sabine Women smiled sublimely at their rapists.

Lisbet despised it all suddenly, loathed the gilded cage Sylvan had created for her in an effort to make her happy. He had ordered almost every piece of furniture and accessory in the room, choosing from exotic import catalogues, then having the items delivered to her as a surprise. She had never had the heart to tell him her tastes were much too simple for such extravagance.

Hearing his footsteps proceeding up the stair now, she stiffened. Through the slim crack above the threshold, she could hear his shuffling gait halt. She could hear him breathe, hear him sigh. And then he began to wail wildly in lament.

" 'Thus much and more; and yet thou love'st me not, and never wilt! Love dwells not in our will. Nor can I blame thee, though it be my lot to strongly, wrongly, vainly love thee still.' "

Lisbet bowed her head in self-reproach, condemning herself because she could not love her husband as he wanted to be loved. She made him wretched, she knew—as wretched as he had made her.

And yet she had made a bargain with him, and in a bare few months, regardless of her unwillingness, would see it kept.

After her husband's door had closed, Lisbet sank down upon the bed. She waited a quarter-hour, then a quarter-hour more until the sounds of Sylvan's fitful sleep penetrated the wall.

It would be safe to leave the house now—escape—if only for an hour.

The rain had gone, taking with it all but a few swiftly scudding clouds. The night was full of shadows, shifting, purpled things that made the landscape alive. As if she were a shadow herself, Lisbet flitted through the garden, darting toward the dark snaking water at the end of the parkland. Rain soaked through her slippers and the smell of wet, greening life caught in her hair. She could hear the faint tinkle of a cow bell far away and the drip of weighted foliage.

In the distance the bridge crouched like a humped beast across the river's silver width. Rising above it loomed the Tower, that black finger eclipsing the rising moon. Lisbet began to run, feeling free, excited, as abandoned as she had in the simpler days of girlhood.

Even in the dark she found the path she had trod so many times with Anvil, that furrowed rut soft with sand and edged with bracken. It zigzagged through orchards of apple and peach, climbed a stony hill before descending like an ochre-colored ribbon. She ran until her thin kid soles slithered and sank in rich bubbling clay, until water reeds brushed her skirt, their spiny stalks releasing puffs of speckled umber feathers. Beside her the water was a living thing and so swollen with rain it made a swift rushing sound in her ears.

After traversing a marshy trail, she put her hands before her to part the branches of a willow, then stepped onto a carpet of damp decaying leaves. At last she stood beneath the arch again.

"So . . . you come here still."

Lisbet gasped and whirled about.

Forrest York lounged negligently against a column.

Adjusting her eyes in the shadow, she saw him idly scraping the length of a willow switch with a penknife, the movements of his hand short and sure. His legs were crossed at the ankles and his head was bent low over his task, giving him an aura of unconcern, as if he were simply out enjoying the evening air.

At first sight of him, Lisbet had been about to fly into his arms, but something in the attitude of his posture and in the lazy mockery of his words halted her.

"Did you know I would be here?" he continued in a conversational tone as if they were speaking casually over tea. "Ah," he added, looking up, "obviously so, for I see you still wear your evening finery. You ought to remove that cloak, though, and use the gown on me to its fullest affect."

She stared through the blackness at him, watching as he indolently tossed the willow into the river and pocketed his knife.

"Don't misunderstand," Forrest went on, his voice smooth, "I enjoyed your display this evening, could hardly get enough of it. You chose well for the purpose . . . right down to the necklace."

So he was angry, Lisbet thought, perhaps more than angry. Years ago she had known how to quell his ire, his sullen moods. But she was uncertain of him now, of this boy who had become a man.

Not knowing how to proceed, she shifted in her ruined slippers and drew the cloak more tightly about her shoulders.

"You seem offended," she ventured at last, testing the waters.

"Offended?" he repeated, as if pondering the word. "Choose a more prurient term."

His coarseness pricked Lisbet. In a voice as sensuous as that she had used earlier at the dinner table, she breathed, "No, you choose."

All at once, with one swift lunge, Forrest left the shadows and grasped Lisbet by the arms. Backing her against the arch, he pressed her to its cold decaying stone, then bent his face so close their noses nearly touched. She could see the black slash of his lowered brows, the wildness in his eyes, the savageness of his downbent mouth. He looked malevolent; he looked beautiful. With his countenance of good and evil, his visage of heaven and hell, he could have been either an angel of justice or a devil in charming guise.

"Do you think I'm a puppet to be played with, *Lady* Thorpe?" he demanded through his teeth. "Do you think I'm an amusement, a diversion? Does it entertain you to draw me close and then push me away? Do you think I am *Anvil,* to be used and cast away if the stakes get high?"

He shook her, made her head snap back, and hissed, *"Well, I am not!"*

She drew herself up, her own ire fueled by his roughness. "If the sight of me disturbs you so, *Captain York,* then why did you come to Wexford Hall tonight? Why did you dine with me? You could have declined, you could have said no!"

"And I should have," he snapped, abruptly letting go of her arms. "But pardon my ignorance, Countess. I thought I knew the rules of this asinine game we've been playing. I thought the object was to avoid getting your husband suspicious."

"There are no rules where the two of us are concerned!" she scorned. "You know it as well as I. You know there is some attraction that binds us, a compulsion that tempts us to risk danger—even our lives—to be together. I've tried to ignore it, but I cannot. Neither can you. Had I dressed in black with a collar to my chin, had I sat at the table with my eyes demurely cast down, you still would be standing here with me tonight. You would! Deny that you would!"

He shook his head as if angered by the truth of her words. Behind him the moon slipped from beneath the clouds, striping the river with silver and outlining the broad curve of his shoulder.

When he spoke again, it was in a mocking tone meant to challenge her. "If that's the case, if you think I don't have the will to keep myself away from you, then why in hell did you feel it so bloody necessary to seduce me in the presence of your husband?"

"Because I feared I had lost you!" she confessed with a cry, throwing pride away. "I feared you would go away from me again!"

Hardening his expression, Forrest demanded angrily, "What do you expect from me, Lisbet? *What?* Am I always to stand in the background of your life? Wait there for you? Listen for your call, watch for a glimpse of you when you decide it's convenient to give me one? Is that what you want? Is it!"

"I want . . ." She lowered her eyes and whispered, "I just want you to stay with me . . . be near me."

He gave a short, hard laugh and laid his head back. "Do you know what you're asking?"

"Yes," she said with urgency. "And it's no more than I ask of myself."

He snorted, clasped his hands behind his back, and turned away. "I think it is more. Much, much more. I don't have the saintly, self-sacrificing nature that you seem to have, remember? I'm accustomed to simply taking what I want."

Hurt by his sarcasm, Lisbet stepped forward and, putting her arms about his waist, laid her cheek against the back of his coat.

But he only removed her arms from around his body as if she were a stranger and, with his boots squelching in the clay, strolled a few paces away from her to gaze out across the river.

"I believe it's true that we're bound in some way," he admitted, absently plucking at a blackberry vine twined upon the arch. "Whether it's a spiritual sort of thing—something noble under ordinary circumstances—or whether it's just a rather base obsession gotten out of hand, I don't know."

He shrugged, looked over his shoulder, and slanted a glance at her through his lashes. "At the moment I'm more inclined to think of it as the latter."

Lisbet wanted to argue with him, convince him that their connection was more than that, but she seemed unable to find the words and merely drew the edges of her cloak more closely to her chest.

"May we meet here sometimes?" she asked awkwardly after a while, desperate to pull the threads of their disintegrating relationship back together. "Arrange a schedule? Just sit close, talk . . . remember . . . ?"

Forrest smiled a smile both fond and full of rue. "Are you returning to the role of innocent already, my dear Lisbet?"

He moved close again and, extending a forefinger, ran it from her brow to her chin, then slowly down to the place where the locket nestled. She could not see the shape of his hand in the night, but she knew it well, its lean perfect shape, its clean square nails. With a little sigh she clasped it within her own.

Drawing her face up to his, Forrest bent his head to kiss her. It was an aggressive kiss, deep, selfish, and swift, and when she reached out to embrace his neck and prolong it, he drew immediately away to elude her touch.

At her cry of protest, he laughed wickedly.

"And now, Lady Thorpe," he said simply, strolling away in the darkness, "you find out that two can play the game."

Chapter Eleven

"Perhaps ye'd like ta plant a row or two of cabbages." Agatha poked her head round the back door and, holding out a packet of seeds, waved them energetically.

"I don't like cabbage," Forrest declared. Kneeling in two inches of dark earth, he made a sour face. "I never have."

Lifting up her prim gray skirts, Agatha negotiated a path through assorted garden tools, and, following the border of string and wooden pegs the captain had stretched earlier, came to stand above him. With one hand on her hip and the other dangling the seeds, she announced, "Ye'll like it the way I cook it."

Eyeing her dourly, he reached up with a grimy hand and took the packet from her fingers in feigned ill-temper. "I'm beginning to wonder who's the employer and who's the employee around here," he sighed, slapping an insect from his sun-browned neck.

Agatha sniffed and pursed her lips. "Just as long as yer not wonderin' who's doin' the cookin' and who's doin' the greater part of the eatin'.

Finding himself without a sally, Forrest watched his magisterial housekeeper return to the cottage and, with a sigh, began to trowel yet another furrow. What had started out as a small kitchen garden threatened to become a plot large enough to feed the whole of Her Majesty's Army.

"Next she'll be pestering me to build a conservatory big enough to house half the Amazon jungle," he complained so she could hear him through the open window. "Stubborn woman. Don't know why I put up with her."

Not that Forrest minded the labor. A few weeks ago, when he had seen crocuses and daffodils sprouting around the box borders behind the cottage, he had cleaned out the flower beds, ridding them of straggling brown vines and layers of last autumn's leaves. Seeing his interest, Agatha had seized upon the opportunity to get a kitchen garden laid out and thereby supplement what she bought in the village market. By summer's end Laurelpath Cottage would have what Forrest considered an overabundance of peas, lettuces, tomatoes, cucumbers, new potatoes, rhubarb, black currants, and espalier apples—not to mention at least a dozen varieties of herbs.

"And cabbages," he muttered to himself, tearing open the packet. Sprinkling seeds in his palm, he shook his head at them and added, "A dozen blasted cabbages."

He worked an hour more, until his knee ached from crouching, and the spring heat parched his throat and made him long for a draught of lemonade—in lieu of something stronger.

"Agatha!" he called, directing his voice at the kitchen window. "How about a glass of something cold for the slave labor?"

He thought he heard her mumble an answer, but thinking it most likely of the impertinent sort, declined to ask her to repeat herself.

Standing, forcing weight upon his stiffened knee, he dusted his soiled hands and looked ruefully down at the cake of earth on his trousers. Thinking it too risky to enter the kitchen and use the pump there—considering who was on sentry duty today—he went around to the side of the house to the stand pipe. Stripping off his shirt, feeling the sun beat down upon his bare back, he bent his head and sluiced water over neck, face, shoulders, and hands, growling with the iciness of it. While he leaned forward with his eyes closed, water running in a torrent over his hair, he had the distinct impression he was not alone.

Without straightening, he opened one eye and glanced under his armpit, experiencing no surprise at finding Gretchen squatting behind the shrubbery warily.

"I don't bite, remember?" he drawled, dabbing at his face with a wad of shirttail. "As I recall, last visit you left here perfectly unscathed."

From her holly hedge shield, Gretchen stood slowly, considering him with an owlish tilt to her head. He noticed she wore something different from last time, though no less indistinguishable. Its dark nut-brown layers hung in uneven lengths, creating an unlikely harmony with the tangled mass of her silver hair.

As Forrest shrugged into his shirt, she cautiously approached him, then turned about and pointed to the ground behind her. There, following like a puppy with a perfectly healthy hop, was the hare whose paws Forrest had mended.

He grinned, honestly expecting the creature to have died or, at the very least, be permanently lame. "So," he said, "your friend has had a complete recovery."

With her hands clasped behind her back, Gretchen moved forward in her smooth, sinewy way, smiling a brilliant pixy smile of response. He saw she had jammed several kinds of wildflowers in the nest of her locks, though the petals were so bruised their variety was no longer definable.

"M-my f-friend's name is Ramtiggadin," she stuttered, introducing the hare with such a reverent nod it could have been royalty. "He's magic."

Forrest kept an admirably straight face and replied, "I'm sure he is."

She ventured a bit closer, her soft doeskin boots soundless on the greening turf. "He's been telling me secrets," she whispered, glancing about in a furtive way. "All sorts of secrets. Secrets from people who have sprouted wings and gone to heaven."

Eyeing her as one would a child telling tales, Forrest cleared his throat and mumbled, "I'm sure he has."

She pulled the amulet he had given her out from under her clothes and, admiring it for a few seconds in an absent way, stuffed it back through her neckline.

"The white foxes told Ramtiggadin one of the secrets," she continued importantly, pushing hair from her fey blue eyes. " 'Tis a special secret, and very old, one Ramtiggadin told me not to tell. If I tell, bad things could happen to me—and maybe to Grandfather, too."

"Then by all means," Forrest said, losing patience with her prattle, "keep it to yourself." For some reason mention of the foxes had touched a raw nerve.

Wanting to hear no more of them, he started to excuse himself. But Agatha chose to step out the back door just then, letting it bang noisily behind her apron-sashed hips.

"Ginger beer!" she called, raising the tray in her hand. "Captain York? Would ye and yer guest care ta have yer refreshments served out here?"

Forrest threw her a withering glance. Spending the remainder of the day chatting with Gretchen about secret-bearing hares was not a part of his plans.

Ignoring his fierce looks, Agatha set the tray upon an old rough-hewn table angled between the shade of two flourishing beeches. Then, as if she had decided to transform herself into the most unobtrusive servant, she went to stand with her hands folded at her waist, awaiting orders.

Resigning himself to the inevitable, Forrest indicated with a careless flick of his hand where his lady guest should sit, then waited while she hung back doubtfully. Familiar with her vacillations, he sighed and sat down himself. Thirsty and out of sorts with the afternoon tea party, he drummed his fingers on the table, stared up at the lacy foliage above his head, and wondered if Gretchen would ever decide whether or not to put her backside to the bench, so he could cool his throat.

At last, licking her lips and regarding the pitcher of ginger beer with inquisitive eyes, she slipped into her seat.

With great aplomb, mimicking a servant from a London drawing room, Agatha stepped forward and poured the beer for her. Then, beneath Forrest's jaundiced eye, she did the same for him before offering iced sponge cake and sugared strawberries to them both.

Gretchen accepted a half-dozen cakes, shoved a berry into her mouth, then held up her glass, turning it round and round so that sunlight bounced off the facets. Agatha and Forrest watched her wordlessly, noting that the girl made not the slightest move of concern when a bee landed upon her hand. She studied it with just as much interest as she had the reflected light, sipping her beer while it crawled between her fingers.

When she had finished downing it all, she ran her

tongue over her lips, closed her eyes, and made a sound of pleasure.

"Oh!" she exclaimed suddenly. Dislodging the bee, she raised a finger as if just remembering a topic of importance. Slipping a hand inside her pocket, she withdrew a thin, crumpled piece of yellow parchment, and puffing out her chest with pride, handed it across the table to Forrest.

Curious, he unfolded the stained scrap and read the beautifully scripted hand.

"Baldwin Sedgemoor, Fifth Marquess of Winterspell, requests the honour of your presence at an informal supper tonight at seven of the clock." He looked up at Gretchen, not masking surprise. "The marquess issued this invitation?" he asked, rattling the paper.

She nodded, her mouth crammed full of sponge cake.

"Did you ask him to invite me?" Forrest prodded, suspicious.

Gretchen looked down, her lips curving in the way of a child caught doing mischief. "Yes."

"Why?"

She turned about and pointed to the hare, who contentedly nibbled sweet grass close to her heels. "Ramtiggadin told me to. He said 'twas only right to ask you since you saved his life."

For a moment Forrest caught himself gazing at the hare as if expecting a confirmation. Then he rolled his eyes and muttered, "Next you'll tell me he'll be dressed in a cravat and waistcoat tonight and eating cooked carrots across the table from me."

"Y-you *are* going to c-come, aren't you?" Gretchen stood up, dropping a piece of cake to her lap. "He would be most displeased if you d-didn't."

Forrest considered, feeling Agatha's sharp eyes on

his face. He was not sure whether or not he wanted to sit down at table with the Marquess of Winterspell, dine with that ruthless scoundrel who had shown not an ounce of pity for the boy named Anvil. Of course, the old nobleman could not know Forrest's true identity now, else he would never have extended hospitality, no matter how circuitously.

However, Forrest mused, perhaps the meal would prove entertaining—if not conducive to good digestion.

"Very well, Gretchen," he sighed, draining the last of his ginger beer before setting it down with a thump. "I've always enjoyed a bit of irony. Tell the old lord I would be honored to break bread with him this evening."

Forrest walked the distance to Winterspell Tower that evening and, en route, passed the gates to Wexford Hall. He had made a concerted effort these last weeks to keep Lisbet out of his mind, and though that task had been a vain one, he had at least kept himself from seeking her out. Each week a sour-faced Scottie had come to help him construct a small timber barn, and as Flambeau was now housed within it, Forrest had no excuse to loiter about the grounds of Lady Thorpe's domain.

He looked now at the flying griffins leering atop the twin gateposts of Lisbet's home, then to the upper windows ablaze with the reflected sunset, and experienced a strong shudder of longing.

It seemed to him that the darker elements of his nature were trying to sway him, fight the short checkrein he used to master them. Someday, he feared, he would let go of that rein, defy the consequences in order to claim the other side of his soul—that fairer side who just happened to be another man's wife.

Ah, indeed, the reckoning would come . . .

He walked on. Spread before him on the distant rise, beyond stands of chestnuts, pines, and oaks, and approached by an avenue of dying limes, stood Winterspell Castle. The last light of day cast colors of mauve and violet across its two ranges, dappling crumbling bastions, dimming portcullises, arrow slits, and pierced machicolations. Above it all rose the Tower, that fortress-keep designed by some medieval architect to house the lord's family and retainers against long-ago sieges.

Forrest knew only a little about its history but, with the experience of a military man, guessed the Tower itself could have been defended for months, even had the outer walls of the castle succumbed to attack. Ironically, in the last century or two, the rugged stones had been assaulted by time rather than armies, choked by vine and lichen, and left to crumble. Not even a moat defended it now, Forrest noted, unless of course, one considered the inch or two of stagnant green water choked with algae.

As he neared the fortress, Forrest noted that the bridge leading to the gatehouse was half-rotten as well, and paid particular care as to where he placed his feet. Before he had got halfway across it, he saw the ancient gate rise ahead and a figure scamper out of its deep purple shadow.

Gretchen waved a hand. Narrowing his eyes, Forrest thought she could have been a character from another time, mislaid here by some quirk of chronology. Her gown was a style from the previous century, and upon closer inspection, he thought it very likely she had found it stored away in a moldy trunk somewhere. Threadbare lace fell in abundance from the sleeves and neck, and the stuff of the bodice and skirt was so wrinkled and fragile its merely staying whole seemed miraculous. Forrest thought the garment might have once been pink, as he saw traces of that color in its folds.

With a giggle Gretchen curtseyed, displaying a little lace cap, yellowed and half-unraveled, pinned atop her tangles. Forrest would have taken his hostess's hand in a courtly fashion and kissed it, but she slipped her fingers in his and pulled him forward like a child eager to show something.

She led him first beneath the entrance archway, where her shoes tread upon cobbles worn smooth by the countless feet of her ancestors. It was slimy now with growing mold. Next she took him through a courtyard, where every inch of masonry showed signs of mildew and erosion and where piles of rubbish stank with rot. Wind howled around portcullises and through apertures, causing the debris to swirl in spiraling eddies before swooping down again.

Forrest was astounded at the degree of dilapidation all around. He thought how this would have been a bustling place full of men and arms and destriers once. He thought of veiled ladies in embroidered finery who must have dwelled in tapestry-hung chambers, and of cowled priests hurrying to their chapel for matins. Oblivious to the reverence he felt, Gretchen skipped about with her arms flung out, singing old-time ballads.

By the time they arrived at the entrance to the Great Hall, night had fallen, obscuring the walls just as effectively as a dropped black curtain over a stage. The great oaken doors Gretchen indicated were shadowy and so ill-fitting in their rotting frames that Forrest had to access them with the force of his shoulder. He stepped inside, inside that place that had always fascinated him in some mysterious way. And then he stood motionless.

The ancient magnificence of the place struck him so mightily he felt breath go from his lungs. Rising two stories, paved with gray stone and enclosed by white plastered walls, the Hall was of incomparable size. The ceiling stretched above Gothic arches of exposed oak beams so dark with age and smoke they appeared black, and iron lamps in the shape of wheels hung suspended on rusted chains. Antlers, armor, and shields adorned the walls, together with fine paintings, whose scenes of wild animals glowed even beneath a film of soot. In the medieval style, trestle tables and benches stretched the length of the room, and at its end, raised on a dais, stood the high table reserved for the lord and his family.

Forrest let his eyes tarry upon the fading grandeur, grandeur lamentably dimmed by neglect. It was as if not a hand had lifted to clean it since the days of knights and jousts, for cobwebs festooned every corner, every beam, every ornament. They hung in gauzelike garlands, in long silvered threads and drifting knots. The floor was coated with dust as well, and the air smelled of smoke and dust and damp, of cooking odors both recent and old.

Tilting back his head, Forrest surveyed the oriel window, noting its heraldic design of red and blue, whose brilliant colors were obscured by grime and night. As he stepped farther into this echoing place of ghosts and history, he experienced an odd mixture of emotions. The dread, the faint nausea that he had felt as a child upon approaching the castle plagued him still; and yet, a strange feeling of euphoria came with it. Just as he had always done, he felt a powerful yearning to explore its every stone, to know its rooms, its history, its secrets. He could not fathom the feeling of urgency that suddenly besieged him, the desire to climb the narrow twisted stairs, to search through forgotten chambers and rusted trunks.

"C-come," Gretchen said, forcing him out of his reverie. "S-sit down."

She led him to the tables, where she stood undecided for a moment before indicating with her hand a cracked, food-stained bench. Eyeing it dubiously, Forrest searched for a cleaner spot, invited his hostess to sit, then eased himself down to await developments. When no one stirred at any of the half-dozen passages leading out of the Hall, he took out his pocket watch to check the time and shifted his legs restively while Gretchen hummed off-key in the manner of a bored child.

At last there came a clatter, then a bluster of wind, then a draft which played havoc with the lighted tapers on the table. A stooped, black-clad figure ambled forward with his head bent low as if to watch the progress of his shoes. Dressed quite informally, indeed shabbily, with white hair so wispy and untrimmed it resembled the cobwebs above, the old gentleman came to stand beside the dais. He held in one hand a blackthorn cane, which he proceeded to whack energetically against the dais frame with a feeble arm that shook with every strike. All during this activity, beneath dramatic white brows which met above the bridge of his arched nose, he glared menacingly at Forrest.

"Who the devil are you to trespass in my Hall?" he demanded.

Forrest experienced initial surprise, for he had assumed the man to be some old retainer, a butler perhaps, come to serve the meal. But here stood the Marquess of Winterspell, by all appearances, the very man who had taken Anvil from Lisbet's side, paraded him naked about the streets, and delivered him up for punishment.

Looking at him now, Forrest felt a strange feeling of release, as if some restless demon had been freed from his chest and flown away. Time had made the tyrant impotent.

He rose, giving the man stare for stare. "I'm Capt. Forrest York. And I do not trespass but am here on invitation."

"Whose invitation?" the old man roared.

"G-grandfather!" Gretchen arose from her seat and ran to her relative's side, clutching like a fretful child at his arm. "Y-you said I might invite a guest. You d-did! Oh, please t-try to remember."

The ancient one frowned and began to mutter confusedly, shaking his grizzled head. "I said you might . . . ? When did I say you might? Ah, yes!" he exclaimed, raising up a palsied hand. "This is the suitor you spoke to me about. Thank God you have found one—and not a bad specimen," he pronounced, examining Forrest with a rheumy eye. "But is he rich?"

With a private groan, Forrest looked at Gretchen's innocent face, seeing its physical signs of maturing womanhood. Why hadn't it occurred to him the girl had targeted him for courtship?

" 'Bout time the chit married." With an unsteady step, and mumbling to himself, the marquess proceeded to ascend the dais, sitting down at the high table beneath an ancient portable canopy that was so moth-eaten Forrest wondered it did not collapse.

"Gretchen!" the nobleman roared, banging a fist upon the table. "You must sup up here with me. Have you no sense of propriety? Those tables down there are for the underlings. Damme, but you need a woman to take you in hand! Where is your mother? For that matter, where is my wife, and my brother . . . and his wife . . . ?" His voice grew fainter and fainter and finally trailed away.

"I've told you, they're all gone to be with the angels," Gretchen said, exasperated, scrambling up to her grandfather's side in her antiquated gown.

The two of them, Forrest thought with a twinge of amusement, could have been actors in some half-baked Shakespearean play.

"Where's the food?" the marquess inquired, looking impatiently at the empty place before him. "Must I sack every one of those laggards in the kitchen?"

"Th-there's only Hilda," Gretchen replied automatically, as if she had answered with the same words countless times before. "Remember? We only have her and William and Rose."

"Then we'll get more! Why haven't we more? I'm lord of a castle, for God's sake. I should have hundreds to serve me!"

Forrest leaned back in his chair and moaned privately, preparing himself for a long evening. It seemed Agatha had been right when she called the residents here a mad menagerie.

"You, there!" The marquess fixed his attention upon his guest once more and, leaning far forward, regarded Forrest with what seemed to be more lucidity than before. "Haven't I seen you ere now?" he demanded. "Seems I recall those black eyes. . . . Were you caught poaching in my woods?"

Forrest remained expressionless. Either the old man had an uncanny memory for eyes, or he had hit upon a coincidence. At the age of ten, Forrest had indeed poached a pheasant from his lordship's bountiful woods.

"G-grandfather!" Gretchen interrupted. "Ramtiggadin will be displeased if you offend our guest."

"Stuff and nonsense! Don't start your palaver about

that damned talking hare again or I shall skin him and hang him in Hilda's kitchens. You are the most witless creature I've ever known. Don't understand how my only child managed to beget such a brainless chit. Must've been that scoundrel she married . . ."

Forrest straightened in his chair, disliking to hear the girl disparaged so. He was relieved to see supper being brought in by an aproned maid, though his relief quickly evaporated when the servant came within a few feet of his nostrils. Not only did the unwashed smell of her person blend unappetizingly with the pewter plates of grease-laden food, but she was untidily dressed and so far in her cups he wondered how she stood. Forrest had trouble even identifying the fare she had cooked, and though he had eaten far worse—at least, he thought he had—he admitted he had grown quite discriminating after months of Agatha's meals.

Plopping two plates upon the high table, then another before Forrest, the servant exited, returning moments later with mugs of ale, which she served with similar grace.

Taking one look at his supper, Forrest immediately decided upon a late repast of cold roast beef and potatoes in his own kitchen. But at least the ale proved potable, and he sipped it rather morosely, wondering how soon he could make excuses and take his leave.

It seemed he was in for a wait. Singing to herself, Gretchen plucked meat uninterestedly from a leg of something, while the marquess consumed his meal with a lazy wielding of an unpolished knife and fork. Forrest had already realized making conversation with either of them was pointless and, besides, prompting them to talk might prolong the evening's misery.

After a moment he could feel the marquess's eyes upon him and, glancing up, saw the old man regarding him intently. With a rattle of silver, his lordship threw down his cutlery, stood up, and stumbled down from the dais. Muttering beneath his breath, he hobbled close, peering low to stare into Forrest's face with eyes that had suddenly turned clear.

"I do know you!" he proclaimed with a shout of glee. "You were that blackguard who worked down at the Hall! You were that bastard child the vicar found one day on the church altar!"

Slowly Forrest drew his legs in, then stood until his head topped the marquess's by at least six inches. For a moment the familiar vengeful demon returned to inflame his ire, then retreated one last time beneath a wave of pity. Regarding his enemy of old, Forrest saw nothing more than a half-sane old man in threadbare clothes whose soul was probably just short of a stay in hell.

"They used to call you Anvil," the nobleman continued, letting out a high-pitched laugh to echo round the Hall. "I remember you, by God! I remember catching you with Lord Tattershall's daughter, too—pulled you off her, I did, at the end of my musket. Bold upstart you were to do such a thing! I saw you get what you deserved, of course. I saw you thrown from the gates and cursed by every mouth in Winterspell!"

Forrest faced him with a grim expression and watched while the excited old man stroked his stubbly pink chin and recalled the past.

" 'Course . . ." the marquess trailed, pulling at his lower lip and staring down at his feet. His mind seemed unfocused all at once, as if he had lost his train of thought. " 'Course, they say you'd put a belly on her . . ."

Forrest's head snapped down and his eyes grew bright. Fiercely he scrutinized the nobleman's face, then took him by the shoulders. *"What did you say?"*

Gretchen had been standing with her knuckles in her mouth. Now she rushed forward and began to pry Forrest's hands loose from her grandfather's sleeves. "H-he doesn't know what he says. His m-mind's not right . . . you mustn't l-listen to everything he says."

Hesitating, Forrest glanced at her, then back at the old man. The marquess's shoulders had slumped, his eyes had taken on the appearance of dull marbles, and flecks of spittle ran from the corners of his sagging mouth.

Forrest sighed, suddenly weary. "Is there a servant who can help you with him?"

She nodded.

"Then fetch him," he said, turning abruptly away. "I'm going home."

Feeling numb, he strolled from the Hall and its eccentric inhabitants, opened the great deteriorating doors, and traversed the courtyard. But before he had reached the bridge whose planks were rotting, Gretchen caught up with him, jerking at his sleeve until he stopped.

He did not want to stand and listen to her nonsense or look into her lovely, nymphal face and see it vacant.

"What is it?" he said unkindly.

A sly light came into her creature eyes, that strange shrewd flicker of perception he had seen before when the simpleness of her brain flashed bright with cunning. She lifted her hand, put it to his face, and traced the shape of its bones raptly as she might explore the structure of a bird's wing beneath the feathers.

And then, with her nimble fingers, she reached up, snatched at the buttons of his shirt, and yanked the fabric away.

The lantern mounted on the gatehouse provided

only the feeblest light, but it was enough to illuminate the telling shape on Forrest's shoulder.

Intent, Gretchen stared at the devil's mark, then put her hand to her mouth. Searchingly, she looked into Forrest's hard gaze. Then she took her hands away.

He watched her turn about, nimbly negotiate the bridge as if she knew each unsafe plank by heart, and shook his head in wonder.

Turning his back, he headed home in solitude. There was much to ponder, much to think about . . . not the least of which was the fey lady in her dated gown fleeing back to the secrets of her castle.

Chapter Twelve

Every year in early May the village of Winterspell enjoyed a fairing day, an occasion arranged auspiciously for the purpose of horse trading but primarily for the recreation of country folk eager to celebrate the onset of fine weather. With his own days falling mundanely into the pattern of secluded rural life and his energies restless, Forrest saddled Flambeau and made his way toward the annual event, hoping for diversion.

Fledgling summer had changed the landscape, made it warmly alive, and trespassing over fields of purple thistle and through burgeoning orchards, Forrest breathed deep of the fragrances released by sun-fire on leaf and flower. He saw that the peaches were hard yellow ovals covered in down and the apples nodules of palest green freckled with pink. Fat gold bees hummed in droves over sweet lilacs, dipping for nectar, and once or twice a robin flitted across his path on dark wings. The lazy heat of afternoon and the smell of sweating hide, the steady rock of Flambeau's gait and the sound of his tail switching flies made Forrest relax in the saddle with a whistle on his lips.

However, he was not so relaxed as to lose his instincts, and before he had even covered a mile, he knew he was being followed. Having a fair idea of the follower's identity, he did not bother to turn around. Over the last week Gretchen had dogged his footsteps more than once, trailing him at a distance without a word, but more often than not, he found her simply spying from behind the hedge while he toiled in Agatha's garden or pounded the last nails into Flambeau's barn.

The girl's behavior perplexed him, for since his visit to Winterspell Castle, she had stubbornly refused to come nearer than a stone's throw. Once or twice he had attempted to cajole her into conversing or sipping lemonade; once or twice he had crossly demanded that she either speak up or pack off. She had always chosen to do the latter when pressed, skittering through the dense emerald woods on her gazellelike legs.

Her knowledge of his past identity puzzled him mightily, for she would not have been born until after his exile from Winterspell. And from Agatha's accounts, it seemed the girl had no contact with any of the villagers. He could only speculate that the marquess, during some point in his mad ramblings, had mentioned the foundling boy marked with the devil's brand.

With a movement of his knee, Forrest encouraged the eager Flambeau into a canter across a heather-sweet meadow, knowing that Gretchen, even on her fleet legs, could not begin to keep up. He raised an insolent hand of farewell to her without looking back, and as he left her behind, wondered what thoughts filled her feckless head.

Before long he reached the wide, sun-flooded field marked out for the fairing, and for a moment halted Flambeau upon the rise to peruse the animated scene below. Men garbed in coarse homespuns paraded all breeds of horses, huge ocher-colored Suffolks, sturdy cobs, and fine sleek-coated hacks. In groups they haggled, slapped one another upon work-broadened backs, or lingered about enjoying ale. Women in plain bonnets and shawls loitered in calicoed knots, relishing sweetmeats from the canopied stalls or coyly displaying a ribbon their men had purchased for them.

To one side, drawing the largest crowd, a troop of acrobats performed, their costumes asparkle with sequins, their feet slippered and adroit on low powdered ropes. Within a ring of potted flowers, a woman in red stockings danced upon the back of a galloping gray horse.

Flambeau, pawing and bobbing his huge arched neck, signaled an impatience to move, and Forrest loosed the reins. Slowly they descended the slope, arousing little attention from the preoccupied fair goers. Dismounting on the outer edges of the celebration, Forrest tethered Flambeau to a line strung between two oaks, allowing him enough rein to snatch at the tall lush grass.

A portly middle-aged man wearing the flashy clothes of a dandy stepped forward from beneath a patch of shade. Between fine teeth he chewed a half-smoked cigar and toyed absently with the gold chain of his pocket watch. With a measuring gaze through shrewd brown eyes, he regarded Forrest's horse, walking round and round him from head to haunches as if to judge all angles.

"Fine animal," he pronounced finally, taking the cigar from his lips. "Care to sell him?"

Forrest smiled briefly but shook his head. "No. He suits me too well."

"A hunter, is he?" the trader persisted.

"Aye. Won at Cheltenham a few years back."

" 'Know a retired colonel up north who'd take him. Give you a good price."

"He's not for sale."

The trader nodded, and biting down on the cigar

again, smiled with a show of friendliness. "You live here?" he asked, glancing toward the distant village as if he found it difficult to believe anyone would do so by choice.

Forrest grinned. "Afraid so."

"Care to share a mug of ale and a little horse-talk with a stranger?"

The idea of talking horses with someone who was not a resident of Winterspell and who, by all appearances, was completely ordinary and sane appealed immediately to Forrest. "I'll buy," he replied.

It was while the two of them stood idly savoring ale and watching a farmer put a piebald mare through her paces for a prospective buyer that Forrest saw the Wexford Hall carriage approach. It rolled on well-greased axles over the grassy terrain, its matched blacks stepping high and worrying their glinting bits. Only half listening to the trader's dialogue on the merits of Percherons over Shires, Forrest watched as Scottie scrambled down from his box, pulled out the step, and opened the black sun-burnished door for his lady. After a slight pause, Lisbet emerged from the shadow of the interior to the dazzling brightness of midday.

At sight of her Forrest narrowed his eyes. No drab gray or pale beige did she wear today, but saffron. Her gown was like an inverted buttercup, its silk ashimmer and trimmed in peach. Upon her smooth honey hair she wore a large hat of straw adorned with fluttering blue ribbons and topped with an azure plume of ostrich. Her long-lashed eyes beneath the rim of shade searched the field quickly, almost frantically, before alighting on Forrest like a butterfly fastening to a flower. Her gaze tarried upon his face so long her regard became obvious, noted by all who had paused in their activity to watch her arrival.

Forrest met her stare directly, all his recent rage and frustration with her evaporating in a moment. He wanted to cross the hoof-marked turf and take her hand; he wanted to hold her close and breathe her scent. The need for possession of her flamed high again in the late spring heat, sending his blood coursing.

In his green and gold livery, Scottie helped his mistress to the ground, then handed down her maid. When Lisbet put up a languid hand to anchor her hat, then snapped open a white lace parasol with a graceful flip of her wrist, the fascinated trader was moved to speak.

"Handsome lady." He gave Forrest an expectant stare, as if to encourage a masculine discussion of the beauty.

Forrest said nothing. But he followed Lisbet with his eyes as she stepped across the grass, then halted at a stall hung with embroidered ribbons, cheap trinkets, and ivory combs.

On impulse he nearly joined her, but before he could take a step forward, he caught sight of Agatha and checked himself. She gave him a warning shake of the head, a reminder of the disaster he could cause here, both for himself and Lord Thorpe's wife.

Sighing, he gave his housekeeper a thoroughly insolent salute.

Not cracking a smile at his impertinence, she moved on to buy herself a penny ice, standing apart from the huddles of female villagers, apparently unwelcomed in any circle. Seeing his housekeeper in her plain spinsterish clothes with her dour square face, and knowing the goodness of her soul, Forrest realized she was just as much outside the pale as he had ever been. He felt a swift anger at those who excluded her.

Lisbet was ordering punch from a vendor. As she

passed the tightly bunched cliques of people, Forrest noticed that their heads came up and that conversations halted in mid-sentence, only to be resumed moments later in hissing whispers. Uneasy, he took leave of the trader, then strolled past the gossiping groups of village crows and chuckling roosters to the ribbon stall. Unhurriedly making a few purchases there, he slid them into the pocket of his coat and turned about again. The formation of the crowd had changed slightly; the black-bonneted women were merging into one large mass to watch the progress of Lady Thorpe. Occasionally their eyes would dart to Forrest surreptitiously, then they would nudge elbows and put their heads close to whisper behind gloved hands.

The young men were more uninhibited in their staring: some regarded Lisbet with the unconcealed gleam of lewdness in the depths of their smallish eyes. Beneath such attention, Lisbet's maid trailed behind her mistress with nervous little steps, while Scottie hovered boldly near, challenge in every nerve of his squared shoulders and rigid back.

Walking with her head held high, Lisbet seemed oblivious to the scrutiny. Just as if she were alone in the field, she met no one's eye, stopped to speak with none. However, when she moved to watch the acrobats and politely asked a group of women to let her pass, they sneered at her contemptuously and swept their skirts aside as if avoiding plaguc.

Like a lion on the prowl, Forrest sauntered nearer, on guard.

"Cheap, she is," he heard one old woman hiss to her cronies. "Allus has been. Don't matter a whit that she's highborn, she ain't no better than one of the village sluts, if ye ask me. Aye, she'll lie with anything that wears breeches, she will."

"Includin' that toady earl she wedded," another sniggered.

Behind the stalls a group of idle boys had ceased their game of bowling and swaggered around the milling crowds as if to find a new source of entertainment. One pointed to the Wexford Hall carriage and rounded up his fellows. Scottie gave them a warning glare, receiving in exchange a bevy of crude gestures. None of the boys, however, made a move toward the countess.

Forrest was the first to notice two men detaching themselves from a group swilling ale beneath an open-air tent. One of them walked with a lurch, obviously so filled with drink he was in danger of toppling over. The other, a brawny, yellow-haired brute, was steadier on his feet and strutted about like a cock in a barnyard. His fellows under the tent shouted out words of encouragement, apparently prodding him to some act of mischief.

Shading his eyes, Forrest examined the man's face more closely. "Tom Fenney," he muttered under his breath, remembering him from days gone by.

Spitting on his hands, Fenney slicked back his hair in an exaggerated flourish, then straightened his collar and hiked up his pants, eliciting randy hoots from the ale swillers. Approaching Lisbet, he demanded her attention by pulling his forelock in mock respect, then bid her good day.

"Is yer ladyship enjoyin' the fairin'?" he inquired, earning snickers from the quickly gathering crowd. The onlookers shifted about excitedly as if about to witness a bearbaiting.

Lisbet merely nodded with disdain.

Coming up from behind, Scottie insinuated himself between his lady and her tormentor, his youthful frame appearing ineffectual beside the mature breadth of the man.

"Get away from her, ye drunken sod!" Scottie commanded, raising up his fists.

Immediately his arms were pinioned from behind by Fenney's drunken companion, who apparently had enough strength in spite of his witless condition to hold the young man prisoner. Furious, Scottie cursed and struggled, only to be dragged backwards by his captor and detained.

"Unhand him!" Lisbet demanded, her color rising high. "How dare you manhandle anyone in my employ!"

"O' course, we'll let 'im go, yer ladyship," Fenney said with feigned politeness. "Just as soon as ye and I have talked a little."

Barred from escaping his company by the circling crowd, whose noose closed tighter and tighter, Lisbet stared icily into the eyes of Tom Fenney.

"Ye see," he continued, bending close, "my friends and me, we'd like t' know if ye'd come and join us fer a spell. There ain't none so pretty as ye, and we've all heard as how yer real good at entertainin' the gentlemen."

Like a bull on the loose, Forrest shouldered his way through the line of jeering villagers. Seeing Lisbet as the center of public sport enraged him. Added to that rage was the old unsettled urge for retribution against these people and the need to vindicate the honor of the woman he loved. He knew taking on a group of men primed with drink was hardly prudent strategy and defying them all with no weapon the height of folly. But at this point it seemed he had no choice.

When he stepped before Tom Fenney, he had blood in his eye, and his voice came hard and low. "Leave the lady be."

Fenney reared back his head and stuck his thumbs in

his belt, a slow grin splitting his vulgar red face. "Well, ladies and gents," he intoned loudly, looking Forrest up and down. "See who we got here. We got her ladyship's fine lover come to defend her honor—an officer of the Navy, no less—"

The words barely got out of his mouth before Forrest seized his coat and shot a fist into his jaw, sending the brute sprawling backward against a vendor's cart of strawberries.

Infuriated, Fenney struggled to his feet, further fueled by the cries of the villagers. He crouched low like a wounded bear, circling Forrest, his back stained pink with berries, the corner of his lip bright red with blood.

Stripping off his jacket, Forrest lowered his own stance and faced off, his fists raised and ready.

Every male voice bellowed out victory for Fenney while the horse trader Forrest had befriended quickly registered wagers.

Impatient, eager for a win, Fenney lunged, throwing his considerable bulk forward in order to bring Forrest down. But heavy-footed and ungraceful, he found himself flying through empty air as Forrest easily stepped aside. When the large man charged again like a bull at a waving red flag, he managed to thrust a fist against Forrest's ribs, delivering a punishing blow there. But Forrest was not to be bested and cracked the giant's jaw so hard it staggered the brute.

Lisbet stood frozen in place. Impassioned by the scent of blood, the villagers had all but forgotten her now, shouting wildly for Forrest's defeat, raising handfuls of money to be tossed into the horse trader's hat. Her eyes fastened upon Forrest, her heart pounding in fear. Though he was tall and well-conditioned, a seasoned fighter since boyhood, the odds were against him, for even if he defeated Fenney, others would welcome a turn to brawl. She glanced at the faces of the spectators, seeing viciousness there, and knew they would relish the beating of Lady Thorpe's lover, relish seeing him bloodied—even dead.

With flying fists Fenney came at Forrest again now, but the big man was off balance and befuddled with the pain in his jaw. Using one well-placed blow to the stomach, Forrest brought him down, leveling him like a great stunned animal.

With his head lolling and his bloody mouth agape, Fenney lay still upon the ground.

The crowd grew quiet, angry at not only over their lost wagers, but over the vanquishment of their biggest man.

Beneath sweating brows, Forrest watched them, daring any by his very stance to follow Fenney.

"Someone take 'im on!" a young man cried, eager for more brutal sport. "Someone bring 'im down. He's flagged now, he is!"

As if spurred by the words, a man marched forward, emerging from the group with hands balled and ready. Slightly younger than Forrest, he possessed a lean and wiry body and a tough, coarse-looking visage.

"Eh, Charlie Stark! Charlie Stark!" the crowd chanted. "There's our man!"

Watching his energetic stride and confident smirk, Lisbet felt weak with anxiety. By his posturing, Charlie Stark appeared skilled with his fists. Perhaps, she worried, he had fought in boxing matches and was an experienced pugilist.

Instead of aggressively throwing himself forward as Fenney had, this man took his time, dancing a little to fire his crowd. Everyone cheered wildly, and the horse trader's hat went around again.

Forrest made the first move, and though his right fist

sank deep into his adversary's belly, the fresher man snapped Forrest's head back with a savage blow to the face. Recovering quickly, Forrest engaged him again, and the two of them pummeled each other's flesh with a flurry of powerful fists. For a quarter-hour they fought like snarling beasts, thudding knuckles against ribs, jaws, and cheekbones with no restraint. But finally, with a strong left jab to Forrest's chin, Charlie Stark brought him to the ground.

Lisbet cried out and put a hand to her mouth, watching Forrest push himself to his hands and knees, pausing there with his head hanging low. He was slow to rise, and when he did, Lisbet saw blood coursing freely from his nose and mouth. Sweat dripped off his temples and soaked his blood-spattered shirt so that it clung to his flesh. She could see him favoring his injured knee, struggling for breath and woozily measuring the mettle of his opponent through two swollen eyes.

Confident now, Charlie Stark pounced on him, putting a shoulder to Forrest's middle like a battering ram. But Forrest held his ground and, after receiving a cuff to his nose, delivered a rapid series of brutal punches to Charlie's abdomen.

The younger man reeled, staggered, then flopped backwards like a felled tree. Groaning, he rolled over, hugging his knees to his belly, and cursed.

When he made no attempt to get up, the crowd seemed to let out a collective moan. Each spectator grew still, waiting, barely breathing.

In the midst of them all Forrest stood with chest heaving and blood flowing, yet fiercely undaunted. For several seconds no one stirred or uttered a sound.

Then with a movement slow and deliberate, the victor reached to clench his shirt in both hands and to draw it up over his head. Tossing it aside, he straightened, throwing back his splendid shoulders.

Lisbet held her breath. His skin gleamed gold with perspiration and the veins beneath it pulsed over muscles hard and flexed. With his extraordinary height and breadth, and his dynamic looks, he could not help but command admiration even in the meanest breast. His flesh was naturally dark, darker with the sun, yet the shape of the mark upon his shoulder was unmistakable.

All but the youngest villager remembered it. Lisbet could see they remembered. Each expression changed as they beheld the brand. Most wore looks of astonishment—all wore looks of unease.

No longer was this the village pariah, a boy to be teased and baited, but a man of strength, a man with whom to be reckoned. With his raven hair and fathomless black eyes, his perfectly formed body and unbeatable fists, perhaps he had come back as a dark avenging angel who would demand retribution for their cruelties. Perhaps he was even a ward of the underworld, given the tattoo as a sign of favor with Satan, like a charm or the evil eye.

A few people stepped back and turned their heads away as if frightened to behold him.

Giving them all a raking, derisive glance, Forrest leaned to retrieve his shirt and jacket, then, without glancing at Lisbet, moved to exit. Like the sea parting for Moses, the villagers let him pass.

Lisbet yearned to run after him and beg him to ride home in her carriage. But she dared not. She would only make a spectacle of herself, and he would likely refuse anyway.

Scottie came up beside her now. He touched her arm and, rushing toward the carriage, gestured furiously for her maid to follow.

A few yards away, Forrest limped slowly toward his horse, hoping to God he could stay on his feet. If not, he thought ruefully, he would probably lie where he fell until hell froze over. His knee was all but useless and his ears roared with the sound of rushing blood. He could scarcely breathe with the pain in his chest and, for a moment, had to pause and bend over double to curtail a wave a nausea.

"Don't let 'em see you puking your guts out, for pity's sake," a gruff voice whispered in his ear. "Here, let me give you a hand."

Confused with pain and dizziness, Forrest had trouble identifying his escort but welcomed the much-needed assistance.

After being helped into his shirt and jacket—an excruciating business he protested in an ungentlemanly way—he was propped standing against a tree, then almost shoved atop Flambeau's broad waiting back. Suffering a spell of dizziness, he slumped forward in the saddle, barely maintaining balance.

"I made a fortune off you today," the horse trader confessed, putting a hand on Forrest's arm. "The villagers wagered heavily against you, the stupid fools. Anyway, seems only fair I give you half."

Forrest heard the clink of coins, then the weight of silver in his pocket. Gripping the trader's hand, he said through aching teeth. "Keep . . . your earnings. I got too much . . . damned pleasure out of it to take payment."

With a great guffaw the trader retrieved the silver, then slapped Forrest on the thigh. "Good luck to you then, man. Will the hunter take you home?"

"Aye . . ." Forrest breathed, not really caring at the moment where the hell he went, and the trader slapped the horse's rump to send him forward.

The sun beat like fire on his back, making his heart thrum more heavily and his bruises swell. He put his head down upon Flambeau's withers and closed his eyes.

"You son of a bitch!"

Forrest felt Flambeau halt beneath him, and he raised up his head, thinking fatalistically that the villagers had come to tear him apart like a mangled dog. Looking down, focusing his eyes, he saw Scottie Stone holding the bridle reins and staring fiercely up at him. The young man seemed extraordinarily clean and good-looking in the brightness.

"Well," Forrest muttered, managing to put sarcasm in his tone, "your face looks all in one piece anyway . . ."

"I would've fought, and you know it!" Scottie defended himself. "If that sneakin', cowardly bastard hadn't come up from behind and grabbed me, I would've fought 'em all!"

Forrest frowned. He was having trouble concentrating, and his words came out slurred. "So . . . you're standin' here swearing at me for *that?*" Closing his battered eyes, he let his chin drop.

"Look what you put her through!" Scottie exclaimed hoarsely. "You put her through hell! You've made a laughingstock out of her. They had almost forgotten before you came here—they *would've* forgotten. Now you've started it all over again, made it where she can't even set foot in the village anymore. Always circlin' round her like a randy dog, you are, makin' her look at you. Well, to my way of thinking, you're nothing but a friggin', cocksure bastard!"

Forrest swallowed and leaned his head back in pain. "And . . . what does that make you?" he countered, hardly realizing what he said. He lost a rein, groped for it. "Look . . . I'd like to . . . sit here and exchange . . . pleasantries with you, but I'm not in my best . . . form." Nudging Flambeau, he slumped forward again. "Pardon me."

Scottie let him go and, with a furious kick of his shoe, sent up a clod of turf.

After what seemed an eternity, Forrest realized his horse stood patiently in the drive of Laurelpath Cottage. With his cheek pressed against the animal's hot neck, strands of mane scratching his face, he opened his eyes with difficulty.

The lids seemed stuck together and he blinked the grit away before noting absently that dusk tinted blue the gravel below Flambeau's hooves.

He coughed, then swore and clutched his middle. Grabbing a handful of mane, he drew his leg up and over the cantle, then practically tumbled to the ground like a sack of potatoes. A pair of arms tried ineffectually to cushion his fall.

"Can ya walk?"

Agatha's voice came to him as if from across an expanse of desert.

He squinted at her white, slightly fuzzy face, then grunted. "Sort of . . ."

Sliding a thin arm around his waist, Agatha took some of his weight against her hip, and together they hobbled to the house. When they at last approached the stair leading to the bedrooms, Forrest shook his head and refused to budge.

"Don't need that . . . particular form of torture. The sofa'll do fine."

Pivoting about with him, her slight form struggling with his unwieldiness, Agatha guided him into the parlor, muttering about his ruining a perfectly good piece of furniture with his sweat and blood.

Replying through gritted teeth that it needed a good soiling, Forrest eased himself down upon the cushions with all the stiffness of an old man. He remained upright just long enough to allow the housekeeper to pull off his jacket.

"God . . ." he groaned, lying down on his back before raising his knees up and putting both hands to his head.

Agatha lit a lamp, chasing away with an arc of amber the darkness of the room. Then she brought it close, causing Forrest to flinch and put up his palms to ward off the light.

"Ya look like ye've been run over by a herd of elephants," she pronounced with no attempt to spare his vanity. "Two eyes swollen shut, a split lip, a chin twice its normal size, and a nose that's not so straight anymore." She shook her head. "And that's only yer face. Heaven knows what shape the rest of yer's in."

Forrest seemed disinterested, mumbling through throbbing lips. "I'll take . . . inventory some other time. Just get some salve out of my trunk upstairs. Large green bottle, cork stopper."

With her talent for efficiency and organization, Agatha arranged salve, bandages, gauze, hot water, and antiseptic on a tea trolley in no time, maneuvering it close to her patient.

"Here's some chamomile tea," she offered. When Forrest made no move to take it, she set the cup and saucer on his chest.

He contemplated it through one eye, giving it a jaded look. "Whiskey, Agatha. A man with a bashed body needs whiskey, not tea."

When she sniffed and moved to get it for him, he added with a drawl. "And . . . don't bother bringing a glass."

Awhile later he nursed his bottle of spirits and allowed Agatha to clean his wounds, stifling curses and suppressing grimaces with amazing will as she determinedly wielded a pair of tweezers and plucked bits of grass and soil from the rawest patches of flesh.

When she paused to empty the basin and fetch clean water, she commented, "I won't mind it if ye yell, ye know." She clucked over the inch-long slice in his upper lip. "Where did ya learn ta be so stoical? Did ye learn it in the Navy?"

Forrest managed a half-smile. "Yeah . . . on board ship they give you ten stripes of the cat o' nine for a groan, twenty for a full scream." He paused, then added with a maudlin drawl, "Actually I guess I learned it in Winterspell."

He did not add that had Agatha been anyone else, he would not have allowed her to tend him at all. All his life he had managed alone, licked his wounds without company or complaint, never wanting or asking for sympathy or tender care.

A silence fell between them while she applied antiseptic to his lip. At the sting, he sucked in a breath.

"Agatha," he rasped a second later, opening his eyes and regarding her with curiosity. "Why haven't you ever asked me about . . . her? I know you want to."

Agatha did not pause in her ministrations, but her mouth thinned, and the tiny vertical lines above her lips grew deeper. "None of my business," she replied shortly, unstoppering the green glass bottle and dipping a finger into the salve. "Truth to tell, I don't have to ask ye much. What I haven't got wind of in the village, I can see plain as day in yer eyes."

Forrest lowered his gaze, staring down the length of his chest. "You don't have to keep your censure to yourself, you know. You can say whatever you

Heartfire Romance
GET 4 FREE BOOKS

like. I won't hold it against you."

She applied the salve to his brow with a jerky touch. "It's not my place ta condemn ya, Cap'n York. I can see ya love her. I just have trouble seein' ya disrespected, beat up so on account of everything."

Staring out through the open window, Forrest fixed his eyes upon the moon and one lone star. The night scents were sharp, carrying with them odors of damp clay and moss and the green smell of river water in springtime. He tried to smile, but between the inflammation of his lip and a smarting twinge of deep emotion, the effort produced little more than a twisted grimace. "I deserve them, you know," he confessed in a quiet voice. "The beating and the disrespect. I deserve them—I always have. Always been a rebellious rascal."

Beside him Agatha said nothing. After a moment he heard her quietly collecting the soiled linen and medicants, putting them back on the tray. He felt grateful and wanted to express his appreciation for her care but did not know how. He remembered the sight of her standing alone today, outside the warmth of any human circle, and thought how she was one more casualty of his ill-favored association.

He closed his eyes again, wanting sleep, wanting peace, wanting forgetfulness. "Agatha . . ." he whispered, hardly able to move his bruised and purpling lips. "You . . . you don't have to keep coming here, you know. You don't have to keep house for me anymore."

For several seconds he heard no sound from her. Then her dry, careworn fingers touched his forehead and brushed a lock of hair away.

Her voice was no less tender than a mother's to a son. "Yer the finest, most honorable man I've ever known, Cap'n York." She patted his hand. "Sleep well."

Chapter Thirteen

Lisbet closed the door to the drawing room with such care that the latch barely clicked. Sylvan dozed in his chair with his head drooping to one side and the book he had been reading left open upon the footstool. To her knowledge he had not heard about the scene at the fairing today. With luck, he would not; earlier she had quietly bribed his valet.

If she were fortunate, he would sleep in his chair an hour or so and never know she had gone out into the night, never know she had run to see her lover. She would have to be careful of the servants, though, and slowing her step, she strolled to the open terrace doors as if to take the air. For several moments she ambled about on the flagstones, looked casually up at the blinking stars, and idly leaned to pluck a pink geranium from its marble pot.

This perfidy, this spreading quicksand of deceit she had created over the course of her life grieved Lisbet went entirely against her nature. But she knew not how to free herself from its treacherous mire. Since earliest childhood she had had to employ her craftiest wiles in order to see Anvil, in order to sit beneath a bridge with him, in order to love him. And later she had had to lie at every turn in order to protect his child. Now she was deceiving her husband, and this burden of dishonesty and duplicity weighed upon her conscience more heavily than ever.

Yet she did not stop in her tracks and turn back. Nor did she hesitate, for her need of Anvil was so resistless that nothing—not even the direst threat of consequences—could break it. She loved him beyond all reason.

Down the stone steps she wandered, directionless for the benefit of any eyes watching from the house, then glided smoothly over the sleek manicured lawn, past the tinkling Italian fountain, past the precisely clipped knot garden. Only when she was beyond the garden wall and the rectangles of gold light streaming from the Hall's tall windows did she quicken her pace.

Lifting her skirts to her knees, she ran, ignoring the headache that blurred her vision with pulses of light, ignoring the sense of disaster that warned her away from her mission.

The path leading to the road was so dark she could barely find it at first, and along the way she stumbled gracelessly upon fallen twigs and stones and tangled clumps of grass. She could hear tiny night creatures stirring in the nettles, scurrying out of the path of her pounding feet and seeking safer havens. Once she thought she heard an owl, and twice she caught the hoarse, low-pitched baying of a hound.

After a half-mile she could run no more and slowed, walking briskly, breathing hard. She cursed the distance that ate up her precious, slyly stolen time, the distance that kept her away from Anvil. She could see his cottage now with its twin cedars black against a cloud-mottled sky. No lights shown from any window, giving the house a stark abandoned shape. But she knew he would be there. He could be nowhere else with his body so badly battered.

Circling round to the back entrance, climbing the steps, she quietly turned the latch and let herself inside. For a moment she stood motionless to get her bearings. The kitchen was as black as pitch, and she put out her hands, groping about to meet the shape of table and cabinet. Proceeding through the small dining room, she entered the parlor, bumping into an occasional table before skirting it and sidling through two angled chairs. Then, above the rustling of her skirts, she heard a distinct click.

"Easy target."

Whirling around, she caught sight of a long shadowy form stretched out upon the sofa and, focusing her eyes, made out the shape of Forrest's white shirt, tan breeches, and oval face. In his hand, pointed straight at her chest, he held the Colt revolver.

"Wear black next time," he said with a bland drawl. "And fewer petticoats. They're a dead giveaway. So's the perfume." Unhurriedly he lowered the revolver in his hand and set it aside, but made no move to rise from his prone position.

Lisbet knew immediately he had been drinking. His words were thickly slurred and the room reeked of whiskey.

"This a social call, Countess?" he inquired lazily. "If it is, hope you don't expect me to get up and bow or anything. Ain't up to it . . . have to beg off."

She moved close, standing beside the sofa so that her gown brushed the fingers of Forrest's dangling hand. "I wanted to see how you fared . . ." she trailed off, kneeling down.

He chuckled good-naturedly. "How I fared after the fairin', eh . . . ?" He held his hands up before his face, contemplated their knuckles in the darkness, moving them close, then far from his eyes. "Lost a little skin, looks like. Other than that, I don't feel a thing."

Lisbet laughed, releasing tension. "That's because you're inebriated."

He turned his head, looking at her abjectly. "D'you really think so?"

With a smile she kneeled and took his hand in hers, feeling the roughness of it, the strength of it, the new wounds. "Yes, I think so."

He did not pull away but put his other hand atop hers, and for awhile neither of them spoke. Lisbet simply reveled in feeling his presence near, seeing the dim outline of his long frame, remembering the magnificent sight of it as he defied the crowd today. She yearned to ease down upon the sofa beside him, nestle close, stay forever.

She could see he still wore the bloodied shirt with both sleeves torn; she could see the smear of earth on his breeches, smell the warm male scent of sweat and soap. She laid her head upon their entwined hands, rubbed her cheek against the sturdy bone in his wrist.

"You didn't have to do it, you know," she breathed softly after a moment. "You didn't have to fight them."

His fingers loosened in hers a fraction as if distancing himself. When his voice came, it was steadier than before, with all traces of humor disappeared. "Yes, I did."

She touched his shoulder. "Just as you had to show them all you were Anvil?"

He made a slight movement, like a shrug. "Up at the Tower they already knew. Only a matter of time before the news spread. Already some benevolent soul left a very generous present of horseshoes on my doorstep."

Outside the wind gusted suddenly, billowing the lace curtains at the window so they waved like tall gray ghosts. The air snaked through the room, clammy, cold, and Forrest shivered.

Raising up, Lisbet bent close to see his face, and

though nighttime smudged the planes of his cheek and jaw, she could see their darkly swollen bruises.

"You're cold," she said with worry.

"No," he denied, unconcerned. "It's just a peculiar sort of reaction—my body protesting vigorously against my flagrant disregard for it this afternoon."

Gently she laid her head in the hollow of his shoulder, putting an arm about his chest as if to lend him consolation. "I was proud of you," she confessed, running her fingers over the strong rise of his inner arm. "Very proud."

She glanced up and there was excitement in her tone. "How impressive you looked, Forrest! How disdainful of them all! I watched their faces as they began to realize who you were, and you should have seen the fear in their ignorant little eyes. Why, some of those vicious old crows thought you were Satan come to seek your revenge upon them."

Forrest grunted.

"And your determination as you fought the men . . ." she added, touching his brow, smoothing back the lock of hair straying down upon it.

"You never have lacked for daring, have you, my love? When I was a little lass, I used to watch you fight the village boys and wondered how you could withstand their never-ending jeers, how you could keep from losing heart. I always wished I had half as much courage as you. . . . I still do."

He touched her hair as he was wont to do in younger days, tucking it with tenderness behind her ear. For a moment he grew thoughtful, and when at last he spoke, his voice was very sober. "You do have courage, Lisbet, but in a way that counts for something."

"No. Don't tell me that," she protested sharply. "I've never been as—as pure-minded as you seem to think. Remember how you used to call me 'goody' when we were children, tease me because I refused to go along with some of your impetuous schemes to meet? It really had nothing at all to do with virtue, I'm afraid, only cowardice."

"If you're not pure-minded," Forrest insisted stubbornly, "then it's only because I've corrupted you from the beginning—incorrigible devil that I am."

"Not you," she said, speaking with her cheek against his shoulder. She could feel the heat of him through the shirt, hear the thudding of his heart. "Only my *wanting* of you."

He stroked the hair at her temples, not arguing, and after awhile she sighed, letting slip how her head ached tonight, how it ached every night.

"I've tried powders and drops from the apothecary," she admitted. "All sorts—though Sylvan won't allow me to take the stronger ones. Nothing helps. I just get sleepy with the drugs, so sleepy I fear sometimes I shall never wake up."

At her words Forrest raised up on an elbow and took her chin in his hand. "Then, dammit, don't take any more of the powders—or anything else the apothecary gives you," he commanded. "Swear to me that you won't."

She smiled, pleased with his anxious concern, and, gently prizing his elbow out from under him, made him lie back again.

He let his hand wander to her back and caressed it where the line of pearl buttons stretched, then put his ravaged knuckles to her cheek as if the softness of her would soothe them.

She moved her head slightly, kissed the hollow below his throat where the shirt collar parted at the top. Then, in reverence, she touched her lips to his bruised eyelids, to his damp brow, and lastly to his firm and waiting mouth.

His breathing quickened, and he tensed. Clasping his fingers behind her head, he drew her closer, returning the kiss deeply.

In a sort of loving wonder, Lisbet remembered how he had let himself be bloodied and hurt on her behalf today and, giving way to pleasure, let her fingers slide through the thickness of his hair down to the wide angular shoulders that had gleamed with sweat beneath the sun. She slipped her fingers under the fabric of his shirt, touching the mark he had revealed so tauntingly to all who had dared to mock him.

Her ears hummed with the magic of the thing that bound the two of them together; her heart hammered with the need to get near and nearer still. She was tender in her touching, careful of the bruises he had suffered for her. And he was tender, too, lulled by drink and pain and weariness, yet roused by drowsy passion. Their breaths mingled, the moistness of their mouths met, and for awhile they were lost together in a languorous spell of desire.

And then the clock upon the mantel reminded them of time, of the other world outside. Lisbet straightened and drew away, taking Forrest's hand from the soft curve of her waist.

"I must go. I had forgotten . . ." she whispered frantically. "He will be awake by now." Gathering up her shawl, which shimmered in a tracery of lace at her feet, she flung it around her shoulders.

"Lisbet." Forrest arrested her, shifting on the sofa with a stiff awkward movement. He coughed hoarsely, unable to suppress a reflexive groan at the agony it caused in his ribs.

"What is it?" she asked with anxious concern, sinking to her knees to scrutinize his face. "You're in pain, aren't you, my love? And here I've been so thoughtless. Why, your boots are still on and your clothes. . . . Let me help you, quickly. Let me help you up to bed at least."

"No." His swollen lips curved in a smile, and with possessive fingers he traced a line from her slender waist to the scalloped edge of her neckline. "I would only pull you down beside me and coerce you into staying. Despite the sad shape of my body, you would in short order become another conquest of my day." He hooked a brown forefinger beneath her chin. "Only vanquished in quite a different way."

She leaned to kiss his lips, lingering when he responded with skillful persuasion, feeling temptation chipping away at her resolve.

"Lisbet . . ." Forrest murmured, taking his mouth from hers. He clenched her hand with his, pulling her down to where she lay upon his chest again. Then, locking his fingers behind her head, he drew in her face so that their eyes met squarely even through the darkness.

"There's something I want to ask you," he whispered with a strange and simmering urgency, while letting his lips brush against hers. "When we were together beneath the bridge . . . when we made love together before I was sent away . . ."

He paused, speaking against her mouth with a tender intimacy, "Did you conceive my child?"

Lisbet almost gasped, only her overwhelming fear of discovery keeping her response controlled. Her senses reeled. Almost she gave way to impulse and broke free from his purposeful embrace, rearing back in reaction with a forceful denial upon her lips.

Such a vehement response would have given her away, surely, allowing Forrest's shrewd eyes to read the truth in her own. And yet, in that fraction of a moment, she yearned to scream out the shattering facts. She longed to tell the truth, longed to give him the knowledge of his son, that golden-haired child they had made together.

But she could not be certain of his own reaction. She could not be sure that her revelation would not set chaos in motion and destroy four lives.

So, with practiced guile, she schooled her face, held on to deceit and fabrication and temporization with an iron-fisted hand . . . just as she had always done, just as she must.

Smiling sweetly, smiling sadly, she said, "How I wish it had been so, my love." She raised his hand, kissed each loved, lacerated finger one by one. "What comfort a son would have given me these years . . . what joy."

She saw disappointment come into his eyes and, unable to bear the sight of it, touched his eyelids with her fingertip.

Drawing her down once more, he kissed her longingly, achingly, until she felt his mastery over his own desire for her begin to slip.

Afraid of him and of his undiminished power over her—but most of all afraid of her own defenselessness against it—Lisbet looked one last time into the fine black eyes that were both fierce and vulnerable, and left him.

Left him before she could cry.

When she arrived at Wexford Hall on shaking legs, she had to hide in the shrubbery and catch her breath, clutching at the stitch in her side. Then she pinned up her straggling hair, picked the burrs out of her stockings, and, like a thief, crept into her house.

Peeking into the drawing room, she saw Sylvan had gone from his hearthside chair. Uneasy, wary, she proceeded up the silent stairs, nearly crying out when the chattering cockatoo in the library startled her with its shriek. To her relief, she found Sylvan's bedchamber door closed, and quickly, she darted through to her own and shot the bolt.

Her maid Mary dozed in the dressing room, having first laid out a lawn nightgown and robe on the tapestried vanity bench. Without making a sound, Lisbet pulled off her muddy slippers, opened the door of a lacquered chest, and shoved them deep beneath a stack of clean blouses. Afterwards, she gently shook Mary awake and allowed the sleepy-eyed servant to help her out of gown and petticoats, then dismissed her for the night.

Unable to settle, unable to calm her spinning thoughts, she roamed restlessly about the room. The maid had left her a cup of tea on the night table. Though it was cooled, she sipped it greedily, for dinner that night had seemed particularly salty.

Putting it aside then, feeling hot, she padded to the window, throwing wide the casement to let in air. Leaning out, she fancied she could see Laurelpath Cottage through the black swaying trees, its homely shape welcome, its windows aglint with silver star-shine.

Thoughts of Forrest lying so near both comforted and stirred her senses.

For a quarter-hour she lay in bed, staring up at the inner valance of green Spitalfields silk, at the canopy gathered in an intricately knotted rosette straight above her breast. She thought endlessly of Forrest, of his touch, his warm body that was somehow a match to her own.

But most of all, and with undismissible anxiety, she thought of the question he had asked.

Had some instinct prompted him to inquire about a child of their union? Or had some snippet of tattle reached his ears? She knew there had been ample rumors, gossip concerning the possible birth of a baby after her abrupt departure to the Continent. But it could be no more than speculation. No one but Lisbet and her father and an old Italian midwife had known about the birth of the golden-haired babe. Lord Tattershall had made certain of that.

With a sigh of exhaustion and heartbreak, she slid more deeply beneath the linens, tossing from front to back as the ache in her head increased. Putting her hand to her temples, she massaged them, remembering how Forrest had touched her there earlier and eased her pain. But the ache only grew more persistent, sharper, until she thrashed out her legs and stiffened them in torment. She moaned with the drumming in her head, began to sweat profusely, and flinging the covers back, whimpered and drew up her knees until her body made a tightly coiled ball in the center of the disordered bed.

She could not fathom what was happening to her. Once she had seen a sweet-faced doe pierced through the head by a bullet and recalled the look of incomprehension in its staring, innocent eyes. The poor creature had simply lain stunned and inert. Lisbet kept seeing a picture of it behind her eyelids. Surely, she inwardly screamed, the doe could not have felt more pain than she did now.

Like a cruel tempest it was building a relentless force in her head, so that weird flashes of light danced before her open eyes. The pain of it debilitated her and made her unable to rise or even to cry out for aid.

And then, merciful God, the pain seemed to lessen, leave her to float as if on an undulating wave of water. She rode upon it in giddiness and unintelligibility, and yet, she could distinctly feel the coolness of the sheets beneath her. She could feel warmth at her back, the moving presence of another body against her spine.

"Forrest . . ." In blissful surprise she whispered the

word. She wanted to turn about, put her arms about his neck, but was unable. Her extremities were too heavy, too slow, would not move to her commands. She knew her eyes were open; they saw the objects of her room swirling with brilliant color, but they could not focus on a single object. A leg brushed against her leg; breath stirred the hair upon her neck . . .

And then she saw distinctly the hand twining slyly about the curve of her waist.

She opened her mouth to cry out words, feeling the sinews of her throat strain with effort, but no sound met her ears in response. Slowly the muscles of her body began to grow more and more relaxed, then torpid and numbed. Simultaneously the canopy above her head seemed to come loose from its railings and fall.

Like a great green shroud it descended, transfigured itself into a coiling serpent with flashing tail, then smothered her until all was black.

Forrest had only dozed for a little while when the short length of the sofa and the hunger in his belly insisted that he get up.

Rising was gruesome, much like being beaten up all over again. Every joint, every muscle moaned in protest, and his knee refused to bend at all. His shirt stuck uncomfortably to his skin with a film of dried sweat and blood, and he thought of the copper tub in the kitchen corner with sudden forceful longing.

With a series of hops, he made it through the parlor down the corridor and into the kitchen, bracing himself against the stove to cough, cursing between his teeth at the pain it induced. After lighting a lamp, he put the kettle and a pan of water on to boil and, moving about like a crooked old man, finally located a yellow mound of cheese and a loaf of bread. Chewing hurt his jaw, but his stomach cramped with such a persistent need for sustenance that he ignored the lesser discomfort and wolfed down the food.

As he ate, he pondered the tub, thinking that if he bathed, he would need clean clothes. The next several minutes he spent determining if there was any way to obtain them save hobbling up the stairs.

"Guess not," he mumbled through a mouthful of bread, looking balefully at his raised, useless knee. Of course, he could always wait until morning when Agatha returned. She would want to pamper him disgustingly, and he would let her.

He considered the tub again, seeing it wink at him with red-gold lights cast by the lamp, and cursed it for its seductiveness.

The climb up and down the stairs on one leg and with a thoroughly black-and-blue body was a hellish journey he hoped he would not have to repeat soon. But once he sank down into the warm lapping water of the tub, he smiled and laid his head back in bliss. Besides making him feel human again, the bath did much to ease his aches.

Once dressed, he rummaged through his shaving tackle and retrieved a hand mirror, pulling a face when he inspected the condition of each of his mistreated features.

"Mincemeat," he pronounced, flexing his jaw. "Pure mincemeat." Shaving was out of the question.

He was just putting the mirror back when there came a thudding of hooves on the soft sand behind the cottage. Hobbling to the window, Forrest saw a shadowy horse and rider slide to a bouncing halt. With a jolt to the ground, the rider dismounted and dashed to his door.

"What the—" Forrest rushed to meet the midnight visitor, opening the door only to have Scottie Stone barrel through it like a charging ox.

The young man was half-dressed and obviously agitated.

"Lady Thorpe," he began breathlessly. "She's in a bad way—terribly ill! The master sent me to fetch you to the Hall. Now!"

Without a moment's hesitation or questioning, Forrest followed him out the door, faltering down the steps and out into the fragrant night.

At his halting progress Scottie turned impatiently about to stare. "Lord, man, can you ride?"

"I can ride."

In a show of uncharacteristic cooperation, Scottie threw saddle and bridle on Flambeau, standing aside while Forrest awkwardly mounted. Then together the two of them set their horses forward and hurtled down the moonlit lane.

While his horse covered the ground in gliding strides, Forrest's stomach cramped with fearful thoughts. What had happened to Lisbet? She had only just left him an hour past. She had complained of a headache, of course, but—With a numbing dart of recollection he recounted her words. *I just get sleepy with the drugs, so sleepy I fear sometimes I shall never wake up . . .*

"Has a doctor been summoned!" Forrest shouted as they rode.

"Aye!" Scottie answered. "Axelton!"

Forrest swore, remembering Axelton as a drunken fool. He only hoped that time and maturity had somehow improved the surgeon's skill and lessened his indulgences.

Upon arriving at Wexford Hall, Forrest flung himself from his horse, ignoring the pain it caused, and entered the house without a knock. The butler escorted him upstairs, opening the door to Lisbet's bedchamber with as much grace as if impromptu midnight calls were a perfectly normal occurrence.

With a sweep of his dark violent eyes, Forrest saw that the poor excuse for a village surgeon was bent over Lisbet's bed. Beneath his hands Lisbet lay white and still, her eyes closed, her hair a wild mass of damp tendrils about her head.

Beside her Lord Thorpe stood swathed in a purple embroidered dressing gown, sobbing.

"What's the matter with her?" Forrest barked, making his way quickly to the bed.

Both men glanced up at him and, without speaking, turned their eyes back to Lisbet. Axelton's hands shook so badly while he examined his patient with poking and prodding fingers that Forrest marveled he was sober enough to stand. He would probably take out his knife and basin and bleed her, for God's sake.

"What's the matter with her?" he demanded again, bending low, pushing the surgeon's hands away to feel for a pulse in Lisbet's wrist.

"Who the hell are you?" Axelton snapped contentiously, staring up at Forrest with bleary eyes. "And why are you interfering with my patient? Move aside!"

"Get him out of here," Forrest ordered levelly, addressing the blubbering Lord Thorpe.

With agitated movements Sylvan plucked at the coverlet across Lisbet's knees, looking uncertainly from Forrest to the surgeon and back again.

"Get him out of here!" Forrest repeated through his teeth. "Get him out or I'll shove him out myself."

"Now see here—" Axelton protested, swaying on his feet.

When Forrest made a threatening move, Lord Thorpe scurried around the bed, slipping upon the trailing end of his dressing gown before taking the surgeon by the arm. After several seconds of argument, Axelton wrenched open the door and departed with a series of disgruntled warnings.

Ignoring them both, Forrest frantically leaned over Lisbet, checking her pulse. her breathing, her eyes. An alarming pallor was draining her face, and her lips were rapidly turning blue. Her mouth gaped, yet barely sucked in air.

In and out of war Forrest had seen the approach of death on many faces and knew without a doubt that death was claiming Lisbet now.

"Lisbet!" he cried, fear throbbing in his voice. He shouted her name again and again, scooping her up in his arms in sheer, numbing panic.

But she remained limp, unresponsive, her breath scarcely discernable.

"Lisbet! Jesus! What's wrong with you!"

Even as he spoke Forrest's eyes lit upon the tea tray beside the bed and focused darkly on the near-empty cup. Seizing it with one hand while he supported Lisbet with the other, he put it to his nose, swirling the dregs about.

His eyes snapped to Lord Thorpe, who hovered near wringing his twisted hands.

"You drugged her with laudanum, didn't you?" Forrest bellowed. *"Didn't you!"*

The dwarf's face fell, crumpling.

"Damn you! When? When did you do it? *How long ago?"*

Sylvan shook his head, putting his hands to his face and sobbing. "An hour—two. I don't know! I don't know when she drank it!"

"How much did you give her—how many drops?"

Sylvan's mouth sagged open and his eyes rolled while he shifted back and forth on his little slippered feet. "I don't know, I'm not certain now. Oh, my Lisbet, my love!" he cried, sinking to his knees. "How many did I give thee? Six, seven . . . twice more? I don't know! I don't know!"

Forrest frantically turned Lisbet on her side. Taking hold of her jaw with one hand, he thrust his forefinger in her mouth, pushed it deep until it reached her throat.

At first his efforts produced no response, and he cursed, trying again. Then, feebly, her chest convulsed and her neck strained forward. She gagged and heaved until, finally, a small amount of bile issued from her mouth.

"Get me a glass of water!" Forrest barked at Sylvan. "Now!"

With a hand trembling so violently the water sloshed, Lord Thorpe brought him a measure from the dressing room.

Sitting Lisbet upright, Forrest took her chin and trickled water into her mouth, easing up when she sputtered and would have choked. "Drink it, Lisbet. Drink it," he coaxed. "That's the way . . . a little more . . . a little more."

When she had taken a sufficient amount, Forrest again lowered her to her side and, inserting his finger in her mouth, made her vomit a second time. With a pain-racked cry she hung limply over his arm then, gasping and shuddering as if with ague.

Taking a handkerchief from the bedside table, Forrest dipped it in the remaining water and cleansed her face, then cradled her fiercely against his own battered shoulder. He smoothed her damp unbound hair from her face, rocking her in his arms as if she were a child, murmuring words of love to her with his eyes squeezed tight and his voice hoarse and cracked.

He could feel her pulse thrumming more strongly, and he breathed a ragged sigh of relief at its slightly increasing beat.

At the sound of Forrest's voice, Lisbet's eyes began to flutter, and whimpers issued from her throat.

Putting one of her arms about his neck, Forrest grasped her beneath the ribs and stood up. "Can you stand a little, love?" he asked gently. "Can you come with me to the window?"

She did not respond, but, supporting her weight, he took her to the closed drapes, shifting in order to grasp the cord and draw them wide. Releasing the casements, he flung them open, allowing cool air to wend its way inside the stifling room.

"Breathe, Lisbet," he encouraged, noting with optimism that she attempted to set her feet down and support herself a bit. "Breathe."

She took slow gulping breaths of the night air and, with her eyes half-opened, raised her head up to find his face. Clinging to his shirt, she cried out his name, begged him not to leave, asked him to hold her, keep her safe from the blackness.

He soothed her, picking her up in his arms and taking her back to bed. As her body touched the sheets, she jerked in protest, frantically beseeching him not to go, not to let her sleep again. Hushing her gently, he repeated assurances that he meant to sit close, hold her hand, keep anything that threatened her at bay.

Noting that her gown was damply rumpled and twisted above her knees, he covered her then, glancing up at Sylvan as he did so.

Across the overelegant room, Lord Thorpe sat in a chair holding his wife's ivory-backed hairbrush, turning it over and over in his clumsy hands. He examined it as if it were important to do so, pulling a long silken thread of hair from its bristles and winding it about one finger.

Lisbet, even in her weakened state, noticed the direction of Forrest's regard. Her eyes moved to the corner he watched, and focused. For a moment she gazed at the man who was her husband. Then she slid her eyes toward the strong skillful hand holding hers atop the bed.

There were three in the room . . . a triangle, and she felt the shape of it like a physical thing. She felt the pain in the triangle, throbbing, throbbing at each of its sharp-edged points. She felt the desperation in it, too.

Slowly, as if ashamed, she began to slide her hand purposefully from beneath the warmth of Forrest's.

He looked at her. With intensity he searched her face, read it, and turned his eyes away. She thought there was bitterness in them—that, and equal shame.

At last, Forrest broke the silence with a quiet question to the motionless earl. "Why did you do it? Why did you give your wife the drug?"

Sylvan flinched as if wounded, his great houndish brown eyes meeting the fine black ones. Then he lowered his head again to study the strand of hair. He said nothing.

Forrest looked away from the pitiable sight. The cards were on the table now, he thought, turned up for the three of them to see. He wondered how the game would end. He wondered who would be the first to fold.

Again he addressed the earl, his voice quiet, yet vibrant in the still, tense air. "Why did you have me come here tonight?"

Sylvan stroked the hairbrush with his ill-made thumbs, running them over and over the smooth ivory surface, then bending the bristles down. His eyes never raised from his idle task as he recited:

> She brooded o'er the luxury alone:
> His image in the dusk she seem'd to see,
> And to the silence made a gentle moan,
> Spreading her perfect arms upon the air,

And on her couch low murmuring,
"Where? O where?"

The meaning of the verses was clear to Lisbet. Bleakly she turned her face into the pillow.

Beside her Forrest regarded the speaker through unsoftened, narrowed eyes.

"Because," Lord Thorpe added softly, with a desolation terrible to hear. "I thought if you asked her to live, she *would* . . ."

Chapter Fourteen

From his seat upon the boudoir chair, where his feet in their red Moroccan slippers stopped an inch above the floor, Sylvan gazed at the man reposing with such wary negligence beside Lady Thorpe's bed. Like a hare mesmerized by a hawk, Lord Thorpe examined every feature of the long-legged, godlike being whose bruises of battle seemed only to enhance the very essence of his stark masculinity. Where Sylvan's shoulders were narrow like a child's, the other man's stretched wide, overrunning the breadth of his chair. His neck was a strong straight column, his hair a thick tousle of waves, and surely no ancient Olympian had ever possessed a more classic profile. Even his hands, scraped from fighting for the honor of Sylvan's wife this very day, were nimble-fingered and perfectly made.

The captain's eyes were lowered pensively to the floor, his dark lashes swept down, and Sylvan wondered what thoughts he thought. Usually, with his black eyes flashing beneath those splendid brows, York's visage was a forbidding one, fierce with some torment or purpose. But now, as if he had forgotten the presence of others and let down his guard, his demeanor revealed a hint of underlying defenselessness.

It was that defenselessness that touched a chord in Sylvan's breast, softened his envy, for it meant the perfectly formed being felt pain just as he did, yearned, too, for something just out of reach and yet torturously near.

Sylvan's eyes moved to Lisbet. She quietly sipped a measure of broth, fixing her gaze on the white china cup in her hands as if fearful of giving even one stray glance to either her husband or her lover. Her face was still dreadfully pale, its every feature frail and delicate, the skin as translucent as a piece of alabaster with sunlight shining through. Her arm quivered with weakness and her hazel eyes were overlarge and bright. And yet, Sylvan marveled, she was beautiful still.

She did not often allow him to see her with her hair unbound: now, to behold its twining honey length made him ache. All things beautiful made him ache. Beauty intrigued him, and he liked to surround himself with it, examine its parts closely as if to better comprehend its essence.

Not only was Lisbet a beautiful example of womanhood, she was the only woman to whom Lord Thorpe had ever got close. During the few times when the young, unknown Earl of Tilbury had been invited to attend social occasions, the ladies had either gasped at the sight of him or kept their eyes averted behind fluttering fans, avoiding him as if he were some horrid beast dressed in evening clothes. All his life he had endured that sort of ridicule and ostracism. Even his father had disdained him. And the children he encountered when growing up either screeched in fright or threw stones at his head. None would consent to play with the hunchbacked oddity they likened to a toad.

As an adult, his life had been no less solitary, for mingling with society in any way proved an ordeal. Even his Grand Tour he had cut short after having one of his seizures in a hotel lobby and putting the whole place in an uproar.

When Lisbet agreed to be his wife, he had been incredulous, hardly believing his great good fortune at her meek acquiescence. Naturally Lord Tattershall had approached him first, made arrangements for the match, but Sylvan had not dared to assume Lisbet would follow through with the nuptials once she had seen his crooked shape. And yet, she had. Though her eyes had remained trancelike upon the altar while she spoke her vows, the words of commitment to him had been as clear as a chiming bell.

It had occurred to him, of course, that Lord Tattershall had forced his daughter into wedlock, but Sylvan could never fathom the viscount's method of control. And then, in all the years of his marriage to Lisbet, she had never made mention of coercion. For awhile, Sylvan had actually allowed himself to believe she loved him.

Now he watched her set down her cup and lay back against the pillow, her head like a drooping flower on a slender stem. At last the mystery of her marriage to him was growing less incomprehensible, its substance coming to the fore in the same way cream rises in a vat of milk. He knew now why she had stood at the altar with him—at least, he thought he did.

Never being privy to much gossip, never having had a confidant, Lord Thorpe was isolated from most of society's talebearing. But recently, one surprising source had dared step forward and fill his ears. Scottie Stone had divulged Lisbet's past, repeating the stories still whispered from mouth to ear in Winterspell.

And he had told Sylvan about the boy named Anvil, that boy who had returned as a man and challenged the villagers today.

The knowledge did not change or lessen Sylvan's love for his wife in any way. He loved her no less and felt no less fortunate to have her as his wife. The knowledge did, however, give him a better understanding of Lisbet's nature.

The first time he had ever seen her gaze into the eyes of Forrest York he had seen love, recognized its manifestation. The sight of it in his wife's face, directed at another man, had devastated Sylvan. He had always wanted for himself that look of adoration from her. Its bestowal elsewhere had shaken him to the core, making him wonder how such a love could have flowered so quickly. And that Captain York had so obviously reciprocated was another riddle to ponder—for although the handsome, grim-faced Captain York did well at masking the intensity of his feeling, his very restraint gave him away.

And now Sylvan knew the history of the love his wife and Forrest York shared.

Even now he watched as York took hold of Lisbet's hand and spoke to her in a voice that was tenderly low.

"I must go now, Lisbet. If you need me, send a message and I'll come."

The battered but unvanquished warrior stood, raised to his imposing height, and leaned over the languishing lady's bed. She whispered words to him Sylvan could not hear. In an equally low tone Forrest seemed to reassure her, and then paused for a moment, as if he would have liked to have bent down and kissed her. But he did not.

Sylvan rose and faced his adversary as the captain prepared to leave. Each man regarded the other for several seconds. Neither spoke, and after giving his host an unmistakable look of warning, Forrest quietly let himself out the door.

At its closing, Sylvan turned his head to look at Lisbet. Like a beaten puppy he trailed to her bed, sank down upon the bedstairs like a sinner on a kneeling bench, and laid his head beside her hand.

"I never meant to make you ill," he breathed, his horror over what he had done finally given opportunity for expression. "I did not mean to harm you. It was all a dreadful mistake, the madness of a wretched fool! Forgive me, forgive me—can you ever forgive my selfish folly?"

At first Lisbet found it impossible to speak to her husband. She could only stare in numbness at his shaking shoulders and tightly clenched hands. She kept asking herself how he could have done what he did. How could the meek and uncourageous Lord Thorpe come so near to killing her?

Finally, at his continued weeping and his woeful posture, the ice of her disdain began to melt. Whatever his mistakes, she could not bear to be cruel to him, to punish him with her silence and frigid looks. She found herself stroking the top of his hand in the same manner an angry mother soothes a remorseful child.

"I began to give you the drops on our wedding day," he confessed miserably, still with his face buried in the coverlet. "Just a drop or two to calm you. The drug is from a flower, you know," he added, as if to make his excuse more palatable. "A flower with a large nodding head and vivid color. I thought its drug would be sweet and soothing, would help you. Would make you happier with me."

He looked up at her, the conspicuous rims of his eyes reddened and moist. "And it did, I think. You could sit upon my lap without growing upset. You could look at me as we dined and even hold my hand with no hysterics."

Shaking his head, he exclaimed, "On that terrible night of our wedding, I could not bear it when you cried with loathing at my touch! I never wanted to see such horror in your eyes again."

Shuddering at the memory, he clutched at her hand. "You became addicted to the drug over time. But when I decreased the doses, you suffered such dreadful headaches that I grew fearful and resumed the usual dose just to ease your distress. I was beside myself to know what to do, especially when you insisted upon taking wine or powders from the apothecary after I'd given you a measure. I felt frenzied with despair, my pet, for what had begun as an innocent act grew to be an unstoppable calamity." He kissed her hand. "And ended as a nightmare."

"Last night I gave you far too much, I know. Oh, how I know!" he cried, looking heavenward with penitent eyes. "But I thought . . . I thought—oh, I cannot say! 'Tis too shameful."

Lisbet took her hand away from his touch. "It was a wicked thing to do to me, Sylvan," she accused, recalling the pain and confusion she had suffered for so many years, realizing that his carelessness had almost taken her life. She wondered that she had not suspected his mischief before. But she had been so trusting of his worshipful nature that she had ignored the danger of his fanaticism.

"I curse myself!" he screeched now. "I curse the

shell in which my soul resides! I curse the very day I was born, the day some devil imp conceived me!"

Fearful that he would fall into one of his seizures with such a display of overexcitement, Lisbet took his tear-wet face between her hands. Tiredly she said, "'Tis alright, Sylvan, 'tis alright. I forgive you. I know why you did what you did."

And that was true. She understood him mind and heart. Recalling the small, dark hand on her waist as the drug overtook her, she felt a pang of self-blame. Regardless of his stature and looks, Sylvan was a man, and his desires were those of a man. She had kept herself from him all the years of their marriage, when, by legal right, he could have forced her. Did she now have the right to blame him for an act she herself had driven him to commit?

At her words of absolution, such a naked glow of gratefulness shone from his ugly eyes, Lisbet glanced away. Quietly, she asked him to leave so that she might rest.

After he had softly shut the door, she put her hand beneath her pillow. Finding Anvil's locket, she clasped it tightly in her hand, then pressed it to her lips.

The next morning Sylvan dressed with great care, donning a buttercup yellow waistcoat, pale blue jacket, and sapphire breeches. He fancied the ensemble suggested a summer's day and would lend him a cheerful air.

During the predawn hours he had hatched a plan, designed in great detail, and he wanted to be sure he could carry it off with finesse.

Pacing about his bedchamber now, passing the

painted scenes of Japanese gardens and delicate pagodas on his walls, he experienced alternating spells of feverish doubt and cold certainty. It was a good plan, but its conclusion remained cloudy, like the end of a road obscured by fog. He would have to think on it more: perhaps a solution would come to him in time.

Before the dew had even dried, he rushed about the garden toting a pair of silver scissors, zigzagging between beds of yellow gladiolas, purple bearded irises, white Canterbury bells, and sweet lavender. And then he located the flower for which he had been searching, that perfect bloom to present to his grievously wronged wife. Their tender blooms would tell her of his feelings better than he could ever express with words. Besides, he was a great lover of poetic imagery.

The tiny bleeding hearts fascinated him, they had since childhood, and forgetting his clean breeches, Sylvan sank to his knees in the soil. Putting out his hand, he cradled a blossom. How perfect it appeared against his furrowed palm, how vibrant pink was its color! With its plump, blue-veined shape resembling the sentimental organ beating in every human breast, he wondered if the Divine Mind had formed it in humor or in pathos.

Pursing his lips, he pondered the two mock droplets of blood trailing from its lower tip. "How like my own poor heart," he sighed.

With his silver scissors, he severed a dozen branches from the row of plants, tittering at the sight of so many delightful little hearts dangling from their vines like baubles on a string. Absorbed, he did not hear the buzzing round his ears or see the circling honeybee intent upon the bouquet until the creature hovered just above his hands.

In utter terror, he dropped the flowers to the ground. Stumbling in panic, he screamed aloud before running wildly down the path with his arms flailing like windmills above his head. Since his tenth birthday when he had been stung on the arm while picking berries, he had been mortally afraid of bees. At the time the doctor had dourly informed him that another sting may be a fatal one, bringing death in only minutes.

"Death, death, death . . ." he chanted now, still running.

Suddenly he halted his headlong dash, stopped so abruptly he nearly toppled forward. His mind swirled madly with a notion, and he turned around.

So simply, so innocently, the conclusion to his plan had presented itself, just as if the designers of fate were listening to his troubled thoughts. He almost smiled at the cleverness of the idea . . . and at the same time, he trembled with dread.

When Sylvan tapped upon the door to Lisbet's bedchamber sometime later, he held the blossoms in one hand and a beribboned packet in the other. She bade him come in, and he greeted her with a beaming smile, bowing formally and offering the flowers with a flourish.

"Ah, my sweet," he said as jauntily as he could, "you look much better today. There's color in your cheeks to rival even that of my garden gift."

Giving him a wan smile, Lisbet drew the lace-edged sheet more modestly over her chest and accepted his present.

"They're lovely," she murmured.

"And significant," he added. "So, so significant."

She nodded, finding conversation with him strained.

"There's a crystal vase on the writing desk in my dressing room," she said, transferring back to his hand the drooping blossoms. "Perhaps you could fill it with water and set these over there—beside the window?"

She did not want them near. She did not want to be reminded of Sylvan and his wretchedness.

Though she felt virtually recovered from her husband's disastrous drug dose, except for a sore throat and fatigue, her emotions were in turmoil.

At long last she had been given justification to leave the Earl of Tilbury and run to Forrest. Sylvan had almost killed her, after all. Without Forrest's intervention she would even now be in a glossy black box, lying serenely in the saloon surrounded by lilies. Lord Thorpe could hardly blame her for deciding to leave him. And if he pined for her, cried, tore out his hair, and languished until death, it was just as he deserved, she told herself petulantly.

He had gone to put the flowers in water and placed them exactly where she asked. Turning, he stood with his arms at his sides and his eyes so filled with sorrow and love she nearly flinched.

"I-I brought you something else," Sylvan said quietly, ambling forward on his short plump legs. He laid the packet on her coverlet like an offering to a queen and invited her to open it.

"I know you've longed to travel during the years of our marriage," he commented in a quavery voice as she pulled the ribbon loose. "But through my own selfishness, I . . ." He glanced down. "I have discouraged it."

Lisbet opened up the packet. It was filled with an assortment of travel brochures, train schedules, and advertisements for inns and hotels and restaurants. She perused them one by one, noting all concerned the Isle of Wight.

"I believe it is time for you to have a little holiday," Sylvan said officiously, watching her bemused face. "You've been weak and pale for so long, I think great quantities of sunshine and fresh air are in order. And they say the Isle of Wight has an excellent climate. Look here—" He shuffled through the pile of pamphlets. "In his medical treatise *The Sanative Influence of Climate on Disease,* Sir James Clark recommends Ventnor's air as being supremely beneficial."

Across from him Lisbet sat astounded. Surprise and excitement beset her at the idea. She could not keep her hands from shaking.

A holiday on an island! After so many years a prisoner in Winterspell, after so many years of facing the same landscape, the same people, the same routine, the thought of change almost frightened her. What would it be like to awake and smell the sea, travel on a packet, and dine on pink lobster and champagne in any restaurant she chose? What would it be like to be free of Wexford Hall and her headaches and the sneers of those in the village?

She looked up, staring into her husband's gentle, ardent eyes. Love dwelled in them, deep as ever—that, and true remorse. He wanted to atone and had given her the only gift he knew to give. She realized such a sacrifice would be a great one for Sylvan: to travel, to walk among streets crowded with staring people terrified him.

As if unwilling to spoil Lisbet's happiness with the moment, Lord Thorpe did not attempt to take her hand or touch her in any way. "Take Mary with you," he said softly. "Stay as long as you like."

Lisbet's head jerked up. He meant for her to go *alone?*

"Whenever you feel able to depart," Sylvan continued matter-of-factly, "I'll send a footman to secure your railway tickets."

She nodded, watching him, unaccustomed to this new unpossessive Sylvan.

"They say the poets love the Isle," he mused, toying absently with the lace at his sleeve. "They say 'tis a romantic place to be . . . a place for lovers."

She looked at him curiously.

Turning away then, he left her.

The prospect of a holiday, the first since girlhood, thrilled Lisbet. She could not contain her enthusiasm for the idea and wasted no time in making preparations to depart, sending a footman only two weeks later to secure her traveling arrangements.

During the interim Sylvan had been the epitome of grace, never dogging her footsteps as he was wont to do in the past, never demanding attention from her in the usual ways. His piteous pleas that she sit with him beside the fire had ceased; his ritualistic counting of the days until they should consummate the marriage halted. He was courteous, always near if she requested some advice from him, but otherwise entirely unobtrusive. He would not even dine with her unless she invited him to do so and stayed clear of her bedchamber. There were no scenes, no dramatics, no servile displays of passion.

He could not have shown her more how much he loved her.

On the eve of her departure, her husband politely requested to speak with her in the drawing room.

After pouring her a glass of sherry, he seated himself quite apart and wished her a safe and pleasant journey.

As she thanked him, she fought down a vague uneasiness. It was as if an ill wind had blown in through the open window, whispering the word *disaster* in her ear. A sweeping sense of doom suddenly clutched the strings of her heart.

"And, Lisbet. About midsummer's eve . . ." Sylvan's voice was subdued as if the same sprite of ill omen had passed by his ear.

Lisbet fidgeted with her handkerchief, her face blanching at the mention of the date and its significance.

"I never expected you to love me," he confessed in a sudden burst of words. "I know 'tis an impossible thing. 'Twas only a dream I dreamed. Like a bewitched child, I clung to it irrationally with blinded eyes, expecting a spell to be cast upon you—or upon me—just as in some silly fairy tale. I know what I am, you see. I truly do. I speak with no self-pity, no intent to cause you guilt, but only in sincerity. I want you to go to the island with a free heart, for I have wronged you sorely many times. In many ways."

Until he spoke the words, Lisbet had fully intended to send Forrest York a note apprising him of her journey to the Isle, leaving open an invitation to join her there. Now she would not. She would tell him only that she was away on holiday for awhile.

This sojourn was Sylvan's special gift to her, his penance. She could hardly sully it with a rendezvous of infidelity.

Early the following morning, after her trunks had

been strapped to the coach and Mary settled inside with her bandbox and shawl, Lisbet visited the austere little chapel at the east end of Wexford Hall. Kneeling down before the altar, she lowered her head and prayed, still plagued by a clinging, irrational sense of foreboding. Then, taking from her reticule a missive to Forrest, she hurried to the waiting coach and, before bidding Sylvan goodbye, discreetly passed it to a footman's hand.

"Take care," she said to her husband in a quiet, solemn voice, extending her gloved hand for his formal kiss.

Goodbye, my dear Lisbet," he replied, fastening to her lapel a full-blown rose the color of milk. " 'I love thee with the breath, smiles, tears of all my life!' "

Handing her up then, he closed the door and lifted his dark fingers in farewell. Then, turning to the footman as the coach lurched away, he said, "I believe Lady Thorpe entrusted a letter to you . . . ?"

At the poor man's red-faced nod, Sylvan added, "May I have it?"

Clutching the envelope and with an air of dignity, the small master of Wexford Hall then strolled into his domain alone, going directly to the library. Once there he fed cored apples to his cockatoo and let it sit upon his hand, and afterwards settled down behind his desk to peruse a volume of poetry.

Beside his elbow, his wife's note to Forrest York lay unopened.

An hour later, with his reading accomplished, he at last allowed himself to inspect the envelope containing what would surely prove a most ardent message of love. His fingers quivered as he took up a gold letter opener and slit the fragile piece of stationery. He read aloud.

My Dear Forrest,

My heart is filled with countless tender emotions, countless thoughts of gratitude, and other thoughts I dare not name. And yet my brain seems bereft of adequate words to express them. Even so. I know you understand, for our hearts and minds have always been perfectly attuned, have they not?

I have received a treat. Sylvan has sent me on holiday! I shall only be gone a few weeks, but knowing how you worry, I have sent this note to assure you of my complete recovery.

Take good care of your wounds, my brave, beloved darling. I do not know when I shall see you again. L

Sylvan finished his reading, put down the letter, and shook his head. "No, no, no, my pure, true Lisbet. This will not do a'tall. You have neglected to follow my design. I feared I should have to write the missive for you!"

Crumpling the paper, he reached into a drawer and retrieved another sheet of engraved stationery. Then he took up his pen and dipped it in a bottle of ink.

My dear Forrest (he penned with his dark elfin hand) *I leave this hour for the Isle of Wight. I shall be in Ventnor at the Esplanade Hotel. It is a romantic place, perfect for two lovers in need of timeless nights and countless days. I shall wait for you there. L*

Folding it with two neat creases, Sylvan inserted the note into an envelope, then rang for the footman. Handing it over with instructions to deliver it personally, Sylvan dismissed the servant and closed the door. Then, in an attitude of sheer desolation, he put his uncomely head down upon the desk.

"I love thee, my Lisbet, my life," he whispered in anguish. "I have sought to give thee everything my gold can buy. I have worshipped thee, adored thee on my knees. Forgive me for my desire of you, 'tis base, selfish, impure—isn't it absurd to ask the fairest flower to lie down with a worm? Though I have failed miserably in my efforts at selfless love, I shall attempt a compensation. I go now to give thee thine heart's desire. A goddess deserves a god."

Raising up his head, the Earl of Tilbury then penned the words, sealed them with a drop of red wax, and left them on his desk.

With dragging feet, he went out into the glorious sunshine of spring, smelled the perfume of apple blossoms and lavender and wisteria, and heard the birdsong from a thousand tiny throats.

Through the orchards he trundled, scrambling over an old stone stile, scattering a bleating flock of sheep with his flapping, gold-buttoned coattails. In an open meadow, where clover and alfalfa grew, he paused, spotting two neat rows of wooden boxes. At least a dozen there were, painted white, but he approached the one nearest the sandy path.

For a moment he remained within twenty feet of it, just listening to the wind in the copper beeches, watching the sun turn the surface of their leaves silver, enjoying the sight of a spotted butterfly. Most of all he marveled at the simple perfection of nature.

Then he let his attention fix upon the hive before him. As if mesmerized, he watched the countless, indefatigable bees dart about in their usual industry, watched them scuttle in and out of the hive on speeding wings.

Cautiously he took a step forward, then another and another until the sound of their buzzing became a high-toned drone in his ears. He drew so close to the hive he could see the bees' round gold bodies, soft with hair, in minutest detail. He could see their shiny black eyes as they emerged from the darkness of the box into sunlight.

One by one they began to swirl about his head as if disturbed by his intrusion and warning him away.

He breathed deep, let the song of their wings impassion him. And then, hurling his body forward, he grasped the lid of the hive and flung it open.

Enraged, the inhabitants swarmed.

Screaming like a warrior going bravely to his death, Sylvan plunged his ill-made hands into their precious combs. He buried his fingers deep in sweet amber-colored honey, felt its oozing warmth.

And then, he smiled in pain . . .

Chapter Fifteen

The smell of strawberries filled the kitchen at Laurelpath Cottage. Rows of clean quart jars lined the table, and Agatha, red-cheeked and aproned, vigorously stirred a jam mixture on the range. Forrest had just come inside from scything the underbrush from the outer yard and, with his face dripping from a washing under the pump, grabbed a towel to dry off.

"Umm . . . what's that?" he asked, hovering over his housekeeper's shoulder and peering down into the pot.

"Strawberry jam, and keep your paws out of it," Agatha warned. Fussily she slapped away his hand as he made to dip a wooden spoon into the bubbling pink sweetness.

He avoided her barring arm, swooped his spoon into the syrup, and withdrew a sample.

"Excellent!" he pronounced, ignoring her scowl. "I swear I've never tasted better in my life. What culinary talents you have, Mistress Peacock. Jam maker *extraordinaire!*" He continued with his exaggerated flattery, sidestepping when she made as if to hit him with her spoon.

"Ye're a smooth talkin' rapscallion if ever I heard one," she declared. Then, inclining her head a bit, she peered out the window. "Looks as if ye have a visitor."

Forrest took the towel from around his neck and tossed it aside, proceeding out the door. Immediately, he recognized the footman dismounting from a sturdy cob as a Wexford Hall man.

"A letter for you, Captain," the servant said, stepping up the pebbly walk.

"Are you to wait for a reply?" Forrest inquired.

"I wasn't told to, sir." The footman returned to his horse, gathered the reins, and heaved himself into the saddle.

Noticing Lisbet's engraved envelope and fearing some relapse in her condition, Forrest wasted no time in tearing open the missive. The wind ruffled the single piece of thin paper, and he pulled it more tautly between his fingers, quickly scanning its lines. His expression changed as he read, going from concern to disbelief to cautious exhilaration.

He raised his gaze, and for a moment stood simply staring straight ahead, his fine dark eyes fixed upon, but not seeing, the flowering dogwood at the end of the yard. Refolding the message, he slid it back inside the envelope and tucked it deep within his pocket.

A moment later, with a purposeful stride, he walked through the kitchen with its neat row of hanging copper pots, past Agatha pouring out her jam, and into the corridor.

"I've been called away," he said over his shoulder, barely slowing his steps. "I'm not certain when I'll be back. Look after the place, will you?"

Under the shade of a gauzy parasol, Lisbet sat in a striped canvas chair, feeling the heat of the sun penetrate the light fabric of her gown. She breathed in the smell of the damp sand and salt, tasting it faintly upon her lips. The English Channel stretched luxuriantly before her, white-tipped and blue, its breakers heaving creamy lines of foam atop the glittering quartz and agate shore. Everywhere children screeched, collecting the shiny "Ventnor Diamonds," together with small furled shells washed up by the waves. Hovering close, a bevy of lace-capped nannies kept track of assorted pails, shovels, and forsaken sailor hats.

Behind them all, the Undercliff rose like a convenient sunshade, its magnificent terracelike formation of chalk and limestone stretching seven miles long and sheltering Ventnor's beaches from the chill of the north wind. Tourists strolled beneath it, then up the slope to the pretty town streets, or they lined up to use the horse-drawn bathing machines. Lisbet could hear the shrill cries of pleasure as gently bred ladies were handed down—or shoved—into the water by rough-handed attendants.

Earlier, having noticed Mary's interest, Lisbet had sent the maid to bathe, craving an hour or two of solitude.

Breathing a sigh of contentment now, she closed her eyes against the glare of sun on water, letting the surging rhythm of the waves soothe her. The headaches were gone, the dreadful languor disappeared. She had left them behind in Winterspell.

And Forrest, too, her heart whispered in lament.

She slid further down into her chair, listening to the nearby scraping sounds of a contented child molding a sandcastle, while giving herself up to a different sort of castle-building.

Lost in reverie, Lisbet only gradually became aware that a shadow had fallen across her face, shutting out the sun's warm fire like a mischievous cloud.

She opened her eyes. A man stood before her, his outline dark, the sun a halo behind his head. He was tall, wonderfully tall, with wide shoulders and well-shaped legs planted slightly apart.

She gasped. Slowly he reached out a hand, taking hers from the arm of her chair. His fingers were warm, finely formed, the knuckles still badly scraped . . .

A heady thrill raised the flesh on Lisbet's arms as he lifted her hand and pressed it to his lips. Forrest York stood before her, as real and solid as the earth beneath her feet. Dressed in a cream-colored jacket and trousers with a straw boater tilted rakishly over the back of his head, he had never seemed so disarming. Between the dreamlike quality of his sudden presence and the effect of his dark debonair good looks, Lisbet felt herself grow lightheaded. Her companion's flashing white smile with its bracketing dimples hardly aided her composure.

Gently he pulled her up from the chair. "I'm told this is a romantic place . . ." His voice was low, intimate. His eyes danced with lively black fire. "A place for lovers," he added with a raise of a dark brow. "Shall we find out for ourselves?"

Hardly aware that the words pricked some vague recollection, Lisbet let him guide her away from the chair and in the direction of a less-inhabited stretch of beach. Blinking in the brightness, she could not dispel her bemusement, her notion that her imagination had somehow conjured up reality.

How had Forrest known to find her here?

As if amused by her distraction, he squeezed her hand, making her laugh with sudden, sheer abandon. All that really mattered, she told herself, was that they were together and alone in a time and place that could, at that moment, have been paradise.

Forrest's gait increased, his long legs in their finely tailored trousers moving faster, his limp evident but not cumbersome. Lisbet allowed him to pull her along, lifting her wind-tossed skirts off the sand. They spoke not a word as they passed gatherings of pink-nosed vacationers: they were too intent upon the need for a private place and a private greeting, too intent upon the need to give their senses reign.

At last the cacophony of children's shrieks and laughing voices faded, the rumble of bathing machines and yapping terriers came only as faint echoes far away. Overhead, the undercliff jutted out over the shore like a huge striated balcony, its overhang providing soft shade, its base chiseled with alcoves carved by ancient seas.

Forrest pulled Lisbet into a rocky niche soft with deep sand and saw that she was breathless, her delicate complexion tinted pink and sheened with perspiration. Breezes tugged at the long streamers of her fine gilt hair, whipped to sea foam the hem of her pale green gown, and fluttered the ribbons of her large-brimmed hat. All about her sunlight danced, turning her eyes to silver green and the curve of her dampened neck to pearl.

His hands tensed with the wanting of her, with the need to hold her, touch the skin that would be warm with springtime. Dragging her forward, he arched her slender back, almost swallowing up her body with his own. His mouth closed over her soft rose lips, tasting, exploring deeply while she gasped his name.

As he kissed her, running eager hands over every curve and dip of her willowy form, he was filled with sudden remembrance of her shallow, dying breaths only days ago. Spurred by desolation, he clasped her more roughly to his heart, realizing how fragile she was, how precious, how essential to his being. Then with his breath rapid and hard, he drew back a bit, putting his hands just under her jaw to simply behold the dearness of her face.

As if unable to bear the few inches of separation, Lisbet moved her hands from his shoulders to his neck and pulled him back to her, covering his face with kisses, entwining white fingers in his hair, whispering short sweet syllables of love.

He caressed the length of her soft voile-covered arms, distantly heard the cry of seabirds as she whimpered against his mouth. He smelled the jasmine cologne she had splashed beneath her ear, smelled wet chalk and brine and sand. When she strained against him, he closed his eyes with pleasure, taking her lips again.

A party of picnickers discovered them then and, with sheepish smiles, hurried on. The two lovers grinned at each other, laughed, and kissed again, unable to stem the flow of yearning long.

"Mary will come looking for me . . ." Lisbet breathed against his mouth.

"Give her the day off," he replied impatiently, intent upon his business. "Give her the week off . . . the year off . . ."

She laughed but pulled insistently away. "Let me go and find her. I'll see that she enjoys herself alone today."

"Drop a few coins in her palm to keep her discreet," he murmured, kissing her ear.

She drew back, put a finger to his lips and traced his mouth. "We can get a picnic lunch," she said, "find some place to be alone . . ."

He searched her eyes, reading promise there, and nodded. But as if she were some precious, winged bird likely to soar out of his reach, he held her a moment.

"I'll arrange the lunch," he offered, bending to kiss the tip of her nose. Then, with an almost reverent hand, he touched her face again. "Meet me at the hotel . . . half an hour?"

* * *

Just like any husband and wife enjoying a seaside holiday, Forrest and Lisbet strolled the streets of Ventnor, wandering up Shore Hill to Pier Street, peeking through shady bow-fronted shop windows by cupping their hands against the glass. Even with its proliferation of hotels and boarding houses, the island fishing village had retained its quaint charm, its solid stone cottages with their sash windows and low-pitched slate roofs blending curiously with the whimsical styles of the newer buildings.

Lisbet twirled her white frilled parasol, holding Forrest's arm. He carried the picnic basket and smiled charmingly at the passersby, his dark good looks earning admiring, sidelong glances from every lady.

Here and there vendors dispensed lemonade from fancy urns, handing out raspberry ices to eager children with pennies in their palms. Overhead gulls wheeled, shrieking while street musicians in bright red neckerchiefs played lively ditties and danced jigs.

Enjoying the simple delight of sunshine and sea air, but most of all, enjoying each other, Lisbet and Forrest sauntered along pleasure paths perfumed with roses, letting the length of their arms touch, experiencing a thrilling sense of anticipation. Their physical need of each other was growing more acute by the minute, simmering with the same natural heat of the late-spring day.

Climbing the steep trail to the top of the Undercliff, Forrest guided Lisbet with a proprietary arm about her waist, lifting her now and then over patches of mire. Reaching the pinnacle, they waded through tall waving grass to an outcropping of rock thrusting aslant out of the earth. The view awed them, made them stand motionless for a moment, wondering at the beauty of beaches asparkle with quartz and admiring ocean waves as curled as a French meringue. Occasionally the slick blue-gray arc of a dolphin caused them to point and smile.

Setting down the basket, Forrest clasped Lisbet's hand, looking beyond her wind-whipped hat to the bright hazel eyes shining beneath its shade. The two of them belonged to a place like this, he thought, a place of free breezes and unknown faces and endless horizons. Even now their surroundings drew them into another world, tempted them into forgetting their identities, tempted them to simply love each other as they had been meant to do.

As they stood framed in the island panorama, he felt a need for Lisbet so great it seemed a physical hurt. Always, he had stood on sea cliffs and mountain ridges and desert steppes alone, his enjoyment of their views unshared. At such times he had always wished to have Lisbet at his side, and now he did. His sense of completeness was so wondrous the thought of losing it again made him desperate.

Roughly he took her in his arms, dragging her down amidst the knee-high grass, throwing her hat aside, and putting his mouth on hers. Deeply he kissed her, thrusting his hands into her honey hair and lowering his body atop the length of hers.

When Lisbet returned his attentions with equal ardor, he groaned her name, confessed his love against her ear, and swept a hand from the slender ridges of her ribs down to the swell of her hip. No less kindled, she slipped her own hands beneath his jacket and let her fingers slide over the flexing muscles of his shoulders and chest, feeling the heat of his flesh through starched shirt linen.

Above them they heard the kittiwakes shrill in a hazy sky, heard the seagrass undulating in a nubile dance, and smelled the sea winds mixing with hot earth smells.

Closer and closer Forrest pressed himself into his lover's form, his control held only by the knowledge that this was not a private place. Meeting the constraints of corsets and stays, he yearned to unclasp the buttons at Lisbet's back but dared not. Despite his daze of longing and lack of personal modesty, he was considerate of hers. He would wait until later when he could hold her behind closed doors and upon clean white sheets where she could return his love with no inhibitions.

And afterwards they could speak of love while wrapped leisurely in each other's arms and together plan their futures . . .

Lingeringly Forrest kissed her once more thoroughly, then raised up on an elbow. His breathing came harshly, his dark eyes smoldered. "I am playing the gentleman for you, Lisbet," he announced with a pained sigh. "But I want you to know that it's costing me dearly."

Adjusting his clothing, he sat up, pulling Lisbet upright as well, as if her reclining position was too alluring for his frustrated maleness. Reaching into their picnic basket, he snatched a bottle of champagne, uncorked it with a practiced move, and poured two full glasses.

"Here's to your honor, madam," he said drolly, clinking his glass to hers. "And to my thoroughly forced gallantry."

They drank and she laughed merrily, her voice as bubbly as the refreshment. Then she retrieved his boater and, after plopping it upon his tousled head, reached to repair her hair.

"Don't," he ordered, pushing her hand down with an air of injury. "At least compromise your propriety a little for my sake. After all, think of my own sacrifice."

"Oh, you!" Lisbet scoffed, hurling the champagne

cork at his chest.

Catching it with a swift clutch of one hand, he used the other to seize her chin. With a loud smack, he kissed her hard upon the lips. "For your effrontery," he declared.

She brought her mouth back to his, returning the intimacy with a soft tempting sweetness. "And for yours," she breathed.

He nearly threw caution to the wind at that. But he wanted their coming together to be a perfect, unhurried time, not a furtive coupling in the grass.

"Hungry . . . ?" he asked.

She laid her cheek against the roughened ridge of his jaw, nuzzling him. "Mmm."

"Cheese, bread, fruit, meat pies," he listed, plundering the basket of its delicacies wrapped in cheesecloth. "And chocolate eclairs for dessert."

They found they were hungry once they began to eat. Side by side, they feasted, Lisbet's head resting upon Forrest's shoulder while he leaned against the outcropping of stone. She tucked her feet beneath her fluttering green shirts, and he stretched his legs out, raising the knee of the injured one after a time to ease its stiffness.

"Talk to me about your adventuring," Lisbet said, reaching up to offer him a purple grape from the cluster in her hand.

Taking it between his straight white teeth, he smiled. "You and Agatha . . ." he mused, chewing.

"Agatha?"

"My housekeeper. She pesters me endlessly to tell her my own tales of the Arabian Nights."

"They must be more interesting than the published version."

He grinned with the possibility.

Lisbet put another grape to his lips. "You said

once—with that mischievous glint you have so often in your eyes—that the Navy found you a handy fellow to have about. I've wondered about it."

He quirked a dark eyebrow. "Yes, well. The War Office has this cozy little department called the Intelligent Branch, you know. It seems the admiralty said something to them about my being a likely candidate to do some snooping around in the Middle East." He sipped the champagne. "At first they were happy to have a few maps, a few details as to the military capabilities of one or two countries. Then they decided they'd like very much to know the plans of a certain Egyptian rebel named Arabi Bey. The fellow and his followers were causing havoc in Cairo," he raised a sardonic eyebrow, "making it unsafe for dear old England's loan-mongers and concession hunters, you know."

"I read about him in the papers during the Suez incident," Lisbet breathed, turning to look up into Forrest's face with incredulous eyes. "You got close to him?"

"Oh, yes," Forrest confirmed drily. "So close I was shot by an officer of my own esteemed military force."

Lisbet put a hand to his cheek. "Your knee . . . how dangerous it must have been for you to do such spying. Why did you ever agree to it?"

Forrest gazed at the cloudless sky as if seeking an answer there, its reflection turning his eyes to glittering silver. "The risks appealed to me." He looked at her. "Risk always appeals to me."

She met his intense regard equally, letting his eyes bore into hers, feeling a great passionate attraction to this undaunted, dangerous being at her side.

"Why did you come back to Winterspell?" she breathed suddenly, knowing the answer.

Without blinking, without decreasing the incisiveness of his stare, he put a lean hand upon her hair, stroking it with infinite longing. "For you, Lisbet . . . I came back for you."

Twisting about, Lisbet threw both arms round his neck. For a long while they sat together closely bound, their gazes turned as one toward the sea.

Behind them a few sightseers armed with spyglasses and easels and paintboxes clattered past, then two well-dressed couples came with children in hand. Each remarked over the beauty of the spot, for along the cliff edge a blanket of wild daffodils bent their frilled heads against the breeze, and below on the beach, herring gulls swooped down on tumbled, sea-sculptured stones.

When they were alone again, Forrest ran a hand along Lisbet's arm, speaking low, musingly. "Where would you go if you were free to live anywhere—anywhere in the world?" he asked. "Have you ever considered?"

She smiled, her cheek against his jacket. "Somewhere warm. I'd like never to feel cold again."

As if wanting to grant her the wish that very moment, he tightened his arms, lending her the warmth of his body. "A villa in the Mediterranean," he prescribed. "You could sit on the terrace everyday in the sunshine. Watch the sailboats glide by."

"Is that what you would do?" she asked, toying with a lock of his hair.

"I suppose I could struggle to make a go of it, make such a place enjoyable," he teased. "Of course, the sailing would become tedious and the swimming, and the sipping of ouzo under an umbrella with you, but . . ."

She tugged on his hair.

"Ow," he complained, pinching her through her skirts.

Their sport ended in an interim of kissing, and Lisbet wished their idle dreaming could come true, wished she could forget her other life . . . the other man who waited for her in the cold empty halls of a mansion.

"Will you go back to the military?" she asked Forrest softly, apprehensive of his answer. "Back to the Intelligence Branch?"

Forrest shrugged. "They've offered me permanent employment, but I haven't decided whether or not to accept it. I've always thought I should like to own a little fishing fleet somewhere."

"A fleet?"

He chuckled. "Two or three boats would do."

"Such an occupation sounds rather mundane," she taunted. "With little adventure, little . . . danger."

"Well," he improvised, rubbing his jaw, "there are always hurricanes and sharks and threats of bankruptcy when the catch is poor."

She laughed. "You will make danger happen wherever you go, won't you?"

"Precisely." Rising to his feet, he pulled her up beside him. "Let's see what danger we can find in those shops down there. I saw a gown in a window this morning just your size."

The gown was the pure ivory hue of a bridal garment, and Lisbet looked as ravishing in it as Forrest knew she would.

He was enjoying a Scotch downstairs in the hotel lobby when she floated down the carpeted stairs on satin slippers with her hair in upswept curls. Bowing elegantly, he took her hand and murmured a series of glowing compliments close to her ear. Then he guided her outside and down the walk, finally ushering her into an inn called "The Crab and Lobster."

"My wife and I would like a private dining room if one is available," he requested smoothly of the proprietor, circling Lisbet's waist in an easy, natural way.

Hearing his words, Lisbet colored with warmth,

feeling for a moment as if she did indeed belong to him.

And all the time they dined upon pink lobster and thick chowder, creamed vegetables and luscious fruit, she indulged herself in the pretension that she was indeed Mrs. Forrest York. She leaned close, touched his hand often, and admired him unabashedly in his black evening attire and snowy white linen. With his thick raven hair swept back from the temples and the planes of his chiseled face thrown into sharp relief by candlelight, she had difficulty taking her eyes from him for more than a moment.

Later, when he smiled and brushed her knee with his beneath the lace-draped table, she could hardly eat. With his wit and subtle intimacies, his claiming of her as his wife, he had disarmed her, making obvious his plans for the culmination of the evening.

And his culmination was the same she desired with every part of her heart—save one—that part answerable to Sylvan and Fidelity. All day she had battled hard against temptation, yet she felt herself losing out now beneath an old irrevocable love. How could she stop the ending to this evening, halt the sure and steady course that had seemed her destiny since she was no more than a girl sharing berries with a black-eyed boy?

"Lisbet, love . . . ?" Forrest repeated her name through his broad white grin. "What are you thinking of?" His voice lowered, and he gazed at her with knowing eyes. "Never mind. I can see your thoughts are close to mine. Shall we go?"

He rose up and took her chair, barely keeping his hands impersonal as they emerged outside onto the busy walk. Tucking her hand in the crook of his elbow, he guided her to the Esplanade, where they strolled along beside the sea on the weathered boards.

The evening air was pleasant but crisp enough so that Forrest removed his coat and slipped it snugly about Lisbet's shoulders. She closed her eyes briefly, feeling his own lingering warmth, smelling the fragrance of his soap. For awhile they said nothing as they wandered. Both simply enjoyed the sound of the foam-flecked breakers crashing against a sandy shore, the fresh tang of salt mingling with the delicious odors of cafe specialties.

The intimate night made them tense with a heightened physical awareness of each other. When Lisbet's hand tightened about the crook of Forrest's arm, his muscles contracted until the heat of the contact moistened his shirt sleeve. She let her silk-draped hip brush against his, tilting her head so it rested upon his shoulder. Darkness had drawn its veil, and it seemed nothing existed around them but ageless seas, stars, and earth.

"Lisbet?" Forrest broke the silence with the quiet, thoughtful query.

"Yes?" She looked up at his face as they walked, arrested by the sudden somberness of his tone.

As if reconsidering his question, he hesitated briefly, then said, "Why in heaven's name did Sylvan feel it necessary to give you the laudanum?"

Lisbet stiffened, her step faltering on the planks.

"You know why he did it, don't you?" Forrest pressed, his ever-perceptive eyes fixed upon her face. "I could tell you knew by the way you looked at him just after recovering from the overdose." His voice hardened. "You can be sure I won't allow you to return to him if I judge your life to be threatened in any way. If you doubt my seriousness, you should know that I didn't leave Wexford Hall without bribing a servant to watch every bite of food and drink you took to your lips."

Strangely Lisbet was unastonished by such a confession; indeed, the thought of Forrest's protectiveness gave her a warm shuddering thrill. But she knew that now he had posed the question concerning Sylvan's disastrous error, he would not let it pass. She must explain with caution.

Taking a breath, she swallowed and watched her slippered feet move upon the uneven grey walk.

"Sylvan began to give me the laudanum when we were first wed." Her admission was heavy with mortification. "I was very young, you see, inclined to be a bit irrational and . . . excitable. When he . . . touched me, I sometimes grew distraught, unmanageable. Naturally he thought to calm me with the drug, keep me from my girlish hysterics. 'Twas all quite logical and innocent really," she added lamely, coming naturally to Sylvan's defense.

Forrest halted their progress, took her by the shoulders, and turned her until she faced him. The glinting of his eyes pierced even the darkness. "And later—years into the marriage—did you continue to grow hysterical over his touch?"

She grew quiet for a moment, groping for a way to explain. "No . . . at least, not in the same manner," she stammered, knowing she was about to reveal one of the secret shames of her marriage. Lowering her lashes, she forced the words from her mouth. "Though he would like to, Sylvan does not touch me in . . . that way. As a high-strung bride of only fifteen, I-I couldn't see my way to being a proper wife. We made an agreement to postpone that . . . part of our marriage until midsummer's eve this year—"

Forrest gripped her shoulders and frowned. "My God, are you telling me he has never been a husband to you?"

She nodded, unable to meet his gaze.

Letting his arms drop from her shoulders, Forrest

ran a distracted hand through his hair, then released a long slow breath through his lips. After shaking his head in disbelief, he stated, "Then . . . I've been the only one . . . I've been the only one to love you." Every syllable bespoke of his elation and possessive pride.

Despite the fact that Forrest had not posed the sentence as a question, she gazed up at him and nodded with solemn eyes.

Music drifted to their ears, snatches of a waltz. They had wandered far where few others strolled, where only faint sounds of civilization intruded upon their privacy. Though Lisbet felt awkward having made her confession, Forrest tenderly drew her forward and into dance. It seemed a natural act, the gentle swirling together of their bodies, this waltzing to sea surge and song. Their steps were attuned, each glide they made one fluid motion of harmony. Forrest's eyes never strayed from hers, nor did his hand on her back yield its pressure.

When the music ended, he moved close and swayed with her, putting the length of their bodies together, bending his head so that his lips caressed her nape. His kisses were gentle at first, then rough and demonstrative. He pulled their hips together and pressed her to him tightly, then with a low sound in his throat, broke away with an abrupt gesture.

Taking her hand, speaking not a word, he guided her back the way they had come.

She knew what he intended, knew, too, that stopping him would be difficult, perhaps impossible. She had set an inevitable conclusion into motion and halting it would surely draw them into a scene of bitter words and accusations.

And so, although Sylvan's plaintive voice seemed to cry out to her in some corner of her consciousness, she almost found herself running beside Forrest's long determined stride. She went with him to the hotel, up the plush crimson stairs, and to her room. He unlocked it for her, and before they had barely crossed the threshold, he shut the door and pulled her into his arms.

His caresses were fueled with hurried aggression, as if he had gone far beyond patience. She felt the strength of him, the purpose of a man intending to fulfil his love, and she gave herself up to it, felt swept along beyond the point of no return.

The room stood darkly, silently, except for the ever-present ocean surges and the sound of rapid heartbeats. Forrest pushed his coat from her shoulders and tossed her shawl to the floor, his hands already working the fastenings at her back, his mouth hardly lifting a fraction from her own.

Clinging to him, she allowed it all, gloried in the feel of him, the taste and smell of him, the power in his hands. He touched her with such an urgency and strength she almost feared the maleness of him; she certainly feared herself and what she was doing.

Their coming together was right—yet not right, she told herself. Once it happened they would never have the will to deny it again. There would be endless, furtive rendezvous, fevered snatches of love, crafty strategies to elude discovery. Their relationship would be as it had in childhood, a thing perceived first as naughtiness and later a union condemned as sin.

Did she desire this present love she had for Forrest to descend to such depths again? Already she had crept about Winterspell to meet him, been wrongly branded by the villagers as the captain's whore. Did she now in truth intend to become an adulteress?

Could she lie down with her lover while her husband waited faithfully for her return?

No. She would stop this madness. The love she had for Forrest was not worthy of degradation. She must stop it now.

As if reading her thoughts even as he held her in the intimate blackness, Forrest murmured persuasively against her mouth. "Your marriage to Sylvan isn't a legitimate one, Lisbet. You know that don't you? It's not legitimate because you haven't done this with him . . . only with me." He bent her back so her body arched to his. "Only with me. You're mine—you always have been. *Mine,* no one else's . . ."

Cupping his head between her hands, she whispered in anguish, "We should not do this, Anvil. We shouldn't. . . . we shouldn't . . . ." Closing her eyes, she repeated the words over and over, knowing even while she spoke them she did not really want to stop him and push his hands away.

Forrest kissed the place where his locket lay, letting his hands wander over the smooth silk gathered across Lisbet's belly, then bent his head so that he might search her eyes.

"You've only to ask me to stop, Lisbet," he muttered, as if the offer were being forced from his lips by some last, begrudged vestige of honor. "And I will stop."

Enveloped in his arms, Lisbet hesitated.

Forrest lowered his face, trailed his mouth along the smooth line of her jaw, and muttered, "When I received your letter, I hardly dared believe it. Must have been a wrenching decision for you, but I swear you'll not regret it. We can leave Ventnor tomorrow if you wish—go anywhere, do anything you like. You've only to tell me."

The gaslight shining through a window illumined the paleness of her throat and shoulders. He ran his hands over her flesh, desperate to know again every inch of her body, desperate to lie with her through the night.

"What did you say, love?" Lisbet repeated confusedly, clinging to his words. She touched his face. "What did you say about my letter?"

At the bemusement in her voice, Forrest lifted his head up and leaned to stare into her face. With his heart thudding with desire, he responded impatiently, "I spoke about the letter you sent, the one asking me to meet you here."

Perplexed, she shook her head, recalling exactly the penned words of her hasty message to him. "But I didn't ask you to come—"

As soon as the words were out of her mouth, Lisbet regretted saying them. Their impact was shattering.

"Of course, you did." Forrest's sudden suspicion turned the words into a growl. "Your letter specifically named this hotel. You asked me to meet you here. How else would I have known to come?"

Lisbet stiffened, fearful now. Someone had arranged this assignation, had carefully orchestrated it.

"I-I don't know," she trailed, putting a cold hand to her throat. "I can't think who . . ."

Seeing her anxiety, sensing her sudden distance even as she stood facing him in clothes mussed by his eager hands, Forrest felt his chest constrict with a bitterness of dashed hopes. Both thwarted love and burgeoning rage seemed to rise up from his chest and strangle him.

She had not asked him to come. She had meant to be here alone . . .

"What a damned, skirt-chasing fool I've been," he snorted in self-derision, slowly shaking his head. "I swear, I could be bashed upon the head with the truth and still come back for more."

"No!" Lisbet cried, clutching desperately at his sleeve. "It doesn't matter about the letter. It—"

"Maybe it doesn't matter to you," he snapped, bending to retrieve his coat and thrusting his arms through the coat sleeves. "But it matters a hell of a lot to me."

"But I did send you a letter," Lisbet argued in a beseeching tone. "It explained Sylvan's sending me on this holiday. It—"

"It did not happen to include an invitation for your lover to join you, though, did it?" Forrest interrupted scathingly.

Jerking his coat closed, he fastened the buttons, turning his back to his forlorn companion in the process. He was sick to death of her teasing, her indecision, her evasions, her damned martyred loyalty to Thorpe. And yet, in spite of it all, his love for Lisbet was such a raw excruciating thing, he wanted to go down on his knees and bellow with the agony of it.

A knock rattled the door, startling them both. "A message for Lady Thorpe," a voice called.

"Go the hell away," Forrest barked.

"It's urgent, sir."

With an oath Forrest yanked open the door, snatched the note from the startled man's hand, and tossed it at Lisbet's feet.

Hot tears streamed down her cheeks at the wreckage of her love, at Forrest's cold belligerence. Numbly she reached to pick up her shawl and draw it about her shoulders in the modest way of a woman suddenly at odds with her lover. Then, wiping the damp, straggling lock of hair from her face, she read the folded slip of paper through bleary eyes.

"Oh, my God," she gasped. *"Sylvan!"*

Chapter Sixteen

"I'll make travel arrangements for you." His voice toneless, Forrest bent mechanically to pick up from the carpet the black tie he had earlier discarded and flung it about his neck.

Lisbet still stood disheveled in the center of the room, her face streaked with tears beneath a wild tangle of hair. "Forrest . . ." she said with pain in her voice, reaching out a hand.

His fingers paused upon the door latch at her plea, but he did not deign to turn around and face her.

"Will you travel with me?" she asked softly, "Will you take me home?"

Forrest's laugh was short and unsparing. "My dear Lady Thorpe. You want to journey across half of England, arrive in Winterspell, and then proceed directly to your husband's sickbed escorted by your lover—and I do use that term loosely, of course." He raised a mocking brow. "Hell, that plan offends even my immured sensibilities."

Throwing her hair back from her eyes, Lisbet clasped her shawl close to her chest and ran to him, stopping just short of reaching out a hand to touch his broad, rigidly held back. "We can get a private coach," she implored. "Mary can travel apart from us. When we arrive in Winterspell, we can part ways."

"It seems to me we've already parted ways, my love," he answered with no attempt at mercy.

"Forrest . . ."

The hurt in her voice racked him, and his fingers tensed about the door latch. He wanted to go, of course, spend a few more stolen hours in her company, even if he must do it in stony silence and without laying a finger on her. God help him, he was like a starving man standing at a bakery window slavering over some unreachable pastry.

Speaking flatly, still facing the door, he said, "I'm not your damned lackey, you know."

She put a tentative hand upon his arm at that, and he steeled himself against the contact.

"Please . . ." she whispered in a desperate tone, insinuating her lovely, fragile body between him and the door. "I—I need you with me."

"In what capacity?" he asked coldly, his eyes meeting hers now, searching them beneath black lowered brows.

Her own eyes filled, spilled over, but remained unwaveringly locked with his. "No capacity. I need you simply because I love you. Nothing has changed that," she breathed. "Nothing ever will."

"You love me only when it's convenient for you, Lisbet," he countered in a weary tone, pressing down on the latch. "When circumstances get a little too uncomfortable, you run in the opposite direction. You leave me dangling like a puppet on strings, refusing to make the decision you must make. I'm damned tired of your toying with me. For God's sake, he almost killed you, and still you won't leave him. I would have taken you anywhere in the world you wanted to go, cherished you, made a life for you." His eyes hardened, growing pitiless. "You say you love me . . . ?"

Seizing her by the arms, he yanked her forward and pulled her hips into his, putting his mouth within an inch of hers. "Very well, then tell me something. Would you have stopped me? When I held you in my arms, there—" he jerked his head, "would you have asked me to stop what I was doing?"

She stood staring up at him, heartsick, unable to say the words.

Forrest's lips twisted in a cruel half-smile, and abruptly he released her from his grip. "I thought as much."

He left her then, stalking out the door in his long, furious stride.

"You don't understand!" Lisbet hurled the words after his back, ignoring the staring passerby in the corridor. "You don't understand, Forrest York!"

An hour later, shivering in the damp cold outside, Lisbet watched Forrest toss her portmanteau into the carriage, then hand Mary up. She did not know how he had managed to rent the equipage in the middle of the night, especially since they would be leaving it at the pier in Shanklin in order to catch a steamer to Ryde. But, observing askance Forrest's harsh, forbidding expression, she could only speculate he had either threatened the owner with his life or sold his soul to him.

A few minutes later, when his hand clasped hers impersonally to aid her up the step, she could not help but grasp it tightly as if it would be the last contact their hands would ever make. With a distinct move, he disengaged it. Then, seating himself in the carriage, he took up the lines, his speed through the night on unfamiliar roads so daring Mary sat with her eyes squeezed shut.

When they arrived at Victoria Station many hours later, Forrest purchased their tickets for a northbound train. He secured a private, first-class compartment at her request and, after ushering her inside, shut the door and took the seat opposite, pointedly extending his long legs away from hers.

During the first half of the journey, he had spoken no words, save impersonal conversations regarding meals and comfort, and the resulting strain between them stretched so tightly it seemed a tangible thing. Lisbet found herself hardly moving, barely breathing, for fear it would somehow snap. So much remained unsaid between them, she thought sorrowfully, and yet at the same time there seemed nothing more to say.

With her heart in her eyes, she gazed at the man she seemed ever fated to hurt. He was staring out the window, silently watching the crowds of travelers milling about the station, watching them slide out of view as the train rolled forward. In his effort to arrange the speediest transportation possible, he had taken no time to change his clothes. He still wore his black cutaway coat with the elegant fit, and the starched band of shirt collar seemed to lay whiter than ever against the darkness of his neck. Fatigue etched his face and a day's growth of whiskers shadowed his jaw. Faint traces of his recent battering at the fair still marked his chin and cheekbone. When he absently rubbed his knuckles with their healing scars, Lisbet's own fingers twitched with a longing to embrace them.

Suddenly he turned his head and caught her staring at him. At the touch of his gaze, she felt color rise immediately to her face. Surely he could see the remorse shining in her eyes, surely he could see her begging him for even the smallest tender gesture.

But if he did, he refused to bestow it. His face remained impassive, all its emotion carefully wiped away.

Just to break the terrible hush, just to establish some sort of dialogue between them, Lisbet voiced her fearful thoughts. "I—I can't think how Sylvan could have been stung by a swarm of bees," she began tentatively twisting her handkerchief and lowering her eyes, suddenly disconcerted by Forrest's lynxlike stare. "H-he's mortally afraid of them. He explained to me once that he'd been stung as a child. It made him ill, and his doctor warned that the poison could be fatal to him a second time." Shaking her head, she added, "He's never gone within a mile of the hives at Wexford Hall—indeed, he rarely ventures even into the garden during the flowering months."

She turned her eyes toward the window, watching building and trees and earth speed by. "Poor Sylvan," she breathed almost to herself, belatedly realizing the awkwardness of the topic. "What a wretched existence . . ."

She did not expect Forrest to respond to her brooding conversation. She guessed his anger over their ill-fated relationship swelled so strongly he did not trust himself to speak; he seemed to be brooding, though, turning thoughts over in his mind.

A moment later, his low voice shattered the stillness in the coach, interrupting the rhythmic clacking of the train. "I acknowledge the fact that you care for your husband, Lisbet," he said quietly, as if needing to express his thoughts. "I can't even pretend I don't respect you for it. For whatever reasons, you chose to wed him, and now you are determined to keep your vows. Very admirable, I'm sure. At the same time it should be no surprise to you that I hardly consider myself the magnanimous and noble-minded type, and I certainly don't thrive on celibacy and solitude. I suffer jealousy just like anyone else—maybe more." He tightened his jaw. "To put it bluntly, I resent the hell out of your unshakable loyalty for another man."

Lisbet clenched her hands, affected by his words but

not knowing how to respond to them.

"I'm going to put a question to you," he said directly, waiting until she had met his eye again. "And I want an honest answer. Out of love, duty, or conscience—only you know which—you care for Lord Thorpe so much you won't leave him. You won't give him up even for us, for the life we could have together. So be it. But I'm puzzled by one point."

He leaned forward slightly, giving her a penetrating scrutiny. "If you are indeed so reluctant to abandon your husband, then answer me this: why did you step off a precipice and into a frozen river?"

Lisbet was caught off guard. Heat rose responsively to her cheeks, and she cast her eyes downward in confusion and shame.

"I have no doubt the drug had a great deal of influence on the state of your mind," Forrest conceded, though his tone remained quietly unyielding. "But your swim in the river was no accident, milady, and you have been wasting your time pretending otherwise with me."

Lisbet shook her head, then bowed her neck to put her face in her palms.

"Why, Lisbet?" Forrest pressed, bending forward, putting his hands on her knees. "Why?"

She opened her mouth, closed it, and gripped her fingers more tightly in her lap. Even to her own mind the reasons remained hazy and uncertain.

"There were many factors," she began haltingly. "You were correct when you said the drug had much to do with it—the pain of my headaches had grown unbearable. Sometimes it was so excruciating I nearly screamed aloud. And then," she went on, beginning the unsavory confession she had never expected to share, "there was Winterspell. It's a gloomy place, is it not? So melancholy and cruel. I'd never realized just how cruel until the day you returned. Earlier Sylvan and I had ventured into the village—it had taken me weeks to persuade him to go out. We went into a shop and bought some confections, and when we stepped out into the streets again, a crowd had gathered."

With an absent gesture she smoothed a wrinkle in her skirt. "Two of the villagers had dressed themselves up in a mockery of us. The fellow who characterized Sylvan toddled about in gaudy clothes too big for him, his shoulders humped in exaggeration. All during his antics the crowd laughed uproariously. Upon his arm preened a woman who was supposed to represent me . . ."

Lisbet took a breath. "She wore the paint and clothes of the crudest whore."

Across from her Forrest stiffened with anger as he listened, his eyes growing metal-hard.

"Until then," she continued, "I hadn't really paid the villagers much attention when they scorned me—I was accustomed to it, after all. But the sight of their mockery that day wounded me deeply, perhaps because I realized just how isolated I had become from everyone in the world save Sylvan. When I returned to Wexford Hall, I experienced such desolation that I felt somehow . . . *compelled* to run toward the precipice. 'Twas an irrational act, a desperate act, I know, and I'll always be deeply ashamed of it—appalled at my own weakness."

"But you asked me a question," she said quickly, seeing that Forrest was about to speak. "You asked me where my loyalty to Sylvan had gone when I stood above the river. And I shall answer you."

Raising her head, Lisbet looked hard into his eyes. "Will it satisfy you if I say I had abandoned loyalty? Will it satisfy you if I admit that my act was blatantly selfish and would have caused Sylvan terrible grief? If so, then I will say it."

Her tone remained steady, her gaze candid as she continued to explain a reasoning complicated with emotion. "Sylvan—who has suffered much adversity in his life—would have understood a plunge into the river as an ending to pain. Had I left him that way, he would have accepted it, I think. However," with a lowering of her voice she gave significance to her next words, "if I were to abandon him for the arms of my lover . . . well, to my conscience, there's a very crucial difference."

Though he did not take his eyes from her face, Forrest slowly leaned back, removed his hands from her knees, and returned to his contemplation of the window.

He had no countering words.

Assailed by utter weariness and overcome by emotion, Lisbet rested her head against the backrest. She had not slept at all on the harrowing journey, and the sudden need to close her eyes overwhelmed even her desire to spend this last precious hour with Forrest. The vibration of the rails lulled her and, seeking contact with him, however minuscule, she slid her foot forward so that it rested against his shoe.

Forrest did not miss the gesture. For a long while he let his eyes tarry on the woman he loved, noting every stray curl beneath her hat, every twist of braid edging her taupe jacket, her discarded gloves and the oval nails on her loosely folded hands. He examined the soft arc of her lashes, the sheen on her closed lids, the sadness in her full reposing mouth.

Quietly raising up, he shifted to the other seat, then eased down and very gently took her shoulders in his hands. Without waking she slumped in his circling arms, and he gathered her close, shutting his eyes, breathing as if in pain. The bow of his head, the posture of his arms, the tenderness on his face all bespoke of anguish.

If this was all he was ever to have of Lady Thorpe, he thought, he would take it.

Just before the train began to grind to a halt, Forrest eased his precious burden down and out of his arms, then with a heavy sigh, stood up. Glancing out the window, he got a glimpse of the Wexford Hall carriage waiting on the station drive. On Lisbet's behalf he had sent a wire from London earlier announcing her arrival time.

She stirred now, aroused from slumber by the shrieking iron wheels and cessation of movement. With a start she sat up, passing a hand across her eyes as if to fling off sleep. Suddenly oriented, she stood up, her face stricken.

Sylvan . . . Had she arrived too late? And Forrest . . .

Immediately her eyes went to him. He stood with his back to the compartment door, one arm braced against the wall, his head bent slightly to accommodate his height. She would have to say her farewells now, quickly, stealthily. Then she must rush off the train alone and on to her husband's bedside.

Forrest watched her, his dark eyes unfathomable again, his unshaven jaw clamped so tight it pulsed. Lisbet's throat swelled with grief, with remorse over their wretched disharmony. She could not bear to leave without touching him, drawing him close to her, even if no words came to her lips. Even if he pushed her away.

Stepping forward, she reached up and took his face between her palms. The muscles in his cheek flinched and his posture grew stiff.

"Don't . . ." he breathed, drawing his head back even as she raised to kiss him. "Don't do this, Lisbet . . ."

But she ignored him, throwing her arms about his neck and kissing his mouth until he gave way and seized her by the waist and returned the intimacy feverishly.

They kissed for the time they would be apart, they kissed to heal the discord, but most of all, they kissed for what might have been.

Finally Forrest put her away from him and opened the door. "You'd better go. Your coach is waiting."

Disconsolately, she nodded and smoothed her skirts with trembling hands. Then one last time she gazed into her lover's eyes and bid him goodbye.

It seemed no other passenger but Mary was to depart, which meant the stop would be a brief one. Waiting as long as possible so as to avoid being seen, Forrest slipped off the steaming black train and into the night shadows. He noticed immediately that the Wexford Hall coach had been moved from its former position and now blocked his exit out of the station. Swearing under his breath, he turned to retrace his steps only to catch Scottie Stone's attention just as the young man climbed aboard the carriage box. The groom looked fully into his eyes.

Caught but unabashed, Forrest stood his ground and returned the hard calculating gaze until the other turned away and flapped the lines.

Despite his fatigue, Forrest walked home, his mind full of fragmented pictures of a ruined plan, one he should have known better than to create. Entering through the front door, he found the house waiting dark and silent. With a sigh, he set down his portmanteau, feeling the sudden acute strike of loneliness. It seemed unfair that no pretty children rushed forward to greet him, to search his pockets for hidden sweets, to bid him sit down while they fetched the post. It seemed unfair that a wife did not appear with a lamp in her hand and a tender smile on her face—it seemed unfair that he could imagine that smile as no other's but Lady Thorpe's.

Running a hand through his hair, he sank listlessly into a parlor chair. For awhile he simply sat alone in the darkness. He hardly even heeded the sound of quiet footsteps crossing the hall. But when the spare, gray-garbed form of his housekeeper appeared on the parlor threshold, he raised his head to look up.

He had always known Agatha Peacock possessed an uncanny ability to sense his moods, and when a black one came upon him, she usually kept to herself. So when she ventured into the dark parlor instead of discreetly turning her back, he was vaguely surprised.

"I thought I saw ya come inside awhile ago," she began in a slightly awkward tone. "I . . . just came over to feed yer horse."

"Thank you." The words came out of Forrest's mouth so low-pitched and thick he was unsure she even heard them.

Crossing the shadowy room, she went to the cabinet on the opposite wall and, taking up a decanter of brandy, poured a full measure into a glass. Wordlessly she offered it to him.

He regarded her soberly for a second, then reached out a hand to accept it. Grateful for her thoughtfulness, he sipped, welcoming the fire as it chased downward to his belly, welcoming any feeling over numbness.

He was glad Agatha had not lit a lamp. He did not want her to see the wretchedness in his face. But it seemed she sensed it just the same, for she moved forward to stand beside him as if wanting to speak but uncertain what to say.

Finally she simply placed a warm hand upon his shoulder and held it there . . . comfort to a friend.

The pounding of hooves sounded upon the road outside then, dispelling Forrest's mood. He rose abruptly, expecting news from Wexford Hall, and before the rider had even dismounted, he waited at the door.

Scottie left the heaving horse to stand, and stalked up the path, obviously seeing the older man framed in the doorway. Even through the darkness Forrest could discern the hostility in the groom's expression, the tenseness of coiled hatred in the jerkiness of his gait.

"You have news?" he asked him sharply.

"Aye. I have news," Scottie barked, stopping a few paces short of the step. "Lady Thorpe asks that you come to the Hall." He spoke tightly, with resentment, as if each syllable were being forced out of his throat against his will.

"Lord Thorpe . . . ?" Forrest inquired, the words hanging in midair.

Putting a foot on the step daringly, Scottie sneered. "He's not dead yet, if that's what you're hoping."

Exhausted, anxious, his never-even temper already stretched to a breaking point, Forrest struggled against reaction. His fighting reflexes had become so automatic over the years that controlling them in the face of such insult was an effort. His arms convulsed with the need to strike the ill-bred brat and give him the manly thrashing he so well deserved.

"Now you've delivered your message," he ground out, just mastering control, "get the hell out of here."

"I have another message to deliver yet," Scottie announced, raising his lip in scorn. "A personal one. I saw you get off the train tonight, just when she did. You've been with her, haven't you? You've been with her on that island. You followed her just like you always do, because she would never have arranged it on her own. Admit it! Admit that you're nothin' but a low-born, filthy *adulterer!*" he bellowed, throwing out a fist and punching Forrest in the jaw.

Blocking a second, wilder punch, the older man seized the youth by his shirt collar and slammed him against the cottage wall, pressing his own body so close the weight of it made Scottie sag. "You smart-tongued little devil!" he hissed, ramming the boy's shoulders against the brick again. "I ought to take you down for that! Show you what it's like to fight a man. That's what you want me to do, isn't it? You've been wanting it since the day I came."

Forrest shook him, and Scottie slumped beneath the violence of his hands.

Breathing hard, his fury high, the older man commanded, "Never cast aspersions on Lady Thorpe's behavior again. *Never!* Do you understand!"

Even as he spoke he dimly heard a cry. Agatha stood frozen in the doorway gaping at him, her face white with fear.

Did she think he was going to do murder, for God's sake?

Forrest looked from her to the boy.

The youth stared fearfully back at him, his eyes clear and thick-lashed and wide . . .

Forrest blinked and felt perspiration bead upon his brow. All at once the fury seemed to drain from his nerves, leave him weakened by a strange sense of shame.

Nonplussed, he let his hands relax on the boy's torn shirt, then watched the groom lean to pick up his hat, rub a hand over his throat, and stumble toward his horse.

Agatha continued to stare at Forrest from the step, giving him an odd, incredulous scrutiny he did not understand. He experienced a vague confusion at it and wondered why his harsh treatment of the insolent boy had left him with such a disoriented feeling all at once.

Growling, he pushed past his housekeeper and reentered the cottage, making for his bedchamber. Once there, he opened up his trunk of medicines and scanned its contents, searching through the trays with purpose.

At last his hand found a small green vial. For a long moment, he considered it, turning it about in his fingers. Then, with a thoughtful frown, he dropped it in his pocket.

Lisbet waited at the window, straining her eyes through the blackness hoping to catch sight of a tall, beloved horseman on the drive. Behind her Sylvan lay motionless upon his bed. She could hardly bear to glance at him, so grotesquely swollen and wealed was his face. His congested breathing reached her even across the length of the room.

Since her return, her husband had drifted in and out of consciousness, moaning pitiably and reaching out his blotched, inflamed hands with their countless fiery stings. When he had opened his eyes for the first time, focusing them on her anxiously lowered face, he had seemed chagrined, even distressed by her presence. But after a time, after she had soothed him with soft words and stroked his head in a reassuring way, he had calmed, but only to mumble strange utterances garbled by delirium. Once he had even begged her to leave him alone, take a train, and go back to her holiday.

Grieved, Lisbet had questioned the servants. Presumably, only moments after the dreadful attack had occurred, a gardener collecting barrows of sand had discovered the prostrate Lord Thorpe lying beside the unlidded hive. He had carried him back to the Hall, throwing the household into panicked confusion.

"The master had honey all over his poor stung hands, he did," the gardener had told her, scratching his grizzled head. "I can't think what he was about. Meself, I thought he was afeared of bees."

Lisbet was no less puzzled. She knew Sylvan's terror of bees reached almost to the point of a phobic avoidance of the outdoors. So why had he been near the hives on such a bright spring day? And how had he managed to get his hands covered in honey?

Doctor Axelton, summoned immediately after the accident by the Hall butler, had been able to offer no clues. Irreverently he had mumbled that Sylvan was half-mad anyway, in his opinion.

"He was on the verge of shock," the tipsy old surgeon had informed her at her arrival. "Could hardly breathe. The poisons had closed up his throat, you see, and his heart was beating twice the normal rate. Had to bleed him," he had added importantly. "Only way to get the poisons out."

And then, a few hours later, the surgeon had bled him yet again. Uneasy, Lisbet had cut the session short, suggesting he put away his lancet and basin, and, as the hour was late, go downstairs for a meal. Avidly Axelton had accepted the invitation and, at last report, still tarried in the dining room enjoying his after-dinner brandy.

Lisbet feared to let him near her husband again. She had read accounts condemning the practice of bloodletting years ago, proclaiming it no longer an acceptable treatment even in extreme cases. Perhaps Doctor Axelton had already harmed Sylvan in some way, done him far more damage than good. She did not know, nor did she know what advice to follow.

She glanced over her shoulder now at her husband's small, motionless form, then peered anxiously back out the window. In desperation, she had sent Scottie to Laurelpath Cottage, needing Forrest's good judgment, his presence of mind, his steady nerves, recalling how he had saved her from certain death only two weeks past. She knew it was somehow unconscionable to ask him to come here to Sylvan's deathbed; she knew it was beyond decency to beg her lover to help save her husband's life. But she had already gone far beyond honor days ago.

Spotting him on the drive, she ran quickly to the more private south-east door of the Hall and motioned him inside even before he had time to dismount.

Striding forward, Forrest took her hands and peered down into her face concernedly. The very nearness of him made her faint with relief in the way of an exhausted combatant upon the arrival of a militia.

"Your husband . . . ?" he asked quietly.

Not wanting to speak where they could be overheard, she shook her head and ushered him hastily inside a small seldom-used parlor at the rear of the house. Then, turning about to face him, she took up his strong lean hands in hers again and met his eyes.

"I fear Sylvan is dying," she said bluntly. "Will you help me?"

Forrest regarded her silently for a few seconds, his face grim. "What would you have me do?"

In a rush of grief she raised his hand to her cheek, laying her head against it. "I don't know, I hardly understand myself why I asked you to come. I have no right, God knows, except that if anyone in this village can help my husband, 'tis surely you."

Forrest sighed and pulled his hand away. "I'm not a physician, Lisbet. It's true I have an interest in medicine. Having been in so many isolated places—dangerous places—I made it my business to learn some rudiments, but . . ." He turned aside and braced a hand on the window frame. "I can hardly perform some . . . miracle and save your husband for you."

She said nothing, and he brushed a knuckle across

the corner of his lip, tasting blood. "Indeed, a short time ago it was brought vividly to my attention that the death of your husband would be to my distinct advantage."

"Oh, Forrest!" Lisbet cried, distraught, clutching at his coat sleeve. "Don't say such dreadful things! I can't bear to hear them."

Bowing her head as if appalled at her own speech, she whispered, "God forgive me, but I've thought of his death myself, even thought that Sylvan himself would consider death to be a blessing—" She threw up her hands in disquiet. "Lord, but I can scarcely believe I'm even voicing these wicked thoughts. They're not really as they sound. And the irony of it is—"

She stopped in confusion, her eyes tragic but soft as she gazed up at the pair of black eyes so bleakly regarding hers. "In my own way, I do love him, Forrest."

He took hold of her arms. "You don't have to confess to me or plead for my help, Lisbet. Despite my faults, I'm hardly a monster. And though it's a poor, worn-out thing by now, I still possess a conscience, believe it or not."

He took a breath. "I'll do whatever I can for your husband."

Unable to express her gratitude, her depth of love for him, Lisbet simply took his hand in hers and led him through the door.

As they hastened up the grand curving staircase to the master bedchamber, she related all she knew of Lord Thorpe's condition, then added, "Doctor Axelton's still here. In the dining room drinking."

"Foxed as usual," Forrest observed contemptuously. "Has he done anything at all for his patient?"

"He's bled him," Lisbet answered worriedly. "Twice. And I fear he means to do it again."

"Good Lord," Forrest growled. "He's probably weakened Lord Thorpe to the point of death. Axelton should be locked up in a cell somewhere and the key thrown away. There's no guessing how many poor wretches he's murdered with his drunken ignorance."

They had arrived at Sylvan's room, but before Lisbet could proceed through the door, Forrest put a hand out to halt her.

"Are you certain you want me to go in? Are you certain it's wise for him to see me here?"

Lisbet replied soberly. "There's little choice, is there?"

Upon his entrance Forrest beheld the monstrous canopied bed with its carved headpiece and golden plumes. Within its depths lay a frail, hideously swollen presence, the presence who stood so indomitably between Forrest and that which he most desired.

Moving closer, observing the poor man's condition, Forrest could not help but wince. At least Sylvan reposed quietly for the moment, his inflamed eyes shut, his mouth opened to take in rattling breaths.

"I saw a calvaryman die of a bee sting once," Forrest said quietly to Lisbet, pondering. "But he did so immediately, within minutes of the attack. He went into coma and died before I could even move him. Seems a hopeful sign your husband has survived to this point."

Kneeling to feel for Sylvan's pulse, he noted the oozing red slash on the small arm and swore under his breath. "That half-witted sot Axelton! He's probably done more harm than the damned bees. Bind the wound—not too tightly, and get as much liquid into him as you can. Keep him still, resting so he can regain some strength."

Standing up, Forrest shook his head tiredly. "I know little more to recommend."

Lisbet sank down upon her husband's bed, weariness

so evident in her drooping neck and slumped posture that Forrest feared she might crumple at any moment. He noticed she had changed from her traveling garments into a fresh gown of lavender, but he doubted she had taken a bite of nourishment or a moment of rest since her arrival home.

Noting his considering regard, Lisbet swept her own gaze over his tall frame. He stood above her, his hair wildly tousled, his fine dark eyes shadowed and grim, and he still wore the black evening clothes of the previous evening.

She could not help but remember sitting across a softly lit table from him, flushing beneath his charm. She could not help but remember his attentive presence as they strolled the Esplanade, and his commanding kisses there.

And then there were the sweet, dangerous moments they had spent amidst a quiet room filled with the scent of ocean tang . . .

Forrest read the thoughts swirling behind Lisbet's eyes, remembered all the enchantment she remembered, experienced all the regret she experienced, and felt the same desolation in his chest that she felt in hers. Simultaneously their eyes slid to the uncomely form lying so vulnerably upon the bed.

No words needed to be said.

Slowly Forrest slid a hand into his shirt pocket and withdrew the vial he had tucked there earlier. "Give him this," he instructed levelly.

Lisbet stared at the tiny, curious bottle made of dark green jade and sealed with a stopper carved in the shape of a coiled snake. "Where did you get such a thing?" she asked, vaguely repelled.

He shrugged and gave her a wry, yet enigmatic smile. "Begged it off a snake charmer in Tangiers. The fellow assured me it was a most effective antidote against any sort of venom. He should know, don't you think?"

Lisbet looked at him sharply, unable to determine whether he spoke in seriousness or not. He quite resembled a man who had just lost his entire fortune in a wager and was putting up a sportsmanlike front to hide the devastation.

She had not yet touched the vial he held, so he took her hand and firmly closed her fingers about it.

"I'll throw Axelton out on my way down," he said tonelessly, walking to the door.

Before he could open it, Lisbet put a restraining hand on his arm, looking deep into his eyes. Never had she loved him so much.

"Thank you," she said, the words nothing more than whispers. She had uttered them more with her spirit than with her lips.

Forrest put a hand out to touch her face, stroked it, and, with an unreadable expression on his face, turned to leave.

Chapter Seventeen

Sunlight sparked off the water in a million dazzling shards, dancing from wave to wave, then up the bank to reflect off the petals of countless bellflowers. Willows bowed low over the river as if dozing in the heat, idly trailing their slender boughs in the cooling current. Dragonflies zipped from bank to bank while an occasional fish broke the surface with its iridescent tail.

Forrest cast his line from the shore, slowly reeled in, and, feeling no promising tug, cast again. A few hours ago he had taken a break from his writing, having just finished the tedious detailing of a military map drawn from information gathered in the interior of Egypt.

His work for Headquarters was fast drawing to a close, and he calculated that by summer's end his compilation of various documents, charts, and technical comment would be complete. He would then need to make a decision about his future. Even now a letter from Lieutenant Colonel Bevins lay on his desk, asking when he would be ready to return to active duty: the Intelligence men had an assignment in mind for him. God only knew what, and where, it would be.

The sun burned hot beside the river, and pushing back his straw hat, Forrest wiped his brow, eyeing the water with a refreshing dip in mind. He would need to hurry. The afternoon waned, and if he planned to dine upon his catch, he must clean the lot and cajole Agatha into heating up her frying pan.

With a whoop he threw off the hat, dragged his shirt over his head, and pulled off his boots, tossing them aside. With hands on his waistband he hesitated, glancing at the dense woods with their convenient hiding places.

Like as not, Gretchen crept about somewhere close, either gathering berries, rescuing half-dead hares, or spying on her favorite victim—him.

Disgruntled, he left the trousers, and, sprinting toward the river, dived in with his head tucked low between his shoulders.

On the opposite bank, Lisbet halted her horse. Putting a hand to her brow to shade her eyes, she followed the swimmer, watching the long easy strokes of his arms, and saw the river drops glisten on his hair as he paused to tread water. Plunging back into the depths then, he disappeared for a heart-stopping interval before resurfacing further downriver.

She glanced at Scottie where he sat his own horse a few paces away. Though the groom usually maintained the proper distance when escorting Lisbet, he had just nudged his mount close, noting the direction of her gaze. She sometimes wondered if he sensed she was his mother, wondered if some instinct told him so. Certainly he showed an attachment for her far stronger than a servant would ever have for his mistress.

With troubled eyes, she contemplated him across the space of waving grass, observing the hard set of his mouth and the brightness of his gaze as it fixed upon the bronzed arms pulling through the slow-moving water downstream. Her son's hostility toward his father greatly pained her.

"Why do you dislike him so?" she asked suddenly, unable to suppress the question.

Scottie clamped his jaw, and in that moment Lisbet felt her heart turn over. Had she a mirror she would have handed it to her son so that he might see his likeness to his sire.

"I'd rather not speak about him," he answered tersely, without looking up.

"You disliked him from the start," she admonished. "Before you'd even got a chance to know him."

"I knew enough."

Lisbet bent her head and smoothed the soft oiled reins threaded through her hands. She longed to speak with Scottie about Forrest, longed to make the boy respect and admire the man, even if he could never know the truth of their relationship. "I knew Captain York long ago," she said carefully. "I knew him long before you were born. We grew up together and played as children here, along this very river."

Scottie turned his head away to stare at the muddy ground beneath his horse's hooves. "I've heard about that." His words were hard, betraying his knowledge of all the sordid gossip.

"You mustn't believe all you hear. Most of it is just malicious talk repeated by narrow-minded people who have no care for the truth."

The young man made no reply to that, but his expression remained mulish.

Lisbet sighed. Her eyes had never left the distant figure across the river. It had been a fortnight since Forrest had come to Wexford Hall to help her husband, and she had not seen him since. After their time together on the Isle of Wight, she was not quite sure how to go about resuming the relationship. More to the point, she was not quite sure if Forrest would want to resume it.

Turning to her son again, she said, "I would deem it a favor, Scottie, were you to treat Captain York respectfully. Regardless of what you believe, he is a fine man."

Scottie swung his gaze to hers accusingly. "He is not your husband."

"No," she conceded quietly, her eyes fastened to that spot where Forrest had disappeared into the deep violet woods. "He is not my husband. But," she finished in a barely audible voice, "he might have been . . ."

At Laurelpath Cottage Agatha had made a fine dinner out of the fish. Forrest heard her pattering about in the kitchen, cleaning up. He sat at his desk, absently perusing the letter from Lieutenant Colonel Bevins again, wondering if it would not be best to return to London and take the assignment offered after all. It would be the least complicated thing to do, if not the easiest.

Lifting his eyes to the window, he found the dying sun hovering just above the roof of Wexford Hall, casting it into sharp silhouette. For a long time he looked at it, then clamped his jaw and returned his eyes to the letter in his hand.

Suddenly a tiny clattering sound interrupted his pensiveness and he glanced up, just able to view the front door from his vantage point. It stood open to let in the late afternoon breeze, and through it, he saw a child enter his house, toddling inside on plump, unsteady legs.

His brows lifting in astonishment, he walked toward the tiny girl, expecting to see a frantic mother charge through the door after her offspring at any moment.

Knowing little of children, he could only surmise the tot to be somewhere between one and three years of age, certainly too young to be wandering about on her own. She wore a plain, none-too-clean smock, scuffed black shoes, and a bedraggled white bonnet. Beneath its brim a riot of gold curls bobbed.

Dragging behind her a twig covered in dusty lavender blooms, she ambled about the foyer, looking curiously at each piece of furniture. Spying Agatha's hat on the hunt board, she raised on tiptoes and snatched it up.

Forrest approached the little girl and, kneeling down on his sound knee, spoke softly. "Have you come a-calling, milady?"

Showing not the least twinge of bashfulness, the toddler stared at him through round blue eyes, inspecting his face in the candid way of most children. Then she proudly held out Agatha's hat for his admiration before yanking off her untied bonnet in exchange for the more matronly headpiece.

When it slipped down below her eyes, stopping at her small up-tilted nose, she giggled in delight, throwing her head back to view Forrest beneath its brim.

He laughed as heartily as she, the deep bass sound from his throat mingling pleasantly with the other's tinkling chime. "You must see the effect for yourself," he said, adjusting the hat on her head. "Every lady needs to primp a bit."

Picking her up by her chubby waist, he let her appraise her image in the mirror above the umbrella stand. The sight of herself in the hat sent the child into another gale of laughter.

Thoroughly into the game now, Forrest removed his own tweed cap from a peg and, putting Agatha's aside, gave the lady a new look.

"No," he declared seriously, cocking his head to the side. "That won't do either. Now here's the thing."

Reaching for the bowl of yellow daylilies on the hunt board, he pulled one blossom out, then tucked it coquettishly behind the child's ear just as Agatha came up.

"Why, Cap'n York," the housekeeper exclaimed, putting her hands to her cheeks. "Wherever did ya find that child?"

"I didn't," he said, balancing the subject on his shoulder. "She found me."

Agatha rushed to the door, peering this way and that. "But someone must be beside theirselves lookin' for her."

He did not answer. The little girl had discovered his pocket watch chain, and he was busy disengaging it from his waistcoat for her.

Agatha stood silently for a moment, observing while he kneeled down and opened the face of his watch. Patiently he pointed out its features to his enthralled guest, whose grimy fingers immediately smudged its polish. After answering her every lisping question regarding its operation, he reached into his hip pocket and, finding a peppermint, helped her tiny dumpling hands to unwrap it.

"Now don't swallow the thing whole," he instructed. "It's much better if you make it last."

"You should have a family."

The housekeeper's words came softly, disconcerting him. He let his eyes wander over the child sitting on his upraised knee, noting the remarkable fairness of her cheeks, the length of her lashes, smelling the plain soap rising up from her warm damp neck. He would like to have a child like this one, he realized, a dimpled little personage to reach for him with tender arms and hold him tight. It would be a fine thing to have someone who *belonged* to him.

"Oh!" a voice said from the doorway. "There she is!"

With no more greeting than that, Gretchen entered the cottage, her figure swathed in another ancient gown that surely had seen duty a half-century ago. Meant for wear over several petticoats, the dress trailed at least four inches below her shoes. She walked gingerly so as not to trip herself.

"I'm minding her," Gretchen announced importantly, indicating the child.

"And exceedingly well, too, I've noticed," Forrest drawled. "Whose daughter is she?"

"The servant's. I l-like to play with her. Her name's Abby."

Forrest gathered up the sticky-faced Abby and gently deposited her in Gretchen's arms. "See that you look after her with more vigilance from now on. She could have fallen in the river, for God's sake."

Looking contrite, Gretchen lowered her eyes. Then, noticing the flower behind Abby's ear, she plucked a daylily from the vase for herself. She admired her image for a moment in the mirror, turning this way and that while Forrest and Agatha exchanged amused glances.

"Oh!" the marquess's granddaughter said suddenly, turning from the mirror. Shifting Abby in her arms, she fumbled in the skirt pocket of her once-blue satin gown and withdrew a piece of folded paper. "Ramtiggadin asked me to give you s-something. He assured me it was quite important." Her long slanted eyes darkened secretively. "He said to give it to the f-foundling lad with the mark upon his shoulder."

Regarding her through narrowed eyes, Forrest took the proffered scrap of paper. Brittle with age, it crackled beneath his fingers as he unfolded it, and the ink of the copperplate hand was so faded he could scarcely read it.

"The Journal of Lady Anne Sedgemoor, Marchioness of Winterspell," he read aloud, looking up expectantly at Gretchen. "It appears to be a title page to a journal. Is it supposed to mean something to me?" As he spoke, he stretched out a hand to return the paper to her.

But she put up both palms, refusing to accept it. "Ramtiggadin said for you to k-keep it. If you'll close your eyes and hold it tightly to your heart, it will speak to you."

"Of course it will," Forrest muttered under his breath, tucking the paper into his shirt pocket and glowering at Agatha's twinkling eyes.

Adjusting Abby in her arms, Gretchen made for the door in a swirl of faded skirts before pausing to instruct blithely. "Come up to the Tower tonight, *Anvil*. C-Come after eleven of the clock, when Grandfather retires, and you shall read all of Lady Sedgemoor's journal." Tilting her head, ignoring his sharp black glance, she viewed Forrest through her lashes before giving him a canny smile. "Ramtiggadin says you'll find it m-most interesting."

"Curious . . ." Agatha commented, watching Gretchen sway down the path, her unlikely gown dragging raggedly over the pebbles. "Do you intend to go, Cap'n?"

"On the advice of a magic bunny, Agatha?" he chided, quirking a dark eyebrow.

"No," she returned with a serious expression. "On the advice of an intuitive old woman."

Giving her a considering look, he shrugged. "I'll think on it."

Twilight had fallen and Flambeau had yet to be fed. Proceeding to the stable, Forrest scooped oats from a storage bin before dumping them into the feed trough. With eagerness the thoroughbred thrust his muzzle into the grain and began munching, undisturbed when his master smoothed a dandy brush over his sleek chestnut shoulder.

The activity helped to calm the restlessness that had plagued Forrest all day, a restlessness stemming from both physical and emotional sources. Since his return to Winterspell, he had felt as if his life hung suspended, without the least direction, and though he had often lived day to day in the past, his sensibilities suddenly seemed to demand more. Agatha's earlier comment regarding a family had sharply echoed his own recent thoughts, his increasing need for a home and family, for permanence and for people who belonged with him.

But until he could free himself from Lisbet . . .

Shortly after his last visit to Wexford Hall, she had sent him a message informing him of Lord Thorpe's slow but definite recovery. That had been the last communication he had received, and he had made no attempt to see her. He was struggling to distance himself, knowing there must be an eventual severance of their futile relationship, a severance that would have to be sharp but final.

He fully realized that the ghost of his love for Lady Thorpe would never leave him entirely—he would carry it with him just as he had always done. But he was an iron-willed man, and he knew it was time for his will to override the wishes of his heart.

Flambeau had finished his meal and, swinging his head around, blew gently against Forrest's hip pocket, seeking treats. Digging deep for the sugar lump hidden there, Forrest held out his palm, let the horse nibble the sweet, then ran his hand down the warm muscled neck. Darkness had fallen, rendering the landscape sapphire, and with a long sigh indicative of his heavy thoughts, Forrest turned to go inside. But before he had taken more than a few strides, dainty footsteps sounded behind him. Pivoting, he saw the shadowy figure of a woman cloaked in black standing upon the edge of the wood.

It was Lisbet, and she met him just as he latched the paddock gate.

Stretching out her hands, she laid them upon his own, drawing close so that she could better view his face.

He held himself stiffly in check.

"I was out for a walk . . ." she contrived awkwardly, having expected him to take her into his arms. "It's been so many days since we saw each other last that I thought we could take a stroll together, talk—"

She broke off, for he had glanced significantly toward the illuminated kitchen window.

"This is not a private place," he warned. "Shall we take a walk through the woods?"

Wordlessly Lisbet followed him, not attempting to touch, for she had caught her lover's mood. He was detached, and the coolness in his eyes chilled her, filling her with apprehension.

With his long stride measured in consideration of her slower step, he led her down a narrow, mazelike trail where the sound of croaking frogs and whirring crickets filled their ears, where the odors of decaying bark and greening life made them both recall the past.

"Lord Thorpe . . . ?" Forrest ventured at last, his eyes fixed ahead and his voice low. "Is he well?"

"Yes," she answered briefly, for she did not want to speak of Sylvan. She wanted to speak of Forrest and herself; she wanted to speak of their dreams again, those dangerous dreams they had enjoyed upon the island. "He is recovered, though his spirits are still a bit low."

Forrest made no comment, and they walked on. With each step Lisbet grew more certain that he had something significant upon his mind he wished to speak to her about, but was loath. In the face of his reluctance, his unusual remoteness, her anxiety increased.

"I received a letter today," he said at last, holding aside a low oak branch so that Lisbet might pass beneath it. "It was from a staff member down at the Intelligence Branch. Impatient fellow. He's getting anxious for my return to service. Seems to think my knee has enjoyed enough leisure time here."

Beside him, Lisbet felt the color drain from her face. *He was leaving.*

"Before the summer's over I should be finished with the journal I've been working on," he proceeded, still speaking matter-of-factly. "They prefer that I deliver it personally, of course, not trusting military information in the hands of the post. Not only that, but I suspect they have a new assignment for me that is so godawful they feel they need to persuade me in person—over a fine meal served with plenty of champagne, no doubt."

He took a few steps more, then delivered the blow. "After that, I'm afraid there's really no excuse for my coming back to Winterspell."

Lisbet stopped in her tracks, turning on him. "What do you mean, there's no excuse for your coming back?" she demanded, her voice low. "What are you telling me?"

Putting his hands upon her shoulders, Forrest spoke with all the pent-up impatience of the last days. "I can't stay on here permanently, Lisbet. For God's sake, surely you can see that! I simply can't exist in a rented cottage, putter about the garden with no occupation, with no future. I—"

He cut off the rest of the sentence, lifted her chin with a finger, and gentled his voice. "This is no good, Lisbet—what's between us. It's no good."

For a moment she could not speak. The foreboding

of his words caused her blood to freeze, and she swayed a little on her feet. "What are you saying, Forrest?" she prodded, refusing to make it easy for him. "Tell me! I want to hear it clearly from your lips."

"Then you shall. I'm saying that sooner or later we have to have an ending, Lisbet. Can't you admit it? We have to have an *ending*."

In the darkness she searched his face. He gazed back at her steadily. She could see love for her in his eyes clearly, but she also saw hardness and a determination that she feared. Perhaps, in some part of her heart, she had always known he would leave one day. But she had pushed the idea away, pretending it would never materialize.

Overcome, she swung away from him, refusing to break down. If she did, he would take her in his hard arms and, in a voice carefully devoid of passion, attempt to console her. She couldn't bear it.

He had moved to stand close behind, so close she could hear him breathing. Her anger snapped. How dare he leave her here again, just as he had done before! How dare he cause her pain again, trying to break a bond that could not be broken!

"You cannot go, Anvil." Her words were an imperious command to the boy she remembered.

"Damn it, Lisbet!" he exploded. "Have you no understanding of my nature, of my pride?"

"I don't care about your pride! I care only for you and I, for what is between us!"

"There's nothing between us except your *husband*." He spoke coldly, his gaze piercing the darkness, daring her to counter the truth.

Her breast heaved with such strong emotion she could not speak. But what was there to say? How could she deny his words? Hadn't she been the one to determine the course of their relationship? He had given her a choice, offered to take her away, make a life for them, but she had refused. She had made her decision. Did she now have the right to blame him for his own?

She opened her mouth to speak, looking into the fine dark eyes she loved so well. They were sad and knowing.

Turning away, she plunged through the tangled blackness alone, her silence a confirmation of all he'd said.

With bleak eyes, Forrest clenched his fists and let her go.

The clock in the parlor chimed eleven times. Forrest sat at his desk over a half-finished letter to Lieutenant Colonel Bevins, his evening companions a lamp and a bottle of whiskey. Pushing the communication aside, he slid his hand into his pocket and, removing the odd yellowed scrap there, unfolded it.

"The Journal of Lady Anne Sedgemoor, Marchioness of Winterspell . . ." he murmured, staring at it as if to glean some piece of significance. "Why the devil did that mischievous girl bring this to me? It's God knows how old. Why should I care what it says? Has nothing to do with me."

And yet, in spite of the irrationality of it all, he rose, extinguished the lamp, and swigged down the remainder of the whiskey in his glass.

A few minutes later he was striding down the lane to Winterspell Tower.

As if knowing he would come, Gretchen awaited him at the gatehouse. She held a lantern, and its glow cast itself over her figure, revealing the shimmering ball gown of gold she wore, its style aged but magnificent. Dipping low over her young bosom, it framed its fullness, belling out from a narrow waistline. For once her hair was pinned up, only a few wayward curls straggling down her neck.

Forrest had had no lack of beautiful women on his arm over the years, but as he beheld Gretchen, he thought he had seen few with such a carnal allure. That quality contrasted strangely with the creature innocence in her eyes, the mental immaturity that had never ripened in the way her body had. He wondered if it ever would.

"Ramtiggadin is waiting for us," she said softly, coming to take his hand. Raising her eyes to the somber tower, she added, "He's up there."

Still holding his hand, she pulled Forrest through the gatehouse, through the decaying courtyard to an open door at the base of the Tower. The pungent odor of damp and mold drifted outward from the aperture, and holding the lamp higher, Gretchen proceeded on, bidding Forrest to follow up the spiraling stone steps leading to the turret.

Feeling a sudden uncommon chill and assaulted by the familiar lurching sickness he always suffered within the castle's sphere, Forrest climbed. His legs moved with inexplicable slowness. When at last he and his escort reached the summit of stairs, Gretchen took a large rusted key from her pocket and, inserting it in the oaken door, sprung the catch. Then, shoving the portal wide, she moved dramatically aside so that Forrest might enter.

The room was large and cold, its tapestry-hung walls and neglected furnishings lit feebly by two candelabra. A thick coating of dust and countless garlands of cobwebs lay upon everything—the canopied bed, the dressing table, the Louis XIV chairs, and the twin clothespresses. Even the perfume bottles and brushes upon the table showed a film of grime as did the decanter with its evaporated contents on the writing desk.

Beside the bed-stairs, Forrest saw an elaborately styled infant's cradle, its head intricately carved and crowned by a rosette of netting. Near it, the hare whose paws Forrest had mended, and who Gretchen called Ramtiggadin, stared at him with fathomless eyes.

"This was the marchioness's room," Gretchen explained, setting down her lantern and whirling around in the center of the turret. "She s-spent much of her time here, reading and sewing, and looking out the window toward the road. She d-died here, too."

Forrest did not reply. From the moment he had entered the room a myriad of odd sensations had set his nerves on edge, and his belly was still knotted with its nausea. He took several deep breaths, needing air, feeling as if his lungs were being squeezed from the inside.

"S-she loved her husband the marquess very much," Gretchen went on, idly examining a silver letter opener on the dust-shrouded table. "You know the way I mean . . ." she smirked, glancing at him slyly. "The way Lady Thorpe loves you. But the marquess went away to India in the Queen's Service. Every day Lady Sedgemoor gazed out the window there, watching for his return, praying that he would arrive in time for the birth of his baby . . . b-but he never did come back. He died in India—some s-savage put a bayonet through his heart. Word of his death came only a week before—"

She broke off, smiled sheepishly, and finished, "Well, I should let you r-read that part for yourself."

Scampering to the clothespress, she threw its door open, showing him the assortment of exquisite garments. "Here are her gowns. I wear them s-sometimes because they're so lovely."

Even as she spoke her pale eyes widened in alarm. "Y-you don't think she'd mind, do you?"

Forrest shook his head distractedly. A queer sense of unreality gripped him, causing him to feel as if he were on the verge of discovering something vital, something that would change his life. He was not usually prone to fancy, which made his sense of presentiment even more disturbing.

"Lady Sedgemoor detested m-my grandfather, you know," Gretchen chattered on. "That's why I'm not certain if she would like me, approve of my wearing her clothes and t-touching her things." She shrugged, her elegant shoulders cream-colored in the candlelight. "Of course, she was afraid of my grandfather, and I'm sure she wouldn't be afraid of me. I would have helped her, had I been here. I would have kept Grandfather away. He was naughty, very naughty. But now," she concluded matter-of-factly, "he's only mad."

Forrest had been staring at her, trying to make sense of her words, arrange them into some sort of cohesive story.

"Gretchen," he said. "Where is Lady's Sedgemoor's journal?"

The corner of her mouth lifted into an impish smile, and she raised her gilded skirts to twirl about again. "She hid it."

Forrest hoped she did not intend to make a game of this, and though some part of him burned now for possession of the journal, he kept his voice calm. "Where did she hide it?"

"Somewhere s-special to her. Ramtiggadin only found it the day you came back to Winterspell. Sshh," she hissed, putting a finger to her lips. "G-Grandfather doesn't know about it."

"Where, Gretchen?"

She clasped her hands behind her back, rocking on her heels, considering him through her lashes. Then, as if deciding she had stretched his patience with the game as far as she could, she went to the cradle and knelt down. Lifting up the neatly folded linens there, she removed a leather-bound book, its edges cracked and peeling, the gilt on its spine fading away.

Mutely she offered it to Forrest.

Taking it, his hands instinctively reverent, he sat down upon the bed, causing a faint cloud of dust to rise up from the counterpane and wend about his head.

Gretchen brought the lantern close, holding it while he opened the cover of the journal and began to read.

The first entry was dated nearly forty years from the present, when Anne had arrived as the bride of Lord Gregory Sedgemoor, Fourth Marquess of Winterspell. The author had spared few details regarding her husband's appearance, describing him as "a fine-looking man, as dark in hair and eye as I am fair."

Little marred their happiness in the first years of the marriage, she wrote, except the bitter scenes between Gregory and his younger brother Baldwin. Baldwin indulged in frequent bouts of drunkenness, it seemed, and though he was often away on pleasure jaunts to London, he always returned to interfere in the running of the estate. And his borrowing of money was incessant.

Later, when Gregory dutifully prepared to leave for India at the Queen's request, he had banished Baldwin from Winterspell until his return, but the younger brother had come riding disobediently back not more than a fortnight later.

Anne had been with child, and fearing Baldwin's inebriated states, his temper, and cruel tongue, she had moved into the Tower, spending much of her confinement sitting beside the window waiting for her husband's homecoming.

Her excitement over the upcoming birth was evident in her sentimental entries, and an entire page of the journal was dedicated to the listing of prospective names for her future child—one column masculine, the other feminine. In each, she had circled a name: Elizabeth on the one hand and Nicholas on the other.

On the day of her delivery, she had made a short entry: "Nicholas is born! I pray to God that I live to see him grown . . ."

After that ominous line two days went unrecorded before the final entry, its script so feebly set down Forrest could hardly decipher the words.

"Baldwin has taken Nicholas from me. He tells me the baby died, but I do not believe it, for he was too strong, too vital, his cry vigorous. However, if he truly lives, I fear I will never know, for I seem unable to recover from the birth. Even writing these lines is effort for me. I pray for my baby's safekeeping, for his growth into manhood, for his happiness. . . . I pray Baldwin is merciful to him.

"He only let me hold him once, but I should know my son anywhere. Upon his shoulder he carries a mark—queerly shaped. I shall draw it here."

And she had. In the middle of the page, as an end to her journal, as an end to her life, Lady Anne Sedgemoor had sketched the shape of an anvil.

Chapter Eighteen

Forrest closed the book and, numbly laying it aside, leaned his temple against the post of his mother's bed.

He was not Forrest York, he was not Anvil. He was the son of Anne and Gregory Sedgemoor, Lord Nicholas Sedgemoor, the Fifth Marquess of Winterspell. The realization was so fantastical he could not digest it, and he reviewed the lines in the journal again and again, searching for a possible misconstruction. In the end, after many long moments, he found himself simply staring at the sketch Lady Sedgemoor had drawn at the end of her diary, knowing there could be no mistake.

He had gone through life having no inkling of his identity, of his day of birth, of his parents and heritage. Now, suddenly he knew it all, everything.

Lifting his head, he stared at the room again, only this time through much different eyes. He had been born here. And in a sense, he had also died here.

Gretchen had slipped out, and raising up slowly now on stiffened legs, Forrest began to wander amongst the dusty furnishings, touching the gowns his mother must have worn, the chair by the window where she must have sat, the pillow upon which she must have died. He wondered what sort of woman she had been, whether her manner had been meek and serene or dynamic and restive. He wondered about her family home and lineage, her parents and siblings and grandparents. In the days and years ahead, he would have much to discover.

After he had reverently opened drawers and cabinets and boxes, examining the things that had once been a part of his mother's life, he found a trunk of his father's belongings. It gave him a curious feeling to touch shirts and cravats and boots, to hold in his hand the silver-handled riding crop and the gold stickpin his father must have used. It gave him an odd start to find a miniature framed in leather depicting a man whose eyes and mouth resembled his own. But most of all the touching of these things left him with a sense of loss, a sorrow that he had never known Gregory and Anne Sedgemoor.

Walking slowly across the room, his boots leaving trails on the gritty floor, Forrest halted at the cradle. Here he had begun life. Here, for a day or so, at least, he had been the well-loved heir to a title, the child desired and anticipated by its mother and father. Had he stayed here, he would have galloped happily about the estate under the watchful eye of a carefully selected nurse; he would have likely been educated at Eton, then Oxford, done a Grand Tour, and finally, upon his majority, acquired full control of the estate of Winterspell.

There would have been no boyhood of deprivation, ostracism, and degradation. There would have been no cause to beg in indifferent streets, no cause to steal a meal of bread, no cause to wander about the world without a place to call home. Instead his life would have been spent in the most elite circles, full of soirees and sumptuous dinners and bevies of uniformed servants. He would have been considered a most eligible bachelor during the London Seasons, and Lord Tattershall of Wexford Hall would have bent over backwards to wed his precious daughter to the young optimally bred Marquess of Winterspell.

With the wriest of smiles, Forrest set the cradle rocking with his foot.

Devoid of misfortune, how different his life would have been.

Ah, but didn't the world's most respected sages insist that difficulties produced a greater character, made one resilient, resourceful, and wise? Didn't they say it was like testing the purity of metal in a crucible?

Well, damn it all, he didn't view it quite so charmingly. It seemed to him that the hardships of youth had bred nothing but rebellion in his heart, causing him to spend the whole of early manhood regarding the world through angry eyes. It seemed to him that the deprivation had robbed him of all innocence. And though he had long ago put self-pity aside, bitterness he found less discourageable.

Moving from the still-swaying cradle, he stepped to the window, that place that had been his mother's constant vantage point. Looking down, he saw the chimneys and slate roof of Wexford Hall, the snaking silver river, and the arches of an ancient bridge.

With a fist he pounded the wall.

His birthright had been stolen from him and would have slipped forever through his unknowing hands had not a fey yet clever young girl happened across his path. He wondered what was left of that birthright now, a birthright flaking and crumbling beneath his very gaze. Was there nothing left but a disintegrating old jumble of stones and a history long forgotten? By his absence, unwitting or not, had he failed his parents, his ancestors?

Moments later Forrest closed the door upon his lost past and descended the stairs. The nausea that had so plagued him had left his belly now, banished perhaps by the cleansing of revelation. Crossing the courtyard, he headed toward the northeast corner of the compound, the corner housing the family crypt. Built of stone, the place was accessed by an ornate iron gate, now so rusted and sagging on its hinges that the slightest breeze made it creak. Shoving it aside, Forrest entered the cold spacious mausoleum tinted violet by dawn light filtering through blue and crimson glass. His purposeful stride lapsed into a more reverent step as he approached his mother's coffin and gazed upon her reposing likeness with the eyes of a grieving son. As a boy he had crept into these chilly confines often, staring with morbid fascination at the gray marble effigies lying atop their stately biers. He remembered the serene profile of Lady Sedgemoor, her folded stone hands, and the date of her death.

Swinging his eyes to the small coffin resting beside her more imposing one, he examined the precisely carved cherub with its neatly furled wings. Its inscription read, *Infant Son of Lord Gregory Sedgemoor, the 4th Marquess of Winterspell, and Lady Anne Sedgemoor. Died 12 January 1847.*

No infant had ever lain inside, of course. That infant had been abandoned dispassionately upon an altar, sacrificed to mercy.

With a growl Forrest pivoted about and, bursting through the doors of the Great Hall a moment later, startled the unkempt maid who crouched before the smoldering hearth.

"Where is your master?" he bellowed, his voice reverberating off the walls.

She raised a hand, pointing one dirty finger in the direction of the stairs.

He took them two steps at a time, making his injured knee pull its weight. Then, after opening and slamming at least a half-dozen doors on the second level, he hit upon the chamber he sought.

The old man sat upon the edge of his bed, garbed in voluminous bedclothes the color of ivory, his fine white hair standing on end beneath a wrinkled nightcap. He squinted at his intruder, then heaved himself up, bawling out curses at the interruption of his privacy.

In three short steps Forrest crossed the room and, grabbing a handful of the ample linen across his uncle's breast, hauled him close. "Do you know who I am?" he demanded through his teeth. "Do you have enough intelligence left in that pickled brain of yours to recognize me?"

Beneath pink wrinkled lids Baldwin stared back at him for a moment, then blinked and slid his gaze away. In spite of their rheumy glaze, the spark of craftiness, of cruelty, glinted still within the depths of his brownish eyes.

"You knew who I was the night I came here to dine, didn't you?" Forrest accused. "You remembered well the despised little village pariah you'd helped to create. Did you ever wonder where I had been these many years, whether I lived or died? Did you feel smug that your secret was safe, or did you ever fear?"

Shoving his uncle back so that the old man sprawled helplessly upon the bed, Forrest leaned over him like a towering avenger. "I want some questions answered, and you'd damned well better cooperate. If you don't, I shall have no qualms about jogging your memory for you."

Holding up his withered palms, his mouth sagging with fright, Baldwin began to blubber, setting the flesh beneath his bewhiskered chin aquiver. "I did not kill the brat," he protested in a whine. "I only took it to the church, gave it to—to—" He raised a quavering finger. "To God, you might say, yes—"

"Did you murder its mother—help her to die?" Forrest demanded.

"N-no! No!" Baldwin answered quickly, struggling to his hands and knees until he wobbled upon the shifting feather mattress. "Sh-she died of the childbed fever. Quite natural. I-I never touched her. But that's when I got the idea. I needed money, that's all. Quite a handsome young blade, I was, avid for the races and gaming hells. I simply needed the ready. Gregory had never allowed enough. And I had always wanted his title—why should the brat have it?"

He lowered his wild hawkish brows and, staring hard at the floor, seemed to fall into a state of meditation. "Gregory died, she died. . . . That left only one squalling whelp standin' between me and Winterspell. The woman who attended the birth—Lady Sedgemoor's maid—" Baldwin smiled slyly, revealing three yellowish teeth, "she'd been warming my bed for months, she had. Quite mad for me. I had no trouble bribing her to say the baby had given up the ghost. Axelton signed the necessary papers—" He put a hand to his mouth and snickered. "He likes his comforts, too, he does."

"So you got your hands on the estate," Forrest pronounced with contempt. "*My* estate. How much is left of it?"

The old man shrugged, plucking at the folds of his bed gown distractedly. His eyes seemed to grow vacuous, his expression blank. "Th-the steward knows. I can't be bothered with all those account books anymore. I have my pleasures to keep me occupied, after all . . . the wine a-and the ladies. There was a Lady Faltingham once, very pretty with a ravishing figure . . ."

Forrest left him to his ramblings, then strode out of the room and down the stair to seek out the maid again, hoping to God she would prove more help than the benighted scoundrel upstairs. She directed him to the estate office, where it took Forrest less than an hour of examining the books to realize the steward had been robbing Winterspell blind for years.

After locating the man the following day, Forrest promptly fired him. Then, gathering up every account, deed, and legal document he could find, he packed them with his mother's journal into a trunk and set off for London. He would hire the most prestigious law firm the city could offer.

A fortnight later, the Fifth Marquess of Winterspell returned to take his rightful place at last. He brought with him a respectable household staff hired in London, whom he felt were capable of making the castle habitable in a reasonable amount of time. The lawyers had disclosed that the fortune of his father's time had been drastically reduced by Baldwin's squandering and mismanagement, and by the steward's outright theft. The coffers would allow for a meager staff and some urgently needed repairs, but little else.

However, the land had not been put to full use in years. Fields lay fallow and the livestock had been reluced to no more than a few head of cattle, two lozen sheep, and three tired horses. A careful master ould eventually make the place productive again, retore the decaying masonry and leaking roofs, and hough the holdings may never be what they had een a half century earlier, they would suffice to keep Winterspell afloat.

Forrest had been back barely an hour when he etched Agatha from Laurelpath Cottage and led her lirectly to the Great Hall. There he bowed, and, vith a roguish grin, introduced himself as Lord Nicholas Sedgemoor, the new Marquess of Winterspell.

His announcement and the resulting explanation eft his housekeeper flabbergasted.

"Never have I seen you at such a loss for words, Mistress P," he teased, amused at her pinkening heeks. She was gazing up at him as if he had suddenly sprouted a bejeweled crown and scepter.

He rolled his eyes. "Endeavor to find that cheeky ongue of yours on the double, will you? After all, you now have a considerable staff to command, and—" he swept out a hand, "an atrociously filthy heap of stones to set in order."

With her mouth agape, Agatha slowly swiveled about to view first one end of the gloomy Hall, then the other, taking in every bit of its size and degree of disorder.

"Of course," Forrest shrugged, perfectly straightfaced, "if you feel you can't manage it . . ."

Drawing herself up, Agatha puffed out her chest and put both hands to her skinny hips. "I can manage, and well ya know it, too," she declared, her old self quite restored. "Where is this staff yer speakin' of? I hope they're not a lot of worthless dillydalliers."

"I believe they're lounging about in the kitchen
taking tea, now you mention it."

"Hah! I shall have to set them straight," she an
nounced importantly, marching off only to stop i
her tracks and ask stiffly, "Where are the kitchens?"

Laughing, Forrest pointed her in the right direc
tion. "Watch that butler," he advised with a twinkle i
his eye. "He's the most supercilious one I could find

The remainder of the day Forrest spent closeted i
the estate office, grinning occasionally at the sound c
Agatha's imperious voice echoing round the corri
dors. Besides the usual staff, he had engaged an at
tendant to care for Baldwin, whom he planned t
house in the east wing of the castle, being disincline
to endure the old devil's company. For Gretchen h
had hired a lady's maid, advising her he wanted th
young woman properly clothed and groomed, an
taught the rudiments, at least, of social etiquette.

Now, as he gazed through the sun-bright windo
of the office where leather-bound books recorded hi
impressive lineage and the considerable boundaries o
his inheritance, he shook his head. The full realiza
tion of his fortune was still difficult to comprehend
Accustomed to owning little but the clothes on hi
back and having had no property to call his own i
the past, the thought of such a vast and proud inheri
tance disconcerted him somewhat. He felt the burde
of it, felt an undeniable urge to put it back to right
as quickly as he could.

He wondered if Lisbet had yet heard the news; h
would have liked to have told her himself, arranged a
rendezvous, taken her in his arms and shared th
wonder of his fortune. He would liked to hav
brought her here, squired her about the great empt
corridors, and explored with her the chambers locke

or countless years.

He longed for her just as consumingly as he had always done. The few weeks separation they had endured and his resolve at distance had not dimmed his yearning one measurable jot. Indeed, it seemed to have sharpened it more.

With late sunlight slanting across his shoulders now, he observed the neglected gardens. Scrubby plots of land they were, full of thistle and bindweed and twining honeysuckle. Tired roses struggled valiantly to raise their tender heads out of the tangle. The once-glorious yews strangled beneath strong tentacles of ivy. But he could not spare the capital to bring in an army of gardeners to clear it all, replant, and prune—not yet, anyway. Perhaps later, next year, or the next . . .

He found himself unable to look much beyond the present hour. When his future should have stretched promisingly before him like a straight, wide avenue lined with opportunity and privilege, it did not. It remained just as nebulous as ever.

While he silently pondered the landscape, a movement caught his eye, a darting flash of color. Leaning closer to the window, he peered through glass so old and bubbled it distorted the view. A figure hastened through the knee-high grass of the lawn, then angled along the path leading to the old gnarled arbor.

Forrest frowned. What business had Scottie Stone here?

Halting beneath a tree, the young man glanced about before idly reaching to steal a peach from its ripening boughs. Then he crossed his legs at the ankles and tipped back his cap, obviously waiting.

Presently Gretchen appeared, floating through the tussocky grass in yet another of Lady Sedgemoor's gowns.

Forrest narrowed his eyes, immediately suspiciou
He considered Gretchen his ward now, assuming re
sponsibility for her welfare in the face of Baldwin
incapacity. Besides, he had grown fond of her an
owed her an incalculable debt of gratitude which h
intended to repay with a most caring guardianship
Temptingly beautiful, innocent of mind, she had n
reason to meet a young man alone in the arbor, espe
cially one with Scottie Stone's insolent, undiscipline
manner.

Forrest sighed. The lady's maid would have to b
routed out from Agatha's command and sent imme
diately to fetch the young minx. And in the futur
Gretchen would need to be closely chaperoned.

He never finished his errand. Just as he reache
the Great Hall, a commotion sounded in the court
yard. Forrest was not only surprised but quite grati
fied to see the butler glide from the shadows and
with all the polished efficiency of a well-trained ser
vant, open the door with a dignified nod. He ushere
in a gentleman and a lady. The former Forrest recog
nized as Lieutenant Colonel Bevins of London.

The middle-aged officer, wearing country tweed
and an abundance of side whiskers, seemed for a mo
ment nonplussed. With his head back, he peruse
the height of the vast, ancient hall. Then, seeing For
rest's approach, greeted him with uncharacteristic ef
fusiveness.

"Captain York, old chap! Well, I scarcely expecte
this. Went to the village to ask where I might fin
you, and a gent directed me *here.*" He cleared hi
throat, still obviously confounded. "You've been hold
ing out on me—a marquess, no less."

Forrest put a hand on the man's shoulder. "I assur

you, I only just found out about the title myself. A case of mistaken identity, you might say," he added vaguely, not inclined to share detail.

His eyes moved to Bevin's companion then, a young woman in a genteel green traveling suit with a sweetly expressive face and hair the color of Lisbet's.

"Er—pardon me," Lieutenant Colonel Bevins blustered. "Forgot to introduce my daughter."

Her name was Beatrix, and Forrest judged her to be no more than twenty-one years of age. Quiet and graceful, she had a wide intelligent brow and an unpretentious air that—for the second time—brought Lisbet strongly to mind.

"We're sorry to intrude upon you, Lord Sedgemoor," she said demurely. "We were on our way to Scarborough to visit relations, and as Father had business to discuss with you, we hoped you wouldn't mind our calling." She dipped her head slightly, her eyes flicking about the dim, debris-strewn space. "I hope we haven't caught you at an inconvenient time—"

"Not at all," Forrest said easily, wondering where the devil he could comfortably seat his guests without dust choking them or cobwebs clinging to their clothes. Finally he opted for the terrace. Its paving stones were cracked and sprouting weeds, but at least a regular rainfall had kept them clean.

"I'm on holiday for the month," declared Lieutenant Colonel Bevins, settling himself down in an ornate cast-iron chair overlooking the disorderly garden. "Thought I'd take Beatrix up north to visit her mother's relations. I'm afraid we've neglected them a bit since Mrs. Bevins's passing two years ago."

Forrest murmured an appropriate condolence and glanced at the gentle-eyed Beatrix, thinking her period of mourning a possible reason for her unmarried state. She was very pretty, with a profile remarkably like—

With a frown he forced his eyes away.

"I decided to come and speak with you in person," Bevins continued. "Not only am I eager to get my hands upon those files of yours, I thought to persuade you to come back to London before long." He twisted his head about, his eyes scanning the venerable gray walls rising upward at his back. "But it rather seems you have a more attractive option, blast it all."

Forrest chuckled. "Nonetheless, I'd like to hear you out."

Bevins considered him. "Been chasing high adventure too long to settle easily into the life of a country gent, eh?"

Forrest's eyes flickered across Beatrix's face again. "Something like that."

"Well, then. Perhaps my case isn't so hopeless after all."

Forrest was relieved to see a maid and a footman wheeling out a trolley of refreshments then, though the tray creaked on ungreased wheels and the linen napkins showed threadbare in the sunlight. The cake looked appetizing enough, however, and steam wended invitingly from the silver teapot.

He rubbed a hand across his mouth, hiding a smile. He could just imagine Agatha somewhere deep in the bowels of the great house, barking out orders like a tyrant while her ever-slippery spectacles threatened to fly off her nose.

"Ever been to Afghanistan, Captain?" Bevins asked, eagerly helping himself to two of the cakes.

"Once or twice," Forrest replied, seeing the sunlight

glint gold off Beatrix's hair.

"Thought so. Know the language?"

"Passably well."

"Care to go back?"

"Maybe."

Beatrix looked up at her host at the words, and their eyes touched briefly before Forrest returned his gaze to her father's face.

"Would it be a long assignment?" he asked.

"A few months at most—depending, of course, upon your level of success. How's the knee?"

"On the mend."

"Good." Bevins suspended his chewing and raised a bushy eyebrow. "No new encumbrances, I presume. No wedding in the offing?"

Noticing that Beatrix was keeping her eyes carefully lowered at the question, Forrest replied, "No."

"Don't know how you've managed to elude the old noose this long, but I can't say I'm not glad. Makes you perfectly qualified." Bevins nudged his daughter's elbow. "In Captain York's—er—profession, it's best not to have a family. Makes a man a bit less daring and leaves a wife fretting back home, if you know what I mean."

She raised her lashes, looked fully into Forrest's eyes with a clear green gaze. "I'm sure I do."

That evening at dinner Forrest found himself astounded at the efficiency of the staff. A dining saloon, much smaller and more comfortable than the Great Hall, had been swept and polished, and the food, though a simple repast, proved delicious. The servants were liveried as well, their blue and ivory jackets obviously relics Agatha had dug out of a trunk somewhere. None of them fit; in fact, the taller footman, standing in breeches three inches too short for his legs, wore a perpetually red face. Embarrassed for the fellow, Forrest made a mental note to allot money to Agatha tomorrow for the making of new uniforms.

Once he had gotten over the initial pleasure of the improved state of his residence, he found his attention turned once again in Beatrix's direction. On impulse, he had invited her and her father to stay not only the night, but on their return journey if they liked. At the conclusion of the meal, he realized with disquiet that he had spent the duration attempting to discern exactly what it was about her face that made him think of Lisbet. On more than one occasion he had had to tear his eyes away from the contemplation of her eyes, brow, nose, and lips.

When he gallantly offered her his arm for an evening stroll in the garden and felt glad at her acceptance, he had the fleeting thought that she could have been dark-haired and coarse-featured and he would still have seen Lisbet's image somewhere in her demeanor. He would have seen it because he wanted to see it, was starved to see it.

The evening was cool and tranquil, as if settling down for the night. From the gardens the river winked through lacy trees, and Forrest could hear clearly its eternal swishing current. He could smell the damp moss of its banks as well and knew the blackberry vines clinging to its bridge would be burgeoning with purplish fruit. The cattails there would be tall and fuzzy brown, the sand warm.

Breathing deep of the spicy air, he experienced a heightened awareness of the woman who walked at his side. He was attentive to every tap of her slippered feet upon the paths, every ripple of her swaying skirts, and every dip of her smoothly coiffed head. As they meandered about the abandoned, dusk-shaded paths fragrant with wild carnations, he felt her soft hand upon his sleeve, heard her quiet voice in his ear, and knew it was not really Beatrix's hand he felt or her voice he heard. It was not really Beatrix's nearness that aroused his physical senses, sent desire rushing through his veins until he grew warm with it.

It was not the lieutenant colonel's daughter at all. It was Lord Thorpe's wife.

She was near. He could feel her presence, but though his eyes keenly scanned the darkening copses and cool blue fields, he could not catch even the merest glimpse of her.

But Lisbet saw him, her lover, strolling with another on his arm, one pretty and very young. Lingering beneath the canopy of a spreading oak near the bridge, dressed in a summer gown of rose, she watched. She had come to find him, her yearning past endurance. All afternoon while she had paced the gallery at Wexford Hall on restless feet, the river had seemed to call her out, whispering where to wait in order to get a glimpse of Anvil. She had not eaten, then refused to settle in the parlor with her needlework. Finally, after Sylvan dozed in his chair, she slipped out.

Now she followed Forrest and his companion with her eyes, losing sight before locating them again on the dusky terrace. She saw him open a pair of French doors for the lady and put a hand to her waist briefly, before escorting her inside to a room where warm light spread a fan upon the ground without.

Lisbet lingered an hour, watching the white petals of a rose turn sapphire with night, watching the nettles close up and the ferns droop with dew. She had hoped the river would call to Anvil as it had done to her, make him feel the same yearning she had felt. But though she waited, he did not come.

Turning, she trailed down to the river's edge, putting her back against the bridge, feeling its stones still warm from the day's vanished sun. Perhaps she had lost the love of her youth, the love of her life . . . lost him finally, forever. Not from distance or time or even circumstance. But simply from her own act of will, that choice of honor over heart she had made on the island.

As a result of that choice, Anvil had determined to make an ending between them—and the ending, it seemed, had truly come.

The possibility stunned her. She had never really credited it. These past weeks, in fact, she had clung strongly to hope after hearing of the strange quirk of fate that had changed Forrest York's life. He was the Marquess of Winterspell now, and surely he would not abandon a birthright so long deserved. Surely, with a private smile of irony on his face, he would stay and be its master. And with his staying, would he not want to resume the furtive, painfully sweet meetings he had always shared with her beneath the bridge? Could he resist the spell?

She breathed a deep and painful breath. Perhaps he could. Lord Nicholas Sedgemoor was a most eligible man now, owning vast properties that should be passed on through his line. He would need to take a wife. Already he strolled in the intimacy of evening with a lovely young woman. Would she be his marchioness soon and bear him heirs, heirs he could hold and love . . . and claim?

The sound of footsteps, slightly uneven on the

spongy path, alerted Lisbet, causing her to turn about and stare breathlessly through the darkness.

He approached.

He did not pause in his progress upon finding her, nor did he utter a word. He merely strode forward, took her roughly in his arms, and, with a violence akin to a dam bursting beneath a tidal wave, kissed her.

Her neck strained back with the force of his assault, and he supported her head with one hand, pulling her hips abruptly into his with the other. He seemed unable to touch enough of her, his fingers going first through her hair until it half-tumbled down, then to the curve of her waist, then to the swell of her hips. His kisses grew harder, more urgent, and she closed her eyes in both bliss and sweetest relief, knowing Anvil had been unable to break the bond that held them. He had been unable to break it with dispassion, with resolution, or even with the iron of his damned male pride. It was as alive as ever, and indestructible.

There was an anger in his body, a primitive masculine questing for dominance, perhaps even punishment. But she did not protest it, knowing from what source it sprung. He had failed in the attempt to stay away from her, and that failure of mastery over himself fueled his desperation.

Kissing her neck, lost with the wanting of her, he began to unfasten the buttons at her throat. He would never cease in his endeavor to posses her, she thought wildly, elatedly. He could not.

Clasping his hand, she drew it regretfully to her lips. "Should I call you Nicholas . . . ?" she breathed, reining him in from the racecourse he had been hurtling down.

In spite of himself, he smiled against her lips. "No. You shall call me Milord."

"Oh, Anvil!" she exclaimed, drawing back from him with an excited laugh. "Isn't it astounding? I was stunned to hear of it. The *Marquess of Winterspell!* Just imagine."

For a moment they did, both thinking how changed their existences would have been had Lord Nicholas Sedgemoor never been robbed of his rightful place.

"But however did you discover it?" Lisbet pressed after a moment. "I've managed to get only a few details."

Needing to touch, Forrest reached out and took a lock of her hair, letting it slide silkily through his fingers. "Have you ever made the acquaintance of Gretchen Sandown?"

"The poor, half-witted girl—"

"She's not half-witted," Forrest cut in, surprised at his own defensive urge. "She's just childlike in a certain manner. At any rate, she discovered a journal written by my mother, a journal which happened to mention—" he tapped his shoulder, "this not-so-cursed mark, as it turns out. I have no idea how the girl saw it in the first place, but suspect she spied on me while I worked shirtless out-of-doors. With a very mysterious air, she invited me to read the journal, assuring me I would find it most interesting. Which I did."

"And the old marquess . . . ?"

"He is my uncle, of course," Forrest explained, going on to detail his relative's treachery.

"What will you do about him?"

Forrest shrugged. "I'll not throw him out. He's in his dotage, after all. But over time he has managed to bring the estate to its knees. 'Twill take years of careful management to bring it back to the profitable enterprise it once was. And the repairs . . ." He broke off with an expressive sigh.

Lisbet bent her head, slanting her eyes to watch the tiny black pool of water eddying near her feet. When she spoke, both hope and fear made her breathless. "So, you'll stay on . . . ?"

Forrest did not answer. Instead he said with seduction in his voice, "I didn't come here to talk, you know. . . . I came here to do this."

Demonstrating, he took her lips, groaning when she gave him measure for measure and slid her hands behind his head. She wanted to press him for an answer concerning his staying on; she wanted to ask him about the woman he had escorted only an hour ago. But she did not. Time was too precious tonight, and quickly running out.

"What's that noise?" Lisbet asked after a moment, drawing slightly away.

Listening, they both discerned a burst of soft but distinctly feminine laughter, accompanied by a rustling in the underbrush not more than a few yards away.

"That bothersome girl," Forrest grumbled, assuming Gretchen had come to spy again. "Follows me as closely as my own shadow. It's long past time to curb her."

Striding up the path toward a likely privet, he glowered, hearing the laughter again just a few feet away. He parted the long shielding boughs of a willow and, behind it, discovered not only his ward but . . . Scottie Stone.

Shirtless, the youth lay atop Gretchen's half-garbed body, so intent upon the fulfillment of his passions he was unaware of an onlooker's presence.

The sight of him enraged Forrest. The young blackguard was ever overstepping bounds, disregarding authority, defying respect. He had prodded Forrest, goaded him, even punched him in the jaw. Now he sought to dally with a girl who was not only Forrest's cousin, but a girl who could not possibly understand the significance of the liberties being taken with her.

Ignoring Lisbet's cry behind him, he seized Scottie by the arms and hauled him roughly backwards. "Get away from her!"

The lad's immediate reaction was to lash out a fist, which Forrest dodged before countering another more collected attack.

Breathing hard, his reddening face twisted in rage, Scottie bawled out, "You have no right to keep me from her!"

"I have every right," Forrest declared calmly. "She's my responsibility, and I shall protect her from unprincipled boys like you seeking a night's diversion."

Gretchen had been crouching beneath the hedge. Now, unfolding long legs, she emerged, taking a significant stance at Scottie's back. In the manner of a thwarted guardian, Forrest glowered at her, but she only returned the glare with unintimidated defiance.

Her show of loyalty toward the youth caused Forrest chagrin and angered him all the more. Obviously Scottie had manipulated Gretchen into a relationship over which she could only lose. Once he had deflowered her and bragged about it to the village lads, he would have no more to do with her. Or so Forrest assumed.

"I love her," the young man proclaimed in a challenging tone, dissolving Forrest's line of thought. "I intend to marry her, elope if need be."

A terrible sense of the past began to prick Forrest's consciousness. As he stared at Scottie's rebellious face, his disheveled state and possessive stance, as he took in Gretchen's tousled fair hair and bewildered eyes, he experienced a sharp and sorrowful empathy for the pair.

Immediately he gentled his rigid tone. "She can't be a proper wife to you, lad," he said, trying reason instead of force. "She can't be a proper wife to anyone. She's—"

"She's not daft like people think," Scottie cut in defensively. "She's bright and clever, and she cares for me just as I do her. It's true she's not like everyone else, but we'll go away, we'll go where no one knows us, and I'll take care of her. Her grandfather can't object on the grounds of her being Quality, because no top-lofty lord would marry her for the reasons *you* say."

Leaning to jerk his shirt from the ground, Scottie firmed his jaw and snapped, "So leave us alone."

"No." Forrest moved solidly to bar his way. "I could never allow it. Gretchen cannot possibly understand the level of commitment marriage requires. She is too innocent in mind, a child in many ways, and it's likely she will always be."

Balling up his shirt, Scottie stepped forward, and in his eyes Forrest saw a more manly determination than he had ever seen there before, a maturity previously lacking.

"She's young and free of ties," the lad proclaimed firmly. "And so am I. We're hurting no one by what we do."

Distraught, Lisbet stepped closer so that her shoulder brushed Forrest's sleeve. The thought of her son's leaving shook her, and she felt a great sadness that he had never confided his secret relationship with Gretchen to her. If he had, perhaps she could have helped them, found a way . . .

Scottie's eyes were fastened solemnly upon Lisbet now. Within them she saw his great love for her, an abiding love, and yet, at the same time, the gleam of accusation.

She opened her mouth to speak, to explain somehow, but he only turned his gaze to Forrest, uttering one quietly brutal sentence: "At least I'm not committing adultery with another man's wife."

For a moment the ugly words hung suspended, vibrating upon the air. Lisbet stared at Scottie, a cry of profound hurt dying in her throat.

Forrest stepped forward, his face grim and hard, his eyes condemning Scottie in the harshest way. "You have done her a grievous injustice, she who has given you nothing but care and love. Other than the services you've been amply paid to perform, what have you given her in return?"

When the young man said nothing, Forrest went on. "I'll tell you what you've given her. Duplicity. You've carried tales to her husband—who is not as imperceptive as you think—reported facts to him that seem what they are not. You've made your motives seem pure when you knew they were nothing more than retaliations toward me. Well, your talebearing has hurt me not at all, but it has caused both Lord Thorpe and your mistress great unnecessary pain. You, Mr. Stone," he finished with damning condemnation, "are lost to all sense of honor."

The words seemed to devastate the youth. For a moment he appeared shaken. And then, as if energized by a sudden rush of helpless fury, he struck out at his accuser with a fist.

Forrest reacted, countering the move with a strong upraised arm.

"Nooo!" Lisbet screamed at him, horrified, her voice shrilling with anguish and despair. "For God's sake. Forrest! Don't you realize he's your son!"

Chapter Nineteen

The very air seemed to freeze. If the wind whirred, if a night bird fluttered, if the river continued in its babbling flow, the sounds were never heard. No one heard anything but the echo of Lady Thorpe's words. Even the silver-horned moon rising behind Winterspell Tower seemed to pause in its ascent and listen.

As if pushed by an unseen force, Scottie Stone took an unsteady step backward, his face paralyzed into lines of disbelief. For endless moments he simply stared at the man who had just been named his sire, seemingly searching for confirmation that Lisbet's announcement had been untrue.

In the darkness Forrest's expression was undiscernible, but Lisbet knew his eyes were fixed levelly upon Scottie's face, penetrating the blackness like twin torches. In that instant she guessed he was mentally computing the boy's age, comparing it to the date when he had lain with her beneath the bridge. She could see him fit the pieces together one by one: her going away to Italy, her resulting marriage to Lord Thorpe, her special and heretofore inexplicable attachment to an undisciplined young groomsman.

Though little light aided him, and though Scottie's

face was pale with hostility, Forrest could see the mother's features in the son's, see them just as if his eyes had only a second ago been opened. He could see his own there, too, blended with Lisbet's in the creation of a child. It solved the mystery he had mulled over; it answered so many previously unanswerable questions.

As he stared at the young man, a barrage of conflicting emotions besieged him. He felt shame over his lack of love and tenderness toward the boy, chagrin at his frank dislike. He felt a fool, as if he should have somehow sensed this most elemental relationship. But most of all he felt immense remorse that he had been denied the opportunity to be a father, hold this once golden-haired babe, nurture and direct him through his life. Fate had done more than deprive Forrest of property and title: it had deprived him of his son.

"It's not true!" Scottie shouted, his outrage vibrating off the arches of the bridge. Helplessly he glared from Forrest to Lisbet and back again, but neither the grim black eyes nor the swimming hazel ones gave support to his negation.

" 'Tis true, Scottie," Lisbet said somberly. "You must believe it."

In fury he turned upon her. "Why should I believe it? Why? Why should I believe that you've kept your son a groomsman all his life—a bloody hireling—while you lived the life of a queen in your palace?"

"Scottie!" Anguish throbbed in Lisbet's cry. "Do you think I *wanted* to keep hidden the secret of your birth? Do you think it was some whim of mine or that I was ashamed of who you were? Well, I was not. I have loved you always, but I was a child when you were born and under my father's harsh control.

Indeed, there was a time when I feared he would take you from me forever. I did the best I could for you, always longing to confide the secret of your parentage. And now I regret that the knowledge had to come to you so shockingly. But yours was an illegitimate birth, and proclaiming it would have ignored all wisdom." Remembering Anvil she murmured, "You would have been shunned."

"I still resent your keeping it from me!" Scottie shouted, his emotions putting him beyond reason. "It clearly served your own best interests, not mine!"

Forrest stepped between them. "You must trust her judgment, Scottie. You do not know the details of your mother's predicament."

"I trust her not at all now. Why should I trust her?"

"I should think you would feel honored to have her for your mother," Forrest replied gravely.

"With you as my father?" The youth gave him a bitter laugh. "Should I be happy about that? Are you happy to discover that I am your long-lost by-blow?"

"For the love of God, Scottie . . ." Lisbet gasped, her face stricken. "I beg you to rescind your words!"

"Let it pass, Lisbet," Forrest cut in, imperturbed. "I don't blame him. God knows it's not difficult to understand how he feels."

Instead of softening the edge of Scottie's umbrage, Forrest's tolerance seemed to provoke the boy's resentment to greater heights. "Perhaps I should feel quite proud," he countered with a sneer. "After all, I have a countess for a mother and a bleedin' marquess for a father. Between them, surely I can manage to get a head groomsmanship, maybe even a room of my own before long."

"Your bitterness can serve no purpose," Forrest

warned. "I suggest you take a day or two to reflect. Perhaps then you'll view things in a different light. All three of us have much to sort out between us."

"Then you must sort it out without me," Scottie declared, taking Gretchen by the hand. "I'll make it easy for you—I'll leave Winterspell and never return. Oh, and don't worry," he answered with a contemptuous smile, "your secret is safe with me. I wouldn't dream of letting the cat out of the bag, tell anyone what *noble* blood runs in my veins."

With that, he started off with Gretchen in tow, and though Lisbet would have followed and begged him not to leave, Forrest prevented her with a barring arm.

"Lisbet, let him go."

She struggled against the grip of his fingers to no avail. "That is an easy thing for you to say!" she exclaimed bitingly. "You have no liking for him, none at all!"

"And how the hell could I?" he demanded in exasperation, clasping her arms in a steely hold. "You have denied me knowledge of him until any reconciliation is impossible. Why, Lisbet, *why?*"

"Need you ask?" she cried, staring up at him with incredulous eyes. "Only think on it a moment with that calculating brain of yours and my reasons should be obvious."

"Don't fling your sarcasm at me, milady," Forrest upbraided, tightening his hold of her arms. "You bore my son, for God's sake, and I demand to know why you kept it from me until now. How much longer would you have gone? Judging by the impulsive nature of your revelation, it's damned obvious you didn't intend to speak of it tonight. Did you plan never to enlighten me?"

"I am astounded by your complete lack of understanding," Lisbet railed. She was indignant over his accusing manner and his callousness for her plight. For nearly twenty years she had protected Scottie's identity single-handedly, and now, when she had shared it at last with the man who should have welcomed the knowledge, he had reproached her for it.

"And why, milady, should I be understanding?" Forrest retaliated, his eyes fierce beneath their handsome brows. "You lied to me. I asked you if you had borne my child, and quite coolly—with touching sentiment, as I recall—you flatly denied it. Why? Were you so displeased over having to bear my son that you thought to square accounts by withholding the knowledge of his existence from me? Or did you simply distrust me, assume I would use the knowledge to hurt Scottie in some way?"

Lisbet glared at him with unforgiving eyes. "Well, you certainly did not use the knowledge wisely, did you? You did not embrace him or give the merest sign that the relationship pleased you. You could have restrained him," she cried hotly. "Instead you have driven my son away!"

Wrenching her arms free, Lisbet whirled from him and, in a billow of light summer skirts, fled down the pathway toward Wexford Hall.

Instinctively Forrest reached out a hand, intent upon detaining her. Then he checked himself, letting his hand drop away as he watched her disappear like a shadowy wraith through the black-green foliage.

Feeling drained of emotion, he turned away after awhile and slowly went home.

Upon his return he was relieved to find that, in his absence, his guests had gone up to their hastily cleaned rooms to retire. Yanking the tie from the colar of his black evening attire, he limped down to the itchens in search of Agatha.

She was there, standing before an open cupboard otting down notes on a pad of paper. Her usually vell-restrained mousy hair was in disarray, and the vhiteness about her mouth showed she was on the rink of exhaustion. Even though his mind was louded with other thoughts, Forrest marveled at all he had done in one day—organizing a staff, preparng a dinner and chambers for unexpected guests, nd then assigning accommodations for the tired serants. He hoped that the expensive butler he had ired would assume much of the more taxing responibilities from Agatha on the morrow. He did not inend that she be overworked.

The housekeeper noticed his presence and turned bout from her task. "Cap'n! I might still call ya that, nightn't I?" she inquired a bit stiffly. "Or do ya preer the grander title now?"

He sat down at the long kitchen table. "Call me vhatever you like, Agatha."

"I was just makin' a list of supplies," she explained, vaving her paper and pencil. "Fair boggles my mind ust thinkin' about all the food them high-nosed Lonlon servants will be wolfin' down three times a day. And, o' course, I'll be wantin' ta serve you and yer guests fancy meals. At least that cook seems ta know vhat she's about."

"My compliments to you all," Forrest said sincerely. And most especially to you. Get a good rest tonight. And tomorrow don't tire yourself out. That's an orler."

Already she was bustling about putting a kettle on o boil and setting out a cup and saucer. When she urned about again, she caught sight of his hollowed face and creased clothing and contemplated him silently for a moment before asking, "What is it, Cap'n? I swear, you look fair flagged." Her voice held all the quiet concern of one who loved him dearly.

Rubbing a hand over his jaw, he regarded her through bleak dark eyes shadowed with fatigue. "I must ask a favor of you tonight. Is there a male member of the new staff, a footman perhaps, who you feel you can particularly trust?"

She thought a moment and then nodded slowly. "Yes."

Forrest withdrew a slim leather purse from the inner pocket of his jacket and laid it upon the table. "Then I would like you to entrust this to him and send him on a mission posthaste."

Reaching out a hand, Agatha took the purse and slid it inside her apron pocket.

"It's to be given to Scottie Stone," Forrest instructed levelly. "I suspect he's at the railway station waiting for the morning train. He has Gretchen with him."

Agatha could not contain her astonishment. "That young scoundrel isn't makin' off with her?" she gasped, putting a maidenly hand to her throat.

"I have no reason to doubt that she's going of her own free will."

"But you'll never let her . . . ?" The housekeeper exhibited shock at the mere notion.

"I am not taking this lightly, Agatha, believe me. But Gretchen's of age. Short of making a prisoner of her in this place, there's nothing I can do to stop her going. If I hauled her back now, it would only be a matter of time until she flew the coop again."

The kettle began to sing a shrill note, and with an impatient hand, Agatha went to take it from the fire.

quickly pouring a cup of tea for her employer and setting it down before him.

"But the girl is—" She halted, as if unsure what adjective to use.

"I know." Forrest watched the steam rise up from his cup before continuing. "And yet, I wonder if we haven't all misjudged her, underestimated her in some way. After all, she's lived most of her life with a half-mad, irresponsible old man whose given her little encouragement toward education and no chances at all for socialization. Perhaps in her loneliness she's created a fantasy existence for herself as a comfort. Now with the attentions of a man who cares for her and a more normal life, we can hope she will develop to be more normal herself."

Agatha appeared doubtful. Sliding the spectacles from her nose, she rubbed them vigorously with a corner of her apron as if to give vent to her agitation. "And Scottie Stone? Do ya honestly believe he cares for her?"

"He says he does."

Replacing her spectacles, the housekeeper sighed, then patted the purse in her pocket. "Should I go now ta fetch the footman?"

Forrest nodded. "You remember the gown Gretchen was wearing? Describe it to him and he should have no trouble identifying the pair. And Agatha—" He looked hard at her. "Once the man has confirmed their names and handed over the money, he must not say that it comes from me. He must say it comes from Lady Thorpe. You must make that clear."

A silence fell while she regarded him keenly.

Beneath her discerning scrutiny Forrest ran a hand over eyes that were suddenly haunted. His voice came thick and strained. "I want the two of them to have a chance, that's all . . . the best chance possible."

His strong shoulders slumped then as if with the weight of the world, and he added, "Scottie is my son."

Immediately Agatha reached to put a hand upon his own, "I know, Cap'n York," she said with infinite care. "I could've told ya that. I could've told ya the night he came to the cottage and struck ya with his angry young fist."

"Well, my dear pet," Sylvan pronounced, coming out onto the dawn-tinted terrace at Wexford Hall the next morning. "I know you'll take this news dreadfully hard, but your young groomsman has run off, it seems."

Lisbet sat at a table, listlessly holding a cup of cooling chocolate in the palm of her hand. "Yes," she said with no emotion in her voice. "I heard."

Moving closer, he stuck both thumbs in his waistband and stared silently out at the view of the river, acting as if he wanted to speak but was unsure of what to say. "I know you had a soft spot for him in your heart," he offered at last, understanding in his tone.

Lisbet nodded, not wanting to make comment, relieved that her husband would be spared the knowledge of her secret. She felt numbed of all emotion, having spent the night shedding tears over the loss of her son and bitterly lamenting the argument with Forrest. Though she had always attempted to use good judgment where Scottie's identity was concerned, trying to spare the feelings of all involved in her complicated net, she knew she had thoroughly failed both father and son.

Sylvan pulled up a chair beside her and sat down, the young summer sun sparkling off the rainbow of rings he wore upon four of his stubby fingers. Reaching out a hand, he gently placed it atop his wife's, as if sensing her private distress but judging it best not to question it.

She wondered at the change in him. Since his recovery from the bee stings, he was quieter than she had ever known him to be and prone to frequent bouts of pathos. Even more disconcerting was the alteration in his manner toward her. Though he was deferent in the extreme, his sad eyes no less adoring he made no demands upon her time as he had done before. Even as midsummer's eve—and all it signified—now approached, he made no reference to it, giving her both guilty relief and unnameable concern over these changes. She realized Sylvan's garrulousness and high emotional states had all but disappeared, only to be replaced with a strange depression.

"I believe I should like to sketch this view," he said now, nodding toward the gardens with their undulating borders abloom with colorful flowers. "I particularly like the play of light beneath the hydrangeas. Can you see it shifting, my dove?"

She smiled at him, glancing at the distant blooms. After the accident Sylvan had never explained, she had ordered all flower urns removed from the terrace, and the beds nearest the house had been dug up and replanted with nonblossoming shrubbery.

"I'll go and fetch your paper and pencils for you," she offered, putting down her cup and rising. She was happy to find him regaining an interest in his old pursuits and would take what steps she could to encourage it.

Gliding along the cool polished halls, she entered the library, greeting the cockatoo on his perch before proceeding to Sylvan's desk. As always, it was orderly, with recent correspondence tucked neatly in one drawer, pens and ink in another, and creamy stationery in the lowest. She counted out four or five sheets of sketching paper and was on the brink of closing the drawer when a letter caught her eye. Wedged between the drawer and the desk frame, it was torn nearly in half. Thinking it must have slipped into the crevice unnoticed, she carefully eased it out so as not to cause further damage to it. In doing so, she caught sight of her name neatly scripted at the top, and idly read the message penned below it.

I love thee, my Lisbet, my life. I have sought to give thee everything my gold can buy. I have worshipped thee, adored thee on my knees. Forgive me for my desire of you. 'tis base, selfish, impure—isn't it absurd to ask the fairest flower to lie down with a worm? Though I have failed miserably in my efforts at selfless love, I shall attempt a compensation. I go now to give thee thine heart's desire. A goddess deserves a god. S

It was dated the day of his accident.

For a moment Lisbet was incapable of movement. Her eyes scanned the words again and yet again, until the terrible significance of what she had discovered fully penetrated her understanding.

"Merciful God . . ." she breathed finally, staring unseeing now at the paper. Sylvan had devised it all, encouraging her holiday on the island while arranging for her to have an intimate rendezvous there with Forrest. How could he have done such a appalling thing! *Why* would he have done it?

She knew the answer to that grievous question

even as it flashed across her mind. Sylvan had arranged the holiday because he had witnessed the love she and Forrest shared and thought to aid it.

Though they had both attempted to exercise constraint while in his presence, Sylvan was ever shrewd and intuitive. He had surely read in their eyes what they had foolishly believed was sealed in their hearts. And though the episode of her near-fatal bout with laudanum was a hazy remembrance, she knew the intensity of feeling between her and Forrest must have been a glaring thing to even the most imperceptive eyes.

And then, of course, there had been Scottie's talebearing to Sylvan, his likely embroidered speculations inflaming a cuckolded husband even more . . .

She looked again at the letter in her hand, its full significance shattering her composure.

Her husband had thought to free her, thought to give her one last gift, the greatest gift he believed he could give—his death. He had failed, thank God! But how he must have suffered to have fallen into such a mad, self-martyring state.

Shaking her head in wretchedness, Lisbet laid her face in her hands, stunned by what she had learned, stunned that Sylvan had nearly destroyed himself so that she might have what she wanted most.

"Every life I have touched has been blighted," she whispered brokenly to herself, gripped by the most anguished form of self-condemnation. "Every one . . ."

She told herself she should have left Scottie with his foster parents, anonymously sending him money for expensive schools and luxuries, leaving him to grow up without her. But she had been too selfish, wanting to keep him as close as possible, wanting the pleasure of watching him grow, wanting to enjoy his presence even if that must be accomplished through deceit.

As for Forrest, since his return to Winterspell she had gone to great lengths to see him, keep him near even though she had nothing but stolen moments and sad rejections to offer him. She had caused him torment, sought to keep the bond that tied them secure at any cost to his own peace of mind.

And Sylvan . . . What had she done to Sylvan?

With trembling hands she wedged the letter back in place, then shoving the drawer shut, hastened from the room. Down the corridors she ran with lifted skirts, passing empty chambers and echoing galleries. Crossing an arched passageway, she at last arrived at the austere little chapel, where she slammed the heavy doors behind her, turned the ornate black key, and went down upon her knees.

Frenziedly she reached for the chain beneath her bodice. Then, breaking it loose from about her neck with a violent yank, she took hold of the dangling gold locket and let it lay upon her palm. With a deep and torturous breath she closed her fingers about the charm, tightening her fist about it until the ring at the top cut into her flesh.

"It must be done," she breathed aloud, closing her eyes and leaning back her head. "It must be done . . ."

In a gesture of supreme significance, she laid the token dearest to her upon the altar.

Forrest had determined to see Lisbet before the day was out. He feared his goodbye to Lieutenant Colonel Bevins and Beatrix was abrupt, but his temper was tightly coiled and his mood impatient. He had already made a less-than-communicative breakfast companion—to Beatrix's obvious dismay—and then had ridden out almost upon the heels of their carriage horses in order to escape the confinement of the house. Pell-mell he had ridden over hill and meadow, venting frustration till Flambeau's chestnut hide had gleamed with flecks of sweat and foam had gathered beneath his bit.

All the while, Lisbet's words drummed in his head, keeping a persistent rhythm with the hammering of the steed's hooves.

Do you realize he is your son . . . ? Do you realize he is your son . . . your son . . . your son . . . ?

Swerving off the road at last, Forrest rode toward Wexford Hall, halting upon a heather-quilted rise giving clear view of the estate grounds. He hoped to see Lisbet walking in the gardens or emerging from the stable for a ride. He planned to signal her, take her deep into the woods. There he would hold her, make amends, ask tenderly about the details of Scottie's birth.

More than ever now, he felt bound to her, fiercely protective, realizing what a burden the keeping of her secret must have been. Once he had had time to think, in the quiet hours of night, he knew she had done her best to make the proper decisions concerning Scottie's identity and blamed her for nothing.

When she had not appeared by noontime, Forrest gave up his vigil on the hillside and allowed Flambeau his head to go home. Once there, he hastily scrawled a message and bade the footman see that it was discreetly passed to Lady Thorpe's hand.

Just after eventide Lisbet met him at the bridge precisely as he had arranged. He had arrived an hour before her and sat quietly upon the bank in a place where clover grew lush and sweet. When she appeared against the backdrop of the arches, he stood, and striding forward, he pulled her close into his arms.

"Forgive me, Lisbet," he said, pressing her tightly to his chest. "I spoke to you in anger last evening, lost control of my damnable temper before I had time to reason."

"Let's speak of it no more," she pleaded, the weight of what she was about to do deepening her tone. "It is over."

"No. I insist that we speak of it." He bade her sit down in the place where he had spread his coat. "Tell me about my son, everything about him. From the first."

Lisbet sank to her knees, letting her eyes wander longingly over the length of her lover's legs in their polished riding boots and up to the generous shoulders draped in a white shirt made shadowy-blue with night. Lastly she searched the dear achingly handsome face she loved so well.

"What would you like to know?" she asked, keeping herself a little apart from his warm familiar shoulder.

Thinking her strange remoteness a product only of lingering petulance, he disregarded it, reaching out a hand to pull her close. With a supporting arm about her waist, he said, "I want to know the course of your life from the day I left Winterspell. I want to know about your pregnancy, about your father's treatment of you, and how you came to marry Sylvan. It is time you told me the truth, Lisbet—all of it."

She breathed deep of the night air, her voice trembling with the relief of sharing with the man she loved memories both painful and poignant. When she spoke of their son's birth, she clasped Forrest's strong warm hand, relating the particulars of the event with all the loving pride of any mother. Glad to voice it at last, she went on to communicate the anguish of a young girl tyrannized by an unrelenting father and coerced by him into a marriage she did not want.

All the while Forrest held her with tenderness, stroking her hair, and listening with a frown. A few times he swore beneath his breath when she related some mistreatment at her father's hands.

"After Father died," she finished quietly, "I fetched Scottie from the sponsor family where he had been living. Father had agreed before his death to obtain papers recording Scottie's birth to a soldier and his wife who had both succumbed to typhus. Secure in the knowledge that no living soul knew the truth of his birth but myself, that he would never be labeled a bastard child, I brought him home to me." She bent her head, plucking at the stems of clover. "I had intended to send him to university in a year or two so that he might enter a profession—the master at the village school always said he was a bright lad. But . . ."

She trailed the thought and, staring out at the river, ended softly, "I always thought you would come back. After Father banished you, I listened every night for the sound of pebbles thrown against my window, hoping you'd come to spirit me away. I looked for you in every shadow, in every secret place, and came daily to the bridge. When you never appeared, I was desolate. And then I discovered I was with child and began to love the baby before 'twas even born. I dreamed of the day I could tell you . . ." Her voice quavered. "But in all the years, you never so much as sent a message to me."

Though the words would seem to be condemnation of his neglect, the bitterness Lisbet had once felt had long since healed, leaving only sadness to subdue her voice.

With gentle hands Forrest pushed her back so that the two of them lay side by side, Lisbet's head pillowed upon the firm curve of his bicep, her hands entwined with his.

"I was a boy of sixteen, Lisbet," he said after a moment, speaking with his lips against the top of her head. "Friendless and without a penny in my pocket. How could I have snatched you from beneath your father's watchful eye? And if I had, what means would there have been to keep you? Think on it. Lord Tattershall could have moved heaven and earth to find us, and I've no doubt he would have."

For a moment she lay still, feeling the strong pulse of his vein against her ear, hearing the rush of the river that swelled just inches from their feet. "I suppose I understood the futility of our situation, even at fourteen. Yet I always hoped I'd find you waiting here for me one day, your arms outstretched and beckoning, that devilish grin dimpling your face."

"And now, I am here," he whispered, raising up on his elbow and bending over her. "Now I am."

He kissed her with a lingering sweetness, no hurry in his manner, as if he meant to keep her long and savor every moment of it. With reverent hands he touched every plane of her delicate face, explored the arch of her neck, put his lips to the hollow below each ear. He wooed her with more patience than he had ever done before, partly out of remorse but mostly out of poignant love.

Against all reason she embraced him wildly and with breathless urgency, knowing time was on the verge of ending for them once and for all. With a cry she drew his face to hers one last time, looked into the dark depths of his eyes, and traced with her fingers the firm curve of his lower lip.

"Anvil . . ." she breathed in utter anguish. "I cannot come here to meet you again."

He put his mouth on hers, kissing her, failing to understand. "We'll find another place . . . a more private place."

"No." The agony in her tone arrested him, causing him to draw back and search her face with consternation.

"My beloved . . ." she said with torment, taking his face between her hands. "You told me once that there must be an ending between us, a final parting. And though I wish to God it could be otherwise, I have come to realize you were right in your judgment."

Forrest sat up, his movement violent, his tone both harsh and disbelieving. "What are you saying?"

Slowly Lisbet arose as well, leaving the tender clover where they had lain together, her body's imprint still upon it. "I am at a crossroads, Forrest, and must make a cruel decision. Only today I discovered that Sylvan tried to take his life—he deliberately allowed himself to be stung by the bees hoping to die. He even arranged our time together on the Isle of Wight. I'm certain it was he who sent you the letter asking you to come to Ventnor."

"Are you saying he wanted us to be together?" Forrest asked, ready to discredit the notion.

She nodded, shifting to her knees. "I found a letter he had written, one he had obviously intended me to find only after his death. In it, he expressed his love for me, his own sense of unworthiness. Through suicide he thought to give me freedom from our marriage and from what he considered to be his loathsome presence. He said—" She faltered upon the remembered words. "He said that a goddess deserved a god."

Forrest spoke sharply. "Are you certain this is not some clever ploy of his to—"

"No." Her tone was definite. "It was quite genuine. I have made him wretched, Forrest!" she cried. "While he has done nothing but adore me, I have repaid him with selfishness. I said vows with him, vows I have never honored. Upon finding his letter today I realized it's time I did."

In one agile move Forrest stood up, dragging her to her feet with him. "What are you telling me?" he demanded in a dangerous tone.

"I am saying that it's time I became a proper wife to Sylvan," she announced with quiet conviction. "It's time I gave him the best of myself for the years we have left together. I intend to go to him tonight, I—"

"The hell you do!" Forrest shouted in a furious voice. "You belong to me and no other. Deny that you do!"

She said nothing, but her face was grave with resolution.

"What of your vows to me, Lisbet?" Forrest asked more quietly then, anguish so clear in his eyes she had to look away. "What of those?"

"Spoken long ago by children," she breathed.

"Children who *loved!*" he countered in gathering ire, "Children who made a *son* together."

"And where is that son now, my beloved?" she posed quietly. "Where is he now?"

She could see the pain come into his face at her accusation; she could feel it in the quiver of his hands where they so savagely grasped her arms.

"You are strong, Forrest," she said almost as a plea. "You always have been. No matter what trials life has thrown your way, you've managed to survive them all. You will find a way to bear the pain of this . . . just as I will."

"No!" Seizing her by the waist, he crushed her to him, the violence in his body causing him to bruise her flesh with his hands. "I'll not let you go, by God! I'll not let you walk away. You'll not go writhe in the bed of another man while your lips are still hot from mine!"

She struck him, struck twice the face she loved so well.

"We are no more!" she shouted at him ruthlessly. "Do you hear? *We . . . are . . . no . . . more.*"

She thought he could not have been more stunned had she thrust a sword through his chest. He stared down at her with eyes so fiercely black and yet so vulnerable she had to turn away to keep herself from crumpling at his feet.

She heard him cry her name—heard him cry it twice, thrice—but she refused to heed him. Instead she fled on trembling legs, running from the man she had loved and wounded, running to Wexford Hall.

Before she had quite reached the gates, before she could pass through them and slam shut their clanging locks behind her, a sound pierced the air. It was long and low and masculine.

And she knew from whence it came: she knew it was the howling sound of Anvil's heartbreak.

Chapter Twenty

With nerveless fingers Lisbet set the hairbrush aside, drew her silken wrapper more closely about her shoulders, and stared at herself in the looking glass. Her face was pale, her eyes large and dark, their expression almost blank. She had such a tight rein over her emotions she could see strain pulling at the corners of her mouth. Later she would let her grief free, shut herself in her suite of rooms and scream if necessary to ease the pain. But for now, she must bury it.

She had made a decision and she would carry it through to the finish. It gave her no comfort that her choice had been the most honorable one, the most unselfish. And it lessened the agony not at all to know that somewhere in the ancient walls of a castle not far away, another shared her sense of loss.

With movements slow and mechanical, Lisbet stood up from the tapestried bench, opened a drawer of her vanity, and removed from the scented paper liner a length of ribbon. Blue, it was—for fidelity. Tying it about the long fall of her hair, she crossed the room, opened the door of the adjoining master dressing room, and stood with a cool hand upon the latch of Sylvan's chamber.

Then she entered.

She had always found her husband's room particularly curious. He had collected pieces exported from all parts of the world and, in this one crowded space, amassed them. Rattan from India, lacquered chests from China, Louis XIV chairs, a black oak bed from Scotland, and Japanese silk-screened wallpaper all vied for attention. Silken fringes and braids of gold edged every fabric, and a crystal chandelier dripped from the ceiling. Two granite pharaoh hounds did sentry duty on either side of the bed, while a collection of porcelain elephants paraded trunk to tail across the mantel shelf.

Most impressively, twin Ionic columns purchased from an antiquities dealer in Greece rose upward to the ceiling, lending a look of ancient grandeur. Between them Sylvan had positioned a temple chair once belonging to a Turkish sultan, and he sat upon its tasseled cushion now, facing away from his visitor.

Apparently her quiet entry caught his ear, however. "Have you had a pleasant evening, my pet?" he inquired solicitously.

Lisbet made no answer but went instead to a beryl inlaid cabinet and, opening it, removed a bottle of brandy and two crystal snifters. She poured a measure in each and, after crossing the floral-patterned carpet, handed one to Sylvan.

Carefully he marked the page in his poetry volume and set it aside. Then he stood and bowed eloquently from the waist. "Thank you, my dear," he said, raising up his glass. "Shall I make a toast in your honor?"

She met his eyes and, searching them deeply, thought the warm brown depths more doleful than she had ever seen them.

"To you . . ." he said simply, waiting for Lisbet to touch her glass to his.

As they each sipped, she had no doubt that Sylvan knew her reason for coming to him tonight. Never had she previously entered her husband's quarters unless it was to tend him in sickness or to admire some new treasure he had acquired. Moreover, her appearance would have told him much, for not only was she attired in a sheer crimson wrapper and gown, her hair was unpinned. She had rarely allowed him to see it thus, the few times she had being accidental occasions when he had caught her unawares.

To add to her sensuous demeanor, she was perfumed and barefoot, having just bathed the soil of the riverbank from her skin. And if these were not enough clues as to her purpose, Lisbet sensed Lord Thorpe's uncanny intuition alone would have given him the foreknowledge.

After they had drunk a little of the brandy, Lisbet set down her glass and unhastily, as if in ritual, went to extinguish the single lamp illuminating the room. With no ado, Sylvan went to open a drawer to his desk, retrieved a match, and lit a pair of tapers. After carrying them to a table beside the scarlet-hung bed, he sat down upon the coverlet and, saying nothing, waited.

Lisbet moved to draw back the linens and set aside the bolster, her hands cold but steady, her mind fixed only upon the fulfillment of her obligation, an obligation she hoped would finally eliminate the despair from Sylvan's eyes—and, if the truth were admitted, eliminate her own burden of guilt once and for all.

"You have sent him away from you." Sylvan's bald statement interrupted the heavy hush, arresting Lisbet's hands upon the ivory satin pillows.

She looked up from across the length of the bed and, with no emotion, said, "Yes."

He shook his head sadly. " 'There are two Souls, whose equal flow in gentle stream so calmly run, that when they part—they part?—Ah no! They cannot part—those Souls are One.' "

"Sylvan . . ." Coming around the footboard, Lisbet took hold of her husband's crooked hands and raised them to her cheek. "This is our night together, the night we should have shared many years ago. It serves no purpose now to speak of subjects painful to us both."

"Ah, no. I think you are wrong, my pet," he argued gently, his smile fond but very sorrowful. "I think we should have spoken of the painful things—all of them—right at the beginning. Instead, for a very long time, we have had to play an exceedingly pointless game of charades, have we not? Complete with false smiles and elaborate masks."

She knew he did not condemn her but only voiced regret.

As was his habit, Sylvan rubbed his thumbs over his wife's slender white hands, marveling at the perfection of the fingers and the oval nails. For a moment he turned her left hand this way and that, so that the candle rays reflected off the ruby clasped within its golden serpents' fangs. Then he said softly, "Why did you never tell me Scottie was your son?"

Lisbet only stared at him, both astounded and dismayed at his knowledge.

"Did you think I did not know?" he asked with soft reproach. "How could I not? The boy's eyes were thine, and his hair. Ah, and his mouth and form were Captain York's. Even if there had been no resemblances, your devotion to him would have betrayed you. For years I tried to goad you into telling me your secret, hoping that you would either slip in anger or come to trust me. Why did you never fly into my arms and confide? Had I not adequately proven my love to you? Had I not shown well enough that I would have given you anything your heart desired? Surely you knew I would have taken your son for my own if you had but asked me."

At his gentle admonishment Lisbet bowed her head, her sense of failure more acute than ever. "I thought the lie would save you injury," she murmured at last.

"No." He sighed. "It injured me more not to be told."

Lisbet looked up at him, her hazel eyes full. "You have a great heart, Sylvan."

Then, uncinching her wrapper, she slid it slowly from her shoulders and, standing apart from him, dropped her gown.

Sylvan gazed at her long, reverently, without touching. "Are you certain, my dove?" he asked at length, his voice aquiver with emotion, his dark twisted face anxious.

For a fraction of time she hesitated, her body tensing and the part of her that belonged to Anvil crying out against what she was about to do. But her husband must not know what this night was costing her . . . what it had cost her already. Drawing in a breath of silent anguish, Lisbet nodded.

As the winds of autumn cooled the air, withered blooms, and thickened the coats of cattle, great changes were wrought in Winterspell. There was more work to be had than ever before, for at Winterspell Castle the great wheels of operation were slowly, laboriously beginning to turn again.

Lisbet stood on a ridge overlooking the gardens of the great estate. In the crook of her arm she held a large basket, and her hands were gloved in kid the color of wheat. Upon her head she wore a velvet bonnet of russet with ribbons to match her darker gown.

She came often to gaze at Winterspell Castle from this distant vantage point; she came often to survey the scaffolding rising all around the castle, to see the progress being made. And some days, if she were lucky, fortune even allowed her a glimpse of a tall familiar figure striding round his property.

Her eyes softened with pride. Anvil would make his inheritance grand again, he would restore it, see it prosper. He would go to London and be welcomed by the city's highest circle, be feted and flattered. And there would be no lack of lords' daughters with which to fall in love.

He deserved it, she thought, he deserved it all.

The wind gusted suddenly, lifting her skirts and tugging at her bonnet brim until she had to reach up and secure it with a hand. Taking a deep breath, she turned away from the sight of the castle and, traversing the steep hill, descended into a meadow fragrant with the smell of burning leaves. A large curl of smoke drifted blue above a line of brilliant red oaks. Leaning down, Lisbet retrieved one of the pretty-hued leaves that had escaped the flames and added it to her collection in the basket. Since Sylvan rarely left the confines of Wexford Hall, she brought nature inside to him whenever possible, arranging huge bowls of autumn leaves or making wreaths of pinecones and walnuts if wild flowers were not in season.

Her efforts to cheer him were tireless, her patience never ending.

And yet, each day he seemed to fall more deeply into a chasm of melancholia she could not penetrate. He loved her more than ever, she knew, his fawning obsession having transformed gradually into a softer affection. But Sylvan nursed a private torment Lisbet seemed unable to release. Whether it was a torment always there, born of his afflictions, or newly come, she was not sure.

The night she had gone to him had been a tragic one; instead of bringing him joy and completeness, it had only brought him shame in the most excruciating form. He had been unable to fulfill the passion which had consumed him for so long; he had been unable to be a husband to her. And that failure had nearly undone him.

"I am no man!" he had cried in utter mortification, prostrating himself on the bed and pounding his fists into the mattress. "You see what a wretch I am? Not only am I a monster to behold, my flesh is so worthless it cannot love!"

When Lisbet had attempted to console him, he had flown into a maddened rage, flinging her silken wrapper at her with a demand that she cover her woman's form. And then he had immediately grown contrite, weeping upon her breast like a heartbroken child until the coming of dawn.

Remembering, Lisbet reached to arrest another leaf in flight. It spun like a pinwheel across the dry meadow grass, its vivid scarlet and gold resembling fire colors, reminding her that Sylvan would likely be sitting beside the hearth now, waiting. Not that he ever insisted upon her company these days or made her conscience-stricken if her absences were long, but she knew her presence at tea was one of the few occasions that gave him pleasure. He had abandoned his sketching, his buying of treasures, even his poetry reading lately, so that most of his time was spent sitting in quietude in a chair beside the fire.

This morbid unhappiness grieved Lisbet, causing her such anxiety that she did not often leave his side. And yet, only once had she ventured into his bedchamber again, for on that occasion he had received her so coldly she had clutched her wrapper about her chest and fled.

The smoke from the leaf burning floated downward in a cloud, its pungency pricking Lisbet's nostrils and stinging her eyes. She blinked, wiped the moisture from her lashes with a handkerchief . . . and looked up to see a figure striding out of the woods a few yards away.

Tall, this figure was, splendidly tall, with shoulders broad beneath a brown tweed coat. Buff-colored breeches defined the well-conditioned legs and tapered down into polished riding boots the color of richest mahogany.

Lisbet swallowed and let the basket drop from her arm, her eyes fastening to the picture he made. He had a rifle slung casually over one shoulder and at his heels bounded two large hounds with flapping ears, their paws stirring up the crackling layer of leaves upon the path. He wore no hat, and his hair was so black it seemed to shimmer with highlights of blue wherever the sun touched it. When one of the dogs chased its tail, he laughed with deep abandon, his smile flashing brightest white.

Lisbet closed her eyes and took a breath, struck painfully by his handsomeness.

And then, Forrest caught sight of her. He arrested

his step. Across the smoky haze, their eyes met and held.

For long moments, neither moved, neither broke the power of feeling that held them captive. They did not raise a hand or nod or make the slightest utterance of greeting. Nor did either step forward.

She heard one of his hounds whine. It nuzzled his hand, circled him twice, but he ignored it. His eyes remained intent upon her, his stance so unwavering and still that Lisbet began to grow unnerved.

Quickly she turned away from him, began walking at a brisk unsteady pace in the opposite direction. But she could not resist one last fleeting glimpse and, looking over her shoulder, met his eyes again. She found them glinting with satisfaction, as if he knew she still suffered keenly for want of him.

Breathless, Lisbet carried her basket of colorful leaves inside Wexford Hall a short time later and, taking a large lead crystal bowl from the dining room sideboard, emptied them into it. Her hands shook as she transferred the container to the parlor, and she had to gulp a few deep breaths of air to calm herself.

She was surprised not to find Sylvan sitting beside the fire. Already the tea things waited, his favorite pink-iced cakes covered with an embroidered square of linen.

"Sylvan . . . ?" she called curiously. She crossed to the library, then the saloon, and lastly to the terrace in a vain search for him.

Backtracking to the dining room, she arrested a housemaid polishing a brass wall sconce. "Have you seen his lordship, Dora?"

"No, my lady. Perhaps he's gone upstairs."

Beset suddenly by a sharp inexplicable apprehension, Lisbet hastened up the stairs, running down the second-level corridors with such speed she was breathless by the time she reached the master bed-chamber.

"Sylvan . . . ?" she called, rapping forcefully on the panel of his door. "Are you there?"

Receiving no answer, she tested the latch. Locked! Going around to her own bedchamber, she passed through the dressing room and tried the inner entry, only to find it barred as well.

Frantically she jerked the bellpull and, upon the arrival of a footman, ordered him to get a set of keys from the housekeeper. While she waited, she called incessantly to Sylvan, rattling the latch and hoping in vain to receive an answer through his portal.

At last the footman returned with a key. Inserting it with a trembling hand, Lisbet pushed the door wide.

Immediately a piercing scream of horror rose up from her throat.

Between the two Greek columns, dangling from a satin drapery cord, Sylvan hung by the neck.

Lisbet ran to him, crying his name, setting upright the upset chair beneath his feet. Wildly she cried to him to get himself down, her brain denying the finality of what she saw. Scrambling upon the cushion, she raised her arms, attempting desperately to disengage her husband. But his weight was far too great for her strength, and the cord was tied so tautly about a ceiling beam it would not come loose with her frenzied jerking.

It was then she noticed the note he had pinned to his chest.

A goddess deserves a god . . . a wretch deserves oblivion.

She read the words aloud, crying out fiercely against their terrible meaning.

Sobbing, realizing that her husband was far beyond saving, Lisbet pressed his poor cold hand to her cheek and wailed her awful grief.

"Mary!" she screamed then, shouting for her maid. *"Mary!"*

Having heard the earlier scream, the servant stood poised upon the threshold, her face frozen into lines of terror and repugnance.

"Help me, Mary!" Lisbet implored, tears streaming from her eyes. "I cannot get him down without your aid!"

The maid merely stared at the slowly rocking body, at its grotesquely bulged eyes and the stain of moisture upon its breeches. Shaking her head, she gasped, "I—I . . . c-couldn't. I—I just couldn't, mum . . ."

Lisbet felt her head grow dizzy, and she swayed, nearly falling from the chair. Bending to grasp the cushion, she climbed down, holding her temples so as not to faint. Weakly she sank to the floor at her husband's suspended feet.

"Then get someone . . ." she breathed. "For mercy's sake, get someone to come and cut him down."

Resting her head upon the edge of the chair, she waited, breathing deeply to keep herself from swooning.

But none of the footman, nor the butler, nor any of the servants arrived to disengage the master's stiffening body from its cord.

Instead, a half-hour later, Lisbet saw through swollen eyes a pair of mahogany-colored boots crossing the carpet toward her. She stared dazedly at them for a few seconds, seeing the dust from the woods upon them, seeing splashes of mud from the riverbank drying upon their tops.

Slowly, then, she lifted her head to look into the dark worldly eyes of their owner.

There was pity in the black depths, she thought numbly, a terrible sort of pity.

Bending, he slipped an arm about her waist and scooped her up, laying her gently upon the bed before returning to Lord Thorpe's body. She watched while he stepped upon the chair and, with strong, careful hands, freed her husband's corpse from its deadly noose.

One red slipper dangled from Sylvan's misshapen foot, and his garish yellow cravat was all askew. Even in death he was so tragically inelegant. How ironic, she thought, that the strong-armed Anvil should carry the little Earl of Tilbury, Lisbet's ill-starred husband, from his chamber of treasures.

It was a picture she would never forget.

Chapter Twenty-one

Autumn shivered into winter, Christmas came and went, and February settled her cloak of white across the land. A heavy crust of snow lay on the stable roof at Winterspell Tower, frosting the copper weathervane atop its steeple, stiffening it so even a persistent wind could not rattle it loose. The wide double doors of the structure were latched tight to keep out the chill, and the rough shuttered windows gave no more than a crack or two of access to the icy gusts.

Within, their strong jaws grinding, a half-dozen horses enjoyed a morning ration of oats, their ears unbothered by the now-routine ringing of a hammer.

With a stack of new lumber to utilize, Forrest refurbished the framework of the double row of loose boxes, a task that by late spring should finally be complete. He had been laboring hard here, as he had everywhere about the estate, doing outdoor repairs when weather permitted. When it did not, he spent long hours ensconced in the study with his steward, planning livestock purchases and determining the number of tenancies the land could provide. All in all, he had made great inroads into the business of revitalizing his inheritance, and the progress pleased him.

Now, after positioning one last nail and pounding it into place with a few forceful strikes, he set the hammer aside and swiped an arm across his eyes to clear them of sawdust. He was tired. His days invariably began before dawn and ended after midnight, their hours punctuated by hastily taken meals and too many cups of cold black coffee.

But there was so damnably much to do, and for some reason, he felt a pressing need to accomplish it all as soon as possible.

Of course, though he hated admitting it to himself, there was another reason for putting his nose to the grindstone. Leisure time had become anathema to him. For after the newspapers were perused, after a solitary game of billiards were played or a wild ride over the fields accomplished, he too often ended up rambling about the empty walls of his castle and ruminating.

And his ruminations would inevitably turn in one direction.

Running a hand through his hair, Forrest sank down upon a mounting block and drank the last of his cooled coffee. With a baleful eye he glanced at Gretchen's hare, the one she had called Ramtiggadin. As if it were some privileged personage, it lay stretched luxuriantly upon a pile of straw nearby, its head raised at a haughty angle and its pink nose atwitch. After the girl's departure, the animal had attached itself to Forrest, materializing whenever he worked outside.

"And Gretchen touted you as such a brilliant conversationalist," he commented scornfully. "I've yet to hear you utter a blessed word."

With its eyes as dark and enigmatic as ever, the creature returned Forrest's regard, not a hair on its plump gray-brown body stirring in answer.

The sudden creaking of the stable door caused For-

rest to glance up, but in the slice of gray winter light i
was only Agatha's spare figure standing in silhouette.

With a grumble Forrest cursed himself. Would hi
gut never stop tensing in hopeful expectation at th
opening of a door?

"Cap'n?" the servant called in a querulous voice, he
spectacled eyes blinking in the dimness. "Are you i
here?"

"Aye," he said, stepping out from the loose box. "Bu
what are you doing out in the weather, Mistress P?"

"I came ta tell ya there's another one of them two-
faced ne'er-do-wells up at the castle askin' for work."
She sniffed and raised her nose. "Disgraceful, it is. No
a one of 'em would have given ya the time o' day afor
ya came inta yer title. Now look at 'em, bowin' an
scrapin' like they meant it. Why, the old bugger waitin
up there now even made eyes at me." She crossed he
arms and huffed. "Thinkin' to have me use my influence, no doubt."

Forrest grinned, raising a teasing brow. "Well, you
influence is considerable, by all accounts."

"Poppycock! You no more listen ta me than tha
high-nosed butler ya brought here from London."

"Why, Aggie" Forrest deviled her, "I've seen old Butterton duck his head between his shoulders and loo
sheepish at a mere cross word from you."

She flapped a hand at his smiling face. "Oh, go o
with ya, Cap'n."

Forrest lifted his black greatcoat from a bridle peg
and, shrugging into it, threw an incendiary remark
over his shoulder, "He's set his cap for you, there's n
denying it."

Agatha appeared horrified. "He never has!"

Maintaining a perfectly serious demeanor, Forrest
spoke to her with raised brows. "Ah, come now, Mistress P. Surely you're not surprised. How would you ex-

pect a bachelor such as Butterton to feel about an attractive, unattached lady such as yourself?"

He slid on his gloves, watching his past middle-aged housekeeper blush in the furious manner of a schoolgirl.

As always when she grew flustered, Agatha searched for something to occupy her hands, and thrusting fingers into her serviceable gray coat pocket, she withdrew an envelope.

"It came in the post this morning," she said. Offering it to him, she waited for his reaction with a keen-eyed appraisal.

Forrest turned it over, seeing immediately it was a letter from Beatrix Bevins. Ignoring Agatha's interested scrutiny, he opened the missive and scanned it.

"She and her father have invited me to spend some time in London," he said, appeasing her curiosity. "Seems they're having a soiree or some such social occasion."

Refolding the letter, he slipped it into the envelope again and shook his head. "That Bevins is a relentless rascal. Obviously he's had no luck in finding any other fool willing to be packed off to Afghanistan."

"That's as may be," Agatha said. "But I would say Miss Bevins is just as relentless as her father, in her own way." Her pale eyes studied his face.

Saying nothing, Forrest moved to open the stable door for her, and the two of them stepped out onto the snow-rimed cobbles. The wind had died, and the flakes had ceased their fall, so that only the clacking of brittle black branches broke the hush of the winter afternoon. A few brown sparrows wheeled overhead, fluttering down to peck at the ice beneath a fir tree, and Gretchen's fat hare, who had come out of the stable with Forrest, darted off to vanish in the shadows.

Above, the Tower rose tall, its structure repaired

now, its stones remortared and cleared of their smothering cloak of ivy. Together Forrest and Agatha ascended the hill toward it, and though they crunched through the snow in companionable silence, the thoughts of each had turned in similar directions.

"So," the housekeeper said finally. "Are ya interested?"

"In what?" Forrest asked unnecessarily.

"In Miss Bevins, of course."

Tilting his head back, Forrest took a breath and released it in the frosty air. "I don't know. The idea of courting her has crossed my mind. Rattling around in those cavernous halls up there makes a man lonely, to tell the truth. And after all," he lifted his mouth in a remote smile, "I'm hardly getting any younger, am I? Still . . ."

Though Forrest left the sentence unfinished, he knew Agatha could have concluded it for herself. Not that he had divulged the barest detail about his broken relationship with Lisbet; he was too private by half to hold his heart up to view. Besides, Agatha would only pity him, fussing over him like a mother with a downcast child, and he was too proud to tolerate that.

With an inward cringe he remembered her mawkish looks last summer just after Lisbet had declared her intent to end their relationship. Of course, his reaction to that crushing blow had been anything but mild. He had spent two days holed up in his bedchamber with an abundant supply of whiskey, turning Agatha away from the door with curt words and the smashing of an expensive collection of porcelain plate. When he had finally emerged from the depths of his drunken rampage, he had been cold sober and uncommunicative. But his housekeeper had contemplated his drawn visage and bleak expression with tender, discerning eyes that had cut him to the quick.

As if reading his thoughts now, Agatha shoved her hand into her pockets and asked, "Do ya think you'll ever . . . forget?"

At the words Forrest's eyes instinctively turned toward Wexford Hall, then grew hard with feelings he did not bother to hide. "I only wish to God I could."

In an anteroom off the Great Hall, a man in worn corduroys waited with hat in hand. Forrest stepped in, greeted him briefly, and asked his business.

"I'm wantin' work, my lord," he explained, pulling his forelock respectfully. "I heard you were hirin' for livestock, and I've got experience with sheep and cattle both."

Already scores of Winterspell residents, men and women alike, had come applying for positions, for most made meager livings in and around the village. Having heard from the recently hired London staff that the new marquess was generous and fair, they had wasted little time in clamoring for work.

"I say, the old place is lookin' dandy," the fellow fawned now. "Haven't none of us in Winterspell seen it so grand since your father's day."

Forrest was hardly surprised at this glaring example of hypocrisy, indeed, he would have expected little else from the denizens of this crooked little hamlet. Where his physical strength and dangerous looks at the fair had brought him a measure of respect, even fear, his title had brought on a nauseating unctuousness from his former tormentors. Ironically this change in attitude gave Forrest no smug sense of satisfaction or enjoyment of justice. It amused him in a perverse sort of way, but, more than anything, amplified his cynicism toward them.

"My steward will take down your qualifications and

consider you for work," he said noncommittally to the man. "We'll be hiring next month."

After the applicant had been escorted to the steward's office, Forrest sat down to take his lunch, sprawling his long legs and eyeing the double line of empty newly polished chairs with vague distaste. Though he had never remained in one place long enough to acquire close attachments, there had rarely been a lack of jovial companions or lively courtesans to keep him company when he desired it. He found his current solitude oppressive.

Pushing his plate aside, he took Beatrix's letter from his pocket and idly reread its neatly penned lines. He sighed, thinking a man would have little trouble living in contentment with such a lovely, gentle-reared lady. She was young and fresh, would bear plenty of pretty children, and would be warm company between the sheets at night.

Refolding the letter, Forrest put it aside, knowing he would decline the invitation.

Fool that he was, he had believed for a time that Lisbet would return to him. After the tragic suicide of Lord Thorpe, after Forrest had grimly removed his body from its noose, galvanizing the squeamish servants into action with harsh commands and then going for the vicar, he had patiently awaited word from Lisbet. He had not expected her to communicate with him right away, knowing she would need time to recover from shock and bereavement. And, of course, it was only honorable that they refrain from contact for a time. Thoughts of her abrupt and shattering severance of their relationship he had even pushed aside, believing she had been prompted by the same desperation to end the hopelessness that he had experienced himself after their time on the Isle of Wight.

Now, though, his hope had begun to wane. Over the

last weeks, in brutal realization, he had concluded that Lisbet had indeed finished with him. Perhaps she even blamed him indirectly for her husband's demise. And was he to blame? Had he not cruelly declared once that he was a danger to Lisbet, that dire consequences might result before there was an end to their relationship?

The harsh demands of his life had rarely given Forest time for much reflection, and conscience was a thing he often ignored in order to survive. But suddenly he felt the weight of self-condemnation descend upon him full force.

Turning about, he began the long climb to his chambers, passing the shields representing the noble name of Sedgemoor, passing the stained-glass window upon which his ancestors wielded swords in some ancient battle.

He sighed, wondering exactly when it was he had made the decision to leave it all . . . every last bit of it.

Telling Agatha of his plans to depart would not be an easy task. When he called her into his study, he took one look at her familiar face with its sprinkling of powder and found himself at a sudden loss for words.

She stood before him, impeccable in her black gown and starched white apron, not a gray hair out of place. With a pang he recalled the first time he had seen her in her prim bonnet and gloves. He had been no more to her then than a gaunt-faced stranger just back from a war zone, but she had cared for him in a hundred small ways, risking icy glares in the village because she worked for "Lady Thorpe's lover." And later, when Forest had come to inherit the monstrous pile of stones called Winterspell Tower, she had toiled inexhaustibly to make it a home for him.

She had been a mother to a man who had neve known one, and he felt a great affection for her.

Putting off the moment of his news, Forrest talked c mundane matters, informing her that all was proceed ing well with the tenancy plans and that the stewar would be buying livestock at the market next week Then he asked her if all was going well with the staff, i she needed any supplies or household money, if sh were taking proper rests.

He could see she grew impatient with his aimles queries and, after a moment, realized she was not eve attentive to him anymore, but gazing fixedly out th window.

"The deuce, woman," he complained. "Am I talkin to myself?"

"Look!" she exclaimed, pointing, her eyes fixed to ward the wintry landscape. "Do you see them – the tw white foxes!"

Forrest tensed at the mere mention of the creatures Swiveling his desk chair about, he rose and reluctantl joined Agatha at the window.

Eventide had fallen, rendering the snowscape in a thousand shades of orchid and blue, tinting the sky mallow pink. Every tree, every shrub, even the billowy clouds resembled a painted scene, a giant canva spread out for the mortals' view by some creative mas ter hand.

Forrest narrowed his eyes, scanning the eerie scene He saw the cursed oddities, saw their pale undulatin forms dashing over the deep snow of the shrouded gar den. They ran in tandem, the action of their slende legs and flitting tails so perfectly coordinated they could have been not two, but one.

All at once, as if ensnared within the pool of warm light cast by the study lamp, they paused, growing as still as statuary adorned with glittering topaz eyes

Only their long whiskers, drooping with a glazing of ice, moved.

"I've never seen them before . . ." Agatha remarked with awe, her spectacles reflecting their ghostly image. "I never believed. Only a few in Winterspell have ever sighted them, their appearance is so rare. There's a legend about them—do ya know it?"

"Aye," Forrest said curtly. "I know it." His eyes flickered as he spoke, and he looked hard at the animals, hoping perhaps to find that they were really only ordinary foxes made spectral by some trick of light. Once, as children, he and Lisbet had seen the pair, and she had been terrified, clinging to him and insisting that the sight of them caused grievous ill luck.

Lisbet.

Realizing that she had crept into his thoughts again like an insidious shadow, Forrest clenched his jaw and turned away.

He moved restlessly to the mantel, his long legs in their tan breeches more lean and muscled than ever from his labors, the injured one barely faltering, as sound as it would ever be. Broodingly he retrieved the poker from its brass stand and proceeded to rearrange the dying logs.

"Ye're leavin', aren't you, Cap'n?"

Plagued by thoughts of Lisbet, Forrest had almost forgotten the presence of the housekeeper. She stood behind him now, and her soft words had been spoken with such a poignancy that Forrest suffered a pang below his breastbone.

For a moment he found himself unable to turn about and look at her.

At last, after clearing his throat, he replaced the firetool and raised up. His eyes met hers directly. "Aye," he confirmed. "I am leaving."

Her face paled with bewilderment and dismay. "But

yer place is here—you have a home now, a real home. Ye're the marquess," she argued, raising up a hand in appeal. "You belong to Winterspell."

"No, Agatha," Forrest replied quietly. "I've never belonged to Winterspell."

Rubbing a hand across his neck, he continued. "It's strange, isn't it? When I returned here I had no identity except the one I'd created for myself—and, of course, the one the villagers had so obligingly given me at birth. And now—" he smiled thinly, "I have a decidedly auspicious title I don't even care to use. Disgraceful of me, isn't it? My father and mother are likely frowning somewhere in heaven. The thing is, I know I should feel bound to the land, I should feel anchored by some sense of belonging to it all. But," he shrugged, "I simply don't. Perhaps—"

He let the thought die.

"And so . . ." Agatha concluded, taking a deep and shaky breath. "Ya'll be goin' on ta London."

"In the morning. Early." Forrest paused, feeling his chest constrict at thought of what the next few minutes would hold. "I'm leaving everything in Carson's hands. He's an excellent steward and will be forwarding reports to my accountant in London. Of course, there won't be a need for a large domestic staff anymore, just a few maids, a gardener or two, and . . ." He looked at her, then clamped his jaw for a second to stop his lower lip from quivering. He offered her his hand. "And a very efficient housekeeper. I—I don't expect to come back, Agatha."

She swallowed, a few tears sliding from beneath the gold rims of her spectacles. Putting her careworn hand in his lean calloused one, she squeezed it hard. "I've loved ya, Cap'n," she said candidly in a creaking voice. "Loved ya like a son. I—I only wish—"

Her voice broke upon the words, and Forrest drew

er into his arms, closing his eyes tight against the rick of moisture there.

A moment later, when he left her sitting quietly lone in the study, he realized it was one of the most ifficult things he had ever had to do.

Chapter Twenty-two

Agatha wasted no time at all in paying a visit to Lad Thorpe. She wondered if the countess would turn he away, or, if she did not, how she would receive the news

She knew Lisbet had been doing hours of charit work since the suicide of her husband. There were som in the village who made jest of it, thinking it quite fittin that Lord Thorpe's widow gave money and time to th malformed children of the union workhouses. It wa "deliciously appropriate," the gossips declared wit spiteful smiles.

At Wexford Hall the butler escorted Agatha into small parlor and announced that the countess woul join her momentarily. When that lady entered, Agath thought she had never seen anyone with such sorrow struck eyes.

The servant quickly stood to introduce herself, bu Lisbet interrupted, her voice full of apprehension. "I Forr—Lord Sedgemoor unwell?" she questioned.

"He's well."

Relieved, Lisbet smoothed her skirts and, inviting th housekeeper to sit down again, poured tea for both o them. The older woman's agitation was apparent, an though Lisbet was anxious to know her reason for call ing, she attempted to put the woman more at ease.

"The work on the Tower seems to be going well," she aid by way of opening. "Lord Sedgemoor is putting it in ;ood order again by all accounts I've heard."

"And a fine job he's doin', too," Agatha declared, making her pride in her employer evident. "O' course, at irst, I feared the man would work himself ta death. He lever stopped. Stayed out in the fields so late he went vithout dinner half the time. I swear he did the work of hree hired men."

Lisbet clasped her hands tightly in her lap. "But he is vell?" she asked again, sure that the housekeeper had :ome to deliver some disturbing news.

"He's not ailin' in a physical way," Agatha replied :risply. "But whether or not he's well is a matter of opinon."

Leaning forward, Lisbet put a cold hand atop the ser'ant's white-gloved fingers. "You've come to tell me omething," she said with naked concern in her wide lazel eyes. "What is it?"

Agatha drew a breath. Though she hated to be judgnental, she could not help but blame Lady Thorpe for Captain York's wretchedness. Accusation edged her one. "I've come ta tell ya he's gone. I've come ta tell ya ie's not comin' back."

Lisbet stared at her, the news clearly a blow. All color lrained rapidly from her face. "When . . . ?" she ɔreathed.

"This morning. Very early."

"Where has he gone?"

"London. One of them government fellows has been ɔesterin' him ta go ta some foreign place again. Somevhere dangerous, just like before, I'll be bound."

Rising, Lisbet moved away in a whisper of black nourning skirts. Framed in the cold light of the tall verical windows, her neck slender and bowed, she made a ʼulnerable figure. "Perhaps 'tis better this way . . ." She

uttered the words in such a low, quiet voice she mig
have been speaking to herself.

Agatha knew she had overstepped bounds merely b
coming to Wexford Hall, but she was in the presence
the woman Captain York loved to distraction and, hav
ing begun, she would not waver in her purpose now. I
her no-nonsense stride she went to take a position
Lady Thorpe's back. "Do ya love him?"

Lisbet raised her head at the bold question, and whe
she turned to face the servant, her eyes were very grav
"Yes. And it has cost both of us . . . and others . . .
very heavy price."

Agatha had no intention, nor interest, in gleaning de
tails. Her only reason for this visit had arisen out of
desire to give happiness to a man she cared deepl
about. "That's as may be. But do ya know how much h
still loves you?" she asked with no mincing of words.

With pain crossing her features, Lisbet lowered he
lashes. "Yes. . . . Yes, I do."

"Then why don't ya go ta him?" Agatha exclaimed
throwing up her hands. "I tell ya, he went near mad wit
grief last summer. Like a great, wounded beast, he was
Locked himself away and drank till he was senseless
And many's the time when I've seen him sittin' alone a
his desk at night with his head in his hands, despairin'
He's mad for ya!"

Agatha shook her gray head, her voice aquiver wit
feeling. "And then there was that business about his son
Like ta have tore the poor man's heart out, it did."

"Don't tell me anymore, Agatha—I can't bear to hea
anymore," Lisbet cried, putting a hand to her eyes
"What's between Captain York and me is not as simpl
as you would have it. It has nearly destroyed both o
us. It's better for me to let him go. He'll find someon
else—"

"He don't want anyone else."

Lisbet sank down upon a silk-cushioned chair, gripping its arms with her hands, exposing a share of her private grief. "Because of my love for Forrest, I must forever carry a part of the burden of my husband's death."

"But he didn't die by yer hand. He died by his own."

Lisbet shook her head. "Had I been able to make him happy he would even now be with me. I'm convinced of that. I'm convinced I failed him."

"Are ya saying," Agatha queried in scornful astonishment, "that ye're keepin' away from the captain just as a way of punishin' yerself?"

Lisbet looked into the servant's accusing eyes and conceded, "I will not deny it. It's my way of atoning, I suppose."

Fearing her cause lost, Agatha crossed her arms over her meager bosom and replied tersely, "I don't know about atoning. But I do know that by punishin' yerself, yer punishin' *him,* and that don't seem fair ta me."

She straightened her prim lace collar and picked up her reticule. "The way I see it, you are the only one who can set things right—as they were meant ta be from the beginning. Time has been turned back for ya, and that doesn't happen to any of us very often."

Having now said her piece, the housekeeper retied her black bonnet strings and made to leave. "G'day ta ya, my lady."

Lisbet did not sleep that night. She lay upon her cold embroidered sheets staring watchfully into the darkness, for when she closed her eyes she saw a disturbing vision. It was a vision of Forrest in a distant land she could not name, walking amongst a milling crowd where hatred lurked on every face.

Rolling over restlessly, she put a hand to her eyes. Perhaps the vision was confused, and he only walked in Winterspell, alone amid the villagers.

With her face against her pillows, she cried for him long heart-rending sobs torn from a raw and tightene throat. She longed for the sight of him, ached for hi touch as she had never done before. But the yearnin battled with a terrible self-condemnation and sense c failure from which she had been unable to free hersel these past many months.

Sliding out of bed on a sudden frantic impulse, no stopping to don a wrapper, she hastened to the adjoinin bedchamber. She had not been inside Sylvan's sanctu ary since his terrible death. The mere thought of it ha discomposed her. She had been unable to face the mem ories, the fear that somehow Sylvan's soul would materi alize and condemn her from the grave.

Now, taking these disturbing thoughts in hand, sh determinedly pressed down the latch.

All the Earl of Tilbury's treasures were just as he ha placed them, all those exotic collectibles from the far away places he had been too frightened to see. Lisbe touched them one by one, the hideous jade dragons, th grotesque African masks, the strange, twisted clay idol from the burial ground of some forgotten people. Lastl she let her eyes dwell upon the misplaced Gree columns. With sorrow, she realized they were all a re flection of Sylvan's inner torment, a torment he ha never been able to bury . . . not even with her at hi side.

Had she not done the best she could for him in th months before his death, though? Had she not forsake Forrest in order to stay with her husband, tend him, giv him what love she could? Had she not taken the care t understand his nature when no other ever had?

Perhaps in the end, she thought with sudden wonde Sylvan had failed *her*. . . .

For a long while she merely stood alone in the cente of his chamber, remembering him, speaking to hin softly as if he might hear her words. And as she spoke, she realized other things about herself not faced before in these last difficult months.

For the first time, all the controls upon her life were lifted. No stern sire kept her behind locked doors, dictating to her what she would do, manipulating her choices until they were no choices at all. Nor did the bonds of an unwanted marriage hold her to the needs of a man, to duty, to honor, to decency. No longer was she controlled by anything or any person. Even society had turned its back upon her long ago. For the first time Lisbet was entirely free to make her own decisions, to choose the course her life would take.

And these reins of power, never held in her hands before, were vaguely disconcerting.

Quietly she moved to open the curtains of the windows in Sylvan's chamber, at last permitting the light of dawn to penetrate the gloomy recess he had so often hidden himself within. She would give all the treasures away, donate them to charities and museums where they could be enjoyed.

Thinking Sylvan would approve, she closed for the last time the slim volume of poetry he had so loved. And then she went out and shut the door.

She journeyed to London alone. When the train screamed and puffed to a halt at Victoria Station, she stepped out into the masses of scurrying people and, finding a porter, asked him to hail a hansom cab for her.

She had no address for Forrest beyond that of the Intelligence Branch in St. Anne's Gate, and she dreaded to think what she would do were that office unable or unwilling to aid her.

As she feared, gaining information of any sort from such a secretive department proved difficult, and it was

only by sheer perseverance that she managed an inter-
view with a Lieutenant Colonel Bevins. After kindly
greeting her, he confirmed that Captain York had indeed arrived in London. In fact, he added, Forrest had
only left the office an hour past. Arrangements were being made for his early departure tomorrow from England. Would she like the name of his hotel?

In a fever of anticipation, Lisbet thanked him and
took her leave, briskly walking the distance to the hotel
impatient with the jostling crowds and heavy traffic
which seemed to conspire to hamper her. By the time
she arrived at her destination, she was breathless, her
lungs aching from the frigid winter air. Snow had begun
to fall, powdering the dirty pavement and catching in
the brim of her small plumed hat. Blinking against the
flakes, she checked the address and entered the hotel.

The establishment was a fine one but unpretentious
She took a chance and asked for the room of Captain
York, guessing correctly that he would not use his title
She gave her own name as Mrs. York.

"He's not in, madam," the clerk informed her. "But I
will give you a key."

When she entered the room a moment later and
pulled off her cloak and hat, she found Forrest's trunks
bound and labeled beside the door. The sight of them
caused her confidence to falter all at once. Nervously she
paced about, touching the shaving things he had left beside the washstand and wondering if now he had decided
to leave the country, he had also set aside his feelings for
her. Perhaps she had no place in this new direction he
had chosen for himself; perhaps he would not want to
abandon adventure in favor of a life with her.

Idly she looked down upon the street scene. The snow
fell heavily now, and passersby pulled their outerwear
more snugly about their chests, hurrying to escape the
bitter, blowing wind. She watched passing broughams,

abs, drays, and coaches until her breath frosted the anes.

When a key rasped in the door lock behind her, she asped, wheeling about to face the threshold.

The door swung open.

And there he stood . . . tall, broad-shouldered, as im-ossibly handsome as ever.

The smell of the frosty air came with him, seeming to wirl about the room and make it chilled even as he losed the door behind him. Snow clung to his gray reatcoat, quickly melting in the warmth to form glis-ening beads upon the fabric. The tall black hat on his ead shimmered with moisture as well, as did the trands of hair lying upon his neck. He had removed his loves and held them negligently in the long fingers of is left hand.

In a sort of wonder over his austere beauty, Lisbet ooked up at his face. His cheeks were slightly ruddy rom the cold, and his black thick-lashed eyes still shone rightly from the stinging wind outside, their straight rows a magnificent slash above. His mouth was firm, hadowed deeply beneath the curve of the lower lip.

Though his gaze narrowed upon her unmoving fig-re, she could read not the barest hint of emotion in it. Iis unshakable composure disquieted her.

She realized her unexpected presence had stunned im. She realized by the clenching of his jaw and the ensing of his hand that he struggled not to react impul-ively. But he had always been skilled at dispassion. He vould test the waters, waiting for her to make the first nove.

Forrest had imagined Lisbet standing in his room just his way so many times he feared at first she was no more han an apparition—just like the cursed white foxes. All luring his journey to London he had indulged himself n a series of fantasies, creating scenarios in which Lis-

bet suddenly stepped out of a crowd and rushed forwar
with a confession that she could not exist without him
While he had walked to St. Anne's Gate and back today
while he had sat alone morosely sipping tea in a tea
room, he had pictured her just in the place she stoo
now, waiting for him.

He blinked, hoping she would attribute the moistur
in his eyes to his cold walk. The sight of her over
whelmed him, and he consumed every detail of her ap
pearance, from the edging of delicate lace at her throa
to the black leather of her shoes. She did not wea
mourning but was swathed in a beautifully cut travelin
jacket and skirt of royal blue trimmed in black braid
Though her hair was gathered in a chignon, the win
had whipped much of the shorter strands free, so tha
they fell in trailing tendrils about her cheeks and brow
A flush colored her face, though whether from cold o
high emotion he could not say. He thought her feature
more hollowed then they had been before, but she wa
still lovely . . . the most desirable woman he had eve
known.

He wanted her so badly it was all he could do not t
run forward, bury his face against the softness of he
neck, and dissolve into some despicable blubbering fool
But he was afraid, afraid of being disappointed on
more time and not being able to bear it. He wasn't sur
why she was here, although obviously Agatha had got
ten involved. Perhaps she had come only to tell hin
goodbye. What if he were to lose control of his dignit
and beg her to stay, beg her to love him again?

He was having difficulty looking directly into he
eyes, into those dark hazel depths he loved so much, s
he fixed his gaze just above them, upon her brow, sayin
at last, "So you have come to see me off." His voice wa
hoarse but rigidly controlled.

Lisbet swallowed against the effect of his coolness, he

thoughts of flying into his arms completely dashed away, but she spoke steadily. "No. I have not."

"Oh . . . ?" he asked with a lazy arch of a brow. "A pleasure call, then. One of those dutifully formal little visits made for old times' sake." He lifted his lip in a wry, uncharitable smile. "I'm touched."

Stung, she inhaled quickly to keep from crying, knowing her heart was in her eyes. "I'm here because—" How could she blurt out her love when he stared at her with that cool unnerving gaze? "A-Agatha Peacock told me you had come to London," she temporized, feeling her heart pound so hard he could surely hear it.

"Ah," he nodded, not helping her. "Agatha."

"She was concerned for you."

"Fine woman. I shall miss her."

Lisbet watched his thumb and forefinger sliding over the soft kid of his gloves, watched the way the sinews moved over the fine bones. Her knees quivered so badly she knew the hem of her skirt moved. She took a deep breath.

"I love you, Forrest." The words just hovered in the air, soft soughs from her lips. She had said them because there was nothing else to say, because even if he were through with her, she wanted him to know.

They caused a barely perceptible flinch to pull at Forrest's cheek, but he answered her as if unstirred by the confession. "Should I be astounded? It's no revelation to me, after all. You have always loved me or—so you have said."

He knew his words were cruel, but cruelty was an armor, one which she could easily penetrate if she tried. *Please, Lisbet. Try.*

"Yes . . ." she confirmed in a quavering voice, her self-restraint almost undone. "I have." With a quivering hand she removed a small tattered book from her pocket and held it out for him to see. "I said vows with you from these pages once, long ago. . . . Do you remember?"

His eyes flicked over the volume, then back to her face. "I do."

Lisbet felt her heart lurch. If he played some game of nerves with her, he played it well. But she did not intend to lose to him. If he had hardened himself against her, erected some barrier against his pain, she would find a way to breach it.

Taking a tentative step toward his tall forbidding form, she lifted her face to his. "I would like . . . I would like to say them again."

She saw his fingers tighten reflexively about the gloves, betraying some emotion. His voice came deeper than before. "Then . . . say them."

She looked at him undaunted, meeting his uncompromising gaze. He stood so stiffly he could have been some carved Roman statue draped in modern clothes and gifted with divine eyes.

Fumbling awkwardly, she opened the little book in her hand to a dog-eared page and, in a voice trembling with deep feeling, proceeded to recite from it. Not once did she falter over the same vows she had repeated once before, long ago, to a rebellious, fiery-eyed boy beneath the arches of a bridge.

Forrest remembered them. He stared hard at her while she recited each syllable, watching the movements of her full bowed lips, focusing on them while he listened to the words.

And when she had ended her part of the rites, he continued it in a low resonant voice, repeating from memory every word she had just spoken herself.

In wonder Lisbet stared at him.

Closing his eyes, Forrest took two convulsive breaths and reached out for her. The contact of his body to hers made him shudder, and he cried out her name once, twice, grasping her about the waist and laying his cheek against her hair. His gloves fell unheeded to the carpet.

Throwing her arms about his neck, Lisbet pulled herself so close her toes raised off the floor. For a moment she only clung wildly to him, much in the way she had done in Laurelpath Cottage the day of Forrest's return to Winterspell.

She could smell the soft wet wool of his coat, the soap he used, the lotion he had shaved with. His body was hard and solid against hers, warmly vital, a bulwark made for her. She pushed herself more frantically into it, unable to get close enough.

And then he kissed her, putting his mouth upon hers in a hard twisting way that made her gasp and clutch at his snow-dampened hair. His hat tumbled to the carpet, and without taking his lips from hers, he unfastened his greatcoat. Hurriedly, he slid one arm, then the other out of the sleeves and tossed the garment aside. When Lisbet's lips parted naturally beneath his, he took them deeply.

"I thought you'd finished with me," he confessed against her mouth, his torment still raw and lingering. "Feared you blamed me."

"No, no, my love," she whispered, reaching to stroke his face. "It was my own guilt keeping me away. But now, I'm here. . . . I'm here—thank God I found you in time . . ."

His hand explored her shoulders, her spine, then the line of her hips, which he drew inward to fit better with his own.

She put her hands beneath his waistcoat, reveling in the feel of his warm skin beneath the layer of linen shirt, frantically pressing her palms to his chest, to his ribs, to his belly until he drew in sharp uneven breaths. The expensive wool garment she pushed off his shoulders with impatience.

Shrugging out of it, Forrest released the black silken

frogs of Lisbet's jacket, afterwards dipping both hands inside to the satin folds of her chemise with a long and shaking sigh.

"I love you, Lisbet . . ." He bent his head low, kissing her throat just beneath her chin, following with his mouth the soft downward curve of it. "Say you'll stay with me," he demanded low in his throat. "Say it, say it . . ."

Tilting back her head for his kisses, she cupped his head in her hands, breathing, "I'll stay with you always. I'm yours. . . . I always have been. I've never known another."

He paused in his caressing of her and, with a smoldering gaze, probed her eyes.

She answered his question wordlessly, laying his palm to the place beneath which her heart beat.

As he removed her chemise, she released the buttons of his waistcoat and shirt, drawing it away so their flesh was laid bare to each other. The contact each against the other was exquisite, causing them to hold their breaths and close their eyes with the warm sensual wonder of it.

Outside the snow descended in white blankets, blowing in soft whirls against the window, making arcs upon the panes. The room grew dim, hushed except for the sound of two lovers breathing and touching riotously.

Forrest lifted Lisbet, carried her to the bed, and there removed the last of their clothing. For a moment, he only sat above her and gazed down at this woman he had loved so long and who had obsessed him to the point of agony. She was to be his now and, knowing that, a shiver of deep desire passed through his body.

Reaching for her hair, he unpinned it, spreading his fingers so that it lay in soft disordered curls about her head. He took up a lock, letting it drape over his palm, and marveled at its satiny length and texture. As he did so, she put both thumbs to the mark upon his shoulder, tracing it and kissing it while repeatedly whispering her love.

In one slow adoring stroke he ran his hand the length of her inner arm, across her collarbone, and finally down to touch the fullness of her breasts. Most reverently then, he proceeded with the business of loving every inch of the feminine body he believed fashioned just for his own. Lisbet did the same in turn, only in a more shy, tentative way, which with tender instruction, Forrest turned to a bolder exploration.

Finally, with a gentle urging, he told her it was time to know him wholly again. The words were whispered feverishly against her ear, words to inflame and stir.

She clasped him to her, and with his mouth settling upon her mouth, his hands interlaced with her hands, Anvil moved to possess Lord Tattershall's daughter again . . . at last.

The room had grown dark with eventide, so that the shapes of trunk and valise and discarded heaps of clothing were naught but shadows. Within the bed, intertwined together in the way of sated lovers, lay Lisbet and Forrest.

Her body reposed atop his and her head was cushioned upon the hard ridge of his shoulder. Each breath she took seemed to her to be in tune with his, each heartbeat an answer to the masculine one throbbing beneath her hand. Looking up, seeing a lock of tousled black hair falling over her lover's brow, she smoothed it back with gentle fingertips.

Forrest searched her eyes, found them heavy with contentment, and grinned, capturing her fingers when they traced the deep lines of his dimples.

"Loving is better now we're older, isn't it, my love?" he asked in a low sensual voice.

"In your case, I fear 'tis experience rather than anything to do with age," she replied petulantly, giving him a slanted gaze through her lashes. "It must be true what they say about sailors. Perhaps I should be jealous . . . ?"

He put one hand upon the smooth curve of her hip and with the other shaped the line of her lower lip, which was still slightly reddened from his ardor. "Need I give you more reasons than I have already done this last hour to make you set your jealousy aside?"

Satisfied with the answer, Lisbet lightly nipped his finger, laughing mischievously at his pretended protest. Then she snuggled against him and idly trailed her fingers over the firmly defined muscles of his arm. Feeling warmly euphoric, she began to close her eyes then, but catching sight of his trunks beside the door, frowned with sudden worry.

Forrest had loved her with his body and declared the same sentiment with words, but that did not prevent him from leaving her at dawn in order to complete his mission for the government. Perhaps only a few hours from now she would be left standing upon a dock watching him vanish in a sea mist.

Taking a breath, she ventured, "Lieutenant Colonel Bevins said you were sailing tomorrow."

"Some Intelligence Branch," he grunted, lifting his brows. "Spouting off sensitive information to just anyone off the streets."

Lisbet raised a playful hand as if to cuff him for the insult, but with one adroit turnabout, Forrest pinioned her quite effectively beneath his weight.

Wrestling with him, clenching her fists sportively in a vain attempt to punch him in the ribs, she pouted, "I see I shall have to find some other means of retaliating against your teasing tongue."

He gazed down at her through devilish eyes and

smiled broadly with suggestion. "Believe me, madam, you have ample means at your disposal. You need only choose your weapon."

Raising her head, putting both hands behind his neck, she pressed a wanton kiss to his lips. Then she drew away and smiled at him with brazen meaning.

"See," he responded with affected sullenness. "Already you have discovered the most disarming weapon of all and have no qualms about using it on me."

But he did not seem to mind at all a moment later when she boldly moved to make the counteroffensive.

A time later, as she lay nestled peacefully in his arms once more, Lisbet returned to the subject that so persistently plagued her. "Forrest," she said seriously, "will you leave here on the morrow?"

He spoke against her hair. "Aye. I will leave here on the morrow."

Lisbet's body stiffened in reaction and she turned her head to the side, away from him. "I see."

"Do you, now?" he asked, stroking the curls at her temples.

She moved slightly as if to avoid his touch. "Your words were quite clear."

"Hmm. As I recall, I simply said I would be leaving on the morrow. I did not indicate where I would be going . . . or with whom."

Sharply she fastened her eyes upon his face.

He grinned at her vexation, then lovingly caressed the rise of her cheekbone with his knuckles. "You don't believe I would ever leave you now I've finally got you in my arms?"

She lowered her lashes.

"Lisbet," he admonished sternly, concerned. "Look at me."

When she obeyed, he saw a trace of anxiety still lingering in the hazel depths and gathered her closely to his chest. "We've spent twenty years of our lives apart, my love. That's much, much too long. Surely you realize I'll not allow us to be separated again."

Pulling his rough cheek down to rest upon her smooth one, she sighed, reassured. "Then where shall we go?"

"Would a long honeymoon in Brighton please you?"

She nodded. "Yes. But, afterward . . . ?"

"Do you feel you cannot be happy apart from Winterspell and Wexford Hall?"

Vehemently she shook her head. "Wexford Hall is no longer even mine. As a part of the marriage agreement, it passed from Father's hand into Sylvan's, but now 'twill revert to the male line again—some distant cousin of mine inherits, I'm told. But," she said with a soft touch to his hair, "it should really be you, my love, who decides. After all, you now possess an estate that requires great attention."

Tightening his arms about her in a reflexive action of love, Forrest mused, "Do you know that Winterspell Tower means little to me? That's not to say I don't care about restoring it for the sake of my ancestors—and, of course, my future heirs," he added, squeezing her naked waist. "But I have little feeling for it—no warmth, no particular pride, no sense of belonging at all."

At the sound of regret in his tone, Lisbet brushed her lips against the bristly edge of his jaw in understanding. "Winterspell has hurt us both. It merits none of our loyalty."

They held each other in silence for a while, each remembering, each drawing the other close in mute reaction.

Finally, pricked by sudden apprehension, Lisbet asked, "Are you going to go ahead with your assignment, Forrest? Are you going to take me to some foreign place and then put yourself in danger?"

Forrest answered in a naughty tone, touching her intimately with his hand. "I fear danger and intrigue have paled to insignificance in the last few hours. I've found something much, much more intriguing to do. Old Bevins will just have to be disappointed."

"To Greece then?" she murmured against his lips. "With white terraces, sailing boats, and your fishing fleet . . . ?"

But he was too busy to give her an answer.

Chapter Twenty-three

In Brighton they were married by special license in a small brick chapel with sunlight streaming through its amber windows. Afterwards, they posted a letter to Agatha giving her the joyful news.

"She'll be so pleased," Lisbet commented as she and Forrest strolled along the shops of East Street. He had just bought her a box of candy at a French chocolate shop, and unable to resist the temptation, she delved inside the package immediately and removed a piece for each of them.

"Aye," Forrest agreed between bites. "She'll be pleased alright. And unless I'm far off the mark, we'll be receiving similar news from her before long."

"Oh?" Clutching her woolen tam-o'-shanter against the sea breeze, Lisbet peered up into her husband's smugly satisfied face. "You scoundrel! You have conspired to make a match for her, haven't you? What is the gentleman's name?"

"Butterton," he drawled. "The butler."

"Is he a decent sort?"

"Decent enough to allow Agatha to rule the roost, I'd say. He'll be despicably henpecked before the honeymoon is over."

"Oh, Forrest!" Lisbet admonished.

But he only grinned and reached a thumb to wipe a smudge of chocolate from her lip.

The streets were crowded, for in spite of the chill wind blustering off waves of pewter, Brighton was a favorite weekend resort even in winter. Matrons in sealskin jackets peered through bow-fronted windows to examine silver bric-a-brac for their London drawing rooms, children cavorted willy-nilly with sticky buns clutched in their hands, and newly wedded couples hurried out of Acton's with arms full of pottery.

Forrest and Lisbet strolled past lace shops and antique stores, joining the stream of fashionably dressed tourists and invalids in bath chairs on King's Road. Though it was too cold to sit in the striped canvas chairs upon the beach, the couple sauntered along the esplanade, stopping to gaze out at the galloping gray waves dashing against the Royal Suspension pier. The smell of the water's tang mingled with damp weathered wood was pungent and delicious at once, and though the breeze whipped roses into Lisbet's cheeks, she felt warm and safe encircled by Forrest's arm.

Never able to keep her eyes from him long, she examined her husband minutely. He was trim and dashing in a new navy greatcoat, the white of the shirt beneath it bright against his dark complexion. The creases of strain had gone from his brow, and the drawn look disappeared from his lean cheeks. She was confident enough to attribute it to the love they shared, realizing that he had found peace in the knowledge that he would have her beside him always.

When he glanced her way and smiled softly, she read the love in his eyes. And yet, as he returned his gaze to contemplate the turbulent seas, she caught a glint of pain in the ebony black depths.

Distressed, she withdrew a hand from her muff and put it to his jaw, caressing its tautened ridge in concern. "What do you ponder so glumly, my love?"

Forrest hesitated, unwilling at first to share his thoughts, for he was loath to bring sadness to Lisbet in any form. For a moment he regarded the gentle curves of her face, then the mature hazel eyes that would forever hold remnants of past cares. She was very strong, he realized, marveling that such a delicate frame could hold such strength. She could withstand much in the way of grief and disappointment. Perhaps it was time to share all things with her, even his painful thoughts. She would not want to be protected from them.

"Scottie," he said simply. "It's Scottie I'm thinking of."

Such thoughts were not strangers to Lisbet, and she nodded solemnly, her mother's heart still grieving for the loss of her son. Raising Forrest's knuckles to her face, she laid her cheek against them in shared sorrow.

"I would have liked to have known him, Lisbet," he said, his voice low and remorseful. "I would have liked—"

She pressed her fingers quickly to his lips then and, wanting to ease his regret, drew down his head and kissed him tenderly.

His own response was hungry, passionate, for though they had loved often and long whenever desire took them, Forrest's urgent need of her never waned.

Their hotel was not far, and by the time they reached it, both were gasping with laughter, Lisbet trying unsuccessfully to prevent her husband's public attentions. He had shocked at least one matron on the esplanade, and two young sailors lounging along the rail had whistled encouragement to him with upraised thumbs. She feared he would have her unclothed before they reached their room.

"Forrest!" she exclaimed, batting his hands away when they grew more bold. "That clerk at the desk will see you and be scandalized."

"Entertained, more like." He all but bore her up the stairs then and, after breaching the door, kicked it closed with his foot.

They did not emerge until dawn.

Ten days later, while Forrest completed an errand at the

bank and Lisbet lingered over her toilette, a knock came upon the door.

As she was in dishabille, she called out for the visitor to wait. Struggling with the buttons at her back—for usually Forrest did them—Lisbet hastened to open the door, thinking the porter had come to deliver yet another bouquet of flowers from her attentive husband.

Instead, she discovered her son standing in the corridor, his workman's cap in hand and his rough corduroys clean and pressed.

Her eyes instinctively examined his face and form in the way of a mother, taking in the familiar thatch of fair hair, the serious blue eyes and squared shoulders. He seemed well and had more the look of a man about him than ever before.

Though her joy was unutterable and she yearned to throw her arms about him, she held back, sensing he would be uneasy with such an emotional display. "I'm happy to see you. Scottie," she said finally. "Very happy."

Drawing him into the room then, she closed the door, asking him how he fared and how he had come to find her in Brighton.

"Agatha Peacock told me where to reach you." he answered, standing stiffly in the center of the room. "She said she'd just received a letter."

"And Gretchen . . . ?" Lisbet asked quietly.

"She's in London. But I'll explain about that later."

Lisbet went to pour him a cup of tea from her breakfast tray, but he held up a hand to decline, shifting from foot to foot in an ill-at-ease manner. "I . . . I wanted to talk to you . . ." he began, rubbing a hand across the back of his neck and glancing away.

"Yes?"

"I came because . . ." He paused and cleared his throat. "I came because it wasn't right the way I left you."

Restively he moved a few steps away, reordering the items on the writing desk in a distracted way before going on. "I knew it wasn't right then, b-but I was angry and couldn't seem to think clearly. I—" Running a hand through the thickness of his hair, he tightened his mouth and stared downward at his feet. "I owe you an apology, that's all."

Lisbet put a hand upon his shoulder, her wretchedness coming to the fore. "Perhaps I made a mistake, Scottie," she admitted in a rush. "I've come to believe I did. I could have left you in a foster home and sent money to see that you lived well. But you must understand how difficult it was for me to let you go to strangers. I wanted you near . . ."

She did not finish, for Scottie was shaking his head at her words.

"It's all past now," he said. "You did what you thought was best. I've acted like a sorry beggar, I know, but I'm grateful for your kindnesses. And Gretchen and I would like to thank you for the money you sent."

"Money?" she repeated, bewildered. "I never knew where you went, Scottie. Though I would have liked, I never sent you any money."

He frowned, equally puzzled. "A fellow came to deliver it to me at the railway station the night I left. He told me it was from Lady Thorpe."

Lisbet's eyes softened. "Your father sent it, surely. He would've know you'd not accept it if you knew it came from him."

Scottie's young face fell. Turning away from his mother, he went to gaze out the window, lemon sunlight streaming in banners over his shoulders.

"I've found a very good job in London," he told her. "Managing a large livery there. Gretchen and I are married. I thought you should know. We've found a small place in Clerkenwell."

"Scottie," Lisbet protested, coming to stand beside him. "Your father and I will set you up—you needn't labor in such a way. I had always meant that you should go to university and enter any profession you liked." She touched his arm. "I was only waiting for the proper time to tell you of our . . . relationship. I wanted to wait until—"

"Until I could accept the knowledge like a man?" he finished with rue.

She made no reply and he continued. "I won't take any more money. I'd prefer to work as I have done the last few years at Wexford Hall. I've a way with horses, I like handling them."

"But, Scottie," she argued. "You could return to Winterspell. You and Gretchen could live at the castle—we shan't be returning there. After all, your father will leave it to you one day."

At the mention of Forrest, Scottie's face closed, but not before his mother had caught a haunting glimpse of unrest lurking there.

Below them on the street, the subject of their thoughts had just appeared. Well-dressed in a dark suit of clothes, his head bare, Forrest strode along the promenade watching the early morning activities. He made a striking figure, his ancestry apparent in his tall bearing and aristocratic profile. Pausing, he rested his forearms upon the railing and watched three children and a spaniel at play upon the beach. A moment later, their ball was caught by a gust of wind and it careened out of their grasps. With a quick stretch of a long arm, Forrest reached up to retrieve it for them as it sailed above his head. Grinning, he returned the plaything with an easy, athletic toss of his hand.

Through her lashes Lisbet watched her son, noting that he had not taken his eyes from his father. Impulsively she touched him gently upon his arm. "Go down and speak with him, Scottie. 'Tis time to make peace. He yearns to love you."

The young man passed a hand hastily over his eyes and, after hesitating a moment, bid her goodbye. He let Lisbet hold him briefly and promised to write her letters from time to time.

Unable to hold back tears, she told him she loved him and nodding with his eyes cast down, he went out into th corridor. With sadness, she watched his retreat, hoping tha someday he would find it in his heart to unbend.

Rushing to the window, wanting one last glimpse of he son, she saw him emerge from beneath the striped hote awning. For a long while he merely stood upon the wal with his hands shoved deep in his pockets, his face hidden i shadow but turned in the direction of the rail where hi father lounged.

Lisbet held her breath.

At last, taking awkward steps, Scottie crossed the distance separating him from his sire, calling out some wor that prompted Forrest to turn about.

Lisbet could clearly see her husband's face, read the surprise, the wary hope upon it. For a few seconds neither ma spoke, but only searched the other's eyes.

Then Forrest slowly offered his hand. Scottie moved t take it. But, as if compelled by some sudden instinctiv need, he raised his arms up and embraced his father's shoulders.

Lisbet let out a glad cry, watching the two men of her lif through a spilling haze of warm tears.

"It has come right . . ." she whispered in wonder, instinctively reaching past her neckline to grip the locket restin there. "Somehow, it has all come right for the three us fron Winterspell . . ."

With a great cry of exhilaration, she raised the windo sash and, shouting across the yellow space of sunshine called out her love.